BROOKLYN CROSS

BETRAYAL RIPPED US A PART BUT WE WERE ALWAYS DESTINED TO MEET AGAIN

the consumed trilogy book two

Scorn
WITH ME

BROOKLYN CROSS

To Those That Have Graciously
Allowed Me To Be Part Of Their Circle

Trademark Acknowledgements

The author Brooklyn Cross acknowledges the trademarked status and trademark owners of familiar wordmarks, products, actors' names, television shows, books, characters, video games, and films mentioned in this fiction work.

❀ Created with Vellum

(Standalone Books Shared World Romance/Dramatic/Women's Fiction/All
The Feels- Dark 2-3 Spice 2-3)

The Girl That Would Be Lost

The Boy That Learned To Swim (Coming Soon)

The Girl That Would Not Break (Coming Soon)

The Brothers of Shadow and Death Series

(Dystopian/Cult/Occult/Poly MMF Romance - Dark 3-4 Spice 3-4)

Anywhere (Releasing Jan 15, 2023)

Seven Sin Series

(Multi Author/PNR/Angel and Demons/Redemption - Dark 2-5 Spice 3-5)

Greed by Brooklyn Cross

Lust by Drethi Anis

Envy by Dylan Page

Gluttony by Marissa Honeycutt

Wrath by Billie Blue

Sloth by Talli Wyndham

Pride by T.L. Hodel

Playlist

Burn For You - Jace Everett

Hold On, We're Going Home - Drake

Stranger In My House - Ronnie Milsap

Nothing - Bruno Major

Carry On Wayward Son - Kansas

Flowers On The Wall - The Statler Brothers

What A Wonderful World - Sam Cooke

Inner Ninja - Classified

Watch Me Burn - Michele Morrone

Hot In Herre - Nelly

Heat Waves - Glass Animals

Basket Case - Green Day

Light Em Up - Fall Out Boy

Play With Fire - Sam Tinnesz

That's Not My Name - The Ting Tings

Super Freak - Rick James

Love The Way You Lie - Eminem

Fireball - PitBull

Demons - Joel Plaskett

Funhouse - P!NK

Driving Home for Christmas - Chris Rea

W A R N I N G

This is a dark novel and is intended
for mature audiences only.
This book is for sale to adults ONLY,
as defined by the country's laws in
which you made your purchase.
This book may contain violence,
course language, graphic content that
includes dubious consensual sexual
scenes, alcohol, tobacco and drug use,
and scenses that deal with mature
subject matter and that some
readers may find disturbing.
For a complete breakdown of the
trigger warnings, please see
Brooklyn Cross's website

Aknowledgement

I would like to tell all those that have supported me on my author journey how much I appreciate you and how much you mean to me. The fact that you have stood by my side and told me that I could and would publish my stories when others said I'd fail is the reason I decided to embark on this journey at all.

I'd like to say a huge thank you to those that enrich my life simply by being the amazing people you are. Those that give me a smile or make me laugh on a tough day, offer words of encouragement when I'm suffering with imposter syndrome, and to those that will bring me a fresh coffee at one in the morning just so that I can keep going.

Your souls are beautiful and you honour me.

Chapter 1

Violet

Nine Years Ago

As the second pebble hit my window, I knew I needed to get going or not at all. Stuffing pillows under my comforter, I waved to Becky, who was waiting on the back lawn. I could just make her out, standing in the shadow of the pool house. The lights from the pool cast dancing shadows along the wall, making me shudder. As quietly as I could, I opened the window and froze as it made a squeaking noise. The house made a ton of strange noises for being relatively new. Feeling the heat, I cursed the humid night air. The windows and doors all seemed to shift with the sticky heat.

I looked back toward the door that proudly had my name, Violet, hanging over the top in bright purple letters. My parents thought I just really liked the stupid thing I'd made in shop class, but in reality, it was my little alarm system. Anytime someone was walking down the hall, it rattled back and forth.

As my homemade alarm remained silent, I smiled and slipped out the window to the overhang that traveled the entire length of the back porch. I thought about closing the window, but I didn't. Not wanting to risk making any more noise, I drew my curtains closed to cover my escape. Getting onto my knees, I scooted to the edge of the overhang. I reached over, my fingers brushing the top of the lattice covered in my mother's climbing roses.

"Come down backward. It's easier," Becky whisper-yelled at me.

"I can't. I hate heights." I'd done this a few times now and you'd think it would get easier, but that didn't seem to be the case.

"Just do it."

"Shh, don't wake my parents, or I'm so dead." I glanced at the window further down the length of the house, but no one moved behind the darkened glass.

"Fine, do it your way." Becky huffed. "Just hurry up."

Getting a grip on the white ladder-like wall, I swung one leg and then the other over the side of the roof.

"Ouch." Of course, my hand had to land directly on a thorn. "Stupid roses."

I hated those flowers. Even though they were my mom's, I was the one that always ended up trimming them.

Carefully, I made my way down. When close enough, I jumped to the grass below.

"What took you so long?" Becky said as she ran her fingers

through her mane of wavey brunette hair. "I was beginning to think you weren't coming at all."

I stared at my best friend for a moment. She'd put on make-up and was wearing a cute blue sun dress that matched her eyes. She never did either of these things. I had no idea why she suddenly wanted to try and impress a stupid boy. They were all jerks. I hadn't met one yet that wasn't stupid. They all farted and belched like it was the funniest thing in the world, or they wanted to feel me up—pigs, all of them.

"My parents were being dick-wads about my grades and other shit. They went to bed late," I said, dusted off my jeans, and grabbed the backpack I'd stashed earlier in the day inside the pool house. "Come on, let's go." I headed across the large backyard toward the woods. Becky remained standing in the same spot. "What is it? I thought you wanted to get going?"

"I do."

"Well then?"

"Maybe we shouldn't. You know what will happen if we're caught—you'll be so grounded."

I smiled wide. "I'm already grounded, and yet here I am. Now come on." I held out my hand to my best friend. Becky rarely stepped out of line, and sneaking out to go to a party was new for her. I'd been doing it for months. What I hadn't told Becky was that part of the reason my parents were so pissed off was that they'd caught me skipping school again, and this time it was the police that had picked me up. Coming home in a cop car drunk didn't exactly win you any points. But come on...what did they expect? The stories I'd heard about my parents were worse than anything I did.

Becky glanced at my hand like it might bite, and maybe it would. I tended to party a little too hard, but now that she was out with me, I wanted her with me.

As soon as our hands clasped, we were off.

It didn't take long to get to the small beach cove. It was a hidden gem that rarely anyone ventured to other than us teens. We both started bopping our heads as the music reached us before we exited the narrow path. I smiled wide at Becky as the path opened up to the small sandy area.

"Isn't this great?" I stared at the bonfire and the party that was well underway as people talked and danced. I raised my hands in the air and wiggled my hips back and forth to the Eminem song that was playing.

"What did you say?" Becky said, her eyes scanning the group of people.

"I said, 'Isn't this awesome?' " Her eyes found mine, but she didn't look so certain now that we were here. Her eyes continued to dart from side to side as she stood, arms wrapped around her body. "What's wrong?"

She nodded off toward the far side of the beach. I narrowed my eyes, my hands balling into fists as I recognized Tyler. He was locking lips with Jenny.

"That jerk. Weren't you supposed to meet him tonight?" Becky nodded, her big grey eyes glistening with unshed tears. "What is he doing locking lips with that slut then?"

I took a step in their direction, and Becky grabbed my arm. "No, Vi. Don't."

I glared at my best friend. "He's not getting away with this. I mean, it's one thing to say, 'no, I don't want to go out.' An interesting thing to do—ask you out before he gets help with his project. Now, he has a fucking A plus, and he does that in plain sight for you to see. That's an asshole move, Beck. So I either do it here, or I can do it at school, take your pick."

"Vi, please just leave it. He's not worth it, and I don't need you making a scene for me," Becky begged. Her eyes held so much hurt, even though she tried to cover it up. I couldn't let it go.

"This isn't just for you. It's for every girl he tries to pull this shit with." Grabbing her face, I kissed her forehead. "Trust me. This is going to be good." I smiled wickedly and walked away.

Marching across the grass, I rolled up the sleeves of my shirt. The people that I walked past stared. I was sure they were wondering whose ass I was going to kick now. To say I had a bit of a reputation would've been an understatement. I had an affinity for getting into trouble. What could I say? It found me, and I liked it.

"Hey, Ass-wipe," I said as I reached the couple in the process of feeling each other up. I got to see way more of Jenny's naked boob than I ever wanted.

Tyler broke off the kiss and stepped back from Jenny. His eyes were glazed over. He'd obviously already had way more alcohol than he could handle. "Vi? Vi, what do—"

He didn't get any further before I smiled and stepped in, kneeing him hard in the crotch. The look of pain on his face was instantaneous. He slumped forward and grabbed at his precious cargo.

"Aww, did that hurt?" Making a pout face, I hauled back and gave him a hard right hook across the jaw. He crumpled to the ground, blood seeping from his nose as he cried out in pain.

"You bitch! What the hell is your problem?" Jenny wailed as she dropped to her knees beside Tyler. I kicked sand at the two of them, a good portion of it going into her mouth.

"Call me that again, Jenny, and you'll join Tyler."

"There's something wrong with you," Jenny said as she spat sand out.

Ignoring her, I pointed my finger at Tyler. "You stay away from Becky. If I even see you look in her direction or ask for help with homework from any of the girls at school again, this will be the least of what I do to you. Understand?"

His eyes were a mix of anger and fear, but the fear was winning out as I stood over him. He nodded, and I smiled. "Now that we have that settled. Have a great night, you two."

I skipped away and found Becky sitting on the log, covering her eyes. "Oh, come on, Beck, you know you loved to see him get what he deserved."

She slowly shook her head back and forth. "Honestly, I just want to go home. I only came to see him. The night is kinda ruined for me. Do you mind if we go?"

I sighed dramatically.

"Two songs." I held up my fingers and stuck out my bottom lip. "Please, pretty please, for me?"

"Ugh, fine. But only if you stop making that stupid face."

"Deal!" Grabbing her arm, I dragged her to the dance area and kicked off my shoes and socks.

I loved to feel the sand between my toes and squealed as the cold water licked up over them to splash my ankles. Becky was finally smiling again, and I loved to see the smile on my best friend's face.

There was so much in the world that I wanted to do, and I didn't care that I was only fourteen. I wanted to start now. As soon as I could drive, I planned on buying a van and traveling the world. If I could, I'd talk Beck into coming with me, and my parents wouldn't be there barking in my ear about what I should or shouldn't be doing.

I didn't know how many songs we danced to, but it was definitely more than two by the time we made our way out of the cove, heading for home. We laughed and giggled as we walked down the quiet road that led to the lush golf estates. We had both moved into the neighborhood the same summer and had become instant best friends. She was the Bat Woman to my Cat Woman, and we've been inseparable ever since.

Becky grabbed my arm, pulling me to a halt. "Do you smell that? It smells like smoke." She looked around.

"Sorta. It's probably just the bonfire smell in your nose."

"No, Vi, look." She pointed through the gap in the trees, and there was a bright orange glow. "That's a...."

"Fire," I yelled as I ran for the opening toward my home. My house was the only one near the trees, and with each stride, my heart sank further as panic hit.

Bursting through the opening, I couldn't even make sense of what I was seeing as I skidded to a halt. I stared up at the structure that looked like a gigantic version of the bonfire we'd just left.

My eyes searched the yard, but I didn't see my parents anywhere.

"Mom, Dad," I screamed at the top of my lungs. "Mom! Dad!" I ran around the outside of the house, covering my face from the thick smoke. I couldn't see a way in because the fire was everywhere, and not a single window or door seemed safe. It was unbelievably hot, so very hot that I could feel my skin screaming from the heat when I got too close.

"Violet!" I could make out my father's face in the bedroom window as I ran around to the side of the house once more to look up at my parent's bedroom.

"No, Dad, no!" I ran toward the house but was pushed back by the searing heat. I looked around for any way to help. He was frantically trying to pull up on the window, but it seemed stuck. He slammed his fists against the glass, but it didn't break. They always slept with their bedroom door closed, and for the moment, there were no flames inside, but the room was darkening with thick smoke that was looking for a way out, just like my dad.

"Dad!" I ran to the garden, grabbed one of the decorative gnomes, and hurled it at the window. It made contact but didn't even make a scratch. Frantic, I grabbed another and threw it again like I was trying out for the football team. With a loud grunt, I tossed the next in line, determined that one of them would do the job and save my parents.

"Vi!" My father's muffled yell hit my ears. I looked up and stared into his eyes. "I love you, Vi." He covered his mouth and nose with his shirt, the smoke so thick now that I could barely make him out. His hand pressed against the window, and ever so slowly, he disappeared from sight.

"Dad, no!" There were no more statues, so I grabbed a big rock and threw one after another at that stupid window until I couldn't lift my arm. Not caring, I reached for another when movement caught my attention. I looked up to see a boy, who was about my age, dressed in all black. He had a hood up, hiding his face, but I could feel his stare. As soon as I looked directly at him, he turned and ran.

"Vi, we're coming." My head snapped toward the sound of the voice, and I realized that Becky had gone to get her parents. Other neighbors were now jogging my way. I'd been so focused that I hadn't heard the firetruck until the flashing lights drove up the lane.

"They're up there." I pointed to the window as the firefighters ran my way. They reached me and looked up to see where I was pointing when the whole upper floor made a rumbling noise. I screamed as the firefighter jumped on me and took me to the ground covering me with his much larger body a moment before the entire house exploded.

I didn't realize I was still screaming until Becky grabbed me and shook me. My eyes found hers, tears streaming down both our faces. She wrapped me up in a hug and held me tight as I cried onto her shoulder. I couldn't restrain my hysterical sobs because I was full of gut-wrenching pain.

"I told them I hated them," I mumbled. "I didn't hate them. They died thinking I hated them."

Chapter 2

Violet

Present Day

As I marched down the long hallway, my heels clicked on the stark white tile. Those working in the offices I passed by looked up and then ducked their heads once more. Some things never changed, while others drastically did. I was still at the top of my game when it came to making people around me uncomfortable.

Not bothering with pleasantries like knocking, I pushed open the closed door and stepped into my boss's office. He was on the phone, but I was on a mission. The thick folder I now held, which I'd been collecting items for over the years, slammed loudly on his desk as I smacked it down.

His eyes narrowed as he glared up at me, but I wasn't about to back down. Glancing around the room, I gazed at the awards and photographs lining his walls. I'd lost count of how many times I'd seen the same pictures or skimmed over his many accolades.

"I'm sorry, but I will have to call you back," Mitch said as he glared at me. He put the phone down on his desk with a thud. "Gee, Violet, come on in? Interrupt my important call, why don't you? Don't bother to apologize as usual," he fumed, but I ignored him.

"The window was sealed with some sort of sticky substance. Why was that not in the original investigation report?" I poked at the file.

"Are we on this again?" Mitch leaned back in his chair and crossed his arms over his chest.

"I told you I'm not stopping until I find out who murdered my parents," I said, more determined than ever to figure out who had killed them and make them pay by putting them behind bars.

"Violet, they did a full investigation, and no one was ever found or convicted. There was no evidence to pin it on anyone. The investigation is closed and was ruled a cold case until the police gathered more evidence."

"That's bullshit. You know that they have stopped looking. They have too many other things 'on the go' to be worried about a decade-old, cold case. I'm your best investigator, and I'm telling you that I can find something they didn't. All I need is access to the evidence for the case. There was so much that was missed. It was like as soon as they discovered the one spot that looked like the ignition area, they stopped looking at anything else." I followed Mitch as he grabbed his dress blazer and hat, walking out the door into the hall.

"Really? Tell me one new thing that you've found," Mitch said.

"I just did. There was a sticky substance found around the

windows that was never tested. I would bet my life that it was a glue of some sort. I want the evidence re-tested. Who knows what else I will find? You just need to sign off on it." I pulled an authorization paper out of the file to hand over to him.

"No."

"No? What do you mean no?"

"I'm pretty sure the word means the same thing it did when created. No means I'm not signing it." Mitch pushed his way out the front entrance of the headquarter's doors.

I followed him like a stalker—I wanted answers.

"Mitch, this is the break I've been looking for. I need this tested to prove that I'm right."

Sighing, Mitch turned toward me after he opened his car door and tossed his briefcase inside. "Violet, it has been nine years. You need to let this go. You're consumed with finding answers where there are none to be found. Your parent's house burning down was a tragedy, and I'm sorry for the loss you endured and the fact that you've never gotten the closure you need, but it's time to let it go. It's time to let them go."

"I can't, and if you'd take a look at the notes I made, you'll see a list of things that were overlooked. Please, sign this, and if it doesn't work out, I promise that I will give real consideration to letting it go."

"How many times have I heard that before? No, Vi. I'm done with this. You need to focus on your other cases. If you continue to pursue this, then you will leave me no other choice than to suspend you."

My mouth fell open. "You can't be serious. I complete more cases than anyone else."

"I am serious. This is for your own good since you can't seem to step away. Vi, for Christ's sake, your dad and I were best friends, and I loved him like a brother. I'm telling you he wouldn't want you obsessing like this over something that will never be solved. Now, I have a dinner meeting I'm running late for, so I will talk to you later. Maybe you should spend a little more time on the serial arsonist case I gave you. This guy has killed over three hundred people so far. Now that is a worthwhile use of your time."

Mitch closed the car door, and just like that, he drove away, leaving me staring after his sedan.

My hand balled into a fist. Everyone assumed I was obsessive because I was investigating my parents' death. No one was taking me seriously anymore because I'd hit a couple of dead ends. Yes, I may have a vested interest, but I remember that boy in the hoodie. I remembered how my dad couldn't get his window open. I remembered how the house was fully engulfed, and I'd seen the pictures. I know I could find this guy if I could get full access to all the evidence collected. How did my parents not hear the blaring sounds of the brand-new fire alarm system installed only months earlier? It worked just fine because we could hear it outside. How come they hadn't even tried to make it downstairs or to another room?

No matter what Mitch said, I wasn't letting this go. I was the best fire investigator this state had, and my gut screamed that if given a little more time, I'd catch the guy that had watched while my parents burned to death.

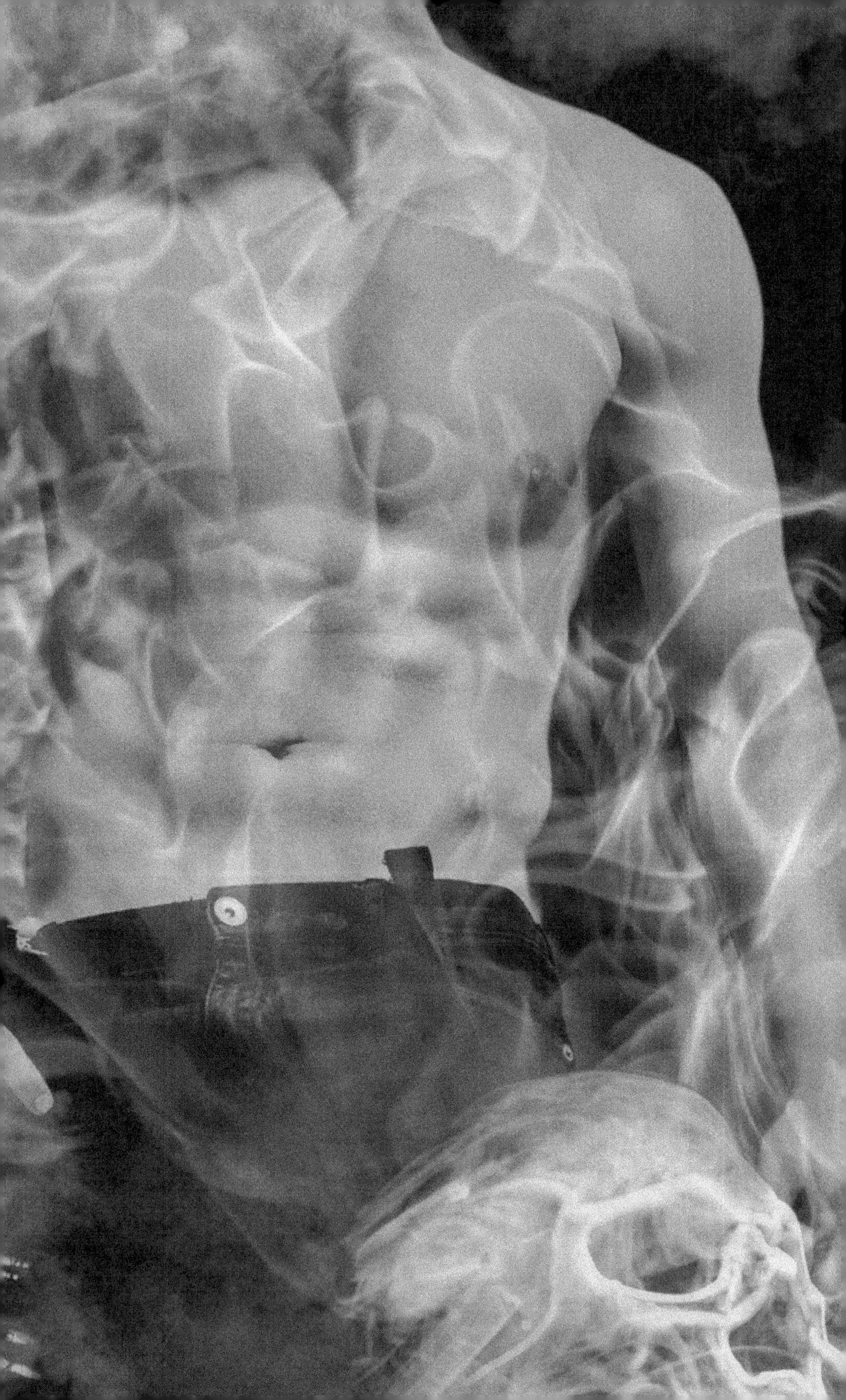

Chapter 3

Asher

I leaned back in the wide leather chair and felt like a damn guard dog as I sat outside the woman's dressing room with a million bags of clothes.

"Who even needed this many clothes?" I stupidly mumbled aloud.

The answer I got was, "well, duh...it's the season change."

What the fuck did that mean? We lived in Florida, for fuck's sake. The temperature ranged from warm, warmer, fucking hot, and so humid outside that you'd sweat your left nut off when you stepped out of the air-conditioning.

"Asher, sweetie, I can't choose," Brit said.

Not that I called her Brit to her face. It was Britnay with an 'A,' not an 'E.' Brit stuck her head out of the door and glared at me like I'd just committed a cardinal sin. "Well, aren't you going to answer me?"

"I didn't realize you'd asked a question in that statement." Irritated, I stretched out my legs.

"Why are you always so sarcastic?"

I cocked a brow at my girlfriend...or, as Brit would say, "my intimate." Labels and I were not friends and I never called Britnay my girlfriend to anyone, but she would make sure to introduce me as her full-time intimate partner every chance she got. It sounded like I was her fucking employee that was only here for her servicing pleasure.

How we ended up together and how two seemingly opposite people became *intimate* had nothing to do with a real connection. She was new to one of the sites I frequented for those in the kink community, and Brit...well, Brit was going to get herself hurt. She was advertising that she wanted a Dom and saying it to all the wrong people.

On the other hand, I am not an asshole, well, not a complete asshole, anyway. As it turned out, Brit was looking for someone to show her the ropes and let her see if this was the life she wanted, and I was...well, looking for someone to fulfill my desires, but outside of the bedroom, we had nothing.

"Wasn't sarcasm. It was a fact. You said, 'I can't choose.' Where in that sentence is a question?"

She rolled her eyes at me before opening the door and stepping out into the sitting area in a sexy little black number. I immediately sat a little straighter. She tossed her long hair over her shoulder and batted her eyes at me as she proceeded to walk past like she was on a runway. I had to give it to her, she had the walk down, and I was enjoying the show of her ass swinging back and forth in the thin material.

Turning at the end in front of the mirror, she smiled that seductive little smirk she'd get whenever she was thinking of doing something dangerous or risqué.

"Fine, it wasn't a question, but you should know by now that I want your opinion," she said. Gripping the front of the dress, she pulled the material up a little higher, and my pants instantly became more confining.

"You tried on ten dresses, and they all looked great on you." Brit did a little bit of modeling, but that wasn't what gave her the money to spend twenty grand on a shopping trip. No, that was her social media platform and the millions of fans who thought she was so adorable.

"You're so sweet." She sucked the end of her finger before slipping it under the material of the dress. I could just see through the material enough that she'd left her underwear in the dressing room.

"What did I tell you earlier?" I sat aside the bag that I'd been holding.

Her cheeks flamed red as she giggled and continued to do exactly what I told her not to do. Such a brat.

"That I wasn't allowed to touch myself," she whispered.

My eyes glanced down at her hand as she continued to play with herself.

"You know I don't like it when you disobey me," I said and slowly stood from the chair. I could almost feel her nervous energy from where I was standing as my eyes narrowed into slits. Her eyes flicked down as her submissive side began to emerge.

"I know, but I really want to," she said. "I'm so horny."

She still didn't remove her hand, and that meant she needed to be taught a lesson. Marching down the short hallway, her eyes darted from side to side, but she didn't try to run as I reached her. Her breathing was fast, and her nipples were so hard that they looked like they may poke right through the front of the dress.

I didn't hesitate and picked her up, tossing her over my shoulder as if this was one of my firefighter drills, and marched her ass right back to the dressing room. Slamming the door in place, I grabbed a sheer scarf hanging on the hook and dropped Brit to her feet.

"Hands." I glared down at her and blocked the door.

She probably would've tried running if I hadn't. She liked the cat and mouse game and would sprint around her massive condo with no clothes on as she tried to get me to chase her down. Sometimes I would, but most of the time, I didn't entertain her and forced her to come to me.

She held out her hands, and I quickly tied them up tight enough so that she couldn't move. Wrapping the rest of the long sheer piece of fabric around my fist so I could keep control of her I spun her around. Pushing her up against the wall I growled in her ear. "You like being disobedient?"

"I'm sorry," she whispered back, but the way her body was shivering had nothing to do with fear.

Grabbing one of the long scarves she had hanging on a hook I held it in front of her face. "Open."

Brit licked her lips and then slowly opened her mouth. I shoved as much of the material as I dared between her teeth and then used my body to push her harder into the wall. "Don't drop it. Do you understand?"

She nodded her head, yes, her nostrils flaring as her pupils dilated with her arousal. "Good girl."

Yanking the short dress up hard, Brit made a muffled yelp as I exposed her naked ass. "Do you know what you get for being defiant?" Brit nodded. "How many should you get? Twenty?" She whimpered and squirmed in my hold, but it was a half-hearted attempt. "Is that a no?"

She shook her head slightly from side to side, the muffled whine telling me she didn't like the idea. Dipping my fingers between her legs, I wasn't surprised to find her already wet and eager for more. Brit wiggled against my fingers.

"Naughty girls need to be punished. Fine. Ten it is."

I didn't waste a second, cracking my hand down hard on her ass. She moaned and her eyes fluttered closed as I raised my hand to spank her again. By the time I finished the ten strikes, both sides of her ass were bright pink.

Unzipping myself with one hand, I removed my cock and thrust into her hard. There was no tentative play or warning. She moaned loudly as I remained perfectly still.

"Don't come until I tell you," I ordered in her ear.

She nodded furiously, knowing this game well. I tapped the inside of her heels with my toe, and she spread her legs wide to give me more room. Thrusting aggressively, I pounded into her as hard as I could. Her body was rhythmically thumping against the wall, whimpering as she begged for more.

"Hello?" A woman's voice called out, and I stopped moving and looked over my shoulder at the door. "Were you needing help with one of the items?"

Holding Brit to my body, I quickly sat down and pulled the fabric out of her mouth before pointing to the door. Swallowing, she undid the lock and opened the door a crack to look out. I lifted Brit with my hands just enough to continue thrusting myself into her while she was forced to keep a straight face.

"Oh no, I'm...good." The tension in her voice was clear as a bell to me. Her voice hitched slightly, and she pretended to cough. "Sorry, I'm fine, really. I just can't decide if I want them all."

"Oh, okay. Are you sure? I didn't see your boyfriend leave. Is he coming back to help you with all this?"

Oh, I was going to be coming alright, and if the lady stood there long enough, she would get more of a show than I was sure she bargained for when she arrived at work today. I picked up my pace and savored the way her breathing changed.

"He went to go get a drink. He'll be back soon, but thank you." I could feel Brit giving the woman a fake smile even though I couldn't see her face.

"All right. I'm happy to help if you change your mind. Just give a shout." Brit locked the door, and I let her drop down onto my lap as soon as she did. She moaned, and I wrapped my hand around her throat to pull her back into my body.

"Fuck me, but be quiet," I growled into her ear.

She immediately began bouncing up and down on my cock, and I could feel myself getting there, but I held off until I knew she was close.

Standing, I pulled her off my lap.

"On your knees."

She dropped like a stone and turned around, expecting me to shove my cock in her mouth, but this was a punishment, and she was way too eager for that. Gripping my cock, I stroked myself hard and groaned as my release landed on the dresses she'd been trying on.

She sucked in a breath in shock but wisely didn't say anything as I continued to unload on the items hanging on the rack. Smirking, I looked down at Brit and held my cock out to her.

"Clean it up."

Her eyes were wide with horror but still held all the desire that I'd intended her to keep. She slipped her mouth around my spent cock and sucked and licked until I was satisfied that it was good and clean before stuffing myself back into my jeans.

Brit shot to her feet as I unlocked the door. "But...but...."

I flashed her a hard stare, freezing whatever else she was planning on saying.

"You disobeyed me, and in public, you don't get to come until much, much later." My eyes flicked to the soiled dresses. "I guess your decision has been made, you'll be getting them all. Now take them up to the register and buy them." I opened the door and stepped out. "Oh, and Brit, don't clean them off."

Okay, maybe I was an asshole.

Not
even the
Devil could burn
the world like
I could

Chapter 4

Derek

The world was blind.

One thing that I'd become acutely aware of since my escape was that for all the cameras and phones and fancy tech that had come about, there were much fewer people that paid attention and more that were content to bop around in their little bubbles of merriment. As if they were ostriches with their head in the sand, they would stay to themselves, hoping that no one saw them. The exact opposite was true. The more they didn't see me, the greater the target they became.

This guy sitting beside me was a perfect example. He had massive headphones on as he softly recited the lyrics of his song. His hood was pulled up on his hoodie while he remained one hundred percent fixated on his phone.

Did he notice me staring when he put in his lock code?

Nope.

Did he notice me reading his messages while he talked to multiple women at the same time?

Nope.

I looked closer. Unbelievable. He relayed the same messages of love and affection and how they were the only one. Did he notice that I heard his entire conversation with his buddy about where they would meet up later and how much fun they would have?

Nope.

In the twenty minutes that I'd quietly sat beside him, I'd learned more about his life than he realized. The other thing I had noticed since being out in the mainstream of society was that people had an arrogance to them now. A 'you can't touch me,' or 'I'm going to tell my mommy' attitude. Here, have a tissue, you sorry sacks of walking burnable flesh. Their arrogance only fueled me further.

They thought they were untouchable, so I made sure to remind them that they were no better than the generation before them and the one before that, and they would burn just as bright.

I was the equalizer that society needed. I was the dragon that had been set loose on the world to remind all those who'd forgotten that even in this new fandangle tech society, there was still a pecking order, and I was one of the few at the top of the food chain.

Asher had gone soft or maybe had forgotten where his roots were. I wasn't sure yet, but he lived in a spacious home inside a gated community. He worked as a firefighter, which made me laugh. But what really burned my ass was the fact that the asshole had grown up to look like a fucking supermodel, and other than one shitty photograph of us together, there was nothing in or around his home that suggested he even remembered me. I planned on making sure he remembered.

I didn't think I could hate my brother any more than I already did for sending me to that fucking nut house and then never coming to see me, but...I was wrong. With each passing week, my hatred morphed into a loathing that was getting harder to suppress.

However, the one thing I did respect about him was his observance of those close to him. His head was always turning, and his eyes searched the faces that passed by him. At least he'd learned one thing from our time as children. I hadn't been able to get close to him, but I'd also managed to go unnoticed as I followed him around, which made my next moves so much more exciting.

Once more, I became the hunter as Asher stepped out of the high-end female clothing store with the woman he was seeing. She was hanging all over him. He looked like a pack mule with all the bags he was carrying, and I dropped my head to look at my own phone as they drew closer.

"Asher, sweetie, I'm parched. Can we go get a drink before heading home?" the woman begged like she was a dog looking for a bone and not a human.

"No, you can wait," Asher said flatly, and the corner of my mouth pulled up as she huffed and made a little pouting noise.

"But, Asher—"

"I said no. Do you need another lesson," he asked, as they passed by and I wasn't sure what that meant, but I found their entire exchange entertaining. A flash of Asher hitting the woman to teach her a lesson flashed before my eyes and my smile fell. I glanced up at their backs and studied the woman closer. No, her body language didn't fit. She looked more like she wanted to toss Asher down in the middle of the mall floor and fuck him in front of everyone.

Their steps receded as they moved further away from my perch. I moved quickly through the department store that would take me to the same parking lot where they were headed. It was best not to look like I was interested in them. Instead, I became a shy introvert just trying to get some shopping done. I grabbed a deodorant and a new T-shirt as I walked toward the exit and quickly used the self-serve checkout.

Dora's cards were coming in handy. My heart hurt as my thoughts drifted to the woman who had seen more than a monster in me. I'd never forget her kindness, and I still kept everything about her farm as clean and neat as the day she died. Her mail was gathered, the car was used, and anyone who saw the daily work in the fields and gardens would think that she was still alive and well.

In some ways, she was.

Pushing my way outside into the hot midday sun, I shielded my eyes, immediately fixing on the couple that was ambling along the row to a car parked at the end of the large lot. I walked slowly toward the bicycle that was neatly chained up and knelt to undo the metal links and watch my prey.

I'd memorized his truck, but that was not the vehicle they

approached. The woman he was with had expensive taste indeed. She got in the driver's side of the fancy red sports car, and I quickly stored the plate number, make and model away in my brain as it approached.

Peddling on my bike, I headed toward the stoplight that left the parking lot and turned in the same direction as her blinker. I cruised down the sidewalk and could hear the sports car's loud motor approaching. It flew past, but they didn't head for the freeway and instead made a direct line for the expensive condos that looked out over the ocean.

Lady luck loved me. I was able to keep a steady pace and keep them in sight as the red lights played in my favor. It took a good forty minutes to reach her condo, and I watched as the cherry red car disappeared into the underground parking area.

I circled the building slowly and picked out all that I needed to know about this spot. It wasn't a good or easy target and as much fun as it would be to see this entire building burn, even the dragon had limits.

It was fine. I had many other ways to make sure that the moment was memorable.

I'm sorry, Asher, sweetie, but I think it was time you learned the lesson. I sneered at the joke in my mind and then cruised away.

A pair of girls on rollerblades made their way toward me in their skimpy bikinis. Their skin had been kissed by the sun, which created a perfect golden brown color. If they had been toast, all they needed was a little bit of butter, and I would've happily taken a bite. But, I didn't need people, and I especially didn't need women. The ice creams they were holding on the other hand...well, those made me smile. Nothing said a hot day in the state of Florida like half-naked people on a beach and an ice cream cone in hand.

Stalking all done for the day, ice cream seemed like a great idea.

Chapter 5

Violet

I slammed the apartment door, and Beck stuck her head out of the kitchen, a spoon hanging out of her mouth.

"Whoa, that's your ugly, 'I'm going to kill someone' face. Who bit your ass?"

"Fucking Mitch. He wouldn't let me re-test the evidence from my parent's house fire. He says I'm being... 'obsessive.' " I grabbed a beer from the fridge and stole a piece of red pepper from the chicken stir fry Beck had made us for dinner.

"You are kind of obsessed," she said as she continued stirring her tea.

I shot Beck a dirty look. "Not you too."

She shrugged and then sighed as she plopped herself down on

one of the island stools. "All I'm saying is that you need to start living again."

"I don't even know what that means. I am living." I patted down my arms to demonstrate.

"No, you're alive, but that is not living. Girl, you never go out. You don't date. All you do is work and talk to your snotty cat."

"Heathrow is not snotty—he's misunderstood. We have that in common," I said as the fat black cat in question walked into the kitchen. Bending down, I picked up Heathrow, who was missing the top of one ear and the tip of his tail. He was a rescue, so I had no idea how either happened, but I didn't care. I loved the fuzzy puss.

"That thing is part demon, but that's beside the point. Vi, why don't you come out with me tonight? It's Friday, and it's just a small group of people from my work. I know you will like them."

I groaned as I pulled the white dress blouse out of my navy pencil skirt. "Thanks, but I want my other three Bs tonight: bath, beer, and bed." I held up my fingers, counting them off.

"Too bad you wouldn't add sex into that list. Maybe getting laid would loosen you up some." Beck smiled as my mouth dropped open.

"Bitch."

Beck laughed. "I figured you wouldn't come. The sticky rice for the stir fry is in the rice cooker, and I made a German chocolate cake, which is hiding in the back of the fridge," Beck said as she stood up from the island stool.

"Have I told you lately that I love you?" I batted my eyes at her, making her eyes roll.

"You're coming out with me one night soon, Vi. You're in your twenties, not eighties." Beck gripped my shoulders. "You used to be the dare devil and the life of the party. Girl, you were the one everyone else wanted to be with because of your fearlessness and drive to see the world."

"That Vi died when my parents died, Beck. I can't rest until I find who killed them, and don't even start with the whole let it go speech."

I placed my hands on my hips and looked at my feet as I tried to organize my thoughts. So much pain all balled up into one burned inside my chest. It was hard to explain it to anyone. "When I close my eyes at night, it's my father's face that I see. It's my final words to them that play on a loop in my head. It's the image of a boy watching my home and my family burn and then running away."

My eyes found hers as I pleaded with her to try and understand.

"I know you think it would be healthier for me to try and move on with my life, but I'm stuck. I'm stuck and still staring up at those flames as my father yelled that he loved me before he died. I need to know who, I need to know why, and I need to see them rot in jail."

Beck gave me a sympathetic look before placing her hands on my shoulders.

"I know all that, and I'm not going to tell you to stop looking, but you also have to realize that if this wasn't an accident... the person responsible may no longer be alive or is already in jail, and you will never have the retribution you want."

Beck squeezed my right shoulder. "As for this boy you mentioned...Girl, we were walking through those woods, coming home from a party. You have no idea if that guy was even responsible or was like us and on his way home when he spotted the flames and came to check it out. Please, please, please think about that before you throw away the rest of what is supposed to be your best years."

"I will, and I will come out, just not tonight. Okay?" I hated that Beck made valid points, but the thought of stopping my investigation made my stomach churn.

"Yeah, that's fine." We hugged one another tight, and then, with a jingle of keys and the click of a door, I was left alone.

Maybe I was acting old and stuffy, but I didn't have the energy to plaster a fake smile on my face tonight. I'd been down that road a few times, and it always ended up the same. Me sitting with people that didn't understand who I was as they laughed and talked about things that didn't interest me in the slightest.

It was like I was there, but I wasn't seen.

I'd have a few drinks, a bite to eat, and have some guy hit on me that didn't hold my interest. Other people loved that shit. Heck, Beck lived off of it. However, the spark that had glowed so brightly within me before my parents died had been snuffed out on the day of the fire. Now, there was nothing left but a charred lump of coal in its place.

Grabbing another beer, I picked up my folder and sat it down on the dining room table before dishing up some of the delicious-smelling dinner that Beck had made. First order of the night, I needed to get out of this female version of a monkey suit and go over my parents' file again. It never hurt to go through the paperwork and pictures once more. There had to be something I was missing, something that I could find and use to have the case reopened. There just had to be.

Burn

"No, Dad! Mom!" The heat singed my eyebrows as I tried to get closer to the bright flames. Movement caught my eye, and I spotted a boy by the tree line. He was laughing, the sound sending a shiver down my spine. Him. This was all his fault. I took off running as he sprinted away into the dark forest.

"Stop. I know it was you. You killed my parents!"

The leaves under my feet crunched from the dry weather, my breathing loud as I ran after the boy that killed my family. Smoke snaked around my feet, and I looked down to see where it was coming from when the trees lining the path burst into flames. I screamed and covered my eyes as the heat was instantly unbearable.

Coughing and choking on the black smoke, I sank to my knees, the sound of laughter drifting further into the distance.

Burn

I woke with a start and stared into the eyes of my cat.

"Creepy, Heathrow," I said to my cat. His nose was almost touching mine.

Man, my head hurt. I lifted it off the dining room table and winced as I peeled a yellow sticky paper off my face. Note to self, don't fall asleep like that again. Who was I kidding? I would do it again, not that my body appreciated it.

I slowly stood, stretching, and then froze. I sniffed the air and looked around for the source of the smoke. I walked through the apartment on high alert, sniffing and looking at every receptacle and touching every wall. Beck still wasn't home, and as I glanced at the time, that said it was two in the morning. The worrier in me had every worst-case scenario going through my mind. What if she got in a car accident? Or, what if someone she met wasn't a nice person and slipped something in her drink? Or what if...

"Okay stop the spiral," I ordered myself. "She's a big girl. She can go out and have fun on a Friday," I said as I continued my search.

Passing the kitchen for a second time, I did a double-take of the window. The blinds were drawn, but there was a soft glow outside that had nothing to do with the string of little decorative lights on the sitting area of our fire escape.

Running to the window, I yanked hard on the little string. The metal slats slapped together as they flew up, and I gasped as I stared at the apartment across the alley.

Sarah, who I'd gotten to know a little since moving in, was trying to pull open the window in her kitchen. Fear, the same fear that had been in my father's eyes, was in hers as the bright flickering light of a fire burned behind her. I could just make out her screaming as her hands pounded on the window. It didn't look like her daughter Kim was home, or if she was...no I couldn't think about that.

This was not happening again.

Not wasting another second, I yanked open my window and stepped out onto the metal fire escape, and the rough metal bit into my socked feet. Looking down through the grating, I briefly considered going down the escape and then trying to climb up theirs, but my fear of heights had the world spinning.

No. You can do this.

Climbing over the edge of the creaking railing, I swallowed hard as I stared down at the alley below. There was not much that I was afraid of other than heights and spiders, and for most, this wouldn't be high, but for me, it felt like I was miles from the pavement below. We were only four stories up, but that was still far enough to kill me and also more than enough to make my muscles quake with fear.

"Get a chair and break the window," I yelled at Sarah.

She ran across the kitchen that was slowly filling with flames that were now beginning to lick along the walls inside the open kitchen archway. I could see her go to the small kitchen set and look around. I couldn't wait any longer.

"You can do this." Rocking back and forth to get momentum, I counted down in my head. *One, two, three,* and I leaped with all I had on three, winced, and swore as I slammed into the metal railing that groaned with my sudden weight. My ribs, knee, and socked feet collided painfully, bringing tears to my eyes. Thank god there were only like five feet between the two fire escape platforms. Any further and I would've fallen for sure.

"Hey, Lady. Are you freaking crazy?" a man yelled. I glanced down to see a firefighter staring up at me. I didn't bother to answer. Gripping the railing, I hopped over onto the metal landing and ignored the pain radiating up from my feet.

"The chairs are gone," Sarah screamed, a hysterical look on her face.

"Move." I waved, and she darted to the side of the window.

Pulling the T-shirt off over my head, I wrapped up my hand and braced myself. Picking what I knew was a weak spot in all windows, I reached back and slammed my fist at the spot with all my might. A tiny crack formed, but it didn't break. I could hear more help arriving below, and the fire escape shook and clanged as they got the ladder lowered.

Once more, my fist hit the same spot. This time, a large crack formed. With a yell, I hit the window again, and it shattered, the pieces falling away. As quickly as I could, I smashed my hand against a couple of jagged shards that were left. Blood started to seep through the flimsy protection of the shirt. I knew I was cut but didn't care.

"Come on, let's go. Careful on the glass." I stuck my head in her kitchen. "Head down the stairs," I said, as I reached my hand in the window to help Sarah out.

I stared at the fire that had wrapped its way around the walls into the room and I swallowed hard. The fire made a deep rumbling sound like a dragon getting ready to roar its fiery breath. I pulled hard on her hand as she moved too slow. "Go, run."

I gave Sarah a gentle push to rush her down the stairs. That sound made goosebumps rise all over me, knowing that the noise meant an explosion was coming. Our feet made the landing of the next floor down when a fire ball burst from the window above.

A heavy arm wrapped around my shoulders just as a jacket draped over my back, and bare-skin like a shield as bits of debris rained down on us.

"That was either the bravest or the stupidest thing I've ever seen," a deep voice said right beside my ear. A shiver raced down my spine at the undeniably sexy sound, and the sudden warmth of the man felt hotter than the fire as we hid under his large jacket.

I glanced over as the unknown firefighter stood, helping Sarah to her feet. My eyes were immediately drawn to the face of the sexy stranger. His intense electric blue eyes and six o'clock shadow proved why firefighters like him were chosen for calendars because, holy fuck! Even I could admit he might be hotter than the fire raging above my head.

Crushing the thought, I knew this was not the time or place for a random flirt session. Besides, I'd never want to date a firefighter. I'd seen them in action, and I didn't mean while fighting a fire. They all held the same arrogance and needed to have multiples of everything, multiple jobs, cars, vacations, women and or men. It was like a prerequisite to becoming a firefighter that one needed to be a cheating asshole. Mind you, they were a step up from cops and paramedics, just not by much.

Besides, flirting wasn't something I did. I'd probably end up saying something random and stupid, like quoting what common chemicals in your cupboard it would take to cause an explosion. Dating wasn't on my radar anyhow. I didn't do the fuck buddy or casual one-night stand shit. People were too fucking crazy to trust, and a relationship was way too much effort.

I followed the small party down the stairs, and water began to rain down onto the building. I looked up at the brick structure and stared at Sarah's apartment. It seemed primarily isolated and could've been so much worse. I tapped my chin as I stared at the flames that were only now beginning to spread. That was strange. Fire didn't choose which direction it was going to head or who it was going to kill, but this one acted like it had been specifically after Sarah.

"Sarah? Was Kim in the apartment?" I said to her as we walked toward one of the ambulances.

"No," she said without any further explanation, and as long as the kid was safe, I didn't need to know anymore.

The same deep voice interrupted my thoughts. "You need to be looked at as well. Come with me over there. Let's take a look at that," the firefighter said.

He pointed to my hand, and it was only then that I realized how much blood I was losing as it ran down my arm to drip to the ground below.

Nodding, I followed him over to the ambulance. He pulled off his jacket, wrapping it around my shoulders. The warmth instantly seeped into my body, and I had to refrain from sniffing the collar as a hint of something spicy joined with the smoky scent that lingered on the fire retardant fabric.

"Thanks." My brain momentarily short-circuited as I stared up at him with the fire burning behind him. He looked like he just walked off a movie set from saving the day.

"What's your name? I have to know who's crazy enough to make that jump and in sock feet." He placed his hands on his hips.

I thought I knew all the firefighters since I'd worked with most of them in one capacity or another over my time working along side them, but this man I'd never met.

Was he new?

My heart pounded a little harder as I stared into those unusual-colored eyes. They were like staring into a crystal-clear lagoon, and I shivered. I chalked up the response to the mass amounts of adrenaline coursing through my veins, not directly linked to the man in front of me.

"I'm Fire Investigator Violet Clarke." I held out my uninjured hand, and he looked at it and then back up into my eyes.

"Ah, well, that explains it. You really are crazy," he said as he cocked an eyebrow at me. Why did it feel like he was scolding me like I was a child and not a grown-ass woman?

My hand dropped as my back straightened at the insult. "Oh, really? And why is that exactly? Don't think a woman can save the day? Only you big, strapping men can do it," I mocked.

He smirked, and I felt it right in the middle of my gut as if it decided to perform backflips.

"No. Because you knew better and still did it." He shook his head. "You had to know that help was coming, and you could end up becoming a bigger issue causing us to spend precious time saving your ass as well as those in the apartment, but you chose to jump and put yourself at risk as well. Not exactly a smart move."

My eyes narrowed into slits as I glared at him and felt my blood pressure rise. "Well, if it had been solely left up to you lot, then she would've been dead, so how about you say thank you instead?"

He smiled, and I wanted to smack myself because I could only think about dragging him into the back of the ambulance. Rolling out his shoulders, he turned and began walking away but stopped and turned back. I was ready for an apology of some sort, but instead, he shocked me further. "I need my jacket back." His tone was so flat and unaffected that my mouth fell open.

Slamming my lips shut, I recovered and stood to step around the paramedic that was trying to wrap my hand, but I pulled away.

"Hey," the paramedic complained, but I ignored him and marched across the few strides separating me from the firefighter. He seemed uninterested in helping me out by stepping closer to me, but I ignored that slight too. With my back ramrod straight, I never took my eyes off his.

"You want your jacket, no problem." Turning around so my back faced the asshat, I flicked the heavy jacket off so it fell on the ground at his feet. Childish, maybe, but it made me feel better. Looking over my shoulder, I smirked at him and then didn't give him any more of my time as I made my way back to the annoyed-looking paramedic. The guy reached into the ambulance and handed over a silver blanket that I quickly wrapped around my body to cover up my lace bra.

As I sat down and held out my hand again, I couldn't help but notice that unknown guy giving me a look I couldn't quite decipher, but it made me want to squirm. The corner of his mouth curved ever so slightly upward, which should've made me want to punch him and ruin that all-too-sexy face, but instead, it did the complete opposite. I bit the inside of my cheek, wondering how his lips would taste and if his body were as cut as it seemed under his clothes.

Bending over, he picked up the jacket and flung it around his broad shoulders, stuffing his arms inside the sleeves. Even that simple act made him look like he was in a slow-action strip tease.

Without another word, he walked away. I made sure to take note of the name on the back. It said West. There was no way I'd ever be interested in an arrogant ass like him. That would've been stupid. Yet,

I found my eyes tracking his movements and making sure I paid attention to what fire station number he joined—station 126.

I had no intentions of seeing the jerk again. It was simply useful information to have.

"You're going to need stitches," the paramedic said, forcing me to pull my eyes away from the sexy asshole.

"Okay, then do it," I said, and he shook his head.

"Not by me. You have to go to the hospital."

"No way." I stood. "Either you fix my hand now or wrap it, and I'll take my chances."

"Unbelievable, you're just like them," the paramedic said and pointed a thumb at the group of firefighters.

"No, I'm not," I complained, annoyed to be lumped in with those heathens.

"Oh yeah? You think any of them would go to the hospital like they should? It's like all of you think I don't know how to do my job and that I don't know what's best. It's actually a little hurtful," he said as he zipped up his large medical bag.

Great, now I was being manipulated to get into an ambulance, but as West looked over his shoulder at me and gave me a condescending look, I decided I never wanted to be lumped in with anything he would do.

"Fine, let's go," I mumbled.

Yay, hours of sitting at a hospital, here I come.

Not
even the
Devil could burn
the world like
I could

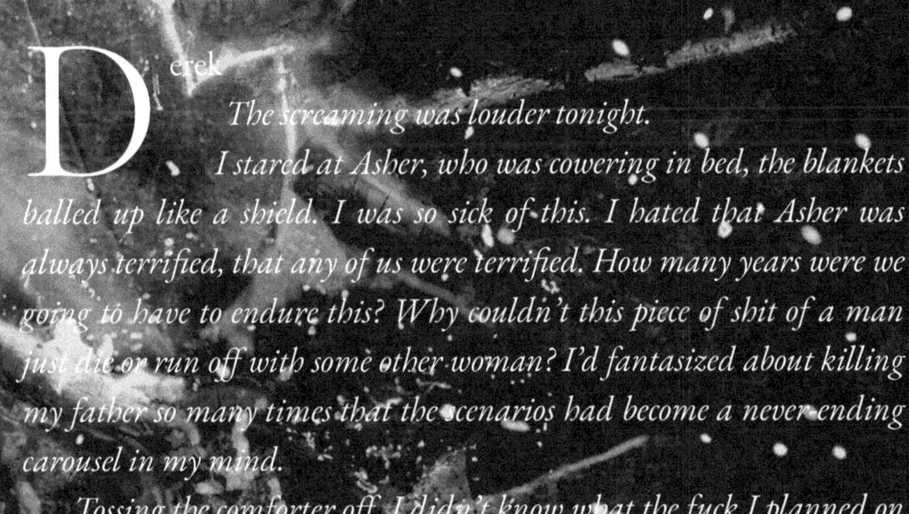

Derek

The screaming was louder tonight.

I stared at Asher, who was cowering in bed, the blankets balled up like a shield. I was so sick of this. I hated that Asher was always terrified, that any of us were terrified. How many years were we going to have to endure this? Why couldn't this piece of shit of a man just die or run off with some other woman? I'd fantasized about killing my father so many times that the scenarios had become a never-ending carousel in my mind.

Tossing the comforter off, I didn't know what the fuck I planned on doing, but I needed to stop this. Either I'd kill him, or he'd kill me, but someone needed to step in. Slamming my always-booted feet onto my bedroom floor, I charged out of the room and stomped down the hall-

way. I learned way too young that it was safter to keep my boots on when I slept because I never knew when I might need to run. However, tonight, I was not running away. I was moving toward...him. My boots were so loud on the wood that the floor rumbled as if I were making miniature earthquakes with every stomping stride.

I found my father standing over my mother, his meaty fist holding her by the front of her sweater. His other fist was cocked back as he yelled about something in his drunken haze.

"Leave her alone!" I didn't think about it. I simply ran at the man who had broken my bones and bruised my body until I didn't recognize my reflection. I ran at a monster that no one would do anything to stop. But I would.

A brief moment of satisfaction washed through my fourteen-year-old body as I watched my father slam into the kitchen counter. The odd bend of his body sent all the dishes in arm's reach, scattering and clattering to the floor. I was breathing heavily, my gaze fixed on the object of my rage and fear.

After a long moment, I knelt and tried to inspect my mother's bruised face, but she slapped my hands away like I was the one that was trying to hurt her.

"What have you done?" Her angry, disgusted tone matched the way her brows knit together. "You've only made it worse. Stupid. Why couldn't you just stay in your room?"

"You think you're tough now, Kid?" my father slurred.

I yelled out as he grabbed me by the hair and gave my side a sharp jab that was still sore from the last round of abuse. All the air rushed from my lungs, and tears sprang to my eyes with the force of the second blow. I screamed like I was possessed.

No more would I be quiet and take his punches.

"Shut up, or I'll give you something to scream about," he snarled like a rabid dog.

I continued to scream and thrash in his hold, my elbow finding the soft squishy part of his belly, and I loved that he groaned at the impact of my blow.

"I said shut up, you fucking piece of shit!" My father dragged me across the small kitchen.

Fear sliced through me at the sound of a click. I knew what that meant. I'd used the stove enough to know that sound with my eyes closed. I turned my head slightly, and my screams got louder as my eyes focused on the glow of the little blue flame.

I became a wild animal and kicked out fiercely. I connected with something earning a loud grunt, but that fist gripped my hair harder and slammed my face off the oven handle, dazing me. Blinking what had to be blood out of my eye, I struggled in his hold as the flame got closer.

"No, Dad, don't," I yelled, bracing my hands on the edge of the stove. My struggles became frantic as fear overrode everything else.

Even as another fist hit my side, I barely felt it and continued to kick wildly at the man that seemed more like a demon than my father anymore. My eyes swung to my mother, who was still sitting on the floor, and instead of helping or saying a word, she looked away before getting to her feet and leaving the room.

"Mom, stop him, please," I screamed and then continued to scream at the top of my lungs.

Another hard shot caught me in the ribs. This time, I heard a sharp crack, the pain stealing my fight.

My scream became a howl of pain as that little blue flame licked a line up the side of my face. The pain was so intense that the adrenaline coursing through my body helped me to push my face away from the flame before it reached my eye. The stench of burning flesh confirmed that this was indeed happening and was not another nightmare. It was real, and it wasn't done. The hair closest to my ear caught on fire, the flame licking upward until it fizzled out, but the stench was strong in my nose. My father's evil laugh was loud, and the dark scent of whiskey was hanging in the air. He went to push my head down again when a new scream joined the mix.

"No," my younger brother yelled as he ran across the room, his face twisted into a picture of fear.

My brother slammed into my father, and my father stumbled back, making both of us hit the wall hard. Losing his balance, he slid down the wall awkwardly and smacked his arm off a small shelf, which sent everything on it crashing to the floor. I watched the small decorative cactus rolled under the table like it was now the thing that was trying to hide from my father's wrath.

His hand loosened in mine, and with a hard pull, I was able to wiggle free from his heavy limbs and large fist. Crawling away, I moved like a dog across the floor, trying to put as much room between us as possible. The smell of him was stuck in my nose, making it feel like he was still assaulting me.

Asher grabbed me under the arm and pulled up hard, yanking me along until we were outside. The sound of the screen door slamming making me jump as I thought that my father was already after us. I turned and looked over my shoulder and didn't see my father, but the moist breeze hit the injured side of my face. I'd thought I knew pain until that moment. My scream filled the air as the warm night air felt like claws scraping down my ruined skin.

"I got you," Asher said as he put my arm over his shoulders to help me run.

He wouldn't let me slow, even though I wanted to lie down and give up. I was so tired and done with the abuse, and I knew I couldn't go back now. If I did...he'd kill me for sure. "Come on, I have an idea that might help you," he said as we pushed onward through the darkened forest.

Burn

I jerked awake and looked around the living room. My heart no longer raced when I had these dreams. Once, I would've woken up screaming and begging for my father to let go, but now I'd embraced the pain and the lick of that blue flame. They were the reasons why I was someone others feared. Even the fiercest of criminals only dared to whisper my name in the shadows. No one was safe anymore.

The little blonde friend of Chase Mathers called me the Dragon. Now, I embraced the nickname, so much so that a dragon-breathing fire was the image I now had tattooed on my back. Was I a man for hire? A vigilante? A demon reborn? I guess I was all those things. I was simply the man who no longer took the punishment but doled it out. The two things I'd never be were an angel or a mother fucking hero.

Reaching over, I lit the candle on the side table and aimlessly let the little light play among the gaps of my fingers. The candles that would flicker around the small room had become my pets that kept me company. Just like any pet, they wanted attention, but also they were beautiful and misunderstood. I knew all too well what that was like, to be misunderstood and locked away. Well, I now knew that I wasn't supposed to stay there, but that was beside the point.

I hadn't always been this way. I was molded from the time I was a child and manipulated into what I am now. Once I'd seen what my pets could do, though...the damage they could cause amongst so much beauty...I was forever changed.

For years, I'd been denied my urges, denying the satisfaction of seeing my flames consume everything in their path. I loved the way they traveled over a body, eating away the fat and singeing the air with the intoxicating scent of charred flesh.

As the heat intensified, I sucked in a sharp breath, and my palm screamed to be moved away, but my cock pounded hard for more as the flame flared against my hand. Fire was pain and pain was pleasure. That was what the world had created within me. I was a man that could take all the abuse this world had to offer and laugh as I fucking jerked off to it.

Closing my eyes, I let my head fall back against the back of the chair to stare up at the plain white ceiling. It was the perfect background for the tableau playing through my mind. My body shuddered as the face of the woman trapped in her apartment danced behind my eyes. Her screams had been so sweet.

Jerking my hand away from the flame, I stared down at the bright red mark that marred my skin. Bringing the palm to my face, I breathed deeply, the scent of the almost burnt skin. It instantly sent another shock of pleasure through my system.

Grabbing the television remote, I flicked it on and found my latest victim. The show was about to start, and another shiver raced down my spine. This woman was a fake, a pretender that, to the outside world, seemed like a loving single mother, if there was such a thing.

It was all a lie. You followed someone long enough, and you would learn things that most other people would only get a glimpse of—a moment equivalent to a photograph. The girl Kim would tense when her mother would touch her, and unless someone was watching, she would glare at the girl with a look that promised pain. I knew that look. I knew it well, so she had to die. Kim would be far better off without a mother like that in her life.

Smoke began to cloud the other windows in the apartment, and then, there she was. Sarah ran into the kitchen and began pounding on the glass. A small tendril of anger rose from the depths of my gut as I stared at her lying face. I craved her death, and the sliver of healing it would provide, but I also wanted the sweet climax that always followed one of my hunts.

I was like the pied piper—my flaming pet following the path I perfectly laid out. Like a great snake, it had wound its way through the apartment, chasing its prey to the only available escape route left and right to where my camera was able to pick up the entire thing.

I sniffed my hand again, taking a long drag of the scent before placing it back over the candle's flame. I watched with amusement as Sarah's expression shifted from relief to shock as the window wouldn't open.

"Yes, that's it. Look over your shoulder at my creation," I mumbled as Sarah stared back at the kitchen doorway, knowing there was no escape. Oh, how I wished I could hear her screaming as the flames devoured her.

"Yes, pound your fists," I mumbled. Groaning, I gave in to the need, pulled my cock from my jeans, and slowly jerked at my hard length. "Ah, fuck."

Removing my hand from the flame's wick, I stared at the little blister that had formed a moment before my tongue licked at the skin. I sucked in a long-ragged breath as I squeezed my cock harder and moved my fist at a blinding pace. If this was hell, then I never wanted to leave. It was where I belonged.

Glancing down at myself, I smiled as the head of my cock turned an angry shade of red from the abuse. Instead of relinquishing my firm grip, I tightened it until it felt like my shaft was gripped in a vice.

"Oh fuck, yes. Scream, Sarah. Get what's coming to you."

Glancing at the television and the image of the burning building apartment, I smiled until movement caught my eye. My hand slowed, and I leaned forward in my chair as I watched as a blonde from the other apartment building leaped across the alley like this was an episode of "American Ninja."

"What the fuck," I growled as I stood and walked closer to the television. "What the hell do you think you're doing?" I asked the screen as I knelt to get a close-up view. She whipped her shirt off and wrapped it around her hand before punching at the window.

"No! Stop! You're ruining it," I bellowed as the window cracked and shattered.

I stared in shock as the unknown woman pulled Sarah out of her apartment, and they scampered down the metal fire escape and were out of sight from the video. Moments later, my pet erupted, and flames reached out of the window, looking for the prey that had managed to escape.

My chest rose and fell with a building fury raging inside me. My eyes were fixed on the spot on the screen where the blonde had disappeared. Grabbing my phone, I opened the app that controlled the camera and turned it as much as I was able to zoom in on my target and the woman that ruined it all.

My hand balled into a fist as I watched my brother take off his jacket and wrap it around her shoulders like she was some sort of hero. She was no fucking hero. She just saved a child abuser and ruined my kill—all my well-laid plans and stalking up in smoke because of her. I memorized every one of her delicate features. Licking my lips, I pictured how stunning she'd look, screaming as her skin melted from her body, the scent of her burning hair strong in my nose.

Yes, she needed to pay for interfering. I'd make sure of it.

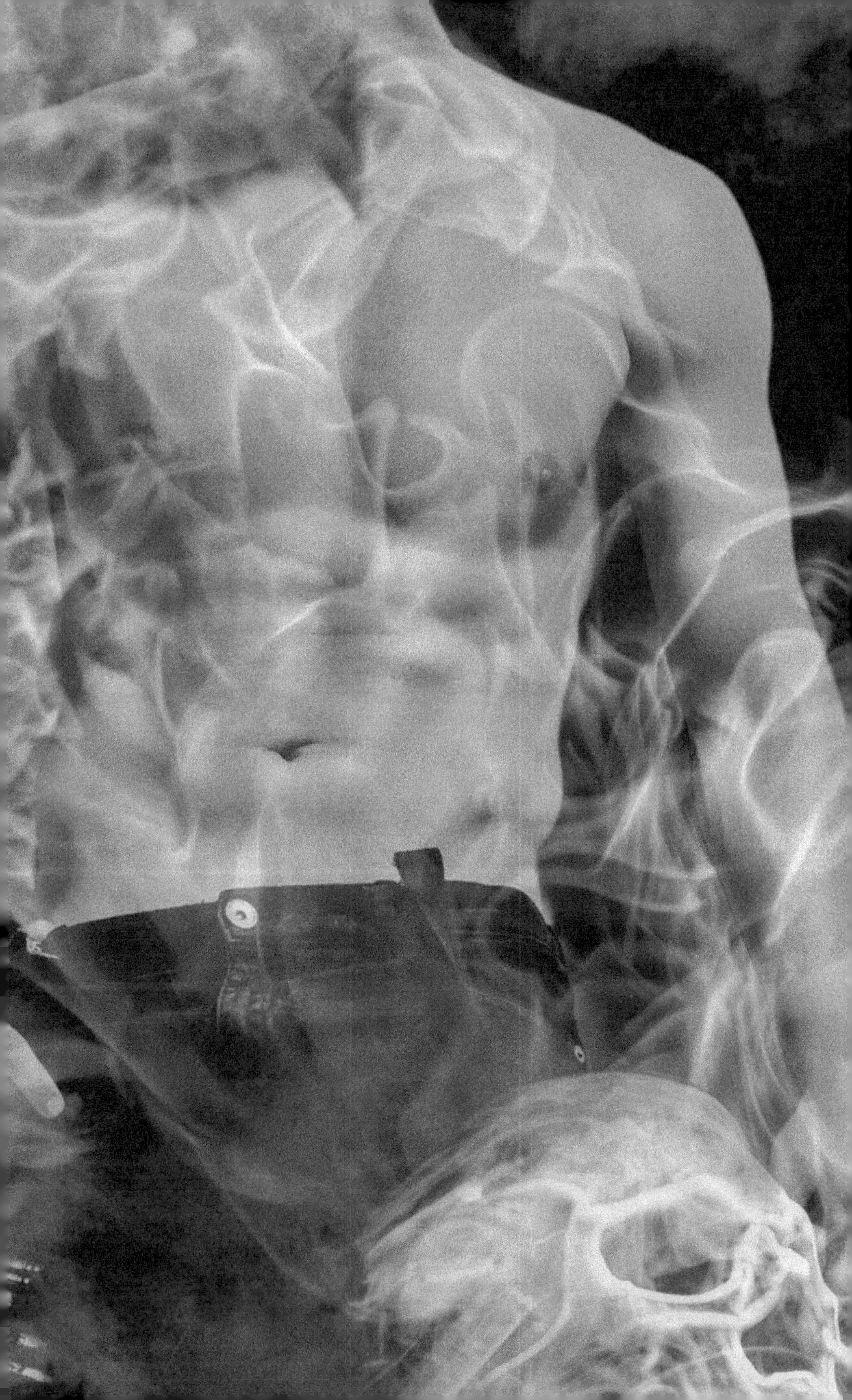

Chapter 7

Asher

"Hey Cap, you good?" Wheels said as he walked past my office.

I looked up from my desk and paperwork to my Lieutenant and nodded. He'd gotten the nickname Wheels because he was always racing from one girl to the next and burning rubber in between them.

"Yeah, I'm good," I said.

"Wanna coffee? I was about to put on a new pot. The way our luck has been running, there won't be any sleep tonight."

"Sounds good. Thanks, Wheels."

I turned my eyes back to the paperwork and the report I was writing about the apartment fire, and I couldn't get past the part where the woman across the alley jumped from the other balcony with seemingly no care for her safety. Even I could admit it was fucking hot, but the look she'd given me when I told her she was crazy was even sweeter.

There was something about her and her blue eyes that seemed so familiar, but I would remember dating or fucking her, so that couldn't be it. Unless...she attended one of the clubs I'd been to on occasion, but I didn't think it was that either. I could usually peg a person's personality pretty easily, but this one felt like a moving target while you were drunk. We hadn't had much interaction, but that didn't usually matter.

For example, Brit was a girl looking for a good time and wanted to explore her sexuality, but she was also spoiled, entitled, and short-sighted. Despite her obvious beauty, Brit had poor self-image issues and was naive as fuck. I knew that about her within the first thirty seconds of speaking to her.

But this one...this fire inspector, Violet Clarke, was...I couldn't put my finger on it. She had a pierced belly button and a wicked tattoo of a fire and a burning house that traveled up the side of her ribcage. She hadn't picked cute little hearts, flowers, or kitty tattoos. No, it was a statement piece. It showed pain and grit because a tattoo like that would've taken hours, especially in one of the most painful places to have work like that done. I couldn't even picture her in one of the stuffy suits like all the talking heads at HQ wore. She had tenacity and a backbone, but there was sadness and heat that burned in her eyes that all swirled together.

It was easy to picture laying her over my lap and tanning her cute ass before fucking her hard as she tried to hit me for daring to touch her. Oh yeah, I fucking loved that image.

Did I plan on seeking her out? No. Maybe. I wasn't sure. To do that meant first breaking off what I had going on with Brit.

Putting the pen down, I gave in to the urge to pull up the internal employee database on my laptop. My fingers quickly typed in her name, and boom, just like that, there she was in her pristine white blouse that was tucked into a dark skirt. She looked exactly like one of the political asswipes that annoyed the fuck out of me, but the heels she was wearing…those screamed, 'I'm a bad girl.' I could easily picture pulling that perfect skirt up and bending her over a desk.

I quickly read over the description of her accolades and wasn't surprised to see that she participated in the "Tough Mudder" competitions. Seems like she would travel to all those held within a day's drive, and the image I found of her covered in mud in a pair of tight shorts and a smile as wide as the entire State of Florida across her face told me that she was so my fucking type.

I groaned as I heard Wheels call out a welcome to Brit, who apparently decided that dropping in on me during my night shift was a great idea. Most of the time, I wondered if she was making sure I was actually on shift. I was many things, but a cheater wasn't one of them, and it pissed me off that she was always questioning me.

Closing the laptop, I returned to my paperwork and managed to scroll my signature across the bottom just before she walked into my office.

"Ever heard of knocking," I drawled before slowly lifting my eyes to hers.

"I brought treats." She held out a small box from a bakery and then proceeded to untie the front of her long coat. Brit looked over her shoulder to make sure we were still alone as she parted the material to show off that she wasn't wearing anything underneath.

This was a new trick. She'd never tried to seduce me at work, and I wasn't exactly opposed to the idea. But because I was the station's captain, I needed to maintain a certain level of professionalism.

"So, you're just looking to be fucked?"

"Well, I thought that was obvious," she purred and ran her fingers down my shirt.

"I mean, do you want to be used? Don't care how, where or who?" I asked and she moaned slightly and sucked in her bottom lip.

That was what I thought.

"Yes. Is this where you force me to my knees again?" She stepped in closer.

"Not exactly. Wheels," I called out.

Within moments, I could hear his boots echoing down the hallway.

"Yeah, Cap?" he said as he reached the door, but his eyes were glued on Brit who'd pulled the material of her coat tight around herself.

Turning my gaze down to Brit, who looked unsure of what she'd just agreed to, I nodded in Wheels's direction. "Okay, go service him then."

"What?" Brit and Wheels said in unison.

Wheels and I had been friends since the last year of high school, and we had shared partners on more than one occasion, and I happened to know he was currently single. I wasn't in the mood for Brit and had no issue sharing her. She was with me to be trained, not to have a lifelong relationship. This was a lesson in learning what you're actually getting into before you agree.

"You said you want to be fucked, right?"

"Well yeah, but I-I thought that meant b-by you," she stammered.

"Did you or did you not agree to be shared," I asked, sitting down again.

"I did."

"Did you or did you not agree that it would be on my terms when and where that would happen?"

"I did," she said a little softer.

"Are you wanting to break our deal," I asked calmly and picked up my pen.

"No."

I pointed toward Wheels behind her. "Well then, go service him. Whatever he wants, you do until he's finished or the alarm goes off for the next call, whichever comes first." Turning in my chair, I moved the apartment fire paperwork into a folder and began writing up the car fire we'd also attended earlier in the evening.

"What if I don't want to?" I could hear her pouting, the tap of her shoe making a loud click behind my chair.

"Then I guess you'll be finding a new arrangement with someone else," I said, beginning to make notes.

"But I'm bratting," she said like that was supposed to get me up out of my chair and lay her over my lap. No, that was precisely what she wanted, so that was not what she was going to get.

"I see that," I simply said.

"Asher, this isn't fair," she complained. "I came here to see you."

"Yes, you did," I said in response, but I still refused to turn around.

"What if I crawled under your desk and sucked you off instead? No offense, Wheels," Brit said, and the corner of my mouth pulled up.

"Is that what you want? What you really want?" I turned just enough in my chair to look at her and lay my hand on my thigh. She followed the movement with her eyes and licked her lips as she nodded.

"Then no," I said.

"What?"

"You heard me." I stood from my chair, put my hands behind my back, and walked forward until Brit was forced to step back and out of my office. "Two choices, you either do what I asked like a good girl, or you get out and never come back."

Her eyes were wide as her mouth dropped open like I'd just told her that her favorite toy had been just thrown out.

"But...but...that's not fair," she complained and tied her coat in place around her naked body.

"We've been together five months now, Brit. You're more than capable of finding a new Dom now, or you can go and do what you agreed to when we first got together. That is the choice you made, so it is fair."

The look of bewilderment on her face told me all I needed to know, so I continued. "I'm not a boy toy or your boyfriend. We had an arrangement that you seemed to think was more than that. This little lesson is to remind you that we don't. I'm your Dom, and I've been loyal to my end of the bargain, but this is also my place of work.

I've told you twice not to come here because I keep my professional life separate from my lifestyle. Yet, here you are."

"I thought you were joking. I thought you really liked it when I showed up."

My brow furrowed as I pictured our last conversation. How the hell had she managed to go from "Don't come to my place of work" to "It was only a joke?" Had I fucking laughed? She licked her lips, her eyes darting away from mine.

"I'm not doing it," she said, crossing her arms.

My hands itched to teach her a lesson, but I knew this would be more punishment than doing anything else.

"Then you know where the door is, use it and don't come back or call me again. We are done. Consider our agreement to be canceled."

Brit's hands gripped my shirt, her eyes filling with tears. "No, please, I'm begging you. I only want you."

"Did I say you could touch me?"

She shook her head no as her hands uncurled from the tight hold she had on my shirt.

"Then you know what you need to do, or there's the door. This is your choice."

I glanced at Wheels, who stood quietly with his arms crossed over his chest, and a curl on his lips. The guy was used to this kind of display. I wouldn't call myself a brat tamer, that term was used for someone with a lot more patience than me, but I did seem to have a type. He'd been part of more than one of these situations and took them all in stride. I had to admit that I'd never met a woman who was so uninterested in Wheels. The guy was hot as fuck, even by guy standards.

"But I love you," she blurted out and then covered her mouth.

I shook my head slowly. "Then it is definitely time for us to part ways. I told you not to fall in love with me and that this was a mutual arrangement. You said and agreed to the terms, and you were supposed to leave if you thought you might be developing feelings, and you obviously didn't. So, it's time for you to go. Please be safe in your journey to finding your next partner."

Stepping inside my office I closed the door and locked it.

"You're an asshole," she yelled and pounded her fist on the door. "I hate you! I'm going to tell the world what an ass you are."

As I continued to ignore her, and with encouragement from Wheels, Brit stormed away. I felt a little bad that she'd fallen in love with me, but I wasn't the falling-in-love type. It didn't seem to matter how many times I made that clear. There were always a few who didn't listen or follow the rules. They ended up angry and feeling betrayed. Brit had never even been to my home, met my foster-mother, or known my birthday. Did that sound like someone interested in a committed relationship? No. But here we were.

Flicking open the laptop, the screen flashed and then settled on the picture that I'd been staring at before I was interrupted. Maybe one day I'd settle down with one partner, but I hadn't met that person yet, and I wasn't rushing out to find her.

I was content with the way my life was.

Violet

"Are you kidding me?" Beck paced across the living room and then back again. Her face was starting to turn tomato red, which was worrying me. I wasn't sure if she was planning on passing out or was going to reach full meltdown mode.

"One night. I go out one stinking night, and not only do you almost get yourself killed, which we will be talking about further, but you didn't get the freaking hot firefighter's first name? I mean, that's like rule number one, Vi." She slapped her hands together, making Heathrow in my lap jump as much as I did. "Are you listening to me," she growled like a parent, scolding me.

"Yes, I think the entire neighborhood is listening to you," I said.

I stroked Heathrow's soft fur as he settled back down into my lap. I think he was the only one enjoying the show from his front-row seat.

"Don't you sass me, Missy." Beck flopped in the large recliner, the thing squeaking in protest as it rocked back. "Do you even know how long it's been since you got laid? I do. Two years, three months, and four days."

My hand stilled. "Okay, that's seriously creepy, Beck. I didn't even know that. I don't think I even cared enough to know that."

"That's because you've forgotten what it's like to get laid by anyone. You need to find this guy. It is like a total must."

"I'm not searching for him. He was a complete jerk. He called me crazy and gave me a look."

Beck leaned forward, her elbows going to her knees as she gave me her death stare. "A look?"

"Yeah, it was like, an 'I'm going to put you over my knee and spank your ass 'cause you did something stupid,' look," I mocked. "It was completely degrading."

"I love this guy already, and you are so finding him." She pointed her finger at me exactly how her mother would do to us. "So here is what's going to happen. First, you're getting his number, or I'm going to start bringing home every random guy I can find to meet you. Hashtag: most-awkward-moments-ever because I will make sure they're all sorts of wrong. I'm talking finger-up-the-nose-and-eating-it while he's talking to you, wrong."

I cringed.

"Or the hand-down-the-back-of-the-pants-to-scratch-his-ass-before-handing-you-your-meal wrong," Beck said, emphasizing each and every word. "You feel me?"

"You've got to be kidding me? Have you lost your damn mind?"

"Nope. You haven't looked twice at a guy in two years—"

I held up my hand to stop her from restating my seriously sad sex life again.

"The point is, this guy made you wet." Beck pointed at me again. "You need to find him."

"Fuck, I didn't say he made me wet. Geez-us, girl, why do you keep pushing for me to see this asshole? He's not a nice guy."

She screwed up her face like I'd just made her suck on a lemon. "Sooo, you know all about him from your five minutes together? And he couldn't be right, considering you could've easily killed yourself or created a bigger problem like breaking your own neck?"

I glared daggers at her. "I was completely fine."

Did I believe the words coming out of my mouth? No. Once I'd arrived at the hospital to have my hand stitched, I realized how big of a risk I had taken. The thing was, I couldn't just stand there and do nothing.

"Okay look." Beck blew air out of her mouth like she was building up to start a huge rant.

I'd never met anyone that could tell a person off for as long as she could in one single breath. It was impressive.

"You never look at guys. I mean, you're surrounded by hotness all the time, and you don't even bat an eyelash. Those men in uniform at fire scenes with their faces covered in ash and soot...." She licked her lips, her eyes drifting off. "Point is, it's like they're completely invisible to you while I'm over here panting and drooling."

I smirked at the imagery. She was exaggerating, of course. Beck didn't have to worry about her supply of men, but she acted like she was a dusty broom closet.

"But your exact words were, and I quote, 'he was pretty damn hot, and you wondered what he tasted like,' " she said, pausing for dramatic effect. "Girl, that is code for 'hells bells, boy, you are fine, and I'm dripping, so get back here so I can fuck you.' " Beck smiled wide as she grabbed the bottle of water off the table and took a swig.

My mouth hung open as I stared at her.

"You're the crazy one. You know that?" I rubbed at my face, and of course, all I could see was Mr. Hottie with the smoldering eyes that promised some form of pleasure. I just wasn't sure I wanted to find out what that meant. "You're not going to let this go are you?"

I wasn't sure if I was annoyed or excited, but I did have a quasi-legit reason to find Mister West. Mitch told me he wanted me to focus my time on the serial arsonist because they still had zero leads. Not that a firefighter helped with an investigation normally, but I could come up with a few questions to ask him.

Was I really going to do this?

"Not a chance in hell. You find him, or I will. That is a promise. And, trust me, if I find him before you, I'll make sure to embarrass you so badly you'll want to move states."

Now, that...I did believe.

I held up my hands in surrender. "Okay, you win. I'll find Mister Hot Guy."

Beck squealed and leaped from the chair, making Heathrow yowl in fright before he took off to another room, and I was pulled into a ridiculous dance party. I had no doubt I looked more like I was getting a monkey hug from a jumping bean than dancing. Beck paused and held me at arm's length.

"Okay, now for the clothes and your hair." She gave my ponytail a flick before dragging me toward her room.

Oh dear lord, what had I just gotten myself into?

Burn

It was easy to get Mitch to agree to give me the apartment building to investigate. I was sure he assumed I was taking him up on his advice and all too happy that I was giving up on my quest to find my parents' murderer.

Although this wasn't my parents' case, I did sort of know Sarah and needed to complete some of the building cases on my desk, and the apartment fire was a good place to start. I stared at the box which held all the fires in the last year that were still unsolved.

"Shit, am I really going to do this?"

Now that I was here, this seemed like the lamest excuse in the world to find this guy. I was positive he was going to see right through it like I was a fake twenty-dollar bill. I was staring at my phone as I thought, not really seeing anything, when a sharp knock sounded beside my ear.

"Shit," I swore as I jumped, grabbing at my chest with a start.

I knew who it was before I looked, and sure enough, there he was —Hot Guy standing outside my car by my door.

Well, I guess that decided for me. Just play it cool, Vi, play it cool.

I gripped the door handle, and he stepped back so I could get out. "Hi there, just the person I was coming to see," I said, trying for cool and unfazed.

West crossed his arms over his chest but didn't say anything. Unnerving much? His sandy blonde hair flopped messily around his face like he'd just had a shower and was letting it air dry. I instantly wanted to run my fingers through it. Was it as soft as it looked?

Clearing my throat, I continued, "I got assigned the apartment case. My boss thinks it might be connected to the serial arsonist that has been very active lately. I need to go back and investigate, but I was hoping to steal a firefighter to go with me."

His lip curled up in a smirk. It was really not fair to command that much attention with one tiny lift of a lip, but fuck, it made me squirm inside. "And you chose me. Why?"

Leaning back against the Jeep, I refused to let him see that he was affecting me. The last thing I needed was for this guy to think I was begging for his attention, hell to the f-ing no. Hot or not, I wasn't the type to beg for a man's attention.

"You're a captain and were there. You know the scene firsthand, who did what at the fire to put it out, and if anyone found anything of significance. You were simply the obvious choice." I shrugged. "So why not you?"

My eyes raked over his body involuntarily like they had a mind of their own that wasn't attached to anything smart or sensible. Placing his hands on his hips as if he was purposely trying to show off his wide shoulders and muscular chest, I had to stop myself from staring or letting my mouth hang open.

Stare into his eyes, stare into his fucking eyes.

He nodded toward my hand. "I see you went and had your hand stitched. How is it doing?"

I glanced down at the white bandage that made it look like I'd broken the thing and not had seventeen stitches instead. "Oh, bit stiff, but otherwise fine. I wasn't going to go, but the paramedic guilted me into going." I shrugged.

West chuckled, and the sound created all sorts of naughty images. "Why doesn't that surprise me?"

He rubbed his thumb over his bottom lip, and I watched it like a fucking cat ready to pounce on a mouse, so of course, that was when my mouth ran amuck.

"Did you know that an average, single sprinkler head pushes out approximately twenty-one point two gallons of water per minute? Well, that's technically only the first pipeline. Then as pressure decreases as it travels throughout a building, it reduces to fifteen gallons per minute." West just blinked as he stared at me, so of course, I continued rambling. "The average toilet flushes one point six gallons in a single flush, so in reality, it's like someone flushed nine-point-three-seven-five gallons per sprinkler head, per minute." I paused which only made the nervous blurting worse. "I wonder if anyone else wonders how many toilet flushes it would take to put out a fire?"

As soon as the words left my mouth, I wanted to crawl under my car and die of embarrassment. What the hell was wrong with me?

He smiled wide, and I could feel my face heating to the point that I knew my cheeks and neck would be bright red. "Fascinating. Are you going to tell me about my hose next? Maybe how much pressure it can hold before it would need to be released?"

My mind went blank as my mouth fell open. I ended up sucking in my lower lip, as my throat went completely dry when he burst out laughing. "Alright, Violet Clarke, we'll start with dinner. If you can convince me why I should help you, then I'll do it."

"Um...but I didn't say anything about dinner."

"Your eyes did. Meet me here tomorrow night at seven. I need to go home and sleep off my night shift, but I'm off tomorrow. We can pick a place to go then." He turned away, walking toward a large pickup truck, and I was left standing there with my mouth open.

"Hey, do I get to know your name, or should I just call you West?" I called after him.

He gave me a cocky smile as he looked over his shoulder at me. "You're the investigator, so investigate."

Son of a bitch.

Violet

I was never letting Beck talk me into going shopping again. She dragged me into one store after the next until I would've agreed to purchase a Big Bird suit as long as it meant that she would let me go home.

Shopping and I were not friends. Much like dating and I were not friends either. Dating and I were like oil and water or vampires and sunshine. Nothing ever stuck. Not one relationship felt like more than I was passing the time with someone just to say that I had a boyfriend. So, my solution had been simple...scratch them all off the dance card, and I'd never be disappointed. So how the hell did I get talked into this nonsense again?

Dinner.

Like a date.

Ugh.

Sighing, I glanced at myself one last time in the rearview mirror. I wasn't sure about the fat curls that Beck insisted on putting in my hair. I felt like a fluffy pixie as a few of the curls bounced around my face while the rest of my hair was twisted up on top of my head. I mean, what was this, a casting for Tinkerbell?

I didn't mind the way she'd done my makeup, though. It wasn't overdone, but it did make my eyes pop. This dress, on the other hand...I was terrified to get out of my jeep. The thing was so short that I was pretty sure I was going to flash the world like I was after a tabloid picture for the paparazzi.

"Okay, you got this, Vi," I said as I spotted West's truck pull into the station parking lot.

Stepping out of my Jeep, I smoothed down the pink dress that Beck insisted I wear. I felt like all I needed was thigh-high boots, and I could've auditioned for the part of Pretty Woman. The little material clung way too tight, and my hand itched to pull at the bottom. Oh, how I wished it was at least six inches longer. I didn't even need to look down to know that I was showing off way more cleavage than I normally would, and I desperately wished I had a hoodie to pull over the outfit and cover myself up.

All hail the grunge look.

"Wow, I was thinking of a burger and fries, but that dress screams surf and turf."

I slowly turned to face West, well, Asher. After only a bit of digging, I'd learned that was his first name. Why did that name fit him so well? Maybe because it screamed that he was made for television.

"You didn't bother sticking around long enough to give me a dress code. I assumed that when you con a girl into having dinner, it would at least have wine." I reached for the handle of my vehicle. "I could go home instead. Trust me. This is not what I would prefer to be wearing."

"I guess it would be a shame if all that went to waste," he said, his eyes quickly scanning over my outfit and making me want to squirm.

"That?" I lifted a brow at him and grabbed the handle to yank open my door.

Screw this.

His hand stopped my door from opening.

"I'm sorry. You look beautiful, really. Like smokin' hot beautiful. I just like bantering with you." I turned and realized how close he suddenly was. I could feel the heat coming off him, and it froze me in place and made my pulse spike.

He reminded me of a lion or some other large predatory animal. It was the way his eyes searched mine while his powerful body loomed over me. Swallowing hard, my eyes locked with his.

"You give it as good as you take it. I like that. Very few are willing to put me in my place, but I have a feeling you're more than willing to push back." His eyes flicked to my lips, and I couldn't stop myself from licking them.

I couldn't tell if he was flirting or simply stating a fact, but it felt like every word was licking its way up my legs. My heart hammered like a drum as I continued to stare into his eyes. I needed to come up with a coherent sentence, and yet very few words were coming to mind other than, 'holy fuck me, you're hot.' Thankfully, I didn't blurt that out.

"Okay, Asher West, where did you want to go then?" I managed to get out and sound like an intelligent human.

Those electric blue eyes danced as a smile played on his lips. "So, you figured out my name."

"Of course I did. I'm a good investigator." I smirked and then laughed, unable to hold a straight face. "Wasn't that tough. I typed your last name into the internal database. Thanks for being annoying, though, and making me do that." My tone was sarcastic as hell, and it was a good thing.

He smiled wide and showed off that he had not just one sexy dimple but two. Of course, he had two sexy dimples that magically made him more delicious. Never mind the strange pull his personality had. It was like he was a magnet slowly sucking me toward him. I didn't like it, and I didn't like this out-of-control butterfly feeling or my sweaty palms. Geez-us, all I could think about was how to talk him into fucking me in his truck. This was insane and wasn't me.

"All right, oh, brilliant investigator, I know this great place on the water where this dress will not go to waste."

He glanced at my hand still on the handle of my Jeep door, and it felt like he was testing me. Would I let go or not? I so wanted to hang on to see what he would do, but it didn't seem like the time or place to continue pushing his buttons. Yeah, I could admit that I was enjoying our little game of tug-o-war. Letting go of the handle, I hit the lock button and dropped my keys into the way too-tiny clutch that Beck lent me.

"Right this way, your chariot awaits." Asher's hand gently grazed my arm as he held his arm out dramatically toward the truck.

I didn't know if it was intentional, but it sent a rocket of heat soaring through my body. I took a steadying breath and followed along beside him.

"I'll be honest, I kind of pictured you as a flashy sports car kind of guy," I said as I stared at the conservative pick-up truck. The only thing flashy on it was the fancy chrome rims and black-out windows.

"Disappointed?"

"Hardly. I was trying to figure out how I was going to fold myself into a low sports car without flashing the world."

Asher laughed. The sound was smooth like butter, creating this thick warm feeling inside me, like sweet caramel that had been seasoned with sea salt. Great, now all I could picture was him drizzled with caramel sauce and licking it off.

"Well, that's a shame. I wouldn't have complained," he said as he held open my door and his hand to help me up.

I didn't bother to retort to the obvious sexual joke, and I ignored his hand and swung myself up into the truck with ease. I caught the hint of humor in his eyes as he removed his hand but kept standing there with his hand on the door as if trying to figure me out. I had a feeling that Mister West wasn't used to a woman like me.

"So, you're saying there won't be any complaining about a bumpy ride ruining your hair? Or saying that you'll look like you've been kidnapped by a redneck?"

I had to laugh. That was a strange visual, and I honestly didn't think anyone would ever say either one of those things with this man behind the wheel.

"Do I look like a girl that complains about my hair?"

Asher's eyes traveled down my body to the strappy little heels I was wearing before returning to my face. "Actually, yes, but then you open your mouth, and it all flies away."

"Now, that is the sweetest thing anyone has ever said to me." I gave him a smile, and it was a real one, something that usually only Beck got out of me.

"Books and covers...I guess I just learned my lesson," Asher said as he closed my door and walked around his truck.

He got in the driver's side, and the already warm vehicle notched up a couple more degrees as he looked over. I realized I was now inside a space smaller than a prison cell with this man who did all sorts of weird things to my body. I was officially his prisoner wherever he decided to take me, which excited and terrified me.

Asher started the truck, the diesel roaring to life with a growl.

"Did you always want to be a firefighter?" I asked as we pulled out of the parking lot.

His body language was relaxed, but his eyes told a different story. They held a dead and pained stare I recognized all too well.

"I had a family incident when I was younger, and it sort of changed me forever. I wanted to be a firefighter from that day on," he said but didn't elaborate any further. I wanted to push to know if he had lived through the same pain I had, but I held my tongue.

"What about you? What made you want to go through the fire academy and put up with knuckleheads like me to become an investigator?"

I looked out the window to the beach, and the water glistened in the late-day sun. My Dad's face flashed in my mind. The sound of him calling my name would never leave me. Maybe that was why I'd accepted my mother's death a little easier. It wasn't that I loved her any less, but I didn't have to see her screaming face or hear her yelling my name. My hand clenched the little clutch tighter in my lap.

"I lost my parents to a house fire, and ever since, I was hooked. If you ask my best friend, she'd say that I'm obsessed, but I just felt the need to find answers for myself and help other people find closure."

"I'm really sorry," Asher said. His voice was soft and sounded genuine without all the teasing or flirtatiousness.

I glanced over at him, and his eyes held understanding. Most pitied me or were even terrified when I told them my theory about my parents being murdered. I got the feeling Asher would believe me and wouldn't run screaming.

"That is one thing you never get used to in this line of work. Seeing people lose everything...their homes, belongings, and some-times loved ones. Seeing their tear-stained cheeks and listening to their pained wails sticks with me," he said.

I stared at the side of his face, and I couldn't tell if he was talking about himself or if he was truly that empathetic.

We ended up sitting in silence the rest of the way to the restau-rant, with just the radio playing an assortment of songs. It wasn't necessarily uncomfortable, but a shadow had descended on the earlier teasing mood. As Asher slowed and flicked on his turn signal, I knew exactly where we were heading. I stared up at the massive boat that had been turned into a floating restaurant. It was one of the hardest places to get a seat in the state.

"You weren't kidding about going someplace on the water," I said as we parked.

Getting out of the truck, I wandered to the driver's side and took a deep breath of the salty air.

"I'll take it you've never been?"

I shook my head no.

"Most of my meals consist of whatever I can grab through a drive-thru or whatever my roommate decides to make." I lifted my shoulder and let it drop.

"Well, you're in for a treat. This place has the best food. Normally, I'd say that it would be impossible to get in, but there is always a table or two for those who know the owner."

He gave me one of those sly smiles that just reaffirmed why this guy had to be a player. That meant I should already be coming up with all the reasons to tell Beck why I decided not to work with him.

"It will be nice not to have to eat noodles out of styrofoam," I said and then almost choked on my saliva as Asher whipped the white T-shirt he'd been wearing off over his head. I was left staring at his muscled back and had to snap my mouth closed as he turned toward me.

"Is that so? What spot is your go-to?" he asked as he pulled out a dress shirt from the back seat like magic. It was as if he was moving in slow motion, my mind making a movie of his too-sexy smile and how he swung the shirt around his shoulders. I could hear the cologne commercial music in my head. All he needed was the tall leggy model walking up and hooking her arm through his to complete the look.

"I'm sorry, what?"

My face began to heat as he let the shirt hang open like he wasn't changing in front of me. I tried not to stare. I would swear on any bible if I had to, but holy fuck, my eyes refused to listen. Those suckers had a mind of their own. His chest tattoo of a fiery skull was so realistic that it looked like it would burst right out of his torso. Then, those amazing pecs flexed for no reason, yet I shamefully watched them, my mouth running dry. I had to admit that I was disappointed the show was ending as his hands were working to close the buttons.

"I asked what is your favorite spot to get noodles?"

It was such a simple question, and all I really wanted to say was something completely inappropriate.

"Um...I...I don't think I have a favorite. It's more about what I happen to be near," I managed to spit out and then bit my lip to keep myself from spewing out something stupid.

"You think this will do?" He smoothed down the front of the shirt before rolling up the sleeves. My mind jerked out of the slow-mo montage it had going on and then scrambled to catch up with what he said.

"Yup, but I'm pretty sure you already knew that," I said.

That mischievous look was back in his eyes, and although he didn't say it, I knew he knew I enjoyed what I was seeing. He unzipped his black jeans, and I was graced with a quick view of a perfect Adonis V before he tucked in his shirt.

Florida was known for being hot in the summer, but I suddenly needed to install an entire air conditioner inside my dress.

"You ready?" Asher pointed to the large boat. "The restaurant. Are you ready to go eat," he asked again as I'd once more drifted off into la-la land where my hands were ripping his shirt off instead of him putting it on.

"Yes, of course. Lead the way."

"Have you lived here your whole life," Asher asked as he held out his elbow.

I stared at it. I'd never been offered an elbow. I was a tomboy, one of the guys. I got punches in the arm and high-fives. Swallowing down the strange nervousness of the situation, I slowly looped my arm through his.

"Yeah, I have."

"Then tell me, how is it that you have not tried, Poppy Cox? I mean, the name alone screams, 'eat here at least once.' " The wonderful aroma of steak and seafood was already wafting toward me.

"I'm allergic to shellfish," I said, keeping my face straight as Asher's fell.

"Shit, I'm sorry. I should've asked. We could go somewhere else? There's an Italian restaurant not far from here or...."

I started to laugh, bringing Asher's rant to a halt.

"You're not allergic, are you?" I shook my head no, unable to stop laughing. "That was just mean," he said, but his look said he was more surprised I'd pulled one over on him. Looked good on him not to be so confident for a moment. It made him feel more real.

"I couldn't resist. Honestly, I just don't go out much."

"I know, but not even a date has brought you here?"

I didn't look up at him. It seemed stupid that I was embarrassed to say that I didn't date much. I mean, it was normal, not everyone had a social schedule they needed a calendar for, but it did feel weird to admit.

"I don't date."

"Oh."

"I mean, I don't do one-night stands or troll the streets. It's not like I'm desperate," I babbled, and I wanted so badly to smack a hand on my forehead. "Let me try that again. I've not had the interest or time to date someone. I like my life the way it is," I said, sounding more confident that time.

"Huh, interesting."

"Huh, interesting? What does that mean?" My back started to bristle for his inevitable, 'you're pathetic speech.'

Asher shrugged. "Just what I said. I find it interesting. You're an amazingly beautiful woman. I'm just shocked, is all. But, I like that you knew what you wanted or didn't and stuck with it."

My stomach took that exact moment to growl like a bear had just stepped up beside us, which was also another reason why I didn't date. This moment right here encapsulated everything I hated about trying to impress another human being. It simply sucked, shit happened, and I always felt like an idiot.

"Well, at least I know you're hungry." Asher laughed as my cheeks heated.

I knew they'd be glowing a bright pink. I wasn't one of those cute blondes that lived in a tropical area that could tan until it looked like they'd been dipped in honey. Nope, I had the type of skin that liked to burn and go cherry tomato red before peeling. Blushing easily in the fire academy had not done me any favors in the teasing department.

Asher nudged my shoulder, and when I looked up, the quick pang of insecurity evaporated. The smile he was giving me was confident with a hint of sweetness. Even though he didn't say it, I could tell that he hadn't made a comment to be condescending. There was something about him that was calming, even with all of his arrogance and sharp wit. I liked that.

He guided the way toward the long gangplank, which was decorated like the rest of the ship. Little white lights lined the railing everywhere like they were guiding our way. It wasn't quite dark enough yet to appreciate them, but an hour from now, they would twinkle as if the stars had been plucked from the sky as decoration. We stepped aboard the tall ship, and I stared out at the ocean. The view was incredible.

Asher walked confidently. His stride was long but not enough that I felt pressured to move faster. I was impressed with how he managed to seem so in control but still completely mindful. He was definitely unlike any man I'd met.

"Mr. West, it is good to see you. Come right this way," the Maître'd said, as we stepped up to the small desk area. She paused and settled her eyes on me. "If you get chilled, there is a gift shop on the top deck that sells shawls."

"Oh, thank you." I looked up to where the elegant woman pointed.

This place was stunning. The tables were swathed in black tablecloths and a matching nautical theme everywhere else. I especially loved the black and white sheers that hung from the rods that ran the length of the sitting area. It was as if the designer had taken the theme and turned it on its head so that it had a high end elegant flare, just like the woman seating us.

We had a lantern on the table shaped like an anchor, and I couldn't help but stare at the little glowing light.

"Flames are hypnotic, aren't they?" Asher nodded at the candle.

I turned my gaze away from the flame to look at him. He, too, was staring at the dancing orange light, a glazed look in his eyes as the flame reflected back at me.

"Sometimes they can feel that way, and sometimes flames are just horrifying," I said. "Is there anything on the menu you'd recommend?"

"Anything, it's all amazing," Asher said. "But if you'd like to try a little of everything, then I'd definitely go for the 'surf and turf' platter. You won't find better anywhere else."

"Now, that is what I like to hear every customer say." A petite woman with her hair done up in a bun and wearing the standard clothes of a head chef walked toward the table. Everything about her announced that she was in charge. "Asher, as always, it's good to see you."

Asher stood and gave the woman a brief hug, his face softening and I could clearly see a different side to the man that wore a mask of indifference.

"Violet, this is my cousin Monique."

"Nice to meet you, Violet." I held out my hand for the woman to shake, and it was shocking how strong her grip was as she reciprocated the gesture.

"Likewise, Monique, but please call me Vi. You have a great spot here." Monique released my hand and looked around at the stunning deck that had been transformed into a magical getaway experience.

"Thanks. It took a lot of hard work, but it's paid off." We all cringed at the sound of glass shattering in the kitchen area. "Well, that's my cue to go and make sure they don't destroy anything else. I know you will love the meal, Vi. Ash, it's on the house," Monique called out, already walking away.

"She seems great," I said and took a sip of the water that had been delivered.

"She really is. She's my step cousin or I guess foster cousin." Asher picked up the wine menu. "She is the daughter of my foster-mother's sister, but when her mother passed away she came to live with us too. Wow I made that complicated."

He smiled and I giggled. At least I wasn't the only one that did that.

"So you prefer to be called Vi?"

"By my friends, yes," I said.

His eyes lifted from the menu. "And what would you consider me?"

"I'm not sure yet. You did call me crazy," I smirked as he chuckled.

"So I did. Alright, I'll take back crazy and say that you were one terrible decision away from never investigating again."

"I'm pretty sure that is not any better, but I see your point." I looked out over the water and the calm waves rolling toward the shore. "I just couldn't stand there and watch her die."

I could feel Asher's eyes on me, but I didn't feel like getting into my story right now.

"Fine, you can call me Vi." My eyes returned to his. "Anything good on the wine menu?"

"Do you prefer sweet or dry, white or red?"

"Tough call. You know the place, how about you choose? I'm

sure it'll be great. I'm not fussy," I said as the waitress approached the table.

"Good evening, what can I get for you," she asked, her small tablet ready for the order to be typed in.

"I'll try the 'surf and turf' platter, all the fixings, and a garden salad to start," I said, and Asher ordered the identical thing and a couple of glasses of wine.

"So tell me, did you already go back to the apartment?"

"Yes, I poked around for a little while before getting ready to come to meet you. The thing is, I didn't find anything that screamed arson. Don't get me wrong. It certainly seems like arson in many ways, but I couldn't find a specific ignition source. The scene is eerie, like the fire simply decided to start everywhere all at once."

"That certainly is strange. Tell me, why do you want me to take a look? What am I going to find that you wouldn't have already found," Asher asked as the waitress set the wine glasses on the table and a basket of fresh bread. "I did a little bit of research on you, and from what I could find, you're an exemplary investigator. You have closed almost twice as many cases than any of the other investigators."

I squirmed under the scrutiny of his stare. The fact that he'd spent time looking me up and reading over my accomplishments was flattering and unnerving as hell.

"I was especially impressed with how you closed the Rogers case," he said. "That case sat open for a few years, and no one had been able to help the police, but you did."

My gut clenched tight, and I could feel my cheeks warming again.

These were conversations I had a million times, yet the way he said it felt much more intimate.

Needing desperately to do something with my hands, I reached for one of the pieces of bread and quickly buttered it. My hands were shaking ever so slightly, and as he watched my hands work, I prayed that he didn't notice.

"I need fresh eyes on this one. I have a past case that could be clouding my judgment. I don't like to make assumptions or fast conclusions," I said and took a bite of the bread.

Asher reached across the table, and I froze. He placed his thumb at the corner of my mouth and gently wiped it.

"A bit of butter." His tone rumbled throughout my body. But then my eyes went wide as he put that same thumb in his mouth. I almost choked because I forgot how to swallow.

"My apologies, that was very forward of me," he said, but the look in his eyes told me he wasn't sorry at all. In fact, he knew exactly what he was doing to me and was enjoying every second of it.

Sitting the rest of the bread down, I cleared my throat, but I was at a complete loss as to what to say. My brain seemed to have short-circuited and all I could picture was a cartoon character getting zapped by electricity. Well, that's what I felt like.

"What is this other case you mentioned, the one that is similar?"

Leaning in a little closer so no one overheard, I dropped my voice. "There are similarities to the fire that killed my parents, but just like their case, there wasn't quite enough to prove that someone had intentionally set the fire. I have no idea if this is the same arsonist. My parents' death was a while ago, but I need another perspective, someone with no preconceived notions."

"Basically, you want someone who doesn't know your story or past to take a look?"

"Exactly. Will you take a look with me?"

Ash sat back in his chair and crossed his arms over his chest. He looked out over the ocean. His eyes fixed on something I couldn't see.

"Alright. I'm not sure how much help I can provide, but I'm off work the next three days, so...."

"Perfect, tomorrow morning it is." I smiled wide as he lifted an eyebrow at my brazen behavior. "After, I'll treat you to the best waffles in the state," I said to sweeten the deal.

"Well, how is a guy to say no to waffles?"

Smiling wide, I laughed and picked up my wine. Holding it out for Asher to clink his glass, he did. Finally, it felt like I was on the right path. What path that was exactly? Well, that still remained to be seen.

Not
even the
Devil could burn
the world like
I could

Chapter 10

Derek

Why didn't it just simply rain in Florida? From the time I was a child, it was so hot and humid that your clothing stuck to you like you pissed yourself, or it would turn into a torrential downpour that would flood the shit out of everything, and you'd become a drowned rat. This was one of those moments. I stood in the alley across the street from the restaurant and watched. Every so often, people would step out and have a smoke, chat on their cell phones and then head inside.

I'd been following my prey since that morning, determined to finish what I'd started. As soon as I spotted her coming out of the back door with an umbrella in one hand, she began fishing around in her purse for what I knew would be her package of cigarettes.

I began to move.

Her car was parked in the next building over in the car park for all those working within walking distance. Crossing the street, I kept pace behind her as she stepped around puddles, but her running shoes were going to be soaked regardless as the miniature river of rain traveled down the sidewalk.

She opened the door to the car park and shook her umbrella outside the door before disappearing inside. Before the door closed, I got an elbow in the way and slowly eased it open. She would be heading to the fourth floor. The place had been packed when she'd come to work, but now it was as empty as a ghost town.

She was waiting at the elevator, but I turned and headed to the stairs. Keeping my hands in my pockets, hood up, and face down, I walked through the open door I'd propped open earlier. I could hear the elevator moving downward, and I raced to the fourth floor to burst out of the urine-stinking stairwell. Her car was parked at the far end, and I walked casually behind the concrete barrier that was out of sight of the lone camera on this level.

The lightning flashed as the storm raged on, and excitement that felt like little electrical currents raced all over my skin. The ding of the elevator arriving was loud as it announced the appearance of the guest of honor.

Pressing myself against the concrete, I held my breath as that sound drew closer. Her foot came into view before her body did, and my muscles coiled and got ready to spring. Reaching out like a snake snatching its prey, I wrapped my hand around her neck and yanked hard to pull her behind the concrete with me.

I was so quick that she didn't even try to scream until I had an arm around her throat and the other wrapped like a vice around her body. My arm tightened and cut off her air supply.

"Don't fucking scream," I growled in her ear. "Do you understand me?" She nodded and I loosened the hold around her throat enough that she could speak.

"Please, please don't hurt me. You can have my purse. I-I have a fifty in the-the wallet," she stammered.

"No, Sarah, that's not what I want from you," I whispered in her ear.

Her body shivered against me, and another thrill shot through my body. The anticipation of what was to come was making me hard.

"How do you know my name," she whimpered.

"I know a great many things about you, Sarah. I know that you leave your daughter Kim home alone all the time to look after herself."

"I have to. I need to work," she cried. "Or we wouldn't have food or a place to live."

"Kim just turned eight. Do you really think she should be in charge of cooking, cleaning, and doing the laundry for the home? How about the fact that she walks to the store alone to get items to make food for dinner in the dead of the night because you don't come home until two or three in the morning. Do you think that is fair?"

Her body shook as she cried. "Who are you?"

"Who I am is not important. Why I'm here is," I growled.

"I'm not a bad mom. I just have to work a lot, but I do it all for Kim," she said, and if I didn't already know better, I would've believed her crocodile tears. The thing was, I'd been following Sarah for far too long for her to pull that card on me.

"Don't lie to me, Sarah. You think I don't know what you're doing at two in the morning? You don't think I don't know the fear that shines in your daughter's eyes when you are home? How you broke her arm the last time you got angry," I whispered, but Sarah's reaction was like I'd yelled in her ear. Her body jerked as if a physical blow had hit her. The demon that lived in my heart began to rise and demand her flesh. "I know all about you. I know that you never wanted your daughter."

"That's not true," she said.

"Do you deny hurting her," I asked and could feel her throat working at swallowing behind the hard press of my forearm. "Do you?"

The anger that burned inside of me was making my body quake as I waited for her response.

"No, I...I have hurt her, but I didn't mean to do it. I just get so angry with her sometimes when she doesn't listen, but I'll do better. I promise that I will be a better mother. Please just let me go," she begged.

So pathetic.

I suddenly felt like I was in the movie, The Crow. Maybe just like the movie if I let her live, she would change her ways, but she wasn't going to live long enough for me to find out. Cause I honestly didn't give a fuck.

"Sarah...do you think it was a fluke that your apartment went up in flames when your daughter wasn't home?" She shook against my body, the tears real now.

Of course the tears were real now.

For all that Sarah was, she wasn't stupid. Her instinct alone would be screaming that this wasn't going to end with me letting her go free. I imagined that Sarah's mind was not piecing together what I'd said and was trying her best to come up with a way to prove how changed she would be after this moment like we were in a Scrooge movie. I was no fucking ghost of Christmas past, present or future, but I was the kiss of death that planned on making her pay for her sins. The same sins my father had paid for with his life.

"No, Sarah, that most certainly wasn't a coincidence. Neither was the fact that your kitchen chairs were missing or that your window wouldn't open. I watched you sleep, and I planned your death with great care. Only fluke circumstance alone is what saved you, but that wouldn't happen twice. I've made sure of it."

"Please don't do this, I'm begging you. I will do whatever you want. Just don't kill me," she blubbered. "Please."

"Mommy, please don't. You're hurting me," I said, my voice rising until I sounded like a child. "I didn't mean it. Ouch! Mommy, please." My arms tightened like a python, and she gasped, trying to pull air into her lungs as she thrashed helplessly against me. "Did you stop?" She didn't answer. Only more of the same whimpering tumbled from her mouth. It didn't matter. I knew what had happened, and I could've told her what had happened even if I hadn't been watching. It always ended the same way.

"You want to run and prove that you're a changed woman?" She nodded as much as she could. "Alright, lets play a game. I'm going to give you a ten second head start. If you can get to your car, get in and start to drive away before I grab you again, then you can consider it your second chance. Does that sound fair?"

"Yes, please...I'll do anything for a second chance."

"Alright, you seem genuine. Put your hand in your purse and grab your key."

It took Sarah a moment to get her shaking hands into the purse and pull the key free of the multiple keychains jingling like a chime.

"Good, now drop your purse and run on the count of three. You ready?" She nodded again, the purse landing at my feet with a thud. "One...two...three."

Dropping my arms, Sarah didn't even glance back as she broke into a fast sprint. "One, firebug," I called out. "Two, firebugs, three, firebugs...."

I watched with amusement as Sarah sobbed, as she ran for her car. She was shaking so much that it took her three tries to get the unlock button pressed.

"Four, firebugs," I yelled. "You better hurry."

Sarah yanked hard on the car door and jumped inside. The distinct clicking sound of the doors locking boomed in my ears. I smirked.

"Five, firebugs...."

Boom!

The car exploded violently as Sarah turned the key in the ignition. The only other car on this level began to wail as the car alarm went off.

"Six little firebugs all in a row. Watching as the woman burns in a show," I softly sang.

Bending over I picked up the discarded umbrella and purse. My black-gloved hand looked large, holding the smaller feminine bag. With deadly accuracy, I tossed the purse, so it landed on the concrete and slid close to the car. I didn't want the police to have any trouble identifying her body. The umbrella, on the other hand, was useful, so I decided to keep it. Never knew when you might run into a little rain.

I stood staring at my work until the sound of sirens reached my ears. That was my cue to go. Head down, I stepped around the concrete barrier and made my way down the stairwell and out into the night before the first fire truck pulled up. They were going to have fun since that truck was too tall to drive up the ramp to the fourth level.

Awe, such a shame.

Whistling, I made my way toward home. I had more plans to make, so many more plans.

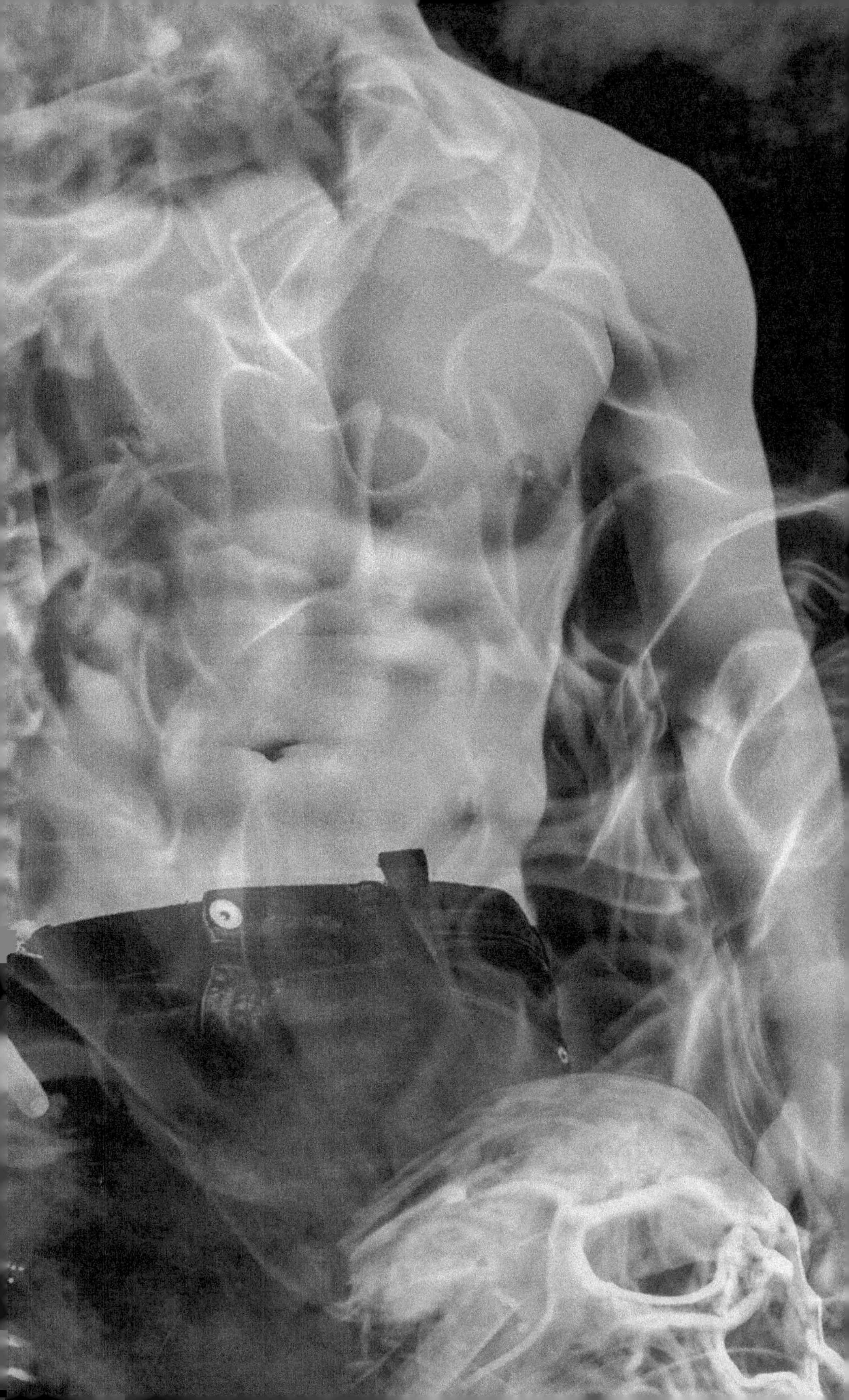

Chapter II

Asher

Vi was turning out to be very entertaining company. She was extremely smart, with a sharp tongue that she had no problem using to put me in my place. Yet, she seemed very rattled and unsure of herself at the same time. As we reached my truck, I handed Vi a hoodie of mine from the backseat.

"Oh no, that's okay, but thanks, I'll be fine," she said, refusing even though I could clearly see goosebumps up and down her arms.

"I was thinking we could go for a walk along the beach before heading back. It's still a nice night," I said, still holding out the garment.

She still seemed reluctant but took the sweatshirt, and I couldn't stop the smirk as I watched her struggle to get it pulled on over her head without ruining her hair. Reaching out, I flicked the hood out of the way and held open the top so she could put her head through easily.

"Thanks," she mumbled, her face that delicious shade of pink.

She looked so fucking adorable in my hoodie that I was tempted to push her up against the truck and kiss her hard just to see how she would react. Taking a deep breath, I held myself in check. Even though her eyes practically begged me to kiss her, it didn't feel like the right time to push that boundary.

My dominant personality wanted to poke at those invisible walls, and I badly wanted to see just how far she'd let me push. Was she a sub, a switch, or a brat? Maybe she was a closet Domme, and she didn't know it. Every instinct I had screamed that she wanted to be a sub, perhaps a bit of a brat, but she also didn't seem to know anything about the lifestyle. Most didn't and blurting out that kind of information could send her running for the hills. So far, I didn't want her to run...well if it was naked through the house, sure.

"Right this way." I held out my arm to her again and gave her a little smile as she took the elbow.

The wooden path led right to a pretty spot along the beach that I knew had a boardwalk and was lit, but it also had places you could venture down to reach the water's edge. We wandered along in a comfortable silence, which was something that I could honestly say didn't happen much for me. Most of the women that I spent time with were interested in being trained to be a sub. Granted, that was the position I'd put myself in, but it did have its drawbacks.

"Do you like living near the ocean," she asked, and I looked down at the top of her head, but she was staring out toward the dark water.

"I've never known anything else."

"Same, but I always envisioned myself living near the mountains. I don't know why. I just love the look of them." Vi looked up at me, and I almost broke my rules as I stared at her full lips, her bottom one playfully held between her teeth.

No one was around, and we were shadowed where we stood. Vi slowly ran her tongue over her lips and looked away from my eyes. Without even thinking about it, I nudged her chin with my thumb and forefinger, forcing her to look at me. She swallowed hard, her blue eyes going wide.

"Don't look away," I commanded softly. Vi didn't nod or acknowledge that she agreed, but she didn't try to pull away either. Fuck, she was so tempting. What was it about her that was so intoxicating? I searched her face. She was beautiful, but I'd dated many beautiful women. So it wasn't her beauty that was drawing me into her.

Against my better judgment, I began to lower my head when a loud rumble overhead made her tremble just before the heavens opened up. It didn't just spit or rain lightly. No, we were caught in a torrential downpour. Grabbing the hood on the hoodie, I pulled it up onto her head, and then I grabbed her hand to run for the truck.

Color me impressed. Vi ran like she was in one of her marathons even though she was in heels. I unlocked the truck and helped her up into the passenger side before racing around to the driver's side and hopping into my seat.

I glanced over at Vi as she pulled the hood down on the hoodie. Her hair was ruined, and her mascara was running down her face. She pulled down the rearview mirror before looking over at me. I wasn't sure what reaction I expected, but a belly laugh was not it.

"I look like a clown from a horror movie," she managed to spit out before she continued to laugh harder. "See this is why I hate make-up," she said through her laughter.

Unable to help myself, I laughed along with her. Starting the truck, I turned the heat on high as she settled herself back into the seat. She pulled out tissues from her purse to wipe at her face.

"I'm sorry. I had no idea it was going to rain."

"It's fine. That's Florida for you." She smiled at me, and I wasn't sure I liked the strange pull in my gut.

She was making me want to break all sorts of rules. Pulling the truck out of the parking lot, I made our way back to the fire station and her car. The rain was loud as it continued to batter the vehicle and make visibility difficult. We'd just pulled into the fire station parking lot where we'd left Vi's car when her phone rang.

She pulled it out, and the name glowing on the screen said, 'Mitch.' A spark of jealousy sliced through me, and I tightened my hands on the steering wheel, holding back a growl.

"Hey Mitch, what's up," Vi asked as she answered the phone. "But I'm off work and...oh...okay, I'll be there as quick as I can."

"Who was that," I asked.

"My boss. He said he wanted me to check out a scene right now. Strange."

As soon as she said that, some of the tension evaporated. But my initial urge to yank the phone out of her hand and tell whoever that fucking guy was to back off because she was taken felt foreign. I shook my head and continued to shock myself further as I wheeled the truck out of the parking lot without stopping.

"What are you doing?" Vi said, her tone unsure.

"Crawl in the back. There is a black duffel with a dry T-shirt, hoodie, and track pants." *What the fuck was I doing?*

I never offered a woman my stuff. That was the boyfriend zone.

"You sure?"

Even though I really wasn't, I nodded.

"Thanks. Here's the address," she said, handing me her phone.

Vi kicked off her heels, and oh sweet lord, she did exactly as I asked and crawled into the back seat. Her short little dress pulled up around her waist on the way. I stared into my rearview mirror at her adorable ass and the even sexier matching pink thong.

"I'm sorry, they make this look so easy in the movies," she said, and I had to adjust quickly as she wiggled her ass back and forth right beside my face. My mouth watered as I turned my head, wanting to nip at her hip. I had to force my eyes away before I did just that.

"Geez-us," Vi swore, and I smirked as she managed to flop into the back and then right herself. Her hair was most certainly wild now as it stood all over the place like she'd just been fucked hard in my backseat. I decided I really liked that fucking look on her. The only difference was that I wanted to give her a reason that didn't have to do with rain or crawling around inside my truck for her to have that look.

Just when I thought I was safe from almost crashing the truck due to distraction, Vi pulled the dress off over her head and sat there in her bra as she dug around in my bag. Holy fuck. The pink bra was completely see through from the rain and her nipples were rock hard from the chill. My cock was hard, too but not from being cold.

I forced my eyes back onto the road before I really did drive into a ditch or light post. Vi didn't know it yet, but she'd managed to gain my undivided attention. What did that mean? She was going to find out, and all of it had to do with her writhing in pleasure.

"I suddenly wish I'd worn running shoes," Vi said, pulling me out of my very vivid fantasy as she crawled back over the seat. Glancing over at her, I fought back a smile. She looked like she was drowning in my clothes, and I liked that a lot more than I should.

"Sorry, that is one thing I don't think would fit you unless you can wear a size thirteen shoe," I said.

"I think I'll pass. As it is, my boss will look at me strange." She looked down at the hoodie. "So you're a Greenbay fan, huh?"

"Don't tell me you like the Patriots? I may have to stop at the side of the road and let you out," I teased.

Vi laughed, and I loved the sound. "Wash your mouth out. No, but my dad was a Steelers fan, so I've kept up with tradition and cheer for them when I have time to watch." She looked at me and smiled as she let down her hair and fluffed it out with her fingers. My pulse jumped as I watched her casually play with her hair and all the while I wanted to wrap it around my hand. "I think that's where we're heading," Vi said and pointed toward the parking tower.

Pulling my credentials out of my pocket, I rolled up to the barricade.

"I'm Captain West from the 126, and this is Violet Clarke, one of the fire investigators. We were called in to take a look." The officer waved us on through, and I parked near one of the fire trucks but kept it out of the way. "Do you see your boss?"

"Yeah, that's him over there." Vi nodded in the general direction of a man that looked to be in his fifties. "Okay, be honest. How horrible do I look?"

I took in the way her hair layered around her face and my cock ached with the urge to fuck her hard. The eye makeup was no longer perfect, but it somehow looked fantastic, and so did the way-too-large hoodie and track pants, right down to the adorable pink heels.

"You look good enough to eat," I said, and her mouth fell open, closed again, and then opened once more. "Come on, we better go. Your boss is staring," I said, fully aware of the pair of eyes watching us.

Getting out of the truck, I looked around at the scene and took in everything. The first thing I noticed was that there were a ton of people lingering on the perimeter. My eyes scanned the crowd. Not really sure what I was looking for, but something was needling my brain. With a serial arsonist that had surfaced a few months back, causing havoc, I now felt like every scene was this person's doing. Sometimes it felt like this person was taunting me. The attacks were more frequent when I was on my shift, and I'd attended more fires in the last six weeks than I had the full year prior.

"Mitch, this is Captain Asher West. Asher, this is Mitch Randall, the head of the fire investigative services." I held out my hand to the man who was all business as he shook it.

"This is interesting attire," Mitch said as he glanced at Vi.

"Yeah sorry. We were out when you called, and I'd gotten wet, so Asher gave me his clothes," Vi said.

I held back the chuckle, but the look on Mitch's face was priceless.

"Oh shit, that sounded wrong. I mean, my clothes were wet from the rain and...." Vi's face was as red as I'd seen it all night as she stumbled over her words. She was so fucking adorable when she did that. In a blink, her spine straightened, and her face was firm. "You know what? It doesn't matter. I was off duty. You going to show me what you wanted me to see or what?"

Gone was the sweet and shy woman that wasn't sure of her own sex appeal, and in her place was a calm and in control woman who was used to giving orders. I was impressed.

"I wouldn't have called you out if I didn't think this was important, but I knew you'd want to see this," Mitch said as we walked into the structure and took the elevator to the top floor.

Stepping out, I was assaulted by two scents: gasoline and burnt rubber. Next was the sweet scent of some form of accelerant. Underneath it all, I could detect the hint of burnt flesh. It was a distinct smell, and it was something you never forgot.

The car had been extinguished, but it was still smoldering, and whoever had been in the driver's seat had already been removed. The doors were blown open, and so had the trunk and the hood of the engine. This vehicle definitely exploded. I wasn't sure whether the fire started and hit the gas tank or the explosion came first, but the small bits of debris that littered the ground told me the car had burned hot and violent.

"Is this our arsonist again," Vi asked as she slowly moved around the car, her keen eyes searching every square inch of the vehicle.

"Maybe, maybe not, but that is not what is so strange." Mitch said walking over to an officer standing guard with an item in a plastic bag.

Mitch put on rubber gloves and reached into the bag to pull out what looked like a handful of credit cards. "I don't think your apartment fire was an accident. I mean, we were pretty sure it was arson, but I'm positive your neighbor was the target."

"Why do you say that," Vi asked, making her way back around the car to where we were standing.

"Because of this." He held up a driver's license. It was easy to tell that it was the same woman. "And because my initial examination determined that there had been a bomb connected to the ignition. As soon as she turned the key, the whole car went up. I have no idea what your neighbor was into or whose path she crossed, but they wanted to make sure she wasn't walking away."

Vi stood with her hands on her hips and stared at the ID. Her body language said she was fine and unaffected, but her eyes told a different story. "Poor Kim. She's so young. I wonder what's going to happen to her now," she said softly.

"It could be a coincidence," Mitch said.

Vi shook her head. "No, there is no such thing. There was a reason her kitchen window wouldn't open and this is why." She nodded toward the car. "She was set up, and she was supposed to die. I screwed that up." She chewed on her lower lip. "I should've seen that coming. I should've had an inkling to warn her. Maybe I could've prevented this."

"No," I said before Mitch could. "The fire at the apartment was professional. You said so yourself. If that person wanted your neighbor dead, then they were going to find another way, no matter what. There was nothing you could say to change that. You can't blame yourself for someone else's actions."

"What he said," Mitch said, putting the I.D. back in the plastic bag.

"I need your full attention on this case and the serial arsonist. I don't know if they're connected or not, but I want you to find out. I need you to figure out who this asshole is. You're the best we have, Violet, and whatever resources you need, you'll have them."

"Sign my form," she said and Mitch's face fell.

"Not this again," he said, and crossed his arms.

I didn't know what they were talking about, but whatever it was, Vi now had the winning hand. It was easy to see that Mitch was going to cave as Vi laid down her metaphorical royal flush.

"You want me on this case and to be one-hundred percent focused, then sign my form," she said.

"You do know this is your job, right?"

"And you know I'll figure out who the arsonist is faster than anyone else. You want the mayor and governor to stop breathing down your neck? Fine, I'll find this guy, and I'll make it my sole mission until I do, but you need to give me this, Mitch. Give me this and I will stop asking for anymore favors to do with the case."

Mitch sighed. "Fine, I'll sign the form, but Vi...this truly is the last time that I'm going to let you pick at this wound."

Vi watched Mitch walk away, a smile pulling at the corner of her mouth, and I'd never been more fucking interested in a woman in my life.

"Why don't I take you home so you can change, and then we can come back here and go to the apartment? I don't know about you, but I'm not going to sleep much tonight."

"Sounds good." Vi grabbed my arm before I could turn to the elevator. "I had fun tonight...before all this." She waved her hand at the car. "Thanks for the great meal and company. You weren't as terrible to hang out with as I thought you'd be," she said and smiled, making me laugh.

Oh, Miss Violet Clarke, you're in very big trouble.

Whether she was looking for someone like me in her life or not, I planned on convincing her that she did and very soon.

Violet

As Asher and I walked through the small apartment space, the charred debris crunched under our boots. I hadn't realized how much smaller the units were in this building. Sunlight was pouring through the broken windows, but everything was so black with soot that it was like hell had touched it.

The saving grace that stopped the fire from moving beyond the two neighboring apartments was the concrete between each unit and on the floors.

Moving my flashlight back and forth in a sweeping motion, I picked out something shiny sticking out from under part of the fallen ceiling. I put the flashlight in my mouth, squatted, and carefully lifted a hunk of sheetrock.

Pulling out my small brush, I dusted away the soot and was surprised to find a framed picture still intact. Picking up the cheap silver frame, I wiped at the glass to reveal the image of Sarah and Kim smiling for the camera.

I stared at the image, hoping that it would help explain how a middle-aged, single mother managed to attract the attention of a serial killer. Had she wronged him? Had she insulted him somehow? Had she been dating him? I didn't know for certain that it was a man, but my gut told me it was. Female serial killers were rare, but one that might be a serial arsonist was like finding a single drop of water in the ocean.

"What do you have?" Asher asked as he stepped into the living room.

I didn't want to admit it, but I was enjoying Asher's company. His insight as we inspected the car gave me some new ideas. Plus, he seemed to know exactly how I liked my coffee, which was strange since I couldn't remember having coffee near him since we met.

"It's a picture." I held up the frame and put it in an evidence bag to be taken with us. "Are you finding anything?"

"Yes and no. You were right. This fire was smart. Too smart for it not to have help. If I didn't know that it wasn't possible, I'd say that the fire had been on a remote control and was chasing Sarah through the apartment as if herding her into the kitchen."

He stood with his hands on his hips and looked around, but I found myself staring at the way his black T-shirt was hugging his body and showing off his muscled arms.

"It also only started in this apartment...hardly spread yet...I can't find a starting point, no accelerant, or extra hot spots."

"So what you're saying is that I'm not going crazy?"

Asher looked down at me and held out his hand to help me up. "No, you're definitely not crazy. This is too perfect. Whoever this is, this person is good. Scary good. Come here I want to show you something."

"I was thinking that as well. It is a little terrifying that this guy has managed to avoid cameras, photographs, or other people. It's like he's a ghost," I said, following Asher into the kitchen.

Everything had been reduced to ash with a few exceptions. Cupboards only had skeletal remains, the dishwasher had collapsed in on itself, and the fridge had bubbled and warped and wouldn't open. It was the only thing had been permanently sealed shut from the extreme heat.

"And it was so hot, like it burned extra hot, extra fast, and then poof! It burnt out."

I stared at the broken window that I'd managed to break and pictured what the fire looked like behind Sarah. The image of the way the fire traveled into the room like it was a living, breathing thing rather than a fire. Thinking back, it had struck me as odd at the time, but now...I shivered. There was something we were missing.

"I'm going back to the beginning," Asher said. "There has to be a trace of what was used to start the fire,"

"At this point, I'd settle for anything useful." I wandered behind Asher, staring at the receptacles and burn patterns on the walls. "I mean, let's think about this for a moment. How does someone set this up?"

"Best guess, they had access to the apartment for some reason that was not nefarious. You'd need time to do this." Asher leaned in close to one of the burned-out walls. "Does the building management chart show any work that needed to be done in here?"

"Ha, we aren't that lucky." I crossed my arms over my chest. "There are no reports of anything needing to be done on any of the units for years. From what I can tell by talking to the neighbors if you needed something done, you had to arrange it yourself."

"At the prices they charge here? That's highway robbery," Asher mumbled. "Totally ripping people off."

"Yeah, I think the superintendent and owners are going to have some explaining to do." I paused as I turned back to face the living room. "I'll be right back."

I marched off and began searching for something specific. I'd seen a white van parked outside the building about a week before the fire. I hadn't thought much about it until now. I doubted anyone else would even remember it, but I had because of a work call meeting I had at home. It forced me to head into the office later than I normally would.

The van had boldly stated Pest Control. I'd briefly glanced at it and thought, 'please don't let that mean there was a rodent issue,' before getting into my car and driving off. No one had been inside but...searching the corners and the edge of the floorboards, I stopped as my light hit the small and now badly charred, insect trap.

"Did you find anything?" Asher said

"Maybe." I stood and held out the small insect trap.

"An exterminator?" Asher furrowed his brow as he stared at the small trap.

"What is it"

He shook his head. "Do you remember that subdivision fire like two months ago now? The one that was all the fancy estate homes?"

"How could I forget?" I said. "The final number was thirty-one people dead."

"Well, I overheard a few people standing around talking as things were winding down, and someone commented that this neighborhood was cursed. First, a cockroach infestation, and now the whole thing burnt to the ground. I didn't think anything of it. I mean, I hear weird shit like that all the time and never bat an eye." He held out the trap for me to take.

"Well isn't that another interesting coincidence," I said.

"I thought you don't believe in those."

"I don't." I shook my head. "I'll pull that file and go through it to see what was missed. If that really is the case, we may have just figured out how our arsonist is moving around and gaining access completely unnoticed.

"Very possible. Listen, I'm starving." Asher rubbed his stomach. "You ready to go? I didn't find anything in the other rooms."

Taking the trap, I put it in a plastic bag. "I need a few more minutes," I said, walking away to go find any more of the little metal containers. "I'm surprised you're giving up so quickly. You didn't strike me as a quitter," I teased, knowing that would get under his skin.

It was actually much later than I'd planned on staying, and my stomach had already been bugging me that it had been a long time since dinner last night.

A snorting sound came from behind me, and I bit my lip not to laugh as Asher took the bait. "I didn't say I was quitting. I just thought we could come back after eating something."

I gave him a smile over my shoulder. "I was just teasing, give me five."

I grabbed the small shovel attached to my belt and began moving some debris. It didn't take long for me to find another handful of traps. It could be nothing. It could be another dead end, but I didn't think so. One thing this job had taught me was to trust my gut, and my gut was screaming that this guy was using extermination as cover. He might even be using other trades like a painter. If that were the case, I needed to review all the cases in the last six months again and see if I could link them.

I was just finishing my inspection of the kitchen when Asher walked in behind me.

"Here, there was one in each of the bedrooms," Asher said, holding out his hand with the traps.

Snapping a few photos, I turned to look at Asher. "I think I need to set up an appointment to speak to Kim. Do you want to come?"

A sly smile spread across his face, and I cleared my throat as I realized how that question must have sounded. "You can get that look off your face. That's not what I meant."

"And what do you think I'm thinking about?" He leaned lazily against the door, and I wasn't sure if hitting him or kissing him would be more rewarding.

"Just answer the question." I flicked my ponytail over my shoulder. As I did, something new glinted and caught my attention outside the window. "What the...?"

I walked away before Asher could answer. I stared at the spot outside the kitchen window across the way from my building.

"What are you looking at?" Asher asked as he came up behind me.

I leaned out the window to get a better look but decided not to try my luck on the unstable fire escape again. Once had been enough for my liking. "Do you see that?"

I pointed at the spot I was talking about, and Ash stared at the same spot. "Not really. What am I supposed to be looking at?"

"Look in the corner of the window of the balcony. You see that black dot with the lens?" I looked up as he leaned out the window, his body brushing mine. Heat seared through me, the scent of his bodywash from the shower he had at the fire station was making me want to lean in and sniff him. I refrained, but I really wanted to and licked my lips as I stared at the side of his neck.

"You must have eagle eyes because I can barely see what you're talking about—it looks like a black dot and nothing more." Ash glanced back at me. As he did, my brain misfired and went blank. He was like a computer virus to any logical thought, and when he was this close, the virus went crazy. The dreaded blue screen and spinning wheel were all that remained.

I jumped a little as his thumb touched my chin and rubbed back and forth.

"You had some soot on your face," he said, his voice a harsh whisper.

All I could think about was grabbing him and kissing him so I'd finally know what he tasted like. The sparks firing between us, at least on my end, were like nothing I'd ever experienced. I bit my lip, and his eyes fixed on my mouth. Forcing myself, I took a step away, and the little bit of space allowed me to draw in a deep breath. He messed with all my normal brain functions. Even breathing became difficult.

"I've always had good eyesight."

"Huh?" he said.

"The lens, the ability to see things others miss. It's a gift. Never challenge me to one of those spot the difference games, you will lose." I smiled wide as Ash laughed.

"You're a bit of an odd one, Vi, but I like it."

Shamefully, I couldn't help the butterflies that took flight in my stomach. Someone other than Beck liked my quirkiness. That never happened.

"We need to figure out if that thing is functional. If so, where the feed leads to—with any luck, it will lead us to who set the fire." I marched for the damaged apartment door.

"I'm not going to get breakfast, am I?" Asher asked as he followed me.

"It's probably going to be more like brunch." I shot him a grin over my shoulder. "But I'll let you eat all you want then." His eyes widened ever so slightly, but the intense look almost singed me to my core. "I...ah...I," I stammered.

"Don't worry Vi, I plan on eating everything that I want," he said, the corner of his mouth pulling up in a cocky lopsided smile.

My throat worked at trying to swallow, but it was suddenly very dry. I had a feeling that he wasn't talking about food anymore, and I was torn between running to my place and locking the door, and laying myself out naked for him like a buffet.

Chapter 13

Violet

"Okay girl, time to spill the tea. How was the date?" Beck was amped up like she was on too much sugar. She was practically bouncing from one corner of the kitchen to the other as I made myself a coffee.

I was a morning person, but she was a morning person on crack. "It was more of a work date than a date-date, but it went fine," I said, pouring the cream into my coffee.

"Fine? That's it? That's all I get?" I could feel her pouting behind me. I could almost feel the frown pressing into the middle of my back as she glared.

Turning, I leaned against the counter and stared at my best friend. "Girl, I don't know what you want me to say. He is very hot, and I do mean sprinklers go off when he walks by kind of hot. But it was mostly a work dinner. That is how I got him to agree to go out, remember? We literally got called to a burning car fire."

There was a lot I was leaving out, but if I even hinted that things had been as interesting as they'd been, then Beck would be planning the wedding and sending out invitations.

She gave me a look like she didn't believe the bullshit I was spewing, so I quickly grabbed my toast and perched myself on one of the island chairs. "So that means you have no interest in seeing him again? The two of you didn't make any other plans?

"We didn't make any other plans, but if he asked...I'd say yes," I said and then braced myself.

Beck squealed loud enough that I was sure all the dogs in the neighborhood just cocked their heads. She wrapped me up in a giant hug, squeezing the life out of me. My phone ringing was the only thing that saved me from complete suffocation. I had to wave at her to quiet down as I picked up my phone and saw that it was Asher's number.

"Oh. My. God! Answer it!"

There were moments in life when you couldn't stop your muscles from doing whatever they wanted, and the ones in my cheeks were doing that right now. As hard as I tried, I couldn't wipe the smile off my face.

"Hello, Fire Inspector Clarke speaking," I said, trying for calm, cool, and collected even though my heart was hammering inside my chest.

"Well, hello there, Fire Inspector Clarke," Asher drawled.

His voice sounded like it had been dipped in honey. I needed to step away from Beck, whose energy was making me more nervous. She followed me to my bedroom, but I made a face at her and closed the door.

"This is Fire Captain West calling."

"Hey, how's it going," I asked and then covered my face, I felt so stupid.

One person shouldn't make you this jittery, but he did. It was like I'd just chugged a dozen energy drinks all at once.

"I hope that it's fine that I called. I don't really believe in the standard rules when it comes to dating."

"I didn't know we were dating," I said and then fanned my face. Glancing in the mirror, I was already going red.

Asher chuckled into the line, and the sound licked down my spine, making me squirm. "True, we aren't, at least not yet," he said but left the rest hanging in the air for me to figure out. "I was calling to see if you'd be interested in spending the day with me?"

"Really. What did you have in mind?"

"Well, since you're such a daredevil, I thought we'd start with some alligator wrestling and end the day by feeding the sharks."

"What?" I burst out laughing and he followed suit. "And you say I'm the crazy one."

"Crazy...I'm rethinking that statement. Overly brave for your own good, most definitely. So what do you say? Hopefully, we won't be interrupted by our very annoying arsonist."

I contemplated all the things I should do today, like how I now had the paperwork to get items from my parents' case examined, but Beck was right about one thing. I'd forgotten what it was like to live and have some fun. The other nice thing about Asher was that he understood my work life. As soon as that call came in, he was all business and helped me work all night and all day yesterday until we were both ready to pass out. It was nice not having to explain the importance of my job or apologize if a call came in. He already understood.

"Okay, let's do it. What do you really have in mind?"

Asher chuckled again, and I was beginning to love that sound. "Do you know how to rollerblade?"

"I do, just not real well," I said, my eyes going to my closet where my blades were stored.

"Excellent. Bring those, dress for the beach, and bring a change of clothes for a casual dinner. I know the perfect spot. I'll be by in an hour to pick you up."

I was utterly blown away. Of course, my mind instantly pictured the man in nothing but swim trunks, and my pulse skyrocketed. Oh fuck, he was going to look like one of those models doing a photo shoot, stepping out of the water like a damn god. My brain was never going to be the same.

"An hour, alright, I'll be ready."

"See you soon, Vi." Asher hung up, and I stared at the phone a moment before Beck burst into the room.

"Oh my god! I'm so excited. Okay, let's get you ready. Where did he say you were going on your date?" She pointed at the door. "I may have been listening."

Oh dear lord.

An hour later, I looked like I was ready for a Caribbean cruise and had a bag packed. I looked down at the canvas bag and knew I could use it to weight lift. I shook my head. It was easier to go along with Beck then try to fight the tide. Why she'd insisted on me wearing these little white jean shorts that looked like my ass was trying to eat them was beyond me. I couldn't wait to get changed as soon as I was out of her sight.

The sound of Asher's diesel truck reached my ears before I could see it coming down the street, and the nervous butterflies took flight all over again. He pulled up the street in front of the apartment building, and I wanted to skip down the stairs like I'd just lost my mind.

Asher hopped out and came around, even though I didn't need his help, and pulled open the back door.

"Here, let me. I'll toss your bag in the back," he said, taking the heavy beast from my hands. If he noticed how heavy it was, he didn't say before turning to look at me.

"You look perfect. I love that you have these over your shoulder so casually." Asher smirked.

He flicked one of the wheels on my rollerblades, making it spin, before taking them from me as well. His eyes glanced over my outfit before our eyes met, and even with the dark sunglasses on, I felt like I was melting under the intense stare.

Once more, I found myself completely tongue-tied.

"Thanks, you look great, too." If there were an award given out for sounding lame, I would've won it fifty times over by now.

Asher leaned in, and I tensed, thinking he was moving in to kiss me, but he reached behind me as his hand went to the handle of the truck It was impossible not to feel the heat coming off his skin and smell the intoxicating scent of the ocean mixed with a hint of fire. That smell seemed to cling to him.

Unable to help it, I took a step closer to the truck, and he pulled open the door. The cool air hit my back, making me shiver. I felt stuck between wanting to leap into the vehicle and being frozen in place, completely trapped by the command of his eyes. It felt like I was waiting for his permission to release me when he hadn't spoken a single word.

"Go on, hop on in," he said, and I jumped into the truck like he'd shot me out of a cannon.

I caught the smirk on his lips as he closed my door. This was all very new for me. The fanning myself and complete mental fog that took over my brain were things that happened to other people. I was in control. I had my shit together and didn't need a man in my life.

I gave myself a pep talk as he rounded the truck and got in, but it did no good. As soon as we were trapped in the small enclosure, my body continued to rebel against me.

"So where are we going first," I asked.

"That is a surprise. I know a great spot where the water is crystal clear at this time of day, and I'm thinking we can start with going for a swim before the beach gets too busy. Then, we'll head to the wharf and skate our way along until we get hungry and then stop some- where to eat. Tonight is open for discussion," he said and smiled.

"Sounds great." I settled into the seat as I racked my brain for a question to ask. "Tell me something interesting about yourself," I finally settled on. It was a safe question.

He looked over at me and cocked his head like he was thinking. "I prefer to be a dominant in most aspects of my life, including the bedroom," he said, and you could've knocked me over with a feather. Okay, so not such a safe question.

I guess he showed me.

I was familiar with the term, but the full meaning was lost on me. "Oh...okay."

"Does that bother you," he asked.

It did a lot of things to me, but I wasn't sure bothered was one of them. "More uncertain about what that means. Are you talking like that grey movie and contracts kind of thing?"

"Sort of. How about I tell you a different fact for now?" I nodded.

I wasn't sure I was ready to process anymore than that bombshell. Beck was going to have a field day with that knowledge. Before I knew it, she'd turn my room into a full kink club if she thought it would make Asher stick around.

"Well, my home life wasn't great, and as I said, I was placed with my adoptive family and am still very close to the woman that became my mom. But before that, I lived for three years on a farm with a really nice elderly couple and helped them with chores in exchange for food and board. I was fourteen when I ended up back in the system and was lucky enough to be taken in by Mr. and Mrs. Pinchin." He took a moment and rubbed the back of his neck like talking about any of this made him uncomfortable.

"I call both Monique and her brother, Ryan, my cousins even though we spent most of our lives living like foster-siblings. It just didn't feel right to call them that and one day, I introduced them as my cousins, and it sort of stuck. I was pretty lucky to find a decent family. At that age, most people are not looking to take on that sort of potential trouble."

"I know that feeling. I don't know where I'd be or what I'd be doing today if it wasn't for my best friend Rebecca and her family. When my parents died, they took me in right away. My closest relative was an aunt who lived multiple states over, and I rarely saw her."

"Sounds like we both got lucky," Asher said.

I wasn't sure about that, but I got what he meant. It could've been a whole lot worse for both of us.

"I like country music," I blurted out. "Well, I like lots of different kinds of music, but I love country."

"Rock mostly for me, but I'll listen and can appreciate everything. Who have you gone to see in concert," Asher asked.

"I've never been to a concert. Just wasn't something I thought much about doing." I shrugged as Asher's mouth dropped open.

"Okay, that needs to change. Do you like Justin Timberlake, Blake Shelton or how about Pink?"

"I love Pink. She is a total badass, and I love her voice. I also adore Blake, and listen to his music all the time."

Asher nodded like he was filing the information away. I really wanted to ask more about what it meant for him to say he was dominant, but we turned off the main road, and I had to grip the door to keep myself from thrashing about on the rough lane. My ass bounced mercilessly over the bumps, and all I could think about was how this felt like an old-style rollercoaster.

"Sorry, but we're almost there."

True to his word, the heavily treed road opened up to a spectacular little beachfront that sat on a tucked-away lagoon. "Wow, this is stunning. How did you find this spot?"

"I like to do some sailing, like the smaller racing boats. When I was nineteen, I took a date out on the boat, but we weren't exactly interested in sailing, if you catch my drift. Anyway, I didn't anchor properly and was a little too busy to notice we were floating. We ended up just outside the mouth of this spot. I was damn lucky that I didn't hit a rock or part of the hard coral because there is a lot of it in this area."

"Why am I not surprised that you found this spot because of sex," I said.

"Why Vi, whatever are you insinuating," he teased as he put the truck in park.

"Nothing. Just that I'm not surprised," I said and shrugged.

He seemed perplexed by the answer, like he'd been expecting something else. The truth was, I'd hung around mostly guys my entire life other than Beck. It would've shocked me if he'd said he'd been bird-watching or wanted a quiet place to read a book, but sex? No, that was what I'd expected.

"Are we getting out?" I said as he continued to sit there, staring at me.

"You're not jealous, are you?"

My eyebrow cocked up, confused. "That's a pretty vain question if I've ever heard one. No, why would I be?" I crossed my arms over my chest, ready to tell him to forget the date. If he thought this highly of himself, then I wasn't interested.

"Usually, when I tell that story, I get a very different response," he said and tipped his sunglasses down so I could see his eyes.

Goodness, they very closely matched the color of the water that was mere feet away from the truck.

"You're just very unique."

"I don't think I'm that unique. You've obviously been spending your time with the wrong women." I shrugged and pushed open the door. "I'm going to go enjoy the water for a little while. Whenever you're done being shocked over the fact that not every woman worries about your bed count or bows down at your feet like a god, feel free to join me."

Jumping out of the truck, I closed the door. Damn, that felt good to shut the door while he sat there with a shocked expression on his face. Plus, being able to get out a firm, logical response out of my mouth that didn't sound like I was panting all over him gave me hope that my brain wasn't permanently fried.

Walking toward the water, I heard Asher getting out of the truck behind me, but I didn't bother to look. If he thought for even a second that I was going to crawl around behind him and beg for his affection, he had another thing coming.

Dominant in the bedroom? Who even says that to someone they just met?

I was definitely avoiding the fact that I wanted to know more about what that meant, but I'd analyze that tidbit later.

Kicking off my sandals, I slipped out of my shorts and pulled the tank top off over my head to show off my bikini. I dropped my sunglasses on top of the clothes and jogged for the rippling waves that were truly picturesque. I ran as far as I could and then dove into the water. The rush of liquid flowed over me before the quiet that always accompanied being underwater. I'd always loved the beach and the ocean. I'd swam with everything: stingrays, dolphins, seals, and even sharks.

Water saved me at my lowest points. The ocean and its ability to survive everything crappy and fucked up that humans and nature have thrown at it filled me with a determination that one day I'd be okay again. That one day, I wouldn't feel like the world or my emotions weren't trying to crush me.

I could hear Asher closing in on my position as I hovered in the crystal-clear water allowing myself this moment of calm. With one stroke, I pushed myself to the surface and came face to face with Asher as he, too, rose from under the waves like some fucking god of the deep. He smoothed his hair back, and his arm muscles flexed with that simple movement. He showed off just how perfect his tan was, along with the body that screamed it was made for pleasure. As hard as I tried, I couldn't look away.

"You're fast," he said, smiling at me.

"I love the water. I'd spend as much time as I could in the pool or at the beach." We fell silent and the current slowly pushed us closer together.

"I apologize for what I said. You're right. It was very...condescending of me," he said, his voice soft. It felt like apologizing was a new thing for him.

"Thanks. I'm not sorry about what I said."

He splashed water at me, and I laughed hard. It was on, and soon I was worn out and out of breath from our frantic game. Flipping onto my back, I stared at the blinding sun and slowly swam for shore until my feet could touch the soft sand.

"You giving up, Clarke?"

"Let's call it a needed breather." I turned to face Asher and wished that I hadn't.

My eyes roamed over the hard abs and the way the water traveled down his body, making me want to lick it off of him. I didn't think it was possible to forget to breathe, but I did. I ended up gasping in a breath as my body reminded me that I needed the oxygen to live.

As if sensing my weakness, he stepped in close but didn't touch me. It didn't matter. His mere nearness was like a caress that I could feel all over my body. As he leaned in close to my ear, his body gently grazed my own, and the tension became stifling.

"What do you want, Vi," he whispered in my ear, and goosebumps rose along my skin. My mouth opened, but no words came out.

"Do you want me to kiss you," he asked, his voice syrupy and rich to my ears.

I instantly licked my lips at the thought of finally tasting him. Still, I said nothing, but I didn't move away. I could admit that I wanted to kiss him. Whether it was a good idea or not was another story.

"I won't touch you unless you say the words, Vi. Do you want me to kiss you? Do you want me to touch you?"

The tension was so thick it felt like I was choking on it. I nodded, my voice seemingly lost to me.

Asher pulled back just enough that he was staring directly into my eyes.

"You need to say it," he said, and even though his voice was low it felt like he'd yelled in my ears.

"Yes...yes, I...ah...want you to," I mumbled.

It felt strange to ask for a kiss and to give permission like that. All the guys I'd dated had taken what they wanted, when they wanted it. Even if I was an uncomfortable kiss in a public line when they knew I wasn't into PDAs. Grabbing or slapping my ass like I was their pet to pat in front of others was also normal. It was also why those relationships never lasted long.

Asher placed his finger under my chin and my heart jumped around like I was in the middle of one of my marathons.

"Are you certain, one hundred percent certain," he asked, his lips so close to mine, and yet he didn't touch me.

My nerves were fraying quickly as my body shuddered in his gentle touch. "Yes, I'm certain," I said.

As his lips touched mine, I instantly knew I'd never known a passionate kiss until this moment. No one else had ever made a fire lick up my spine, leaving me breathless from a simple touch. The kiss started out soft, but quickly deepened as his hands cupped my face. Like a fire burning so hot that metal collapsed in on itself, so too did my insides.

Moaning, I slid my hands up his chest to wrap them around his neck, but his hands quickly removed mine and gently placed them behind my back. He held them easily with one of his hands. His much larger body bent my body back a few inches, breaking the kiss. I was breathing hard, my chest rubbing against his with every inhale. Asher's eyes were as intense as he stared into my own.

"I did not yet give you permission to touch me," he said softly, but there was no doubt this was a command.

My instinct was to bristle against the order, which must have shown in my eyes because I was once again being kissed. I could barely remember why I was annoyed.

"You taste like chilled strawberry wine on a hot June day," Asher mumbled against my lips before he nipped at my lower lip.

My eyes were still closed as I waited for him to continue to kiss me. He'd released my hands at some point, but I kept them in the same position like he still held them. As I opened my eyes, I felt him stepping away. Grabbing for his hips, I pulled him closer. His eyes flared with heat, but he shook his head no.

"You're not ready for that, although you do tempt me, little Firebug, you certainly do tempt my restraint," he said, and once more he pulled my hands away from him.

Embarrassment scorched through me, and I looked away from him, pulling my hands free of his hold. He didn't move, but I could tell he wasn't going to kiss me anymore. Once again, I found myself conflicted about him.

"I see." I crossed my arms over my chest and slowly pushed out a deep breath trying to think reasonably. He made me feel like I was a teen with my first crush all over again, but I wasn't a teen, and I didn't have a crush.

I stepped away and turned to walk toward the shore to sit and enjoy the warm sand. Grabbing my shades, I put them in place, happy to have something to be a small shield between me and his intense stare. Asher remained where we'd been standing for a while as if he expected something else to happen, but whatever it was, I had no idea.

Instead, I watched the water roll up to the sand, making it wet, and then retreat again. I could suddenly relate. The way that Asher pushed in on me and then pulled away felt like he was one of the waves, and I was the sand. As far as I was concerned, he was making me seasick.

"Why did you call me, Firebug," I asked as he came to sit down. One of my eyebrows rose in question when he didn't respond. "That is someone that likes to set fires."

"It suits you," he said. "You are petite in stature, yet you've managed to set a fire to everything you do in a good way. You pave your own path and clear whatever obstacles are in your way. You've also lit a fire within me. Don't you think it suits you?"

My body flushed as heat spread throughout my body and warmed my cheeks with the strange compliment. If this was the case, then why did he say I wasn't ready? Did he think I was a virgin or was this something to do with what he said earlier about being dominant in all areas of his life?

"I don't know," I said and looked away from his eyes.

Laying back to enjoy the sun, I liked the way it dried me off. Asher was a lot more complex than I expected and a whole lot more confusing. If this morning was any indication of how the rest of the date was going to go, I was in for one hell of a rollercoaster of a day.

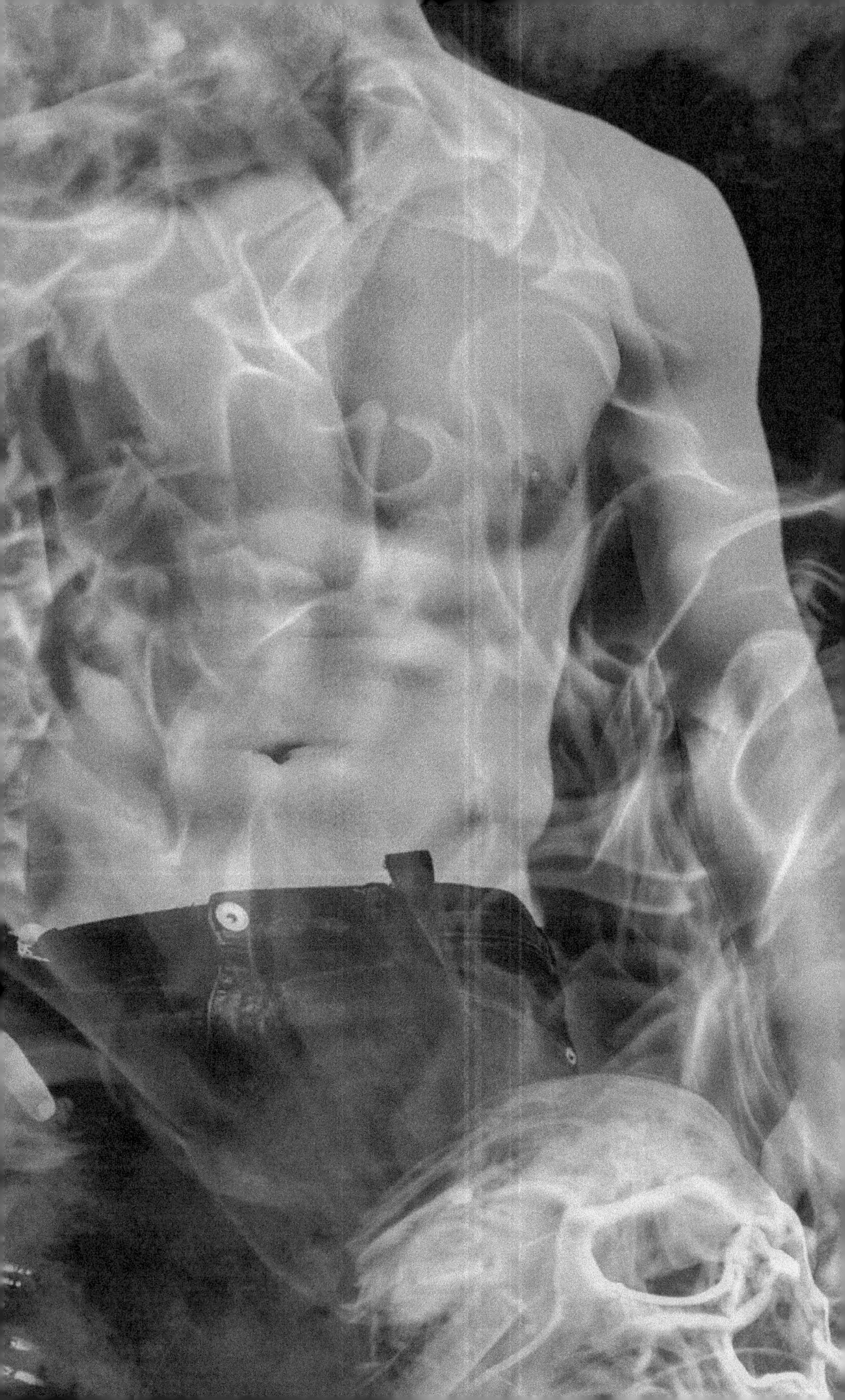

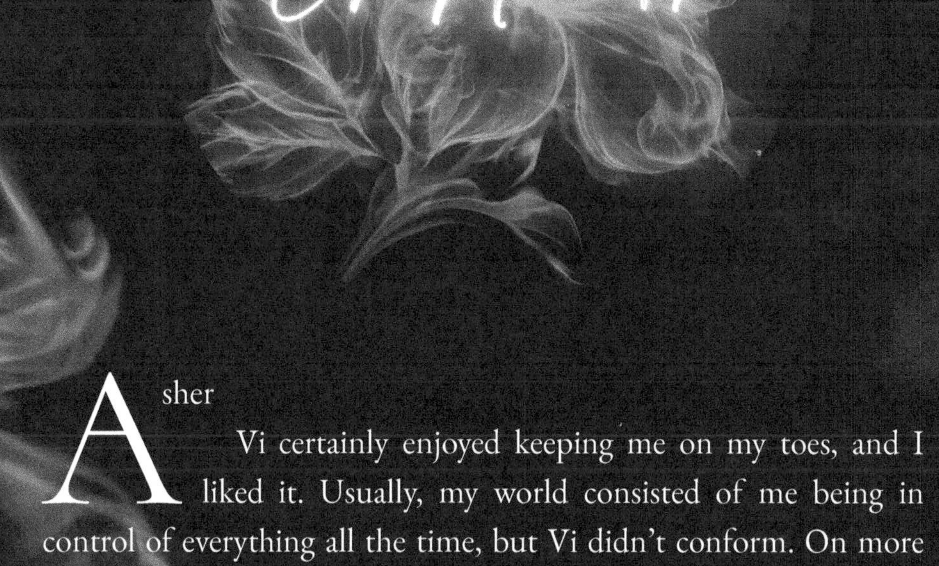

Asher

Vi certainly enjoyed keeping me on my toes, and I liked it. Usually, my world consisted of me being in control of everything all the time, but Vi didn't conform. On more than one occasion, I'd already been rendered speechless.

She was making me want to break all of the rules I kept in place. The present moment was a prime example. She was licking her chocolate-swirl ice cream cone, and she managed to get it on the corner of her mouth but acted like she didn't notice. Unable to help it any longer, I leaned in, kissed, and licked the sweet chocolate off.

Fuck, she tasted so good.

"You had some on your...," I nodded at her lips.

"Did I?"

"Yep."

"Well then…" She booped her ice cream off the corner of my mouth, my eyes going wide. But then she smirked, making me want to teach her a lesson and order her to lick it off.

"You have some on the corner of your mouth now. I'd lick it off, but…I'm not allowed to touch you," Vi teased and licked the entire length of her ice cream cone while she stared at me.

Normally, I'd be annoyed at the brat-like outburst, but instead, I smiled back. She didn't do the things she did to purposely brat, not in the traditional sense. No, she was genuinely a jokester under her tough exterior, but I wasn't sure what to do with it. The fact that I didn't know how to handle this situation perplexed me.

"What the hell, Asher," the sound of Brit's voice wiped the smile off my face as quickly as it wiped away my euphoric mood. "Why does she get to act like that? Why aren't you putting her over your lap to spank her, huh?"

Vi stared over my shoulder, her face was shocked, but aside from that, it was unreadable.

Pushing myself to my feet, I turned to face Britnay. One of the most important rules of this kind of lifestyle was not to talk about it like this in public. Those in the kink community were private people, we kept our relationships, clubs and everything else quiet. Brit knew this well. It was one of the first things I had to make clear when we started our arrangement, yet here she was, coming at me in public about the lifestyle and doing so after our time had come to an end.

"Britnay, what do you think you're doing?"

She had her phone out and was recording me, which was also a huge 'no' between us. "Oh, I just thought that I'd show all my viewers who the jerk was that ended our arrangement."

She was never allowed to livestream us, and she certainly wasn't allowed to livestream anything to do with the community as a whole. If she had been doing so, she did it without me knowing. I looked around confused. We weren't anywhere near her place and it didn't seem like she was here with anyone.

"How did you even find me?"

"I used Find My Phone, and it led me here to find you, but it looks like you've already moved on," she said, glaring around my body at Vi.

"If you want me to speak to you, then you need to put your phone away," I said, trying to keep my tone calm, even though it was becoming harder to do so by the second.

"No, I don't think so. You don't make the rules anymore. Isn't that right? That's how it works, isn't it? Our arrangement is done, so I no longer have to listen to you," she said, her tone snotty as hell.

Her voice was getting louder, and taking a chance that she'd follow me, I turned and marched away from the growing number of spectators. I could feel Vi's eyes on us, and I wasn't looking forward to explaining this.

"Where do you think you're going," Brit asked, but I continued walking at a brisk pace until we were near one of the lifeguard towers, away from the larger group of people.

Turning around, I faced Brit. "If you want to talk to me then we can talk, but not on your live and not if you simply plan on making a spectacle of yourself." I waited to see what she was going to do, and finally, she clicked her phone off and put it in her pocket. "Okay, now what do you really want to say?"

"Asher, I didn't want us to end. We agreed that you'd teach me and guide me through this world, and you just tossed me out the door after I told you I loved you. Doesn't that count for something," she whispered.

I crossed my arms and leaned against one of the wooden legs of the lifeguard house. "Britnay, what part of 'don't fall in love with me' did you not understand? We had an arrangement, and it came to an end. It's that simple."

Brit stepped closer and placed her hands on my chest, but too many eyes were watching, so I couldn't just remove them and force her to take a step back.

"Please reconsider, Asher. We had a lot of fun, and I learned my lesson. You forced me to see that I must do better if I want this life."

She looked over her shoulder, and I could see Vi watching us. The look on her face made me feel uncomfortable in my gut.

Fuck.

"I'll get down on my knees right now and suck you off in front of all these people if you want?"

I rolled my eyes. "No, Britnay, that's not what I want."

"Then name it. I'll do anything."

"Are you listening?"

She nodded furiously like a toddler excited over a toy. "I want you to go home. I want you to think about how right now you're breaking every one of the communities' major rules. Then I want you to ask yourself why I'd ever consider taking you back when you cannot muster the respect for me or for this lifestyle in the first place?"

She looked down, her bottom lip trembling as her hands dropped from my chest. "Asher, please."

"Britnay, you don't need me. You only think you're in love with me, but you're not. It is common for someone new to this lifestyle to think they are in love. And even if you were, I don't feel the same way in return. For me, this was what it has always been and what we agreed on. Now I'm going to go back to my friend." I stepped around her and stopped as she spoke again.

Britnay's eyes narrowed.

"Is she your next victim," she hissed under her breath.

I turned to face her, and her eyes glared holes into me. I knew she was going to hit up one of the clubs and get herself hammered. She had that look on her face that she got whenever she wanted to act out.

"Is that what you think you are? A victim? If you're a victim, Britnay, then you're a victim of your own actions, not from anything I've done. I truly wish you well."

She began to cry, but I walked away, ready to deal with the next angry-looking woman. This lovely day did not turn out as I hoped it would.

Vi had already packed her bag and had it slung over her shoulder.

"I'm really sorry about that, Britnay is my ex in a way and..." I started to explain.

Vi held up her hand to stop the rest of what I was going to say. "You know what, Asher, it's fine. I'm just not into drama. In fact, I kind of despise the entire three ring circus thing. Besides, even if she is your sorta ex, I'm pretty sure I don't want anything to do with whatever that was."

She motioned toward the lifeguard house. I was shocked by how calm and aloof her voice was, and I really didn't like it. Usually, I'd be all for the lack of any sort of attachment, but Vi was metaphorically slamming the door in my face, and it was not sitting well with me.

"Correct me if I'm wrong, but I'm pretty sure all that has something to do with what you mentioned earlier and the whole 'you're not ready' thing." She shook her head and quickly looked at the spot where Britnay and I had been speaking. "If what I just witnessed is someone 'ready,' then I'm never going to be. I'll catch an Uber home." She went to walk away, and I almost grabbed her arm to stop her. My heart was beating much faster than normal at the thought of her leaving and not seeing her again.

"Vi, please let me explain," I asked, surprising myself.

"The thing is, I don't want to know. As I said, I don't like drama and wasn't looking to date someone at all let alone one with a stalker ex and a lifestyle I'm not sure I want anything to do with. That is... not my idea of a good time. I really shouldn't be here anyway. I need to focus on my cases. Thanks for all your help, and it was fun today until...well, just until."

She gave me a weak smile and pulled out her phone as she walked away. I watched her back retreat until I couldn't see her anymore along the boardwalk.

What the hell just happened?

Burn

Violet

Beck picked me up a couple of miles down the road from where I'd left Asher. Her face was worried as I got in and closed the door.

"Okay, what's wrong? What did he do?"

"Nothing, really. It's hard to explain, but I don't thing I'll be seeing him again," I said, my mind already working to push the hot Captain from my mind.

Work, that was what I should've been concentrating on and not some guy. So why did I feel so disappointed? Leaning my head back into the seat, I could feel Beck staring at me, and I knew she was refusing to move until I gave her more information.

Sighing, I collected my thoughts. "The date started out fine. Then when I asked him to tell me something about himself, he blurted out that he's 'a dominant person in all aspects of his life, including the bedroom.'"

Beck's mouth dropped open. "Is that exactly what he said?"

"Pretty close. Why?"

She squealed and bounced around in her seat, which was not the reaction I'd been expecting. People stared as they passed along on the sidewalk, the strange squealing drawing their attention through the open windows.

"Oh my god, Vi!" She grabbed my arm, her eyes wild with excitement. "Please tell me you know what that means?"

I lifted my shoulder in a shrug. "Sorta."

"Of course you don't. You spend way too much of your time working to know." Beck looked around like she was about to tell me state secrets before lowering her voice. "It means he's a Dom, and from what you've already told me, he's a real one, not one of those guys that toss around the word Dom but really is just an asshat."

"Yeah, okay, you've lost me again," I said and then cringed as she shrieked again and clapped her hands together.

Beck pulled away from the curb, smiling wide. "Oh I have so much to explain to you," she exclaimed.

"Do I want to know how you know so much?"

Had this been a lifestyle that my best friend and been living and didn't tell me?

"Girl, how do you not know? I mean, it's empowering and erotic. It's all about owning your own sexuality and learning to let yourself trust or to be trusted." She tapped the steering wheel as we turned onto the highway. "Let me start at the beginning."

By the time we arrived home, I'd received an entire rundown of what it really meant to be in a BDSM lifestyle relationship. Also, I was clear on how much Beck wanted me to call him. She thought it was appropriate that he was the first guy I'd been interested in since my years-long hiatus began and that we were made for one another. I wasn't so sure.

On the one hand, I had to admit the lifestyle seemed interesting and something I'd like to learn more about, but on the other hand, if the girl that stormed in on our date was any indication of what he wanted from me, then he could forget it.

Even though I couldn't hear what she was saying, it was obvious she was begging him to either take her back or maybe she just wanted him to fuck her again. I didn't know for sure, but I never wanted to be 'that girl,' begging some guy in the middle of a crowd to take her back. I'd spent way too much time carving out a piece of this male-dominated world for myself, and I was respected. Becoming his play-thing, pet, slave, or whatever else Beck called it seemed like a step back. No, it seemed like a leap backward.

I wasn't sure I wanted a relationship at all. Let alone one with a million rules, punishments, and everything else that Beck seemed all dreamy-eyed about. It certainly explained his attitude and why he asked to touch me.

Stepping out of the shower, I twirled up my hair into a towel and wanted nothing more than a good night's sleep. As I snuggled into my bed with Heathrow curled up beside me, my phone dinged.

Grabbing the phone off the nightstand, I saw Asher's text. Ignoring it, I placed the phone back down. Whatever he had to say could wait until tomorrow. My brain was way too tired to deal with him at the moment.

My phone dinged again, and I ignored it. But it began to ring. Pissed off now, I grabbed the phone. Just as I was about to hit talk, I realized it was my boss, reined in my annoyance.

"Mitch? What's going on?"

"We have another one."

I closed my eyes. "Text me the address."

Hanging up the phone I was tempted to roll over, pull the covers over my head and go to sleep. This arsonist seemed to be determined to make sure I didn't get a single, good nights sleep, ever again.

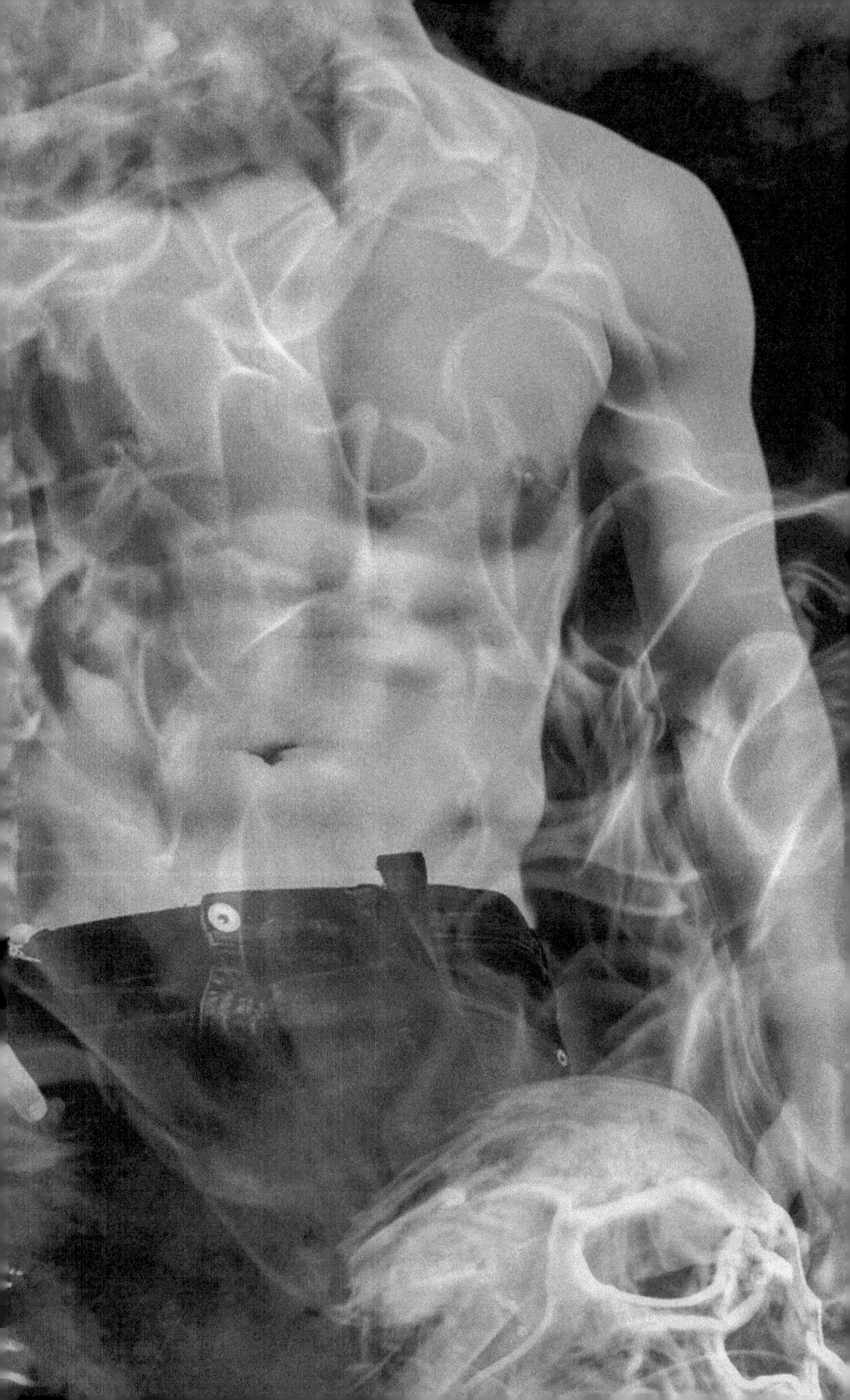

Chapter 15

Asher

"Whoa dude, what is your problem," Wheels asked as he rounded the corner to my office. I was currently glowering at my computer screen. "Everyone is scared to come to tell you that lunch is ready."

Pushing myself back from the desk, I stared up at my friend, who'd decided he wasn't leaving. Unlike the rest of those who worked here, he wasn't smart when it came to staying away from angry things. Probably part of the reason he loved angry sex so much.

"I'm annoyed."

"I can see that," Wheels said.

"And I'm frustrated."

"Why?"

Sighing, I relented. "Have you ever messaged a girl, and she didn't get back to you?" It may have seemed like a stupid question, but this was a new situation for me, and I wasn't sure how to handle it.

"Um...like every day. But that's me, and I'm a pig, so I get it. Why? Who's not calling you back?" Wheels leaned against the door frame. "Whoa, not the girl that was here the other night?"

"No, not Britnay, but feel free to contact her." I tossed the pen I was still holding onto the desktop and pushed myself to my feet. The window allowed me to see the front entrance of the fire station, and I watched the cars as they drove past.

"Naw, she's hot, but not my type."

"I'm not sure farm animal is a type," I said and gave him a smirk.

"Fuck off, man.... Farm animals," Wheels muttered and then laughed. "Okay, that Jersey cow was sexy, man. She had beautiful eyes."

I screwed up my face at him as he laughed. "How are we friends?"

"You're like the only person that will put up with me." Wheels wandered into the small office and flopped down in my chair and then pushed with his feet so it spun in a circle.

"Gee, I wonder why. Anyway, I met someone that is...I don't know."

I looked out the window and watched as an antique, blue truck drove past. It reminded me of the kind Mr. Giltberts liked to take Derek and me to see. I loved going to the car shows. The smell of the old leather and the vibration of all those revving vehicles was comfortable but exciting. Derek hadn't liked going at first, and then he fell in love with it. It was one of the few places we went where the people didn't seem to care about his scar. I hated that I didn't know where he was. I'd tried to find him so many times, but each attempt ended in a dead end. After the police had taken him, he ended up in a hospital and then disappeared.

It was my fault. I did that to my brother, and I had to live with the fact that I'd never find him if he was even alive.

"Did you hear what I said?" Wheels's voice jerked me out of my thoughts.

"What? No, sorry, I was...anyway, what did you say?"

"I said you've never been annoyed by a girl not calling you. In fact, you're kind of the king at walking away and never looking back. I envy the shit out of you for that. The point is that maybe you feel this way because you don't just want the whole 'get on your knees and suck my cock,' routine."

My eyebrow lifted at him. "It's not quite like that."

He waved his hand at me. "I know. It was for dramatic effect."

I shook my head. That was the most ridiculous thing I'd ever heard...or was it?

"Damn, is that her," Wheels asked, his eyes now focused on the screen and the image of Vi on it. I'd managed to snap a photo of her when we were at the lagoon as she playfully smiled at the camera. I got it at just the right time because the next moment, she disappeared under the water again. The woman was like a freaking fish.

"Yeah, that's her." Wheels moved closer to the screen, his mouth hanging open. "Don't fucking drool on my screen."

"Fuck me! How do you get all these smokin' hot girls? I'm mean, Ash, she is on fire. Like wow."

I glared at the back of my friend's head. "As you can see, I don't exactly have her, do I? She won't return my messages."

He looked over his shoulder at me. "You've sent her more than one message? Damn, you really do have it bad. Not that I blame you. If I even thought I might have a chance with a woman like that, I'd fucking put a collar on and crawl around behind her all day." Of course, he turned back to the screen and zoomed in to make the image larger. "Fuck and look at her ink? Damn, this girl is sic. Smokin' and sic. If she doesn't answer you, can I have her number? I'd so tap that."

"Fuck you," I growled out.

My hand flexed at the thought of Wheels touching her. Hell, anyone else touching her had my blood boiling. Wheels snorted with amusement as he stood and stepped out of the room.

"So...how exactly did you screw things up?" I opened my mouth, and he held up a finger. "Don't bother lying to me. How did you mess up?"

"Britnay found me on our date the other day, and she was... unpleasant. Even though I managed to keep the situation civil, Vi said she didn't want any drama in her life. Also, I don't think she was interested in me being part of the lifestyle."

Wheels rubbed his chin. "Huh."

"Huh?"

"Did she throw a huge fit? Vi, I mean."

"No, why?" I said, and Wheels smiled.

"Don't you see?" I shook my head no. "Dude, she is you but much better looking."

I glared at him, but he shrugged it off.

"You don't see the irony here, do you? Her attitude is how you normally are to everyone else. She's the type that isn't going to beg, not unless you give her something to beg for, but simply dropping to her knees and wanting you...to be you...It's not enough. Find out what motivates her, and you'll find the key to unlock her."

"Every now and then, you sound intelligent, and it's creepy as fuck."

"It's a gift I like to keep hidden." Wheels tapped the side of his head. "That way, people don't expect much from me. You coming down for some lunch? Have to eat while we can. With this arsonist still out there, who knows how soon it will be until the next fire."

Wheels started to walk away and then stopped.

"For what it's worth, I'd find a way to get her to listen and change her mind about you. Any girl that can tie the great Asher West up in knots is worth the effort."

As Wheels disappeared down the hallway, whistling as he went, I couldn't help wondering if he was right. I glanced at the computer and the smiling face looking back at me. I pulled out my phone.

"Okay, Vi, you won't answer my messages. Let's see if I can get your attention another way."

Burn

Violet

I was wiped. Not just tired but full-on wiped out. I sat on the ceramic tiled edge of a decorative planter that held a tree and held my head in my hands and rested my elbows on my knees. I couldn't tell if this arsonist was purposely trying to run me ragged or if he was simply this hungry to kill. He was more active than any other serial arsonist I've come across in my career or read about in any book—seven fires in six days and ten deaths. None of the scenes had a single piece of useful evidence, and I'd literally gone from one scene to the next to check. I was really getting sick of the cops groaning when I walked in and their shitty coffee. How was it that not one precinct could make a decent pot of coffee? It all tasted like dirty mud water.

All I wanted was a shower, a hot meal, and my bed.

The sound of shoes stopped in front of me, and I opened my eyes to see an extra large coffee from my favorite spot and sighed. Looking up, I instantly groaned inside as I stared into Asher's eyes. Of course, my pulse would spike, and all my lady parts stood at attention. It was like he held a remote control to my damn body.

"Hey, I thought you might need a caffeine fix," he said and sat down beside me.

"Thanks," I said, taking the coffee from him. Popping the little tab on the top I took a sip and moaned. "Damn that's good."

I glanced over, and one corner of his mouth was pulled up. I had to look away. I didn't need anymore hot thoughts of him running around in my brain, there was already enough in there to create a whole movie.

"Did you get bored at the fire station and thought you'd come slum it with the inspector?"

He chuckled. "Something like that. I needed to hunt you down since you wouldn't return my messages."

"Ah, so you've decided to moonlight as a stalker. Good to know," I teased and took another sip of the coffee.

"Here, I got you this too." He pulled a small paper bag out of his pocket and held it out. "Figured you might have missed a meal or two."

My stomach growled at just the sight of the bag. Reaching out, I took the offering and then groaned as I looked inside and saw the chocolate, raspberry danish. "Oh my god, how did you know these are my favorite?"

Like a rabid animal, I tore the bag open and pulled out the treat. Taking a bite of the soft pastry, I closed my eyes and licked my lips.

"Fuck, Vi." I looked over at him, and his eyes were trained on my mouth. "You make everything sexy," he said, and my cheeks quickly warmed.

"Why are you really here, Asher? It can't be just to offer me sweets and caffeine, although you've certainly segued well."

I took another bite of the pastry. He certainly knew my weak spot cause I was never saying no to good coffee.

"I wanted to speak to you, and I'm hoping the offering is enough to get you to hear me out."

My eyes roamed over his body, and before the words were out of my mouth, I knew this was a bad idea. I should shoo him on his merry way. "Okay, you have my attention until I'm done with my coffee."

He smirked, his eyes dancing with mischief. "First, I want to apologize for what happened with Britnay. It wasn't right that you were put in the middle of that situation."

I looked away from his eyes to watch the crime unit as they worked at gathering their evidence.

"You had an irate ex make an unexpected appearance. No one can control that, but it was the way she did it, Asher. She looked like a dog begging for your affection. If I'm being honest, I'm never going to be the girl that has to ask permission whenever I want to hold your hand."

I shrugged and looked back over at him.

"My friend explained more about what your lifestyle meant, and it doesn't bother me or disgust me or anything like that. I just don't need or want to be ordered around like a puppet all day. I've had men my whole life trying to tell me what to do at work, at school, and the gym. No matter the flavor, I don't need or want that in a relationship."

He nodded as I took another sip, polishing off the caffeine-loaded sweetness that hit the spot. I hadn't realized how hungry I'd been.

"Look," he started. "I don't normally concede any part of my lifestyle for anyone. It's what I live and breathe with someone all day, but...." I looked over at him. He rubbed at his face and leaned forward, so he was only inches away from me. How did he always manage to come across as intense and demanding? "I'm willing to negotiate a different arrangement."

My brows shot up. "What exactly does that mean?"

"I'm not sure, but what I can tell you is that I don't normally date. All my relationships have been arrangements like I had with Britnay. I'd be willing to try the dating thing without all my normal rules outside the bedroom but inside it...I don't think I can give that up, and you may find that you like it."

I bit my lip as I thought about what he was offering. My eyes snapped up to his, and he groaned. "Say yes, Vi. Say you want to try, and then I can kiss you and punish your bottom lip that is begging me to bite it."

The workers, the breeze rustling the tree, and even the sound of cars driving by all disappeared into the background. He slowly moved in closer until our lips were a breath apart.

"Say it, Vi," he whispered.

Maybe he had some sort of vampire-like compulsion in him, but whatever it was pushed me to nod my head yes, regardless of the doubts dancing around in my mind.

"Yes," I managed to get out.

His lips landed softly on mine. I shuddered and moaned into his mouth as he kissed me like there weren't twenty people working a few feet away. The kiss was almost as demanding as the man as he pushed closer into my body. His arm wrapped around my waist and my hands instinctively went to his chest. He didn't push me away, and I melted into his hold.

I felt heady as he trailed his lips across my cheek to my ear. "You make me want to fuck you everywhere in every position possible," Asher whispered. "I'd even take you right now in front of all these people."

My heart jackhammered in my chest, my blood whooshing loudly in my ears at his words.

"That would certainly get people talking," I said, my words hitching as he laid his lips against my neck.

"Trust me, they already are, but I don't fucking care." He pulled back, and all I could picture was getting on his lap and letting him follow through on his idea.

"Inspector Clarke?"

Jerking away from him, I glanced up at the blushing tech. "I, uhm...I'm sorry to interrupt, but we found something," the tech said.

"Duty calls." Standing, I stretched, trying to ignore my own embarrassment. I couldn't help feeling Asher's eyes on my body.

"Want me to stick around and help?"

"I think it's safer if you didn't." I smiled as I took a step away. "But I'll give you a call." I held up the cup he'd given me. "Thanks again for the coffee."

I loved the look on his face. He seemed very torn, and keeping him off balance for once was nice considering he pushed me over the ledge of sanity every time he came around. Dating Asher West? The thought of being alone with him in the bedroom...whew. What exactly would he do? Nervous anticipation swept through my body.

This was going to be interesting.

Sometimes people surprised me, and Asher had done just that. I could see him walking away and as he turned to look back I gave him a smile and a wink.

What the hell was I getting myself into?

Not
even the
Devil could burn
the world like
I could

Chapter 16

Derek

I stared down at the woman that was tied at my feet, my shadow casting a long line across her face. Even in the dim light, I could see her terrified eyes clearly as they filled with big, fat tears. Watching them spill over and leave long black lines on her face was fascinating. Her makeup ran as surely, as she wished she could. I wanted more of her tears.

Crouching down, she made little whimpering noises as she tried to move away. She pushed with her tied feet at the unyielding concrete, her feet kept slipping, so she kept trying. I had to give her credit. She was putting up more of a fight than I expected. It was kind of a shame that her only crime was being an idiot. Well, that and dating my brother.

Reaching out, I snatched her ankles and yanked her close, reducing her hard work to nothing. She tried to scream, and her muffled cries were decadent on my tongue. The tank top she was wearing traveled up her body, displaying her smooth stomach and the glint of a tiny stone along with a brand-new tattoo that said, 'bad bitch.' I could admit she was beautiful, my brother had good taste, and if I'd been a sick kind of killer, I would've taken this opportunity to enjoy the kill differently.

Luckily for her, I only planned on killing her to make a statement. So far, all the little clues I'd left behind for Asher were either ignored or my brother never saw them. This...her...well, that he couldn't ignore. I waited until he was on the night shift and picked this spot in his area on purpose. I wanted him to be the first to find her and finally understand my pain.

"Well, I guess, Bad Bitch, it wasn't so smart to walk around alone at night?"

Her body was shaking. The ripe scent of her fear was strong in my nose. I half expected her to piss herself before the night was through. I leaned over and gripped her hair into a ball, the long strands wrapping around my fist. She tried to cry out through the wide tape covering her mouth as I twisted her neck painfully to sniff at her skin.

"So young. What are you, twenty? No. You're twenty-one because you did the whole cruise party live. You stood on the deck and howled at the moon while you waved a glass of champagne around." I took another deep breath, and my body convulsed with the thought of how she was going to smell burning.

Releasing her hair, I rested my arms on my knees. "Look at me."

She flicked her big doe eyes up to meet my gaze. Unable to hear the words properly, I still knew she was begging for her life.

"You know what I did for my twenty-first birthday?" I asked. She shook her head slightly. "I sat alone in solitary and then was drugged and dragged to a room where I was tortured for hours. Happy fucking birthday to me. Yours looked like a lot more fun."

I rolled out my shoulders.

"I was practically able to live it right along with you." I waved my gloved hand in the air dramatically. "You know this is the problem with this new generation," I said. "Not that I'm that much older than you, but I'm old enough to know what it was like not to have everyone know what you eat or when you shit. Now, you all show every detail online and think that you are invincible."

I held up a finger, and her eyes followed the black leather gloves as they creaked in the otherwise silent warehouse.

"It's like the world has gone stupid. Do you think that people like me don't watch you? Are you really so naive to think that someone isn't watching your little dancing video and jerking off to it? Or do you not care? Then again maybe that's what you want."

I chuckled, and the sound bounced off the cavernous space. She wiggled a few inches away and kept looking around as if a magic door would appear. Too bad for her that the only magic in this world was inside books.

I pushed back the hood on my hoodie and took off the baseball cap before turning my head so she could see the scar that traveled down the side of my face. The shrill noise she made was another shot straight to my cock. I gave it a quick rub, promising it would find its ecstasy soon enough.

Her blue eyes found mine, and I knew what she was thinking, but sex wasn't what I wanted from her. Pussy was boring. Pussy was just a hot, wet hole, or so I'd heard. Her screams of death, on the other hand, that was pure fucking rapture.

"You see what my pet can do?" I gently ran my fingers down the two long jagged scars that had burned more than skin deep. "See what you have to look forward to."

I smiled as she whimpered and thrashed around on the ground like a massive worm. Standing, I took a deep breath, my chest rising with the large intake of air. For a moment, I tried to imagine what I must look like to her. Was I the monster she envisioned living under her bed as a little girl, or was I worse? The blonde tried to curl herself into a small ball like a possum, but there was no playing dead in this game.

There was only death.

Reaching down, I grabbed her tied legs and began to drag her across the concrete floor. Her feet feebly flailed, the initial fear now turning into survival mode. She made little noises like cats did when pissed, and I laughed at the ridiculous sound. She really was quite entertaining. Tossing her onto the metal table, she cried out and tried to roll back off.

"Do you really think rolling off the table is going to help?" I asked, gripping the metal cuffs I'd attached to her wrists and yanking them above her head.

She continued to thrash, but for someone who seemed so fit, she wasn't that strong, and it felt like I was combating a feather as I attached the cuffs to the chain on the table.

I traced a finger down the side of her body, her eyes snapping and glaring at me. She still held the worry that I was going to rape her as she involuntarily tried to cross her legs and would glance down her body.

"Don't worry, Brit-nay. I'm not going to fuck you," I mocked and smiled as her body momentarily stilled as she waited for the punchline. "I'm just going to kill you."

The calm evaporated instantly, and her thrashing became wild, her cute little heels banging on the metal table like a worm under a shoe. Grabbing her feet in one hand, I picked up the next piece of chain in the other. I began to hum and wished that I could whistle. It was something I'd never mastered, but this seemed like such an appropriate time to whistle while you work.

Once her feet were secure, I stared down calmly into her seething eyes. In one quick motion, I ripped the silver tape covering her mouth off. She screamed as it tore at her delicate skin that had never been treated so roughly.

"Why are you doing this to me," she asked through her trembling lips. Her voice hitched as new tears streamed down her cheeks.

"Why? Why ask why? 'Why' is such an overused word. Have you ever noticed that? I mean, people ask 'why' for everything. Why is the sky blue? Why is the grass green? Why do you hate me? Why am I here? Why did you kill those people? Why fire? Why? Why? Why? The better question is, why not?"

"Do you want money? I have lots of money if that's what you want." Britnay nodded her head as she pleaded like that might help her cause. "Or I can make you famous? Or I can hook you up with women, I'm sure you don't get many with...well you know."

My brow arched at her. At least she didn't mince words. "No, I don't want money. Money is just colored paper and brings me no satisfaction. I have zero interest in being famous...well, your kind of famous anyway. As for women....do I look like I want a woman in my life?" I shook my head no. "The only thing I want is to hear you scream while you die an excruciating death. Is that really too much to ask?"

"There's something wrong with you."

"I don't have anything wrong with me." I stood up straight and laid a hand on my chest over my heart. "I'm one of the few that are normal. I mean, look at this world you've surrounded yourself with."

I picked up the sparkly pink purse and dumped its contents on her stomach. "Condoms, a phone, make-up, receipts to fancy restaurants, women's products, an extra thong. Oh look, more condoms, ones with ridges and glow in the dark." I raised an eyebrow at her. "Were you heading to an orgy that has black lights?"

"Leave my stuff alone," she bit out, her cheeks turning a vibrant shade of pink.

"You're worried about your stuff when you're chained to a table? Keep proving my point. What did he ever see in you," I mumbled as I picked up her cell phone and held it in front of her face to unlock it.

Gotta love facial rec technology.

"Who are you talking about?"

I ignored her as I flipped through her phone, which had a million apps on it. "Here we go."

I found her main social media account, which had millions of followers. This was something that I wanted as many as possible to see. "Wow, you're almost at twelve million followers? Not bad."

"Please let me go. I won't tell anyone what you did."

Ignoring her, I scrolled through her posts and held up one of her in a bikini, smiling for the camera as she cocked a hip suggestively.

"Tell me something because I'm truly curious. Do you think any of these people that like and make comments on your photos give a shit about you? I mean, really care whether you live or die? These fake friends in your fake life while you put on a fake smile? Do you actually think that while you sit in your glittering little ball of fakeness, those following you care what gourmet meal you ate for breakfast? Or how you struggled with the loss of your newly polished nail? This is a time for truth." I looked at her social media handle. "Britnay Cutie."

"They care. The people are real. There are always people that say mean things, but most care."

"Oh, they're real people, alright. It's their actions and emotions that are clouding your judgment and making you delusional. No matter. I guess we will find out soon enough." Grabbing the stand I'd brought, I placed the phone in the holder and stood it at the end of the table, ensuring Britnay could be seen clearly.

"This isn't how I chose you, but your social media account did give me a perfect itinerary of everything you'd be doing all day, every day." I looked around the tall phone stand and leaned against the table. "Firefly, two, two, two. That's me. How many posts of yours did I like? Do you even know? Do you know how many times I commented? Said you're beautiful and whatever else I could come up with. Do you even know how many times you placed a little heart beside my name?"

Her lower lip trembled, but she didn't answer. "All of them. I stared at you as you flaunted yourself for your followers, and all the while, I was biding my time for the right moment. See what I mean now? Fake friends. I always wondered how many hard cocks were hidden by screens at a time?" I smirked. "I wonder how many hard cocks there will be when they watch you die."

Firing up the live feature on her feed, I could see people joining and making comments.

Oh my god, Britnay, this is the best yet!

I wondered when you'd show us your kinky side. Love it Queen!

Ohhh lovin' the new look. Gonna need to get me some chains.

I love you so much. Marry me?

You look so fucking hot tied up.

I stared at the comments and read them out to Britnay as they came in. Not one person was concerned about seeing her tied to a metal table with chains or comments about her makeup smeared down her face.

"Please don't do this," she yelled. Fixing her eyes on her phone, she gave the performance of a lifetime. "Someone call for help. Some freak has me and plans on killing me. Help someone, please!"

You're so lit.

I can't wait till you land your first big role. You so deserve it.

Oh, that was sexy. Beg for help again.

"I'm serious. This guy plans on killing me. Call nine-one-one!" She looked around and realized she didn't know where she was. "I'm in a warehouse. Send help now, please," she whimpered.

I kept low, out of the camera range, turned the taps on the bottom of the table, and then wandered around the room to ensure that the lines of accelerant leading to the table behaved themselves. Once finished, I pulled a small ant trap out of my pocket and laid it on her stomach so only my hand would be able to be seen in her camera lens.

I then pulled out the small box that I'd brought with me and opened the lid of the fire-resistant container and laid her driver's license inside. Sitting the box beside her body, I could only imagine the comments, but I had to get moving and didn't have time to look. My little bomb was already in motion.

"Let me go, you fucking creep. Let me go now!" The chains thrashed against the metal. I had to admit the viewers were going to get their money's worth. "You'll pay for this! They'll trace this call and find you, dumbass. My dad will hunt you down. Don't you know who my father is?"

I stared at her indignant expression. I just shook my head no and smiled. The guy could've been the next president for all I cared. The more influential the father, the more coverage my kill would receive.

Her screaming for help resumed as I sauntered across the room and headed toward the area in the back of the warehouse. This was the only exit that existed. I'd spent a great deal of time building a protective wall that would give me more personal viewing time before having to leave.

Picking up the protective mask, I pulled it on over my head and then slipped into the fire-retardant suit. I stared out the small window that gave me just enough visibility to view my work of art. Britnay screamed for help at the top of her lungs and then began to cough as the chemical's fumes slowly slunk across the floor and, rising over the table, found their mark. Smacking my hand on the button on the wall sparked the needed ignition.

Multiple lines of bright orange flames streaked across the space and followed the chemical accelerant toward Britnay. She stopped screaming and leaned over the table as much as the bindings would allow, staring at the floor before the screams turned to high-pitched hysterical wails.

"Oh brother, sweet brother, hear my call. Oh brother, sweet brother, I'll be your fall. Oh brother, sweet brother, feel my pain." I smirked at my impromptu song.

I watched with anticipation as my pet climbed the legs of the table and slowly crawled across her skin. The wails managed to reach heights that even I hadn't been expecting. The sound was racing down my spine like a lover's caress. I shuddered as the shrill screams grew like a crescendo making my cock harder than it had ever been as the pale skin began to bubble.

She thrashed back and forth, mouth open wide as her hair lit, waving like there was a breeze in the room. My hand went to the burn on my face and remembered well the lick of pain that the little blue flame had induced. Her once smooth face began to peel and slide, slipping to the table. The fire moved like a living creature across her body as it did across the room, seeking out more that it could destroy. I wanted to stay and watch the rest, but I would have the video. Glancing up, I peeked at the small camera installed in the corner and sighed. Too bad it would be destroyed before my brother arrived. I'd love to have seen the look on his face when he realized who was on the table.

Pushing open the door, I stepped out into the alley and to my escape vehicle. Quickly undressing from the fire-retardant suit, I slipped behind the wheel of the car and slowly drove away. Every one of my instincts screamed to stay and watch the rest of the show. I'd love to be there when the fire trucks with their flashing lights and blaring sirens arrived. Instead, I kept to my plan. Only the smoke could be seen in the rearview mirror until the finale. With a bright flash, the entire structure lit up as the building exploded in a ball of fiery flame.

Putting my window down, I could just make out the roaring sound of my pet, the fire of a dragon. My only remaining wish was to have been able to smell her better. The mask had hindered the scent of my pet consuming its meal.

Taking my foot off the gas, I let the car coast and stared at the bright fire, slowly getting smaller the further away. I licked my lips as I pictured Britnay's final moments. The way the fire had traveled into her mouth like it was feeding her. I wondered if her viewers had enjoyed the show as much as I had.

Unzipping my jeans, I pulled out my hard cock and slowly stroked the shaft between my legs as I watched the building burn.

Chapter 17

Violet

I jerked awake as the phone I'd set on vibrate did so right off the nightstand and crashed on the floor. Heathrow bolted from the room like his little ass had been set on fire.

"Chicken, what kind of guard cat are you?" Groaning, I leaned over and picked up the phone that wouldn't stop ringing.

"What?" I answered, not bothering to look to see who was calling.

"Cheerful when woken up, I see. I'll keep that in mind."

"No one seems to want me to sleep anymore." I moaned into my pillow. "If you called to see if you could convince me to call you sooner, Asher, you're off to a terrible start."

"No, I wish that was the reason I was calling. I need you to come to see this. It's...it's important." Asher's voice was serious and a little solemn sounding.

I sat up straight.

"What happened?" I threw the blanket off and stumbled quickly toward my closet, yawning on the way.

"I'll text you the address. Our arsonist has struck again and this time...it seems to be a little more personal."

"My hands stilled on the hoodie I was in the midst of grabbing. "Personal, how?"

"You'll see when you get here."

"Asher, tell—" I stared at the phone for a heartbeat as it went dead. "Jerk face." Yanking on the first thing I could get my hands on, I dashed for the door.

"Tell Beck I'm all good," I said to Heathrow, who sat watching me on the back of the couch. "Don't look at me like that. It's not like I'm sneaking out in the middle of the night to have sex with a strange man. Although, I must admit I'd thought about it with this guy," I mumbled, pushing my feet into sneakers. Locking the door, I ran for the car just as my phone dinged with the address. It was an industrial part of town. Not able to help myself, I wheeled into my favorite coffee shop drive-thru and grabbed two coffees.

When I pulled up to the building, the fire was already out, but pumper trucks were still on the scene, making sure that nothing would rekindle. Stepping out of the car, I stared at the grey building with its windows blown out and dark smoke marks decorating the walls. Just like all the others, this fire had burned hot. I could tell before even seeing the inside that it would be black, like how I'd picture the mouth of hell.

Unlocking my phone, I hit the saved number and waited for Mitch to pick up, but it went straight to voicemail. "Mitch, it's me, Vi. I just wanted you to know that I'm taking the fire in the industrial section. I'm pretty sure it's the same arsonist, and I want to get an early jump on it. No need to send anyone else out. I'll let you know what I find." I shut off the phone and dropped it into the cup holder.

I spotted Asher near the door closest to me. He was pointing and giving instructions I couldn't hear, but he was in his element. There was something so deliciously sexy about him when he was all 'domineering' as he put it. He really did have an annoyingly commanding personality that, for some reason, made my inner me sit up and take notice.

I walked in his direction and had to take a moment to control the stupid little pitter-patter in my chest as he turned my way. Soot was streaked across his sweat-covered face. His messy hair looked even more so and way too scrumptious for someone that most likely stank of sweat and fire. The corner of Asher's mouth turned up as he looked down at my feet and then back up to my eyes.

"I'm digging the look, Vi. I didn't realize that this was an option for fire inspections." Asher nodded toward the little boy shorts and then at the tank I was wearing under the zip up hoodie. It was only then that I realized the shorts were about an inch away from showing way more than what would be appropriate in this scenario, and my top was bordering on see-through without a bra.

"Shut it. I wasn't even awake when you called. Here, take your stupid coffee." I held out the offering, trying hard not to squirm under his scrutinizing gaze. Of course, just then, the door opened, and a few more of the firefighters walked out. Their lingering gazes were not lost on me.

"Keep your eyes in your head, Wheels," Asher called out without even looking. One of the firefighters that had been staring like I was a meal swore and looked away. "Don't mind him, he's harmless and if he wasn't I'd kill him if he ever touched you."

My mouth fell open as Asher calmly took a sip of his coffee.

"Come on. We better get in there before everyone is completely distracted by the heat out here." His lip curled up, and I sipped on my coffee to do something with my hands. "I like it when you're nervous, Vi. You look adorable."

"I don't do adorable," I said as Asher pulled open the door. "Is it even safe to go in there?" I looked into the dark space that still had thin tendrils of steam rising.

Asher held out a flashlight for me to take.

"Don't worry. The fire is out. Besides, I got you." His eyes danced with the challenge, and if I could, I would've growled at his all-too-sexy face. Instead, I marched past him and flicked on the flashlight. It was easy to follow the right path as it had been lined with glowing sticks similar to those you'd see at a nightclub.

I didn't have to ask what I was supposed to be looking at because the moment we rounded the corner to the main part of the building, I was able to see a metal slab-like table. The flashlight illuminated the body that was on it, charred beyond recognition. I looked around as we slowly stepped closer, water dripping from the ceiling. I stepped in a puddle more than once, and water splashed up my legs and soaked my feet.

The stench of burnt skin made my stomach churn, and I immediately wanted to gag. It didn't matter how many scenes I walked into like this. I couldn't get accustomed to the smell of charred flesh. Usually, I'd bring something to put up my nose to help mask the scent, but I forgot in my rush to get going. I placed my arm over my nose and took shallow breaths trying to block out the strong smell that was very fresh as the body continued to smoke.

"My guess is female based on the size," I said as I slowly circled the table staring at the remains. "It looks like whomever she was, she was chained to the table."

I flashed the beam around until it landed on a few barrels. Their tops had exploded off, and their structures were twisted from the heat.

"It will be easier to see in daylight, but those look like the source. The way the heat pattern traveled along the floor in almost perfect lines toward the table."

Kneeling, I noticed another canister strapped to the underside of the slab.

"This seems like overkill for one person. Could the killer have known the victim or possibly hated them for another reason? I'm spit-balling here, but this one seemed personal to the arsonist."

"Not to the arsonist," Asher said.

I looked up at Asher, who was staring at the body, his eyes transfixed on what used to be the face of a living, breathing person. "Hey, you okay?"

Ash's eyes turned to me, and I swallowed hard with the intensity of the stare.

"I will be. We found this with her body." He nodded toward the remains, his weight shifting and the heavy boots crunching on debris.

"And, yes, it does seem like overkill, which is what really worries me," he said, holding out a small box.

"What's this?"

"Her I.D."

I took the box and stared at Asher's face, suddenly unsure I wanted to open the blackened lid. "He left her I.D. in a fire-retardant box?"

"I'm pretty sure that was a purse and wallet and whatever else she had with her." He pointed to the floor.

I hesitated a second longer, my pulse pounding hard in my throat. Lifting the lid, I stared down at the perfectly intact identification and sucked in a sharp breath.

"Oh my god, Asher." I looked up into his eyes, and he looked away and blinked away unshed tears. "Are you sure it's her, and this wasn't just left here?"

"I'm not sure, but this is pretty deliberate if it's just a sick prank. No, my gut tells me this is Britnay, and even though we were no longer together and didn't have a...traditional relationship, she didn't deserve this."

"Do you think one of her followers did this, or do you think this has to do with something else?"

Asher's heavy gaze found me again and I wanted to round the table and wrap him up in my arms. His eyes seemed to be holding up the weight of the world.

"I think it is a message to me or us. I think the arsonist knows that we are investigating him, and he's warning us that he knows who we are close to and our habits."

A shiver traveled down my spine, and I remembered the camera at the building that had ended up being a dead end, but at some point, it had been recording all the other scenes we'd been at recently. Was this guy actually targeting Asher and me? Was he angry or feeling threatened by us? That meant we had to be on to something, but I didn't know what.

"Oh shit, Beck," I mumbled under my breath. If he hurt one hair on her head, I would rip his balls off before he went to prison.

"Come here. I want to show you something else that is really fucking diabolical and creepy."

"Like this wasn't? Such a sales pitch." I followed him to the backside of the building. At first, I didn't understand, but then Ash wiped at a square area in the wall, and I gasped. "He was watching."

I flicked my flashlight around for what I was sure I would find, and sure enough, a tiny glint in the corner had me walking closer. "Son of a bitch, this guy is sick. Look up there. That's another camera. No wonder this guy has decided to make us his playthings. We are cats that are getting closer and focusing in on him. We need to figure out the connection that he's worried about and fast."

"Yeah, I see it." Asher shook his head. "I got into firefighting to save lives, and Britnay may have lost hers for simply knowing me." Asher turned back toward the body, his large shoulders slumping slightly.

Reaching out, I grabbed his arm, not sure where we were and what was allowed with our new relationship agreement, but Asher didn't step away. "Don't beat yourself up. First, we don't know for certain that this kill was because of us, regardless of how much it feels like that. Second, even if this guy did target her because of you...

Asher, the man has issues. There is no way you could've ever predicted this in a million years."

"I know," he said and laid his other hand over mine.

"So there was another reason I wanted you to come down here, and it is because of this." He put his hand in his pocket and pulled out something small and round. I didn't need to see the label to know what that was. I'd collected enough at the apartment fire to recognize the bug trap.

"So what, you think it's now become his calling card and not just a way to get access to places?" I asked, taking the small piece of metal from his hand. My thumb gently brushed at the black surface.

"Honestly? I don't know at this point, but even I can't say it is a coincidence. It was beside the table." Ash rubbed at his forehead with the back of his arm. "I do think that he no longer cares if we know. I'm not a psychologist, but that's my best guess."

"You know that is not a bad idea. I have an appointment with Kim and her psychologist tomorrow, I'm thinking maybe I can ask some questions about this arsonist's behavior. Maybe they will have some extra insight that we're missing."

Asher's face remained worried.

"What is it? Do you know something that I don't? I feel like you're holding back."

"There's something about this fire that seems so personal. I know that's crazy, but I can't shake the feeling that this guy is laughing at me." He shook his head and rubbed at his eyes. "You're probably right, and it's nothing. I'm just tired and overthinking it."

"Hey, Captain?" Asher turned in his direction of the voice.

"What's up, Wheels?"

"You need to see this," Wheels called back.

Asher turned in his direction, and I followed him out. There was not much I could do without my tools or more light. The moment we stepped outside, we could hear frantic screaming, and we both looked toward the noise. Another firefighter held up his phone and handed it over as we reached him.

I sucked in a sharp breath as I stared at the woman I'd seen at the beach on the small screen. Her wide eyes were filled with horror as she begged and pleaded. I had to look away as the fire spread across her body, her pain-filled screams loud in my ears. Even though my father and mother had succumbed to smoke inhalation before the blast, it didn't stop my mind from picturing them trapped in the room with it on fire. It didn't stop my mind from conjuring the sounds they would've made and how it lanced my heart.

My dad's yells replaced the young woman in the video. I covered my mouth and closed my eyes as I fought not to cry. I'd never forget the look of hurt on their faces as I screamed that I hated them earlier that day. It was a loop that played like a terrifying rollercoaster going around in my mind, and each time, there was a new twist that made my stomach drop. I hated that I had thought they were trying to ruin my life, my fun. Why had it been so difficult for me to see the reality and that they were just looking out for me? So many times, I wondered if I could've saved them if I'd been home or if I would have perished alongside them.

I sniffed and quickly wiped away the lone tear traveling down my cheek. I wouldn't cry. Tears were wasted on the dead. I'd cried so many times, and it never brought them back or helped me find the answers I was seeking.

A warm hand laid on my shoulder, giving it a gentle squeeze. "You, okay," Asher asked, returning the gesture I'd given him a few moments ago.

"I'm going to get this son of a bitch," I said and stood tall. I looked over my shoulder at Asher. "I will get him."

"No, we will get him. He made this personal. We will get him together."

Chapter 18

V iolet

"So let me get this straight." Beck sat her fork down as she prepared herself for the dramatic scolding she was about to give. "You got up at three in the morning and snuck out of the house wearing practically nothing, and you didn't get laid?"

"Shh, would you keep your voice down?" I looked around the little diner and was greeted with disgusted glares from a nearby set of parents.

Beck leaned across the booth, the old red leather squeaking as she did. "I'm not just worried about you now. I'm also worried about his guy. I mean, how did he not rape you in the parking lot?" she whispered, but the glares spoke louder.

"First, we were at the scene of a murder. Second, he was working. And third, maybe because he has morals."

Beck made a snorting noise and sat back in the booth, crossing her arms. "You are reaching pathetic status, Vi, like seriously."

"Are you going to eat those?" I pointed to her half-eaten waffles.

She shoved the plate at me. "Eat them. I can't now."

"Shouldn't I be the one that is upset and having the dramatic moment here?" I poured a giant swirl of maple syrup on the waffles and dug in.

"And this is another thing. Do you know how much I hate you right now?" She glared at the waffles that I was stuffing into my mouth.

"Why now?" I mumbled around the chipmunk-sized mouthful.

"You eat like a horse and never gain an ounce, and then you waste that hot body by never getting any. We aren't getting any younger, Vi. You need to find a man or woman. Honestly, at this point, I don't care which. Just find one."

I rolled my eyes at my best friend. "Unless I missed something, you don't have a boyfriend either."

"Actually..." She sighed and clasped her hands on the table. "There is something I've been meaning to talk to you about."

I wiped my mouth with a napkin and then prepared myself for what looked like horrible news. The look Beck was giving me, I was expecting an atomic bomb heading my way.

"I've been seeing someone for a few months now, and I really want you to meet him," Beck said.

"Okay, great. Why do you look like I'm going to hate this news?"

My girly senses told me I wasn't getting 'the whole truth and nothing but the truth.' I really needed to watch *A Few Good Men* again.

Beck wouldn't look me in the eyes, which wasn't a good sign. "Because Brian asked me to move in with him as a trial run for, you know...maybe something more permanent, and I said yes."

Her soft grey eyes looked into mine, and I swallowed the lump in my throat. "So this is why you've been pushing me so hard to find someone?"

She nodded. "Vi, I don't want to see you alone. You spend all your time working or obsessing over your parents' deaths, and you forget to live. I just want you to be happy—you deserve to be happy. Even if you don't think so." Beck reached across the table and took my hand in hers. "I can't leave the apartment when I know you will turn into a hermit and block the world out, and don't you say you won't because we both know you will."

A tear trickled down my cheek. I wiped it away. "Beck, you don't need to worry about me. You know I'm a survivor."

"Girl, that is the problem. You only survive. You don't live. There is a difference," Beck whispered.

I stared at her hands as they rubbed mine. How many times had she comforted me over the years? How many times had she been the strong pillar for me and my sorrow or my acting out? If I hadn't gone to go live with her and her parents after mine died, there was a good chance I would've ended up in a very dark place and on a path that would not have me sitting here across from her. I flicked my eyes up to hers and smiled.

"Does he make you happy? This Brian. Is he a good one, or am I going to have to go all Vi on his ass?" I asked, making us both laugh, even as tears streamed down our cheeks.

"He seems to be a really good one, but this is to find out for sure, you know? I wanted you to meet him so many times, but...."

"I was always busy." Beck nodded, and it made me sad that I hadn't even noticed my best friend was in a serious relationship. "I want to meet him, and you move out as soon as you are able. I'll be perfectly fine. I promise I won't turn into a pumpkin in the middle of the apartment."

"You better not, girl. I mean it. I love you too damn much to see you end up sad and alone like some romantic tragedy."

Standing, I pulled Beck to her feet and wrapped my arms around her. "You're the best friend anyone could ask for, and I'm happy that you're happy. I need you to stop worrying about me now. It's time you did you. You've been looking out for me for too many years." Stepping back, I cupped her face, which looked like a mess with all the tears. "Come on, I need to buy you a housewarming gift, and you might as well pick it out because you know that whatever I get, you'll end up taking it back."

She laughed as she wiped away the tears. "That kind of defeats the purpose of it being a gift, you know?"

I shrugged my shoulders. "You've always hated my taste. This way, you'll get something you want, and we will have a girls' shopping day. Win, win in my book."

"You do make a good point."

"Of course I do. I always do." I grabbed my purse and tossed money on the table as she shook her head at me.

I didn't know what I would do without Beck. She was the one

constant that I had in my life, but it was unfair of me to tie myself to her and make her the reason for my happiness. If losing my parents at such a young age had taught me anything, it was that you needed to make the best of what you have now. I had a great friend, a great job, and a potential love interest on the horizon. I had more than most, and there was no way, after all the death and destruction I'd seen lately, that I was going to let another moment pass by for Beck or myself.

Burn

Derek

This place had the best breakfast, I'd eaten here a few times since I started stalking my brother and the food was always the same. That was harder to do than you'd think it would be. My eyes flicked over the top of my coffee mug as I watched my prey from a couple booths away. I had yet to learn her name. She didn't have it on the buzzer in the building, nor did she seem to get any mail delivered to the apartment.

Picking up my last piece of toast and jam, I took a bite as the two women continued to talk. My eyes were trained on the back of her head. Her long blonde hair shimmered in the sunlight. I could just make out the side of her face and imagine her leaping from one fire escape to the next.

She glanced up from her meal and looked at the booth beside them as the baby with its family shrieked. Her eyes were like a bright blue sky. It would be a shame that they would end up burning up with the rest of her. Although, unless I found another reason to kill her, she was low on my list.

Saving Sarah had been an inconvenience, and at the time, I was so angry that I would've squeezed the life out of her. After some reflection, which I had a lot of time to do, I decided that unless she knew what Sarah had been doing to her daughter, then her reaction was something that anyone would've done. My fault was not thinking about the close neighboring building or that someone inside may want to play the hero.

Swallowing the toast, I tilted my head in their direction and held my breath to hear their hushed conversation. I was still only able to pick up parts of what was said. The woman, my prey, sat across from someone who clearly meant something to her.

I loved this part, the game, the hunt, the decision to take their life or not. I liked watching them in their element. Seeing what they did when they thought no one was looking was helpful information to have. But then, I'd rip the curtain back on their ugly. I always took pleasure from their screams of agony. My eyes traced the features of the woman that was my prey's friend. Women were off my list of interests. The two that I'd let into my life hurt me, but...even I could admit that she was beautiful. Her dark hair shone in the sunlight, and the strands glittered like one of the shampoo commercials. Her smile made me want to smile back, and her soft grey eyes reminded me of another pair of kind grey eyes.

She laughed, and a small spark flared in my chest, but I stomped on it as surely as a boot would a bug and turned my head away from the woman before she caught me staring.

My prey looked around the small diner as she scolded her friend, and as her eyes looked my way, I shrank into the hoodie and kept my eyes trained on my phone. It wouldn't do for her to see my face. It was the kind of face women remembered, but only in their nightmares.

The two women stood, and after tossing money down on the table, they slowly ambled to the door. I would find out who she was. I always found out what people were hiding. Everyone had secrets and things they never wanted others to know.

Downing the rest of my now chilled coffee, I too stood and left my payment before heading out the door. I watched as the two women got into my prey's Jeep, and with purposeful strides, I made my way to Dora's little white car.

A shot of adrenaline shot through my body as I now focused all my attention on the blonde and what her secrets would tell me.

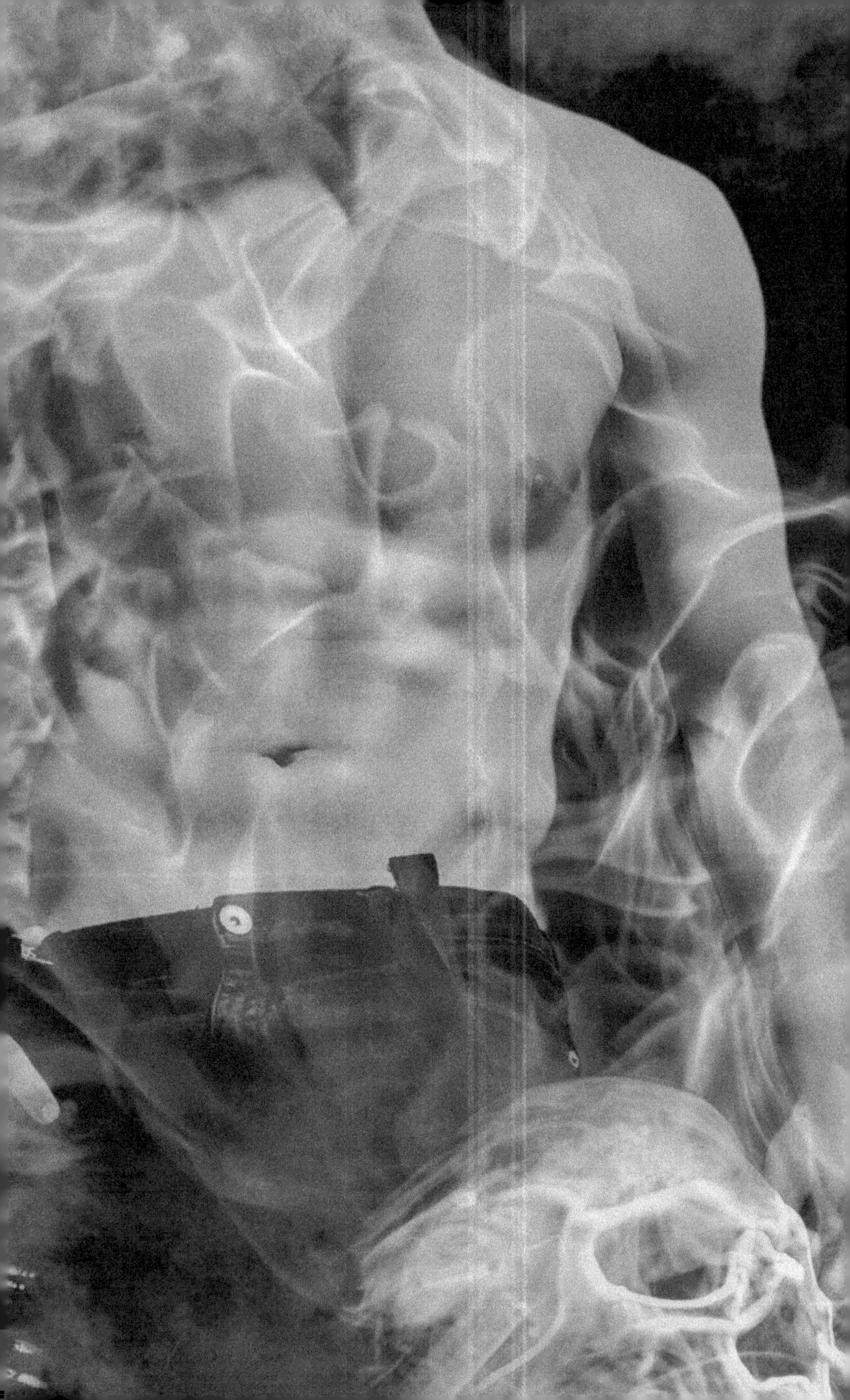

Chapter 19

sher

It was hard to believe that Christmas was right around the corner. Three more weeks and it would be here. The only thing that gave it away was the fake green wreaths with their lights and bows strung up everywhere and the decorated trees in all the storefronts. I always wondered what Christmas would look like in a place with snow. Would it be as magical as it seemed? It was something I wanted to see one year, but for now, I couldn't leave my foster parents here. It just didn't seem right.

Pulling into the parking lot of the doctor's office, I spotted Vi's car and backed into the space beside her. As soon as I saw her face, I felt myself wanting to smile. This was a new experience, and she seemed to be creating many of those lately.

"Hey there, I stopped and got coffee on my way," I said, jumping out of the truck.

"You know me too well, thanks," she said, taking the steaming cup. That was funny because I felt like I didn't know her at all. She was this enigma that had catapulted into my life without even trying, and I was still reeling as I found my footing.

"What are you hoping to gain by talking with Kim," I asked, as we headed toward the medical building.

"I'm not sure. The death of her mother could've been as simple as she caught the arsonist's eye and when she didn't die, he felt compelled to complete the job."

"But you don't believe that."

She looked up at me, her intelligent blue eyes focused. "No, I don't."

We stepped into the elevator, and as the doors closed, I couldn't help myself. "I want to push you up against those mirrors and kiss you the way I should've outside."

My eyes were trained on slowly increasing numbers as the elevator moved up, but even so, I could easily see Vi turn her head and look up at me.

"Then why don't you," she said, her tone seductive but sweet.

I sucked in a deep breath at her little taunt, and I would've done exactly what I said, but the elevator stopped on the fourth floor. With a ding, the doors began to open.

"Because I need a taller building for what I want to do," I said.

We glanced at one another as we stepped out onto the floor. The heat and tension that had formed were thick between us. If it hadn't been for the people in the waiting area, I would've been tempted to follow through. She tested each and every one of my boundaries.

"Hi there, we're here to see Dr. Sinclair. She is expecting us," Vi said to the receptionist working behind the desk. I stared around the office that really could've been an office for anything and pondered if all these buildings got their décor from the same supplier, in bulk.

A hand touched my arm, and I jerked, not realizing I'd zoned out. "The doctor is ready for us now," Vi said.

We followed the woman down a long hallway until we reached an office with a stately-looking woman standing outside. She looked like she'd just stepped out of an old English catalog with her tweed jacket and matching knee-length skirt, and her hair was tied up in a tight bun on her head. This all matched the plain pair of flats and thick glasses she wore.

"Ms. Clarke and Mr. West, it's very nice to meet you. I asked Kim if she would feel more comfortable with just you, Violet, in the room, and she said yes, but both Mr. West and myself will be in the viewing area."

Violet nodded, pulled a notepad and pen out of her bag, but dropped the pen back inside. "I'm ready," she said as she pushed open the door. I could see a girl that didn't look any older than nine sitting curled up in one of the chairs.

"This way, Mr. West," the doctor held out her hand, and I followed her into a small room with a two-way mirror for observation. "Are you one of the fire investigators too?"

"No, I'm one of the firefighters that put out the fire that destroyed Kim's apartment. I'm helping Violet with the case," I said as the doctor flicked on a switch, and I could suddenly hear Violet's voice filling the room.

"Hi there, Kim. My name is Violet. I don't know if you remember me, but I live in the apartment across the way from the apartment you lived in with your mother."

Kim didn't say anything, but she nodded her head not making eye contact with Vi. I watched as Vi opened her pad of paper, looked around, and rummaged through her bag.

"Oh darn, looks like I forgot my pen. Do you have something I could write with," Vi asked, and my brow furrowed, knowing full well that she did have a pen.

Kim lifted her head from her lap for the first time and reached down to a small backpack that had been sitting on the floor and pulled out a pencil.

"I only have a pencil," Kim said, her voice soft.

"That's perfect. I actually prefer pencils, thank you." Vi held out her hand and gave Kim a smile. Vi pointed the pencil at the book sticking out of Kim's backpack.

"Oh, you're reading, 'Mrs. Frisby and the Rats of NIMH.' I love that book. I still have it on my shelf," Vi said, and Kim pulled the book out, showing off the worn edges that spoke to how well-loved the book was.

Vi leaned forward to look at the cover and managed to name off parts of the book that I would never have remembered. As Kim shifted closer and smiled, I understood what Vi was doing. Her genuine warmth was shining through, even through the glass, and she was slowly drawing the girl out of her shell.

"Do you know why I'm here?" Kim nodded. "Do you mind if I

ask you a few questions, Kim? I know this is really tough to talk about, but there might be something you know that can help me figure a few things out."

Kim held the book tighter to her chest and nodded before looking down.

"Do you know if anyone was mad at your mom for anything," Vi asked.

The pencil that Kim had handed over was poised to write.

"I don't think so," Kim answered, her small shoulder lifting in a shrug.

Kim pulled the cuffs of her sweater down until her hands disappeared. There was something about her posture that was calling to me. The way she wouldn't meet Vi's eyes and how she was folding in on herself. There was something she wasn't sharing, but she didn't want to say. I used to make that pose whenever the teacher, social worker, or anyone else asked if my father hurt anyone in my home.

"So you never heard her get into a fight? Maybe you weren't supposed to overhear with someone on the phone?" Again Kim shook her head no. "Was your mom dating anyone?"

Kim's shoulder lifted again. "I don't think so."

A thought came to me, and I quickly stepped out of the room. I rounded the corner to knock on the door that Vi was behind.

Vi poked her head out. "Hey, what's up?"

"Ask her if her mother hurt her," I whispered, and Vi's eyes went wide.

"I can't ask her that. She just lost her mother."

"I know. I need you to trust me," I said.

Vi took a deep breath, but nodded before closing the door to the room again. I quickly made my way back to the viewing room.

"What did you tell her," Doctor Sinclair asked.

"Probably nothing that you're going to like. I'm sorry."

The woman gave me a strange look until Vi opened her mouth.

"Kim, I'm going to ask you something, and it's going to be a really hard question to answer, but I promise you that whatever you say won't ever leave this room. This is a safe space."

"Okay."

Vi leaned forward, her voice lowering to just above a whisper. "Kim, did your mom have a bad temper?"

Kim instantly curled in more on herself, but her eyes lifted to Vi's as she nodded ever so slightly. "Did she ever scare you?"

Big tears filled her eyes, and I knew I'd been right. I hated that I was or even recognized it as a possibility.

"It's okay, sweetie. Here you go," Vi said, reaching back and grabbing a box of tissues. "Remember, whatever you say stays between us unless you want to share it with someone else." Kim took the offering and nodded again.

By the time we walked out of that building, I was strung out and ragged from listening to stories that, in so many ways, mirrored the childhood I wished I could forget. Nothing I did let me forget the sound of my mother screaming or the look on Derek's face whenever he'd push me out of the way to take the abuse.

My hand clenched into a fist, my muscles tight as those images once again danced before my eyes. A dark tableau of blood and pain that cost me so much more than the physical abuse ever could. That was what people didn't see. That was what they'd never understand.

It stuck to you like an inky ghost and would slip into your mind's crevasses and poke out when you were least expecting it.

"Hey, are you okay," Vi asked, her hand touching my forearm. I looked down at her hand and was tempted to tell her to take it off—the old need to control everything once more rearing its head. I didn't just live the lifestyle I did because it brought me pleasure, although it did. I lived it because it helped me harness the rage and the fear that was toxic to my soul.

Instead, I grabbed her face, and her eyes went wide, but she didn't resist as my lips crashed down on hers. There was nothing sweet or romantic—it was all-consuming. Pushing her back, she bumped up against my truck, and as she moaned into my mouth, my body shuddered in response. Vi tasted like so many sweet things that I couldn't pick out a single flavor. She reminded me of spring when so many new flowers were growing that your senses were assaulted.

We were both panting hard by the time I broke the kiss off, but I didn't want to let go of her. I nipped at her lower lip as I enjoyed the flushed look on her cheeks.

"You're such a naughty girl, Vi. I should order you to get down right here and suck my cock for being so damn tempting," I whispered in her ear.

Her hands tightened where they held my waist, and dragging her into the back of my truck became a very real idea in my mind.

"Say it. Say you're a naughty girl."

"I'm...I'm a naughty girl," she said, her voice wavering.

Pulling back, I stared into her bright sky-blue eyes and saw the desire burning in their depths.

"Good girl," I said, and she licked her lips like what I'd just said tasted good. My lip curled up. "You like that, Vi? You like being my good girl?" Her cheeks flamed so red that it traveled right up to the tips of her ears, and I'd never seen a more adorable and sexier sight.

She went to look away, but I moved to follow her gaze and dropped my head to kiss her again, but this time it was slow and soft —a tease of a kiss that promised so much more.

"Do you, Vi," I asked again.

"Yes," she whispered.

"Good, so do I."

She watched me as I moved slowly and laid my lips against the pulse on her neck. The feel of her fast pulse under her skin increased the throbbing in my jeans.

"I think you should come over to my place tomorrow. Have all the cases sent to my house, and we can look through them together. I have an idea forming, but I want to be sure before I voice it," I said, reluctantly stepping back from her body as a couple more cars pulled into the parking lot.

"There are a lot of boxes," she said, her voice a little rough, and it brought me great joy to know that I'd caused that reaction in her.

"That's fine. I'll text you the address, and why don't we make it a late lunch? Say two?"

Vi smoothed down the front of her shirt even though there wasn't a wrinkle to be found. "Okay, I'll be there, but only if I bring the lunch. Do you like Thai?"

"As a matter of fact, I love Thai. Get me anything sweet and a little spicy." I smiled as she cleared her throat and stepped around me toward her car.

"Why do I feel like I'm going to be heading straight into a lion's den," she asked, making me laugh.

"Maybe because you are," I said.

I waited until she was in her vehicle and driving away before I got into my truck. If I had my way, Ms. Violet Clarke would be tied down to my bed tomorrow while I ravished her body.

Chapter 20

Violet

I hated this sensation. My hands were all sweaty and heart-pounding, while my neglected female parts ached and tingled every time I thought about Asher. Was this normal? And if it was, how did people enjoy this feeling?

"Pull yourself together, Vi. He's just a guy," I mumbled as I walked up the steps to his front door.

Not that the pep talk did me any good. He'd already managed to push all my buttons and tie me up inside. The way he looked at me was enough to make me all fluttery. I didn't even know what the hell fluttery was, but it was the only way to describe what I felt around him.

I glanced around the large yard. Asher had a nice bungalow that looked to be sitting on a couple of acres that led down to a dock and a boat. Everything was perfectly manicured. The trees were neatly trimmed, the driveway didn't have a speck of dirt on it, and the flowers were a vibrant rainbow of color and stood out even amongst the overcast sky.

Why had I agreed to this? Why had I demanded to bring over lunch...dinner...whatever this was? I reached out and pushed the doorbell, but as soon as I did, the last of my bravado stood up and ran away. The idea of being alone with him in his home had me turning the other way to bolt, but the door opened just as I spun around.

"Running away so soon," Asher asked. His voice was dripping with arrogance and a hint of sarcasm. My back bristled at being called out. I hated being scared and didn't like to admit it to a man.

Plastering on a smile, I turned to meet his gaze, and I would've sworn he was making me crazy. As soon as I looked at his expression and the calm way he was leaning against the door, I could only think about the kiss yesterday. Forget running. I was tempted to strip out of the stupid dress Beck made me put on and tell him just to take me already. I was sure that would've gotten a strange look from his neighbors.

"I forgot something in the car," I lied. Like I was walking the plank, I took the three steps back up to where Asher stood. Each step felt like I was being reeled in by some invisible line. "Here, you take the food. I'll be right back."

"Are you sure?" He smirked. "I mean, I could be wrong, but you looked more like you were getting ready to take off down the street when I opened the door."

I was really starting to hate how intuitive he was when it came to me. I didn't like people seeing through me, not even Beck. "Oh, I'm sure it did to you, but that's just because you don't know me as well as you like to think you do."

He laughed and took the large paper bag from my hands. "Who are you trying to convince, Vi? Me or yourself," he said, a wicked smile pulling up the corner of his mouth. I wanted to smack that smile off his face. Whipping around and leaving the door open, Asher padded off into his house. He looked way too comfortable in surfer trunks and a T-shirt. My eyes were transfixed by the way his hard ass moved under the thin material.

Fuck it. Who was I fooling?

I closed the door and took off my sandals before following the same path Asher had taken a moment ago. My eyes were instantly drawn to his arms as they flexed, pulling the food containers out of the bag. He glanced at me out of the corner of his eye, and knots settled in my stomach.

"The files arrived right on time. You weren't kidding when you said there were a lot of them."

"Huh?" I said, shaking away the fogginess that had decided to descend upon my brain.

Asher looked at me like he knew all my secrets, and I forced myself not to squirm under his stare as he reached for plates.

"The case files you had sent over. The guy arrived a little before you did to drop them off. I started unboxing them in the dining room. Unless, of course, there is something else you'd rather be doing?" He leaned his hip against the counter, the sexual innuendo not lost on me.

I suddenly felt naked in my little sundress as his eyes roamed over my body as surely as if his hands had. I lifted my chin and placed my hands on my hips as I stared him down. "Nothing else I want to do that I can think of." I tried for sweet and innocent as I smiled back.

"All right, then." He turned and began dishing out the Thai food, and I couldn't tell if I was more annoyed at his comment or the fact he gave up so easily. Asher held out a massive plate that I would never eat. Taking it I waited to see if he would say anymore.

"The dining room is that way," he said.

I took the plate from his hand, and our fingers grazed as I accepted the plate. The brief touch sent a shock of pleasure racing through my body. Asher's eyes locked with mine as he licked his fingers to remove some of the sweet sticky sauce he'd gotten on himself. I swallowed hard as each one of those digits came out of his mouth wet.

"Did you want more?" he asked when I didn't move.

I tore my eyes away from his and looked at the plate that was shaking slightly in my unsteady hold. Not trusting my voice, I shook my head no and exited the room as fast as I could in the way he'd pointed.

I sat the plate on the massive wooden table that looked like it had been carved right out of the center of a tree. Asher had piled the suspected arson files in one pile and confirmed arson cases in another. It would take some time to get through all of these, but we needed to find a link. Whomever this person was, they were smart and careful and had done it many times prior. No one woke up one day and was this great at setting fires without practice.

Looking up from the table, I took the moment I was alone to

admire Asher's home. It was simple, but he had great taste. There wasn't much in the way of trinkets or photographs, but the combination of leather and wood was masculine and sexy. What he did have for decoration all seemed to revolve around boats and marine life. He had a picture framed on the wall of a tiger shark, and I walked closer to read the little plate. My eyes grew wide as I read the date, time, and location of the photo.

"Did you take this photo of the tiger shark?" I called out.

"Yeah. I've gone on a few of the tours where they feed them. It is a hell of an experience," Asher called back.

"Damn, now I'm jealous. That is on my bucket list."

"Really?"

I looked over my shoulder as he leaned to the side to look out of the doorway. "Yeah, why? Do I not look like the type of girl that would want to feed the sharks?"

"More like, I don't know many that would do it, period, male or female. Most are terrified of what's in the water and what they cannot see coming," he said before disappearing again.

Wandering back to the table, I stared at the large stacks and was suddenly happy to have another pair of eyes on these cases. "Thanks for helping me with all this," I said.

"No worries," Asher said, right behind me. I jumped and looked over my shoulder. "This guy needs to be stopped."

His eyes were trained on the piles, but he looked like he was thinking about something miles away. The moment our eyes met, the look washed away, and only the sexy grin remained.

Okay...the grin was there, but his eyes were hard, unreadable.

"Are we sure it's just one guy?" I said to him, wanting to change the topic, and then ate a mouthful of the spicy noodles.

"The fires we've looked at so far don't fit the M.O. of multiple arsonists, and it doesn't work with your theory of how the person is gaining access to the buildings."

"How are you doing? I mean, after finding Britnay and all. I meant to ask you yesterday, but I was so focused on Kim that I forgot. I'm sorry."

"Like I said, we weren't close as you'd expect. I feel terrible about what happened to her, and yes, I feel partially responsible and can't help thinking that if I hadn't called it off with her, she might still be alive. But I didn't want anything more than our arrangement, and she did. I never met her family, and she never met mine. I met a couple of her friends a few times, but that's it."

I stared at him and wanted to ask many questions, but before I opened my mouth, I decided I didn't want to know the answers. There were some things you were better off leaving alone. I took another mouthful of food and then crossed my arms over my chest.

"I hate that I feel like I'm second-guessing myself," I said, changing the topic.

"How about this? You take that pile, and I will take this one. We should create a 'possible suspect' pile and a 'definitely not our guy' pile from the two stacks. We will take it from there, but Vi, don't second guess your instincts. They've been spot on so far," Asher said.

He looked away as I looked over at him, but I couldn't help being affected by the compliment. It wasn't one of his typical—teasing comments. He seemed genuine with his praise, and I liked that.

Why did the fact that he thought I was smart turn me on so freaking much?

That was what I really wanted to know as I watched his mouth chew his meal. Shaking it off, I grabbed my pile and began to read.

"You thirsty?" Asher asked, pulling me out of my reading. I was on the twentieth folder, and I hadn't found any similarities to this arsonist so far. I looked up as Asher walked in with two glasses and two bottles of wine.

"Are you trying to get me drunk?" I took the glass he offered me, and he smiled as he poured the wine into the glass.

"I don't know. Would it help my cause?"

I took a sip of the wine and liked that he remembered how I preferred it with a touch of sweetness. "And what cause would that be?"

"The cause to get you into my bed."

I almost spit out the next sip of wine but ended up choking on it. He laughed. No mirror was needed to know my face was as red as any fire truck, and my body was suddenly as hot as any fire.

"Was that too forward?" He grinned over his glass at me. "I thought I made it pretty obvious that I'm...interested in you sexually." I gulped down the glass he'd given me.

"I think I need more wine," I looked away from his intense stare.

"Was I wrong," he asked.

I'd never had conversations about sex unless it was with Beck, and that was usually her complaining about my lack of it. This was new and made me feel like jumping out of my skin.

"No, you've been clear." I swallowed the lump in my throat. "I just didn't expect you to spit it out there like that."

Asher poured me another glass of wine and then sat down beside me, making my body tremble a little more. Reaching out, Asher moved the strand of hair hanging in front of my face out of the way, and I bit my lip as I felt the urge to spit out something bubbled to the surface, but it didn't help.

"What do you think of all these new electric cars and their lithium-ion batteries? With one of those, it must make any car fire extra sketchy, not being able to put water on it. I wonder if the states will have to make it mandatory to have a truck of chemicals for each station. Bet they didn't think of that and all those chemicals ending up in our water," I rambled as his thumb softly rubbed my cheek.

"I'm not a fan of them personally." I nodded and kept my eyes firmly on that folder in front of me even though the words made no sense to my muddled brain.

"Vi, look at me." I breathed out and slowly turned my head. "I've never had a woman in my home or meet my family. You are the first woman to walk into my home. If you're going to be with me, then you need to know that I talk about everything because I don't like misunderstandings. I want to be clear about where we stand and what I'm looking for in a relationship." He leaned forward, and every muscle in my body froze into place as his lips softly brushed my own.

My heart was hammering inside my chest.

"Yeah, but we're here to work," I said, my voice shaking.

"Are we?"

I opened my mouth to answer, but Asher leaned away and turned his focus to the pile in front of him.

The thing was, my mind kept drifting to the same thing. Hadn't I laid in bed last night thinking about what today would be like? Hadn't I wanted him to kiss me like he had up against the truck? Hadn't I wanted him to take it further?

I managed to get through two more files before I found myself daydreaming about Asher's hands on my body as he was buried deep inside me. My body was overheating, and it felt like he'd ignited a fire in my pussy even as he sat there looking as calm and cool as a tall drink of water. It wasn't fair.

Needing to take a moment to clear my head, I stood. "Where's your bathroom?"

"Down the hall, last door on the left."

As I wandered down the hall, the cool wood floor felt nice on my bare feet. I stopped to admire a small, framed photo of two boys with a woman. It was easy to pick out Asher in the photo. He had the same devilish grin even at such a young age. He held a football in his hands, a wide smile on his face, but the flat expression on the woman's and the other boy's faces told a different story.

My eyes scanned the image with the house and small barn in the background. It was a bright sunny day. The woman I assumed was Asher's mother or maybe stepmother. Either way, she should've looked happy, but instead, her eyes seemed tired, sad, or lost. I'd seen that look before on those whose entire lives had been destroyed by fire, simply gone up in smoke.

The other boy didn't look anything like Asher. He had dark hair like the woman in the photo, he stood taller, and it was easy to tell he was going to be a big man. He stood in a typical teenage pose of defiance. His face was shadowed in anger as he crossed his arms over his chest and glared at the camera. He looked like he was wearing the weight of the world and hated the rest of it. In contrast, Asher's innocence shone like a beacon.

Taking another second to look around I peered across the hall into the large bedroom that had to be Asher's room.

"You find it okay?" Asher called down the hallway to me.

"Yeah, thanks. Sorry. Got caught up looking at a photo." I finished my journey to the bathroom and stood staring at my reflection in the mirror.

Beck was right, my focus was great for work, but everything else in my life suffered. Asher had made it obvious he was more than interested. The question now became, did I want to take that leap? No, the more accurate question was if I was brave enough to take the leap. Something inside of me warned that this one could hurt. I could fall for him, and if I did, and he decided all he wanted was another lifestyle partner...I'd be crushed.

Shit. Do I open the door to that possibility or not? It was an answer my brain and my heart couldn't answer, but by body sure knew what it wanted.

It had been longer than I wanted to admit since I'd teased someone, but how hard could it be? Probably not too hard.

With my decision made, I pulled on the little string that tied the front of the summer dress up and let the ends drop, the soft material instantly pulling apart to show off a lot more of my cleavage and the fact I wasn't wearing a bra. I pulled the clip from my hair, allowing the soft waves to fall around my shoulders, and gave it a fluff. Giving my nipples a tweak so they stood out, I smiled at my reflection.

"All right, Asher, let's do this," I whispered as I gathered my courage and pushed the doubt aside. I took a deep breath, opened the door, and almost slammed into Asher's chest.

Chapter 21

Violet

His hand was raised like he was about to knock, but his eyes found my cleavage. The passion that remained at a low simmer between us spiked through the roof at his close proximity. His heated stare only made it worse.

"Were you wanting me to stay in the restroom?" I said. Feeling very stupid for my silly question, I wanted to smack myself on the forehead.

"You really are the sexiest person I've ever met when you're nervous."

My cheeks flamed hot along with the rest of my body. There was no point in trying to explain my temporary insanity away. He knew I was nervous, so I stepped into his space. Placing my hand on one of his pecs, I bit my lip. His muscles immediately flexed under my touch, and his forearm grew taut as he squeezed the doorframe.

I could feel the rapid beat of his heart, and that knowledge gave me a bit more courage. Sliding my hand up his chest, I softly ran my nails against the bare skin of his neck. His expression darkened and then flared with desire. I could see it burning in his eyes as clearly as any fire.

"Is this what you really want, or are you messing with me? Because you acted like you were unsure a moment ago, so which is it?" His eyes narrowed as they searched my face.

Raising up on my tiptoes, I leaned in as close as I could without our bodies touching. "Why can't it be both things? I'm unsure, but it's also what I want."

I took a shuddering breath and tensed as his fingertips brushed my throat, the darkened look telling me he wanted to do a whole lot more.

My pulse danced as I pictured him tightening his grip.

His arm snaked around my body and spun us around until my back was pressed against the wall out in the hallway next to the door of his bedroom. He was predatory in the way he was staring at me, and I was fucked in the head. I had to be because all I wanted was more.

"I need you to be clear, Vi. I want you to be fully aware of what it means when we go into the bedroom." Asher's voice deepened, and my legs shook as he brought his lips closer to my ear. His thumb was sitting over the pulse in my neck, and I knew that he had to be able to feel how fast my heart was racing. "I need to be in control, but I promise I will make sure you have everything you want and desire, even if you don't know what that is yet."

His lips brushed along the line of my neck, and if my pulse spiked any higher, I was going to pass out. I had no idea why this man affected me like this, but there was no denying what my body wanted.

"Where is that saucy mouth now?"

My eyes narrowed into slits as I glared at him. "You're a conceited asshat."

"There she is. Don't ever lose that mouth. I like it." He nipped my ear, and my knees shook violently. "Are you one hundred percent sure about this? I want you to be sure because there is no going back for me once you say yes. We will cross a new line, and I don't intend to let you run away from it. Do you understand what I mean?" Asher's leg pressed between mine. I had to resist the urge to rub myself on his leg.

"I understand, and yes, I want this, whatever it means," I said, my voice a little firmer despite the quaking in my body.

"No. You need to understand that I will be in control of your body and pleasure. That I want to wrap my hand around your neck and make you come while I'm doing it." A shudder ran through my body.

He was serious.

"I want to smack your pussy and your ass until they are pink and pretty, all while I order you to behave."

He ran his nose up my neck and slid his lips over to my ear.

"I will use an assortment of toys on you that please me, then fuck you until I decide we've both had our fill."

He grabbed my chin with his thumb and forefinger, forcing our eyes to meet.

"Do you consent to those things and more as we go, Vi?"

All I could do was nod. My mouth wasn't working, but my libido was dancing off the charts.

"A headshake is not an answer, Vi. Say, yes, I understand, or no, I do not."

"Yes. I understand."

"Good girl."

That smirk returned to his face. "Your safe word will be popsicle."

"I need a safe word?"

"Yes." He nodded once.

"And you want it to be popsicle?" I giggled. I didn't know why I couldn't just use the word stop or something else that made sense.

"Yes, popsicle and no topping from the bottom, Vi."

I felt my forehead furrow. "No, what?"

"We'll get there."

"Okay, then yes to popsicle. Am I going to have to keep doing this?"

"Doing what?" His eyes focused on mine.

"Telling you 'yes' or 'I understand?' It seems redundant and feels like a mood killer."

"Trust me." He growled. "It's not redundant. I will be in complete control of your body, and you need to understand what that means every step of the way, or I could hurt you."

I swallowed hard and froze. What the hell did he want to do to me that was so dangerous? I'd had rough sex many times, and the guy never asked for my consent or warned me that he could hurt me.

"Last chance, Vi, or there's the door." His eyes flicked toward the front door. "Leave now, or I am going to fuck you like I just laid out."

The only thing I could hear was our breathing. Asher's stare was intense, his body rigid as he waited for me to respond. I glanced at the end of the hallway and thought about keeping things strictly professional.

He was bringing too much emotion to the surface, and I wasn't sure I was ready for more, but the thought of leaving felt like a bucket of water was being poured on my head. He was giving me an out, but...

Did I want this?

Did I want him?

Did I want to take that next step into an unknown world?

I stared into his eyes, trying to convey my feelings, but it wasn't enough. So I crashed my lips to his and kissed him hard. He opened up, and he kissed me back, surprising me.

Breaking the kiss, I said, "Yes, I'm certain."

Slipping my hands under his shirt, I watched his eyes flutter as I slid my hands down his back and gave his deliciously firm ass a squeeze. He arched into the sensation, a small groan slipping loose, and my already white-hot need climbed to an insane level.

Pushing him with all my strength, he stumbled back. His eyes went wide as I leaped onto his body, the two of us colliding into the hallway wall. Locking my legs around his waist, I reveled in the way he gripped my ass, holding me in place.

"Oh fuck," he groaned before he kissed me again.

He tasted so much better than any fantasy I could've conjured. He pulled me hard into his body, the roughness of his hands exciting me as they moved over my skin. I needed to be closer. Wiggling back and forth, I found it impossible not to feel his length poking me through his yielding swim trunks.

"Do I need to strip you," I panted out.

"Not a bad idea." He smirked, and I instantly wanted to smack him.

Why the image was so strong, I couldn't say, but my hand moved before I realized it. He easily stopped me before I could connect my palm with his face. Asher's eyes flared with something I couldn't quite put my finger on, but it made me squirm in his hold.

Ash turned so fast I was once more pressed with my back against the wall as he ground his body into mine. Even the small trickle of fear that came with the understanding that I was giving up all control, something I never did, made me groan. Weakly, I fought the sheer strength of his hands holding me while the idea of being trapped by this man tantalized and terrified me.

"You like it rough, do you? I can do primal." His eyes darkened like a freaking mood ring as his jaw flexed along with the muscles under his shirt.

He breathed out, and I would have sworn he growled as our lips met ferociously. He was like a tidal wave crashing onto the shore, and I was the shore beckoning him. I yelped as he bit my bottom lip, the sharp sting of pain amping up the twin pillars of fiery passion and fear inside of me. Breaking the kiss, he traced his tongue up the side of my neck to my ear.

"Let me guess. No one has ever been able to satisfy you with their placid fucking."

"That's none of your business," I said as he pulled us away from the wall.

Although it was true, I wasn't going to admit that to him.

"Oh, but it is very much my business. You're a lioness that has been choosing antelope to feed on—they kept you sustained but unsatisfied, is my guess."

I gasped as he yanked on my hair, bowing me away from his body.

"I'm no antelope, Vi. I'm a lion, and you've just wandered into my den."

A whimper left my lips, my body shivering in his hold at his words. He was right. I'd always been dominant in everything I did, including sex, but I hadn't wanted to be. I'd wanted to lose control, just for a little while, and hand those reins over to someone else. It was tiring, and I'd been doing it for so long that I was exhausted.

"Have you ever had a real orgasm? One that makes you scream?" He released my hair so I could look him in the eye, but I quickly looked away with embarrassment. I'd only ever climaxed when I masturbated, but never with a partner. For whatever reason, that information seemed mortifying, like something was wrong with me. Like I somehow sucked at sex. It made me feel like I failed at something that seemed so basic.

"Look at me." His quiet command caught me off guard, and my eyes met his again. I couldn't look away from that authoritative stare. "Don't ever feel embarrassed for your past lovers' failures. They weren't right for you."

"And you are?"

"I am."

He began to walk, holding me close to him. I squealed as he gave my body a playful push and I fell backward off of him. I braced for the impact of the floor but bounced as I landed on his soft bed. Laughing, I looked around. The greys and oceanic blues of his room were fitting for the man standing at the foot of the bed.

Asher pulled the white T-shirt he was wearing off over his head and tossed it to the side. My eyes followed every dip and plain of his fit body.

"Take your dress off."

"And if I don't," I asked, feeling particularly cheeky.

"Then I'm going to fuck you in it and come all over it for disobeying me. That's what naughty girls get." He pulled the string on his swim trunks, the tip of his cock poking out of the top of the waistband. I swallowed the scratchiness that was suddenly in my throat. "Get undressed, Vi. Now, or else."

I managed to roll off the bed and stand, feeling a whole lot of wobbly on my unsteady legs. I didn't dare look at him, or I wouldn't be able to get the dress off at all. He was doing something to my brain. No, he was doing something to my entire body.

If I were a cat, I would have hissed at his annoying face and then licked his body just because I could. I felt like pushing him, seeing what he'd do. I'd never had this urge to be so devilish, but the look in his eyes made me want to run down the hall and have him chase me, just to see if he would. Would he put me over his lap once he got me? Would he spank me for being naughty? A shiver ran up my spine at the thought.

Looking over my shoulder, I was treated to plains of muscle and a tan that didn't stop at the short line. That was just not fair. Of course, I instantly wanted to use my tongue to draw wet lines over all that golden skin. My fingers fumbled with the zipper at the back. Beck had helped me get into this thing, but I really should've thought more about how in the hell I'd planned on getting out of it. Once it was loose enough, I managed to wiggle back and forth as I tried to get the snugly formed corset top of the dress over my head.

"Stop." Asher's hands touched my waist, and I jerked like I'd been electrocuted from the surge of pleasure that one simple touch caused. "Let me help. I didn't realize it was going to be so difficult to take off."

I couldn't see him but knew exactly the look he'd been giving me, which annoyed me. I couldn't explain the instant anger, but it bubbled up, and I snipped back.

"Oh, shut up, Asher. Not all of us can be so perfect as—" The final words didn't make it out of my mouth before his hand landed with a hard crack on my ass. "Ah!"

I would've smacked him back if my arms hadn't been trapped inside the dress. I didn't want to acknowledge that the sting was like a blow torch to my libido. "Asshole."

Smack.

His hand landed harder this time, and I jumped forward while he gripped the dress over my head. He effectively kept me trapped.

"Watch your tone, little Firebug, or you will get another one," he said, his tone soft in comparison to the sharp bite of his hand.

I managed to wriggle the rest of the way out. Yanking the dress from his hold, I held it to my chest and stared at him and his sly smile. The look alone gave me pause, but the fact he was naked with his hands on his hips, had me transfixed. I licked my lips as I studied all that perfection, forgetting why I was angry in the first place.

"Come on, Firebug. Come and teach me a lesson," he teased, his eyes glinting with the arrogance that got me so hot.

A flicker sparked in me once more.

I glared even as my body shook in anticipation. "You'd like me to try, wouldn't you?"

"Depends on what kind of lesson you want to teach me. Do you want to teach me what lights your body on fire?" He took a step. "Are you going to teach me how to touch you to make you come?"

He reached out and gripped the dress I was still clutching, the material disappearing as he tossed it behind him. His nearness overwhelmed my senses, and I swayed on my feet, trapped by his closeness.

"Because I would love to learn those lessons, Firebug, but if you're just bratting or trying to top me...." Asher leaned in, nipped my ear, and then took me by surprise as he picked me up by the waist to once more unceremoniously toss me on the bed.

A strangled noise, a mix of wild passion and anger, ripped from my mouth. Why was I angry? I didn't know. I wanted this, I wanted him, but it was there simmering under the desire.

Asher followed me to the bed, but grabbing my hands, he held them above my head and just stared at me.

"Stop Vi, or we'll stop right now."

"Stop what?" I looked away from the eyes that left me naked, even with my underwear still on.

"Do you want this? I told you what I'm like. If you want to stop, you tell me. Remember my rule about misunderstandings? I will not have them between us."

I slowly shook my head back and forth. "I want this. I-I want you. I don't know why I'm angry."

One eyebrow lifted as he studied my face. It was terribly unnerving having him stare at me like that. "I see you, Vi, but if you want this, then you need to let the rage go. Just take a breath."

He gently rocked his hips back and forth, making me gasp. "Relax and enjoy," he said. His voice was soft, yet his words dripped with a command that I couldn't deny.

I took a shuddering breath and closed my eyes as he continued to rub himself on the most sensitive part of my body, and my nipples brushed against his muscular pecks. I needed him to fuck me now.

"I hate you," I said, and he just smiled back.

"No you don't. You hate that I see you. You hate to let anyone in, and I don't let your walls blind me to who you are."

My eyes fluttered open, and as our eyes locked, I knew he was right. "I like to fight back."

He smiled wide. "Do you want to fight me?"

"No."

"But you like to fight?"

"Yes. I used to get into fights all the time when I was younger." I was beyond wet. I could feel it trapped by the lace panties I was still wearing.

"Maybe, I should leave you like this, all pent up. Make you go home instead so you can think about how you missed out on this moment because of your desire to prove you're stronger, faster, better."

My mouth dropped open. "I...I..."

I stopped and looked away, the anger returning. He was calling me out on all the things I did like to bury.

"Please don't," I said instead of trying to argue.

His pearly white teeth flashed with a simple grin, but his eyes held enough mischief to have me worried he planned on following through on his threat. If he left me like this, I might actually murder him.

"All right, Firebug, I know what you need, and I'm going to give it to you, but...." Asher held up a finger. "You need to stay still, or I will do just that."

"What are you going to do?"

"You ask too many questions. This is an exercise in learning to trust me to know what you need and when. Now, just breathe."

I watched him get up from the bed. The sight of that perfect ass was enough to make my mouth water. Once more, the slow-motion movie started in my mind. All I needed was the bow-chicka-bow-wow music to start playing. It was unfair yet so delightful as it flexed and released when he moved.

Meow.

He looked over at me, confusion on his face. "Did you just meow at me?"

Holy fuck, I'd said that out loud.

"No, just...clearing my throat."

A throaty laugh rippled from his mouth. "You're not moving, are you?"

I shook my head no. Every little flex of his muscles drew my eyes to him like a moth to a flame. He dug around in his dresser drawer and pulled out what looked like a leather handle with tassels. My eyes went wide as I took in the painful-looking toy.

He smirked the entire time he laid it out like it was on display on the nightstand. "Remember what I said."

I sighed dramatically. "I'm not going to move."

He nodded, but the look on his face was a challenge, and I scowled as he leaned over to reach under the bed. I couldn't have kept the shocked expression off my face if I tried hearing the sound of chains moving under the bed. I bit my lip hard as he pulled out a long chain with a fur-lined, thick, leather wrist cuff attached to it. As he brought it closer, I saw the 'serious, not getting out' binding on top.

This cuff was not the fun, cute pink fur ones, oh hell, no. This was black leather and metal that clanged with how legit it was as Asher stared down at me. Every nerve tingled, part of me wanted to run for the door as I recognized what was about to happen, and the other part of me wanted to stand up and scream, 'fuck, yes.'

My eyes flicked between the cuff he was holding and his cock that was standing at attention.

"Umm..." I started, and he held up his finger.

"Don't bother asking what I'm going to do or how many people I've had in here. I already told you what I do and never brought anyone else home. I installed these with you in mind."

I swallowed hard. What the hell did someone say to that? The throbbing between my legs steadily grew as well as the sudden feeling of being important to him. Important enough to bring to his home. Granted, he could be lying to me. He might have had a hundred women on this bed, but I didn't think so. Asher didn't strike me as a liar. Besides, I couldn't take my eyes off him. He was like candy, and I wanted to suck on every part of his body. His hard cock was so close that it was making my mouth water.

"It's not very ladylike to drool, Vi. Then again, I wouldn't really call you a lady," he smirked.

"That is one thing we can agree on," I said.

Asher placed a knee on the bed, and my heart rate ramped up.

"You may not be what is considered a stereotypical lady, but you're my kind of lady, Firebug. I could see that the first moment we met. All woman, a tomboy at heart, and the way you sassed me—I wanted to lay you out in the back of that ambulance and fuck you in front of all those people."

My heart stopped beating as he looked down into my eyes. I remembered that night very well. I'd lost count of how many times that particular fantasy had crossed my mind.

"Why didn't you?" I asked breathlessly as he leaned over my body, securing the leather cuff to my left wrist.

"I didn't fancy getting fired and being thrown in jail for rape. Not really my thing. As you can see, I'm pretty big on consent," he said.

It was completely unfair that everything he said made me hotter. If I hadn't been ordered not to move, I would've been tempted to fan myself.

"Fair enough," I said and licked my lips as I held out my wrist to have the leather secured into place.

"Is that too tight?" he asked. I gave the cuff a tug and shook my head no. He slowly wandered to the foot of the bed and pulled out another cuff and chain, attaching it to my ankle.

"But I knew I'd have you." He bent down and repeated the same thing on the other side as he talked. He acted like he was doing nothing more than household chores. I had to wonder if he had a cleaning lady. The poor woman would probably be terrified to miss a single corner after finding chains under his bed.

Asher once more strolled around the bed and looked down at me, his stare so heated and cocky. Normally, arrogance wouldn't do a thing for me other than make me want to roll my eyes, but there was an aura to Asher that was so different. I couldn't put my finger on it.

"Pretty sure of yourself, were you?" I tried to sound indignant, but my quivering legs, shaky voice, and dripping pussy made that a tough sell.

His lip curled up as he checked the tightness of the last cuff. He never broke eye contact as he walked around the bed once more. Reaching forward, agonizingly slow, Asher picked up the leather-looking contraption.

"I was sure of our chemistry. Are those cuffs comfortable enough?" I tugged and then nodded. "Now tell me, my sweet little Firebug, what do you want from me?"

"I thought laying on your bed naked would tell you. Maybe you're not as good as you thought picking up on my not-so-subtle cues," I said as sarcastically as I could muster.

It was my nervousness that was pushing me to lash out more than normal. I hated being exposed, and you didn't get any more vulnerable than being tied up naked to a bed with a man that could seemingly see into my mind.

Asher's face grew serious. "If you keep bratting I will stop, is that what you want, Vi?"

It wasn't lost on me that he used my name and not the nickname he'd given me. He was very serious, and the fact that he could and would walk away sent a trickle of panic spreading throughout my body.

"N-n-no," I managed to stutter as he trailed the leather toy along my legs. The ends were ticklish as much as they were unnerving and arousing.

With a sharp flick of his wrist, the long strands swooshed through the air and smacked off my thigh. I tried to pull on the four restraints but could only move an inch at best. He did it harder, the strands thudding on my thigh but lightly wisping across my hot, wet core, but there was almost no pain at all as the strands hit.

I closed my eyes as my heart hammered—those ends hit again, and my chest rose off the bed in a gasp. I opened my eyes to look up at Asher.

"I'm going to break you, Firebug. I'm going to break you and put you back together again, and you're going to beg me to do it."

He couldn't have said anything sexier and more terrifying.

"Now, let's try this again. What do you want from me?"

I licked my lips and stared into his eyes as he let the long strands of the toy sway by his side.

"I don't know," I said honestly. Emotion gripped me, and my eyes filled with tears. "I don't."

He nodded. "All right, Firebug. From this moment on, your body is mine. You do what I say no matter what, and I don't want any more backtalk from you."

I struggled to swallow but nodded my compliance. I really had no idea what I agreed to, but I realized I didn't fucking care anymore.

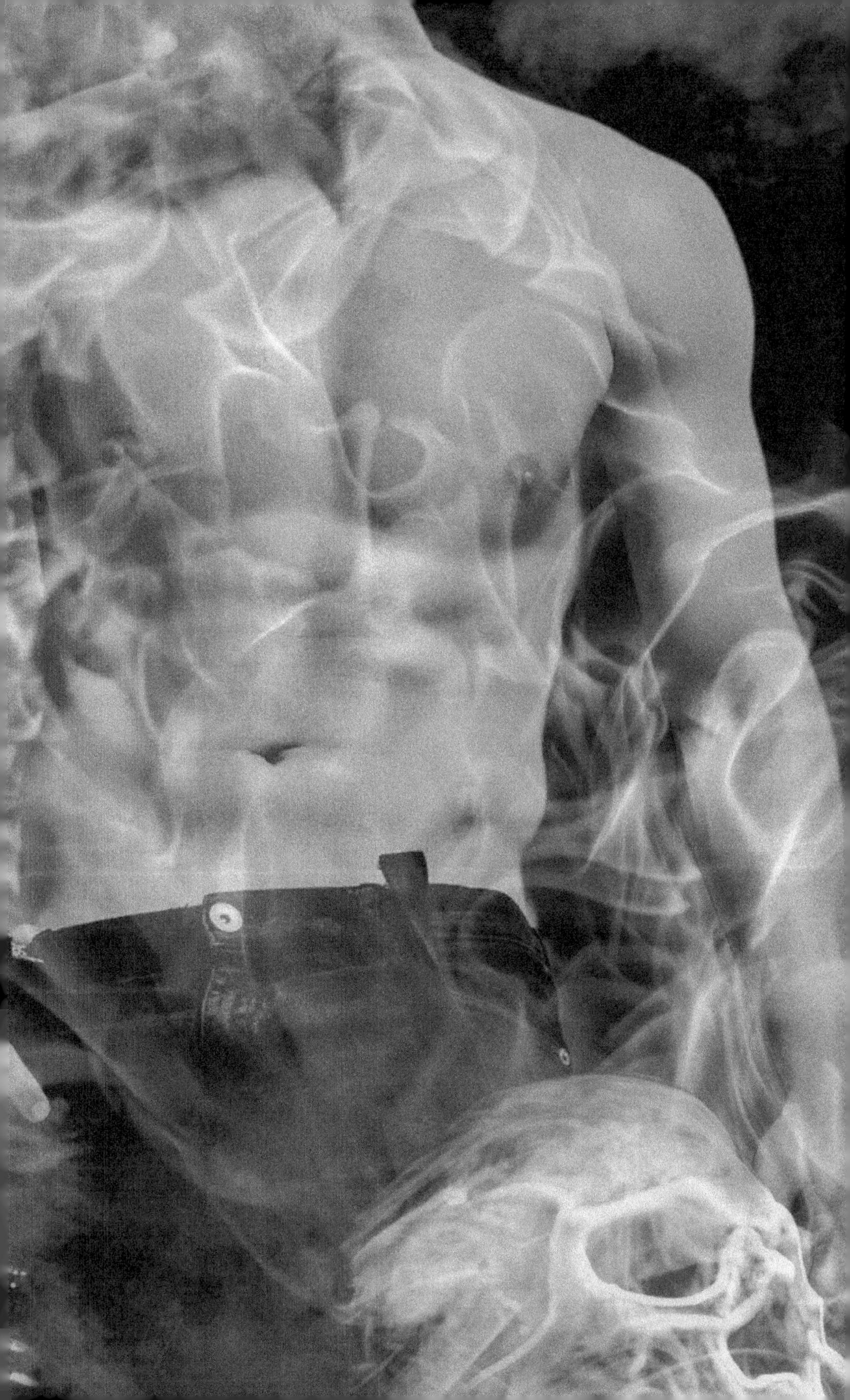

Chapter 22

Asher

Holding out my arm, I let the long strands of the flogger drape across Vi as she wiggled from the light touch. I loved how she squirmed under its gentle caress as I slowly drew it in long lines up and down her body like a painter would apply the final touches to his masterpiece.

"Do you know what this is?" I held it up for her to get a better look. Vi opened her mouth, but no sound came out, making me smirk. She shook her head no. "This is a genital flogger."

She raised an eyebrow as her eyes went wide, making me laugh. "Don't worry. It doesn't hurt, and it's brand new."

I swirled the flogger around her stomach, drawing shapes and designs that only I could see before letting the ends dip into the small valley of her partially spread legs. She was stunning. Everything about her made me hard with anticipation. I'd been planning this from the moment her eyes locked with mine as she sassed me for the second time at the fire station.

With a quick flick of my wrist, the tail ends smacked into her sensitive mound, and she moaned an all too delicious sound and spread her legs a little wider.

"You liked that, did you?" I already knew the answer but wanted to hear her say the words.

"You seemed to like it more...." The rest of whatever she planned to say to me died in her throat as she gave me a hard pointed look.

"Were you planning on saying something bratty?"

Vi pressed her lips tight together and shook her head no. I knew she was lying, but the fact that she caught herself made me smile. She looked at my cock, which was clearly hard and ready, but my needs could wait. First, I was going to make her scream my name. I wanted her high with passion and spent to the core. Vi may not realize it, but she was holding something back, and I could see it in her eyes. Something that was making her wall up and lash out.

I wanted to break her walls down and see what lay beneath. The gentle tickling touch of the flogger disappeared as I gave her two fast strikes. She screamed out as her mind told her that they hurt, and her sensitive system agreed, but this flogger could be used with all my strength, and it would never leave a mark. This was a mental game, a twisting of her body and mind's wires, and I was the one holding the control.

The cuffs did their job, jingling as she gave them a sharp tug. "You like challenges, don't you, my Firebug? You love to win, so I'll make you a bet." Vi was already panting hard as she stared up at me. Her eyes filled with desire and, under that, a thread of fear. I intended to wipe the fear away. Whatever her reasons were for the uncertainty, it didn't belong here with us.

I tapped the leather in my hand, making a dramatic show of it. "I'm going to bet you I can make you come, screaming my name long before I sheath this cock in you."

Her eyes glimmered with excitement and the idea of a challenge. "What do I get if you lose that bet?"

"I won't lose." Leaning forward so my face was right in front of hers, I stroked the ends over her thighs but made sure not to touch her pussy. "Because you want the release, your body is screaming for it."

"We'll see," she challenged back, but there was no hint of the earlier brattiness. She was ready and willing to try and hold off her pleasure to prove a point. It was fucking sexy. I was enjoying this so much more than I ever thought I would.

"First things first...." I laid the flogger down on the side of the mattress before making my way to the end of the bed.

"Lift your ass." I saw by the look in her eyes that she was tempted to mouth off again but managed to bite her tongue.

She lifted her ass up off the mattress, and I leaned forward between her legs and savored the heated look I got in response. Grabbing her lace panties in both hands, I pulled hard. The material ripped in two, the sound of tearing loud in the otherwise quiet room. Vi gasped, her mouth falling open as I held up the two pieces and tossed them aside.

"You can lay back down now," I said and ran the tips of my fingers over the tops of her feet. She jumped as I took hold of her legs.

"Are you scared?"

"No."

"Then relax. I'm not going to hurt you."

She took a deep breath, and I watched her chest rise and fall as she forced herself to settle. My eyes focused on every inch of her body as I studied her. Her nipples were hard little peaks. I could feel her muscles quiver and her legs shift slightly as the tenseness eased. Only when you paid attention did you realize that our bodies speak, and she was talking to me now.

Picking up the flogger, I once more began to trail it along her body. Goosebumps rose everywhere the cool leather touched.

"Close your eyes," I ordered, and it took her a few extra seconds, but she allowed her eyes to flutter closed. "Good girl."

This time when I raised the flogger above my head and brought it down, she flinched but didn't jerk. Soft sweep, hard thud, my wrist worked. I went only as long as it took to make her pant hard, her mouth hanging open as her pulse raced.

"You can open your eyes," I said and was impressed that she'd kept them closed the entire time. Laying the flogger aside, I unlatched her ankles from the cuffs and then slowly pushed her feet up until the soles touched, and she splayed her knees like a butterfly.

"Good girl, my Firebug," I said. "This is much better." I took a moment to admire how sexy she was and how my little warm-up had her dripping and ready for what was to come next. A surge of pleasure raced through my system at the sight. "Keep your feet like that."

Retrieving my flogger once more, I purposely dipped the tails between her legs, but this time I began a hard rhythmic flick of my wrist. The leather tails beat against her swollen and sensitive pussy like a drum.

"Oh my god," Vi mumbled and arched off the bed as I repeated the movement over and over. She shook with each gentle thud that I knew would seem almost painful with how sensitive her body had become.

I stood at the side of the bed and felt like an orchestra conductor. It took care, time, and hours of study to watch another human closely enough to become so in tune with their body that her sighs became my own. I knew exactly when to add the next phase of the play and how much Vi could take before she needed a break. Vi had become the instrument, her body playing the melody while I was the one that knew exactly what strings to pluck.

I let the flogger rest against her mound while I ran my hand over her nipples. Each bud got the same attention before I steadily added pressure to the one closest to me. Vi arched off the bed, pressing her breast and the nipple harder into my hand, but I refused to increase the pressure. I knew that before too long, that beautifully hardened peak of nerves was going to begin throbbing and aching in a way that would drive her crazy. Giving the flogger a quick flick with my wrist, Vi cried out as the leather landed against her pussy.

"Do you like that, Firebug?"

Vi nodded, but I wanted to hear it. "Say the word."

"Yes," she panted.

"Good girl."

I became the metronome her body needed as I picked an even rhythm with the flogger and switched between a gentle caress or a squeeze of her nipples. I swirled the long tails between her legs, and her muscles relaxed, allowing her knees to almost touch the bed as she silently begged for more.

"Does this hurt," I asked.

It was an evil question because I knew it didn't. Her body was so sensitive by now that every little touch would feel excruciating in the best way possible, which only served to confuse her mind further.

"The pressure in my body is almost unbearable," she said, making me feel warm inside. My cock ached, and I wondered if I'd come just from watching her writhe on the bed in pleasure. It was a drug to my system that I craved, but with Vi, the sensation was already so much stronger that it was taking me by surprise. I needed to take a few steadying breaths to continue my work. Vi cried out, almost a growl, as I continued to swirl the flogger on her clit and tease her nipples.

I smiled down at her as her eyes begged me to let her come.

"Easy, Firebug," I said and stepped away from her body to let her breathe.

Vi moaned, the sound so small it was like a whimper. It was time for the next phase. Laying the toy aside, I picked up a blindfold and held it up for her to see what it was.

"Lift your head."

She didn't hesitate this time to do what I asked, which made me smile. It wasn't just that she obeyed. No, it was the fact that she trusted me enough to take away one of her senses. We were protective of our senses whether we realized it or not. It took a great deal of courage and trust to be blindfolded.

As soon as the black blindfold was tied into place, her muscles tensed with the sudden darkness.

"Don't move, Vi. I'm watching you," I said softly, right near her ear. She gasped, her arms tensing for a moment against the restraints. "You're such a good girl, Firebug."

I backed away from the bed, moved around the room, and loved that whether she noticed or not, her head tracked my movement.

"I think we need some music. Don't you, Firebug?"

She was back to nodding, but we were taking steps forward, not back.

"Answer me, Vi."

"Music is fine," she said and shrugged, the chains rattling slightly.

"No moving," I said as her body wiggled a little more. "Don't think I didn't see that. I see everything."

"Asher...I...," she said a hint of panic in her voice.

"Shh, Firebug. Just relax." I flicked on the sound system, and a dark but soothing song filled the room. "Calm your racing heart and listen to my voice. Don't let the fear control you." I returned to the bed, staring down at her body.

For the first time, I was more tempted to come inside Vi rather than on her. The thought was so strong that I had to squeeze my cock to help calm my body. Nearing release too quickly was not an option.

Her muscles quivered as she forced herself to remain compliant. I was more excited than I'd ever been in my life to end the scene and fuck her now. It was unnerving to feel even a little out of control. It had been a very long time since I'd been immature enough that I couldn't handle hours of play before finally taking my final release. Vi did something strange to my perfectly controlled system right from the first moment we met.

I knew she hadn't heard me return to the side of the bed, and it was confirmed as I trailed my finger along her leg.

"Oh god," Vi mumbled as goosebumps rose where I touched.

She moaned, and I could imagine her heart pounding hard inside her chest with the way her pulse was jumping in the side of her neck. Inch by inch, my finger moved closer to where I knew she really wanted me. Vi opened her mouth, but I placed a finger against her lips.

"Shh, remember you need to remain quiet. You'll get what you want soon enough."

My fingers trailed around her nipples and down her stomach until I was able to give her clit the same attention. Her stomach flexed, and I knew that it was taking every ounce of control she had not to move or make a sound. My finger slid lower, and her reaction was like a decadent dessert. Her hands clenched into fists. This was her first time, and she was new to all the sensations bombarding her body, so I let her get away with it.

I made sure to interchange between rubbing small circles along her hard little clit and giving it a subtle squeeze. Vi's mouth dropped open, and she sucked in a deep breath before snapping her mouth shut and biting her lip. I was eating it up. No, I was eating her up.

Slipping a finger into her body, she yanked hard on the restraints, a loud gasp escaping her mouth, and I knew she was getting close to losing control. The question was, did I allow her to release and start the build-up all over again, or did I make her hold off longer? Both ideas were equally tantalizing.

Studying her like a cat would study its prey, I pressed her a little more as my finger smoothly slid in and out of her body and decided that she was too wrung out. Leaning close to her, I blew a cool stream of air on her nipple, and she whimpered under my touch.

"You've been a very good girl. Do you know what you get," I asked, picking up the pace of my hand and pressing a little harder to find her G-spot. "You can answer," I said when she didn't speak.

"No," she breathed out.

I whispered close to her ear and loved that she shivered. "I want you to come for me. Don't fight it. Let yourself go. Allow yourself to feel the pleasure coursing through your body."

I added a second digit to her hot pussy while still using my thumb to stimulate her clit.

"I know you want to come for me." Quickening my pace, I purposely breathed a little heavier in her ear, and I could feel her walls start to tighten around my finger.

I stopped moving, and as I knew she would, Vi whimpered and wiggled her bottom, trying to get me to continue.

"Tell me what you want, Vi," I said and smoothed the soft blonde hair away from her face.

Her body trembled while she continued to try and win the challenge I'd tossed down. It was like watching a perfectly crafted puzzle slowly coming apart. She gave the restraints another small tug, desperate to touch herself.

"Tell me, my little Firebug. Say the words, and I'll make it happen. Just say the words." I kissed the jumping pulse on the side of her neck.

She groaned a deep sound of pure need as my tongue traced a line down to her nipple. My eyes locked on her face, a smirk pulling at my lips as I sucked her nipple into my mouth.

"Please," Vi yelled and arched up.

"Please, what," I asked, breaking the contact only for a second before twirling my tongue around her areola. She was as sweet as I imagined.

"It's okay to lose, Firebug. The prize is well worth it."

"Please, Asher, make me come. Please," she cried out.

I immediately began to kiss her. My mouth drank down the taste of her and her whimpers as my fingers once more began to move inside her clenching pussy. Oh, those moans were so sweet, and I was enthralled with the way she became the aggressor and sucked in my bottom lip like she was trying to ground herself. It was so her and so adorable.

I quickly pulled out my fingers and gave her mound a sharp smack. Vi screamed into my mouth, and the sound shot through my body. Her thighs began to shake as my fingers slid back into her, and I counted to seven in my head and then pulled out and smacked her again. I repeated the process until she was begging.

"Asher, please. I give up...you won. I'm begging you, make me come." Her ass wiggled back and forth, and I smiled at my victory, but it wouldn't be a win without her coming and screaming my name.

"Okay, Firebug, your request will be granted." Removing my fingers, I quickly walked around the bed, laid down between her legs, and took but a moment to savor the sweet pussy that was spread open for me.

I'd have time to savor her better later. But I made a promise, and I intended to keep it. My fingers slid into her shaking body at the same time I took her into my mouth, and this time she cried out, but no words left her mouth as she arched off the bed.

Releasing her clit, I lifted my head to stare at the sexiest woman I'd ever laid eyes on. "Let it out, Vi. Scream for me. Scream my name," I ordered before dropping my mouth to the swollen clit that was unhooded and would be aching.

Vi jerked on the cuffs as she pressed her pussy harder into my face. I groaned, loving everything about this moment.

"Fuck...Asher! Yes, right there, please don't stop. Oh, yes, yes, yes," she yelled, her head rocking back and forth as my tongue continued its assault. "Asher!"

The yell of my name sent a shiver down my spine as she came into my mouth. Gripping her ass hard, I lifted her up like she was my last meal. I'd never been so ravenous in my life, and I had the strongest urge to claim her as my own.

I didn't allow people to put labels on me, and I'd already conceded that we would be considered dating, but it didn't feel like enough. I didn't know what more looked like or how to get there.

Changing positions slightly, I pressed on the G-spot I'd been dancing my finger over and sucked hard. Vi yelled again, and the chains rattled as she pulled on them as another wave of pleasure wracked her body. I repeated the action until she went limp in my hold.

I gently licked the inside of her thighs and messaged her legs as she caught her breath.

Walking around the bed, I left the blindfold on but gently undid the cuffs and laid her arms down on the bed.

"I will be back. You rest."

"Are we done," she asked, her voice wispy.

"No, far from it, but you must let your body come down from the high and rest for a few moments. I'm going to get us some water. Rest."

I wandered out to the kitchen, poured two tall glasses of water, and grabbed the painkillers for later. Better to be prepared.

As I stepped into the room, Vi hadn't moved, but goosebumps had risen on her skin. Sitting the water down, I grabbed the throw I kept in my closet and came back to lay it across her body.

"Thank you," she whispered.

"I have some water. You should take a sip," I said. Vi pushed herself up, and I handed her the glass as I undid the blindfold. Like a magnet, her eyes traveled to my cock, which was still hard and very ready for what was going to come next.

"How do you do that? How do you hold off so long and act so calm," she asked before gulping down a couple of mouthfuls of the water.

"It takes practice, but more than that, I love the control and love to pleasure first. It is what, 'does it for me,'" I said, making little air quotes. "But you almost made me break my control, Vi. That takes more than you'd think." I lifted her chin as she looked away. "You're so beautiful."

She blinked away a tear and smiled.

"Thanks," she said shyly. It was the first real shy thing I'd seen her do. Vi was the 'jump from a building' and 'dive with sharks' type, which made my chest puff with pride.

"You ready for round two?"

That sexy flush deepened on her cheeks as she smiled wide. "Yes. Definitely."

Reaching out, I tapped the metal frame of the bed. "Grip that and get on all fours."

Grabbing the blanket, I tossed it aside and waited as she rolled herself over. She did as I asked and grabbed the bar. My cock jerked against my body at the sight of her taut ass in the air.

The bed shifted as I got behind her, a surge of pleasure shot through my body as my hand lightly slapped her ass, and she moaned.

"Fuck, you're sexy," I said, running my hand in slow circles on the perfectly round globe of her ass cheek.

She wiggled her ass back and forth, willing me to do it again. I smacked the other cheek slightly harder, then rubbed my hand in a circle over the mark. I repeated the process from one cheek to the next, and each smack got a little harder until she jumped forward with the hard crack.

I found her limit.

Rubbing the spot to ease the sting, I backed off the pressure and smacked the other cheek, and once more, she moaned and pressed back toward me. Her pussy was already dripping again, and I was tempted to use my mouth one more time.

I licked my lips at the thought, but the aching between my legs steadily grew and became harder to ignore.

"You ready for me, Firebug? You ready for me to spread you wide and make you come again?"

"Yes, Asher." Vi looked over her shoulder, and the look was heated as her eyes begged for what I offered. I gave my insistent cock a stroke before running it along the outer lips of her pussy, and her body shuddered against mine.

My adrenaline and pulse were spiking much higher than normal, and I needed to take a moment before slipping the tip of my cock into her tight heat. Slowly, with every incredible inch I managed to gain, she gripped me harder and moaned. It felt like she was trying to choke my cock as I worked to get myself fully sheathed. The sensation running through my body was new, and my head fell back as the last few inches finally disappeared inside Vi.

"You're so fucking tight. I love it." I groaned as I bottomed out and just held still. She was moaning, her head down and muscles shaking.

"Please, more," she begged and then whimpered as she pushed back into me.

"Easy, Vi. I need a moment. It's been quite the build-up watching you." Ready to come at any second, I had to give my balls a little twist to get my body to behave. So, this was what it was like to feel nineteen again. Her body clenched hard around me, and sweat formed on my back. I could feel it trickling down as I fought the urge to move.

"Should I be concerned about a short performance," Vi asked, but the teasing look she gave me over her shoulder was more an innocent challenge than brat, and I found myself smiling back.

I made a snorting noise. "Not likely. I promised to break you, and I always keep my promises."

"Oh god, yes," she moaned as I rocked slightly back and pressed into her, testing my resilience.

"You ready for me, Firebug? I plan on fucking you hard and making you scream my walls down."

"Yes, I'm ready," she said and wiggled her ass again.

This time, I smacked her hard, and she jerked but stopped wiggling and hung her head as she moaned again.

I pulled back and slammed forward. Vi screamed and squeezed the bar tighter. I would've asked if it was too much, but I could tell she was having trouble holding still and containing herself. There was no soft sweetness in my demeanor as my test confirmed what she could handle. My hips rocked hard into Vi, the force of my thrusts making the bed squeak as it tried to move across the floor. But, it had nowhere to go.

My hands tightened on her hips as I picked up the pace and let myself go. Vi arched her back and yelled my name as an orgasm stormed to the surface, taking us both by surprise. There hadn't been a warning or build-up, and I was shocked that I didn't feel it coming.

"Again, oh, yes, please again."

Reaching forward, I grabbed a handful of her hair and wrapped it around my wrist as I pulled back.

"Let go of the rail," I growled at her, and she did as I ordered.

The new angle allowed me to see her face. Now, I was able to make sure that she wasn't already in subspace. Her eyes found mine, and there was nothing to indicate that she was, but it still rocked me that I hadn't felt her about to orgasm so soon. I couldn't even describe the level of euphoria I was reaching.

"Do you like that?" I pulled back and slammed into her as hard as possible.

"Yes, I love it."

"Well, you were a naughty girl, and you came too soon. You're going to come again, this time when I tell you, you can."

She nodded her head as our bodies came together over and over until the music disappeared. All that was left was our moaning and the sound of skin slapping together.

I was nearing my own orgasm. The build-up was tightening my balls and my lower stomach.

"Now, Vi! Rub your clit and make yourself come right now," I growled in her ear, and she shuddered against me. She moved her hand to do as I ordered, and I could feel her furiously rubbing at herself. "Yes, that's it. Squeeze my cock, come all over me." I commanded.

Her muscles shook violently. This time, I could feel her body building toward that glorious peak, but I wanted her to do it faster. "I said, come for me, Vi. I meant right now."

I gently bit the side of her neck. She cried out and bucked back hard into me as her body took over. This time the waves that followed were much like her first orgasm and continued to rock her, which was exactly what I wanted.

"Where do you want me to come," I asked, and her mouth moved, but no words came out. "Answer me," I ordered again. We didn't have much time before she couldn't continue.

"Inside me, come in me," she whimpered.

This was also something I'd never entertained, yet here I was about to do as she asked. Letting go of her hair, it fanned down to cover her face as her hands dropped to the mattress. With each thrust, my pleasure was pushed higher as every muscle tensed.

"Fuck, Vi," I yelled and came hard, my body straining.

I held still as the last of the orgasm subsided. I expected to feel unsure about what we'd just done. A hint of fear raced through me about what this meant emotionally for me, but also what it could mean if she got pregnant. As I searched my emotions, I found nothing that resembled uncertainty.

Taking a deep breath, I released her hips and rubbed a slow circle into her lower back.

"You okay?"

Vi nodded, and I reluctantly pulled out of her body and reached out to gather her up in my arms. As soon as I lifted her into my embrace, her eyes met mine. There was the moment of stillness that passed between us, this calm in the aftermath of what we'd done, but suddenly the ecstasy that had been dancing in her eyes began to fade. I could feel her mood shifting as quickly as hurricane winds.

Tears filled her beautiful eyes. "Hey, what's going on?"

"Spank me," she blurted out, but the request was pained as tears began to pour down her cheeks.

It was like an emotional cord inside of her had just snapped. Whatever I'd seen her forcing down was coming to the surface.

"I said spank me," she said, firmer and angrier this time. "You liked that, didn't you? Then do it again." Vi went to get out of my arms, but I held her tight and forced her to continue to look at me. "Stop looking at me like that. Just spank me already."

"No, we're done for the night."

I could sense and see the pain that was bubbling inside of her. What she wanted now was not for pleasure. She struggled harder in my arms, and I let her go. She stormed to her feet and marched over to where I'd left the flogger.

"Do it. Hit me," she yelled and held it out to me.

She wasn't bratting. If she were, she would be tossed out on her ass. This was different. I could feel great sadness and pain inside of her. I wasn't empathic, but I was very in tune with people, and what we'd just done together left me very connected to her emotions.

"I said no, Vi, you've had enough." I stood up slowly.

She was shaking from head to toe.

"Hurt me," she yelled as I walked toward her. "Please just do it. I know you like it."

She was bawling now, the tears running in streams and dropping to her chest to mingle with the sweat we'd just created.

I took the flogger from her hand and set it aside before cupping her face. She kept trying to look away as the tears turned into heart-breaking sobs. She wrapped her arms around herself like she was trying to keep her emotions inside.

"Look at me, Vi. Now." She finally complied and looked me directly in the eyes, so I asked what I needed to know. "Why do you want me to punish you? What do you think you need punishing for?"

She tried to struggle, but it was feeble. I could see her warring between wanting to tell me and keeping it inside, but I knew it would continue to eat at her.

"Please don't make me say it. Please," she begged.

"No, Vi. You need to be honest with yourself and me. Why do you want to be punished?"

"Because I deserve it," she said her voice breaking.

We just stared at one another as all the fight left her body.

"Because I deserve it," she said again, quieter.

"You need to tell me everything, Vi," I said softly and slowly drew her into my body, holding her tight.

"Don't make me say it."

"You need to, for yourself and for us to have any kind of a future," I said softly and rubbed her back as her arms slid around my waist.

"I should have died with them. They died thinking I hated them and wasn't there to help."

"Who, your parents?"

Vi nodded as the tidal wave of emotion burst through the final door, and her knees gave out. Scooping her up into my arms, I walked back to the bed and sat down, holding her to me as she cried. My heart seized in my chest. What I'd learned from Vi so far was that she didn't let people in, and she guarded her heart with all she had. This gut-wrenching display meant so much to me that she trusted me enough to share her agony.

"Vi...you are a smart woman. Do you think your parents would have wished you'd died with them?"

"You don't understand," she choked out. "I snuck out of my house and went to some stupid party. We'd been fighting over my grades, my attitude, and the stupid pair of sneakers that my mom bought because I hated them. I told them I hated the stupid shoes, and I'd be better off if they were dead."

She sucked in a shuddering breath, and I laid my lips on her forehead.

"I came home, and the entire place was engulfed in flames. I tried to get in, but the fire was so hot. I tried to throw stuff at the windows, but nothing worked. My dad said he loved me. How could he love me after what I'd said? I was horrible to them, I was a terrible daughter, and they died thinking I hated them."

I leaned back so I could look her in the eyes.

"I've never shared that with anyone other than my best friend. I... I deserved to die with them, Asher. Please punish me. Please."

She was beating herself up with guilt that she didn't deserve to hold in her heart. Standing, I scooped her up and held her close as I walked to the bathroom.

"Where are you taking me," she asked as I cuddled her to my chest.

"To clean you up," I said, letting her feet drop to the shower floor.

I didn't say anything else as I got the water to a warm temperature and put Vi under the spray. I cleaned every inch of her body and spent time massaging her shoulders and neck until her breathing returned to normal.

I quickly cleaned myself off, grabbed a massive fluffy towel to wrap her up, and guided her back out to the bedroom. She stood there silent while I changed the sheets. As soon as the bed was clean, I picked her up in my arms and cuddled her in my lap on the bed. I rocked her gently, trying to soothe her.

"You didn't and don't deserve to die, Vi, and your parents wouldn't have wanted it either. We will never know if you could've saved them if you were home, but my gut tells me it wouldn't have mattered. I think you know that too. As for what you said, I know you think they thought you hated them, but they were teens once. Do you think they never argued with their parents? You don't think they regretted the shit they said and never meant?"

"I don't know why, but you telling me that makes me feel a little better."

"I wouldn't say this to you, Vi, if I didn't believe it to be true. You need to let the pain go. Even if you want to continue to investigate their death, you need to let the pain that has sunk its fangs into your soul go."

She nodded, and I gave the top of her head a kiss as she began to fall asleep.

"Thank you," Vi whispered.

"Rest now. I've got you," I said as she finally drifted off.

This woman was changing my normal. She was making me want something I'd never wanted. More than that, the thought of her leaving and ever seeing another man sat like rocks in the pit of my stomach. I looked down at her peaceful sleeping form, her beautiful face, and knew there was no way I was letting that happen.

Violet Clarke was mine.

Not
even the
Devil could burn
the world like
I could

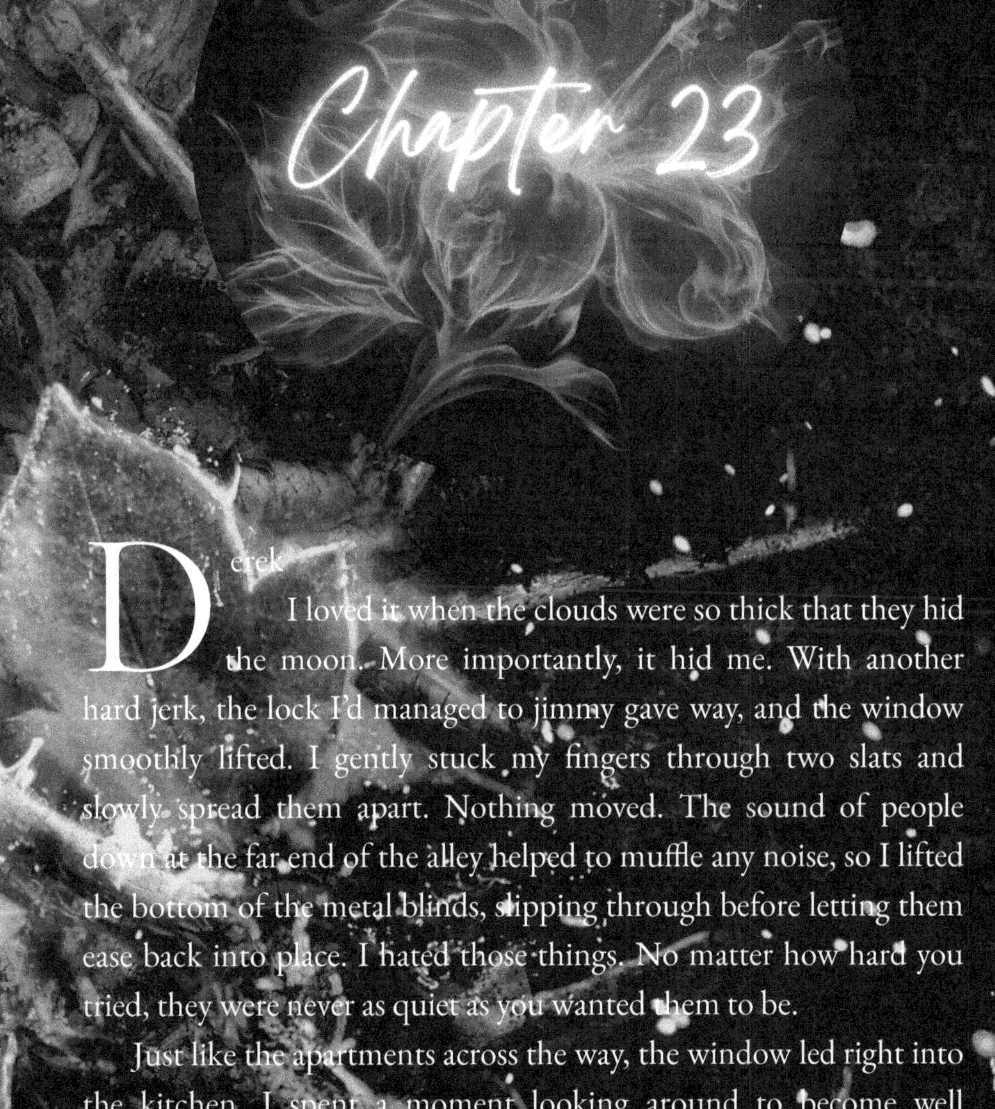

Chapter 23

I loved it when the clouds were so thick that they hid the moon. More importantly, it hid me. With another hard jerk, the lock I'd managed to jimmy gave way, and the window smoothly lifted. I gently stuck my fingers through two slats and slowly spread them apart. Nothing moved. The sound of people down at the far end of the alley helped to muffle any noise, so I lifted the bottom of the metal blinds, slipping through before letting them ease back into place. I hated those things. No matter how hard you tried, they were never as quiet as you wanted them to be.

Just like the apartments across the way, the window led right into the kitchen. I spent a moment looking around to become well acquainted with my surroundings. A soft jingle had me freezing in place. A black cat wandered into the doorway. As soon as our eyes met, it hissed, and its back arched. Those yellow eyes practically glowed in the dark.

"Oh yeah? Right back at ya." I hissed back at it, and the cat took off and disappeared into the apartment.

Pulling the little blue booties out of my pocket, I slipped them on before continuing my hunt. I knew the blonde woman who lived here hadn't come home yet. I'd followed her and her friend into the mall. They went into a massive department store and disappeared, but I now knew what her vehicle looked like, and it wasn't in the parking lot.

I didn't know how much time I had, but it was three in the morning, so I was betting that she wasn't planning on coming home tonight.

There was something oddly satisfying about wandering through someone's home without them knowing. I'd never thought of myself as the stalker type, but these hunts over the last couple of months had been the most satisfying thing I'd done since my job for killing Dr. Wallace. Nothing would ever compare to that moment.

I stopped to stare at the pictures that were hanging in the hallway. Almost every single one of them was of the blonde and the other girl with her. The images looked as if they were taken at different ages and in different parts of the world. The way they smiled at one another screamed that they were sisters, but they looked nothing alike.

I poked my head around the first door I came to and found a decent-sized bathroom. For whatever reason, I found myself stepping into the space and picking up the bottles to sniff. I oddly liked the scent and was tempted to spritz myself. That was fucked up.

Sitting the bottle down, I picked up a small dangle earring that looked like a child's piece of jewelry in my massive, gloved hand. Putting the earring back, I turned in a circle and stared at the plush purple towels and dried flowers in ocean blue frames. I hadn't pictured the blonde that leaped from one balcony to the next, the type to use this sort of color scheme.

There was only one more room at the end of this hall, and the door was halfway open. I gave it a small push and froze as I spotted the person lying in bed. How did she get in here without me seeing? I would've sworn that her Jeep wasn't in the lot. Curiosity had me inching closer to the bed and the sleeping form. There was just enough light coming from a small night light that helped me see all the furniture in the room.

With a moan, the woman mumbled and rolled over onto her back, with one arm flung over her head.

My pulse pounded a little harder as I stared at the brunette's face that had been at breakfast with the blonde. I needed to know their names. It was annoying to think of them as the blonde and the brunette. Not even sure why I stepped closer to the bed, but I did until I was standing right beside it. Her face was relaxed while she slept.

Up this close, I was able to see the long dark lashes lying against her cheeks. They looked like the wings of a butterfly, and her hair splayed out around her like a large fan. She was truly beautiful. For just a single stupid moment, I pictured what it would be like to have someone care for me. Someone like her. Someone not to see me as a damaged thing or a monster to fuck for fun. I thought I'd found that with Adalyn, but then I realized she was almost at big of a monster as Dr. Wallace.

Anger flared in my chest, and my fists clenched tight at my side as I took a step away from the bed and the sleeping woman. My eyes found the incense stick and the lighter on the nightstand. I wanted to grab for it, but I forced myself to stop. I hated that I'd been tempted to kill someone that I hadn't done proper research on yet and certainly hadn't done anything to me. My heart squeezed like it was in a vice, and my stomach twisted up in knots. This girl hadn't hurt me, and from the little bit I'd seen of her, she was a nice person. I was starting to create a code, and she didn't fit the mold.

One step at a time, I backed out of the room.

"Vi, is that you," she mumbled, her voice soft and delicate with sleep.

She didn't stir or sit up, but I stepped to the side of the door to be safe. My heart was pounding like a piston in my chest with the sound of her sleepy and thick tone that was like honey to my ears. I waited to see if she was going to get up. I didn't want to kill her if I didn't have to, but if she forced me to...

When I was sure that she would remain asleep, I made my way back to the kitchen area and wandered to the other side of the apartment. This time, I found the bedroom I was looking for and proceeded to snoop around the space, looking for anything to tell me more about who this woman was. Pulling open her drawers, I sifted through her belongings but found nothing useful. Her closet wasn't any better. Her shoe boxes were filled with useless items. That told me nothing. My eye caught a plastic bag hanging on the back of the door, and I realized it was dry cleaning.

"Huh, a fire investigator," I said as I stared at the arm flash on the sleeve of the dress shirt. Rubbing my thumb over the crest, I had to smile.

"Isn't that fucking ironic. Are you looking for me?" I chuckled.

I made my way back out to the main area, and my eyes scanned the surfaces for mail. The place was as neat as a pin, which was annoying. About to give up, I did one more scan of the area and spotted a brown folder on the small dining room table. Flicking open the folder, my hand froze.

"What the fuck," I mumbled as I stared at a fire file and the picture that stared me in the face was the first fire I'd ever done.

Taking a deep breath, I closed my eyes and could still picture the smell of that fire. How my adrenaline spiked when I snuck in the open window. I'd watched that girl leave. She always snuck out on a Friday night, and I knew it would only be a matter of time before she gave me my way in.

My fingers brushed over the image of the fire and the home that was mostly burned to the ground by the time the photo was taken. I missed this part of the burn. I'd been on a mission and hadn't stayed long enough to see the full aftermath. It was stunning, with the tendrils of smoke rising into the air with the forest in the background. It was exactly as I imagined it would look.

It had been a pure fluke that I saw the social worker who had been to my house so many times. I knew her by name. Vivian had become a constant attendee at my home. She showed up once a month like clock-work, which would've been fine if she'd actually done something to help.

But she didn't.

Instead of pulling Asher and myself out of there like she was supposed to, she sat and drank tea with my mother. They laughed about whatever the fuck women that age laughed about. Then my father would arrive home, treating her like he was a perfect gentleman. He'd fucking smile and shake her hand and say crap like, 'so nice to see you again.'

She never bothered to stick around to see my father's anger every time her ass showed up at the door and who he would take it out on. She never saw how I became the punching bag because she couldn't be both-ered to do her job correctly. She never saw the bruises on my skin, the fear in my brother's eyes, or the cracked ribs my mother had.

Nope, she never saw any of that.

She'd smile and wave and fucking drive off like she was some super-star. Meanwhile, all she did was make my life worse.

I was leaning forward on my handlebars as I waited to cross at the lights when she pulled up beside me in her car. Her windows were down, and the music she was playing was upbeat and happy.

My head turned at the sound of the music, and I did a double take on the face. It couldn't be a coincidence for no reason that we arrived at the light at the same time. No, this was a sign, and I couldn't just let her drive past and disappear.

I couldn't just let her continue on like it was okay that she got to sing like she was a fucking karaoke queen while I was biking down the road after stealing a chocolate bar and a pack of football trading cards to give my brother for his birthday. No, I needed to know where she lived.

Of course, the hood on my hoodie had been up, so she didn't notice me, but I noticed her. My feet pushed hard on the peddles until my legs burned as I tried to keep up with the sedan. She never saw me as she turned into the expensive neighborhood with homes that were the size of four of mine. It was one of those areas that sat in the middle of the golf course and cost a fortune.

All of them had these perfect bright green lawns and pretty flowers. A father was out tossing a baseball with his son, and a mother was teaching her kid how to ride a bike.

I had to learn how to ride a bike on my own, and I fell off and scraped my hands and knees. I'd done it so many times, and all my mother said was, "Great, now your father is going to be pissed that you got a hole in your jeans. Clothing is expensive you know? Go get changed right now."

I'd stopped at the mouth of the court. I watched as the car I'd been following drove up the driveway of a large home that backed onto a forest. A girl about my age came outside and crossed her arms over her chest like she was pissed off. I was too far away to know what was being said, but the two were clearly arguing.

Skulking about the park, I waited until it was dark before returning to the house and saw the garbage set outside for pick up the next day. It took some digging, but I found what I needed. I hit the jackpot when I grabbed an electricity bill that had both Vivian's name on it and a man's name. Vivian and Nicholas Clarke.

It took me a couple more weeks to make my plan, and while I did, I learned everything about the family. I followed them to work, and as it turned out, Nicholas Clarke was a judge in family court.

I sat in the back row and watched the man work. One person after another listened to the gut-punch stories about abuse, but as long as the parents said they were enrolled in programs, he would be lenient and give them another chance with their children.

Was he blind?

Didn't he see that all he was doing was putting those children right back into the hands of monsters?

Most were not as terrible as my father, but some were, and some were worse. I saw the fear in their eyes. They were a mirror of my own soul. It was the same look I'd get every time my father stepped foot in our home.

He couldn't be allowed to continue this. Neither of them could. It was their fault and people like them that forced all of us kids to endure more fear than they could ever imagine. Meanwhile, they would go home to their loved ones, drink beer, and eat fancy foods. We were not really a concern to them. No, we were a job to leave at the door, and the faster they could push us through, the quicker they could move on to the next.

The hatred burned like a fire in my gut, and it was then that I knew what I needed to do. They wouldn't live much longer. I'd make sure of it.

Vivian looked so peaceful when I walked into the room and ever so gently laid the rag over her face with the chemical that would force her to sleep while the house was lit. I did the same to Nicholas and stepped back to watch them breathe in the fumes.

I'd had to break into a vet clinic to get what I needed, but I didn't care if I got caught now. This was my mission, and I wouldn't stop until they were wiped off the face of the planet.

• • •

Jerking, my mind came back to the present. I stared at the top sheet and quickly thumbed through the paperwork. There was a picture near the back pinned to one of the pages, and there she was, the teen from the home of Vivian and Nicholas. I pulled out another picture and held it up, my eyes bouncing between the two as my pulse began to race.

"Well, what do we have here? The lone survivor and a twist of fate have brought us back together. Violet Clarke, it looks like we were destined to meet again," I whispered into the darkness, and a smirk curled at the corner of my mouth.

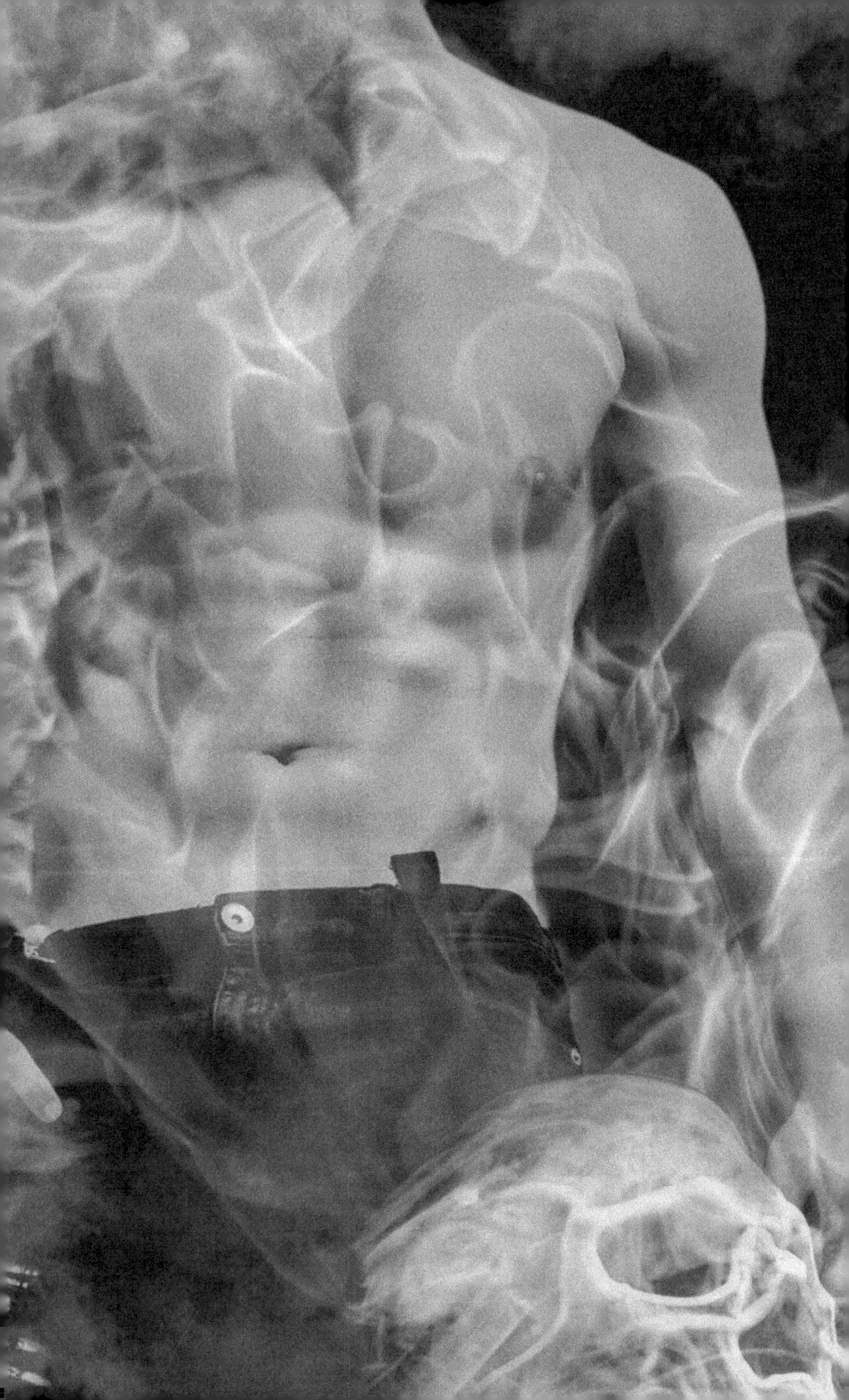

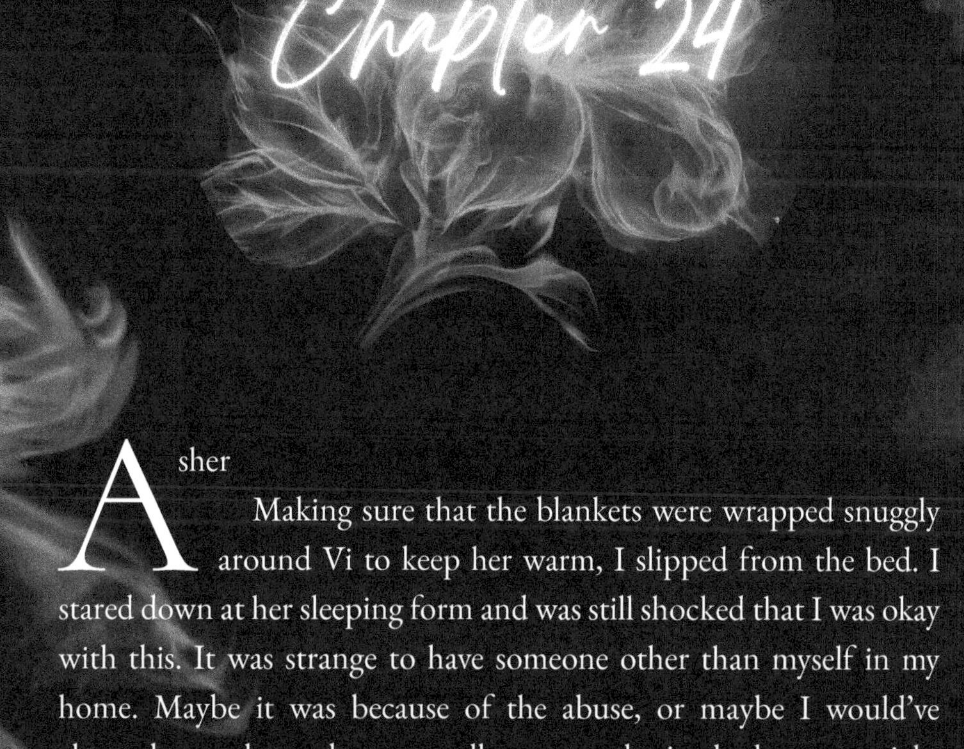

Chapter 24

Asher

Making sure that the blankets were wrapped snuggly around Vi to keep her warm, I slipped from the bed. I stared down at her sleeping form and was still shocked that I was okay with this. It was strange to have someone other than myself in my home. Maybe it was because of the abuse, or maybe I would've always been a loner, but normally anyone else in the house at night would make me restless.

Vi's presence didn't do that.

In fact, I felt calmer with her here.

Pulling on a pair of track pants, I headed to the kitchen and grabbed a bottle of water before making my way to the piles on the table. I had a theory, and the way that we were searching the fires now wasn't helping prove it.

I put all the folders into one pile and started over. Skimming through the entire report and witness statements, I didn't see the needed pattern. It was not in the photos or the write-ups. Opening the next folder, I didn't see anything either, but the third one made me pause. My fingers skimmed over the report as my eyes followed along, and I quickly flipped to the police report that was attached.

"There it is," I whispered.

Placing that folder into a separate pile, I moved on.

"Hey, is everything okay," Vi said, her sleepy voice coming from the hall as she slowly walked toward me. Glancing at the time, I realized that I'd been at this for just over an hour already. She didn't hesitate to slip her arms around my waist and lay her head against my back. I smiled at the gesture.

"Yeah, I think I'm on to something," I said as she moved.

She stopped after she was standing by my side. I pulled her into me, suddenly not wanting to be without her touch. As she looked up, I kissed her forehead and took a moment to study her face.

"You okay?"

Vi nodded.

"You know, I think I'm better than okay. My chest doesn't feel tight for the first time in years. I don't know what kind of magic you have, but it helped. I'm sorry you had to see that, though. It wasn't exactly my finest moment," she said, looking away from my eyes.

"No, don't be sorry. What we did is the closest that two people can get to baring their souls to one another. I'm honored that you trusted me with your past and your pain." I gave her shoulder a squeeze, and she laid her head against my chest.

We stood quietly, staring down at the folders for a few minutes. I realized that this was new for her as well. Vi was not the type to let people in, and her work had become her joy. What threw me off was that I had a new craving simmering in my system. I wanted to become her joy.

"What's your theory," she asked, pulling me out of my thoughts.

Reluctantly, I moved away from her and pointed to the piles I'd already searched.

"I began cross-referencing when this new arsonist came on the scene. I still haven't tracked down what his first fire was, but I'm confident we will get there." I picked up the pile of fires that I didn't think had anything to do with the new arsonist. "I don't think these are him."

Vi's forehead wrinkled up as she looked at me. "Okay, how did you draw that conclusion?"

"I was looking for three specific things. The first was whether it was still deemed suspicious, but with no real accelerant found. Our guy is smart, and he either puts on a display like at the warehouse, or no one ever knows he's coming. Either way, there seems to be a very specific pattern. He sets the fires so they move like they are alive. They don't move like regular fire."

Vi rubbed her arms. "Why is it that just feels entirely too creepy?" I smiled at her.

"It is, and yet it's kind of beautiful in this weird way." She cocked a brow at me. "Okay, creepy it is. Anyway, the next thing I looked for was if someone did indeed die. Not all the fires here have a death, some are just random abandoned buildings, but no one was inside. That is not our guy. Everything he's been doing feels like it has a purpose."

"I feel you getting more excited. What have you figured out?" She looked closer at the sticky notes I'd set up for the piles.

"Excited is the wrong word, but maybe happy that I'm onto something? Okay, what if I told you that I thought that our guy was a vigilante or maybe an antihero type?"

"What do you mean?"

Taking a deep breath I picked up the folders that I was pretty sure were our guy and tried to shake off the unease settling in my chest.

"You'd asked me what was wrong when we went to see Kim. I saw her body language. She had the same reactions I gave people when I was young. My father was not a nice man. Most days, my brother and I called him the monster and for good reason. From the moment he arrived home from work until he left again, we would either hide as best we could or leave home."

"Oh, Asher, I'm so sorry," Vi said, and stepped close to my side, but she seemed to realize that I needed this moment without being touched to get through this.

"It was a long time ago, but those kinds of demons stay with you. The look in Kim's eyes...the point is that this guy went after Sarah, not once, but twice when Kim wasn't around. She was the target. It wasn't random. It's not just the fire that is driving him."

"You think that he's hurting people, that hurt people? How does that explain Britnay?"

"That was the one stumbling block I still hadn't figured out. I'm not sure, but it is possible that Britnay had offended him or was rude to someone, and he saw it. Could also be that he has been watching the fires and wanted to put us on notice that he sees us. I haven't solved that one yet, but if you take her out of the pile...."

I held out the stack for Vi to take. "All of these fires started approximately five months ago. All of these fires, someone died, and all of these fires, the person or persons that died were either charged with rape, assault, gang affiliation, or pedophilia...you name it, and it's in these portfolios."

Vi's eyes went wide. "For him to know that...."

"He's either a cop or he's a stalker. He is hunting them. He knows their patterns, their sleeping schedules, what they drive, and what their homes need. He's a master at making bombs, and that doesn't happen by accident, so maybe he was in the military at some point. All I know for certain is that this guy is going after people he deems toxic to society. Yes, others get caught in the crossfire, but my guess is that he deems them necessary collateral damage to achieve his goals."

I took the top file from Vi and opened it. "This was the subdivision fire that was attached to the golf course."

"I remember. That was when I got involved with this case."

"I don't think it was his first, but my initial thought was this was just mass murder. Some person had wanted to see an entire street burn. Don't get me wrong. I'm pretty sure this guy got off on seeing all those houses go up, but...."

I quickly opened the folder and spread all the files out to show her who had died.

"Every single one of these families has something to do with corruption. You don't see it at first, but this judge was taking bribes, and this lawyer was working for a local gang."

I held up another picture.

"This doctor was charged with rape and got off because the woman was sedated and couldn't prove for certain that the attack happened. This one? The doctor was suspected of torturing patients at a mental hospital. I mean, this is like an all you can eat buffet for someone like our guy. Granted, civilians died in the blasts, but the root attack was specific. He wanted these people to pay for their sins."

Vi took a deep shuddering breath and looked at the dozens of files spread out and then finally down to the armload I'd given her.

"We need to go back to the beginning. We need to find the fire that started all this. If we find that fire, we will find our guy."

"Agreed, I'll put the coffee on," I said and smiled. Stepping away, I got to the kitchen doorway when Vi called my name.

"Asher?"

"Yeah?"

"Thank you for...well, for helping with this and for... you know. I just want you to know that no matter what, I'll always be thankful to you," Vi said softly, and she turned away to continue sorting files.

I wanted to say something profound, but like so many of our conversations, I was at a loss for words, specifically the right words.

Violet

I woke up to the feeling of my body jerking. I was dazed and disoriented, not even remembering where I was. The warmth radiating up into my body and the strong arms around me told me I was lying on Asher. Lifting my head, I stared up at his strong jaw and realized that we were in the same position where we'd collapsed on the couch.

Our eyes wouldn't stay open any longer as one report began to blur into the next. Asher's face looked pained, and his forehead pulled down into a frown. Even in the soft glow of the lone lamp, it was easy to see he was sweating.

"Asher," I said softly, but he continued to mumble something incoherent. He didn't respond, and again, his muscles twitched beneath me. It was obvious he was in the throes of a dream. It didn't look like it was a very good one.

"No, no, no," he mumbled, his head jerking back and forth as his arms suddenly tightened around me.

Reaching up, I cupped his face like he'd done for me. "Asher, wake up. Asher, it's just a dream," I said louder.

Asher jerked as his back arched, and his eyes snapped open. I'd seen way too many people brought back from the brink of death, and the way he gasped and looked around with confusion was eerily familiar. It took a moment before his eyes locked with mine. Asher blinked like he was still confused and then flopped back as recognition kicked in.

"Shit, sorry." He swallowed and ran his hand through his messy hair.

I pushed myself up to straddle his waist and kiss his amazingly soft lips. Fear never left you. It simply dulled or took on other forms to haunt you. This was something that I understood well, and I wanted to kiss away the last remnants of his dream.

"You okay?" I asked.

"Yeah, I am now." Asher pulled me back down so he could hold me. The man I'd first met didn't strike me as someone who cuddled for the sake of cuddling. That knowledge made this moment feel more special.

"Do you want to talk about it?"

"Not really. Just more of the same. It's always the same."

I kissed his chin, and he smirked as his eyes turned down to my face. "After what I revealed to you, I think it would only behoove you to share with me in return."

"Behoove?" He laughed and pulled my body closer to his own. "I'll share only because you use fancy words that I barely understand. So, I briefly told you that I have an older brother, and we were both abused. He was my best friend and the one person I trusted no matter what. So many times, he would protect me even when I didn't fully understand until years later."

"What was his name?"

"Derek."

"Is that him in the picture you have in the hallway?"

He nodded. "Derek is...I don't know where he is. He was arrested, and they told me they would be taking him to a hospital. But then it was like he simply disappeared. No one would give me answers. I tried so many times, but it was like the paperwork just vanished—like he just vanished into thin air." Asher shook his head and laid his arm over his eyes. "I have so much guilt, and it still strangles me."

"Do you mind if I ask what he did?" I asked and reached up to play with the soft strands of his hair.

"He killed four people," he said, and my hand stilled.

My eyes went wide. "Oh my god, Asher, that's...wow, I'm sorry."

He shook his head back and forth before sighing. "Two of the people were my parents. Don't get me wrong, I didn't shed a tear over their deaths. They were not great people, but even so, to murder them? I love my brother, but..." he stopped and looked toward the window.

"It's okay. You can tell me."

"Derek had been protective and would get violent with my dad, but he wasn't a natural bad guy. My father...shit...he did some evil stuff to him and..." Asher stopped again and rubbed his face.

He pushed himself up a little. I immediately moved and let him sit on the couch but tucked myself under his arm. I didn't want him to shut down this time. We had broken down so many walls that I didn't want them to go back up. At least not yet.

"Derek just never got over what happened to him, not that you simply get over the abuse, but he didn't deal with it either. It just festered and turned into something dark until it twisted him into someone I no longer recognized."

I knew what he meant. That could easily have been me after my parents had died. My parents had never abused me, but the trauma from their deaths had pulled at me and made me want to lash out. Beck had pulled me back from the brink so many times that I'd lost count.

"He began doing things that seemed harmless. He set off fireworks and lit the burn barrel we used for garbage on fire, but I didn't understand escalation. I mean, I was eleven at the time. What the heck did I know about anything like that? He needed help, and I wish I'd seen it. I wish I'd found someone for him to talk to."

I held onto Asher tighter, and I could feel him begin to stiffen. Before he could push me away, I kissed the side of his neck. For the first time in a very long time, I felt comfortable with someone, and I'd be damned if I was going to let that just disappear.

"I'm going to assume he only got worse?"

"Yeah, he didn't stop. He turned into a pyro, testing out his abilities. The fires got bigger, and then, just like that, he killed." Asher pushed himself up, and I let him go. "I'm sorry, I'm not sure why I'm telling you all this. I don't talk about this with anyone."

"Maybe it's because you feel as comfortable telling me about what haunts you as I did last night when you helped me open up," I offered, but Asher seemed more torn by that response.It was hard to read what he was thinking or feeling. The stern mask of the arrogant and dominant personality was being pulled into place, and I sighed, looking away from his eyes.

"Could be, I don't know." He rolled out his shoulder, and the conversation just stopped. It was like he'd turned off a switch and no longer wanted to share his past or what happened next. I badly wanted to push, but there was something about the hard look in his eyes that told me he was done talking for now.

"If you'd like me to go, I can." I glanced at the files and preferred just to leave them.

We had a solid day to finish sorting, so I wanted to leave them here rather than packing them all up and moving them to my much smaller apartment.

"Why?" He cocked a brow, and my mouth seemed to freeze.

"Well...I...It just felt like I'd worn out my welcome. You seem..." Uncurling my legs from the couch, I stood, not really sure how to put this. "You just seem like you'd like some space."

Asher rubbed at his chin. It was a little habit he had, but I knew right away that he was thinking about something.

"It's not a big deal. I can come back...."

"What are you doing for Christmas?"

Shocked by the sudden change in topic, I stared at him blankly for a few moments. I swear, he just liked to keep me off kilter. "Um... I guess do what I always do? Grab some takeout, watch "Die Hard" with my cat, and go to bed. Why?"

Asher screwed up his face like he'd just eaten something disgusting. "Okay, first of all please tell me you don't think "Die Hard" is a Christmas movie?" I opened my mouth to argue, and he held up his finger. "On second thought don't say it, we'll be here for hours disagreeing over that topic," he said making me laugh. It was true, it was a conversation I'd argued with Beck about many of a time.

"You are not doing that this year. Come with me?"

This was a man that openly declared he didn't date, didn't bring people to his home, and most certainly didn't introduce them to his family.

"I don't understand," I said.

"I want you to come to Christmas with me. I would like for you to meet my mom. Well, my foster mom. Forget the accurate titles, she's my mom to me." Asher stepped forward and wrapped his arms around my waist before dropping his head to kiss my lips.

Pulling back, I looked up at him, and as hard as I tried, I couldn't make out the expression on his face. "Are you sure about this?"

"Yeah."

"I'm not asking this to jinx the moment, but...."

"I know what you're going to say, and the answer is, I'm doing something completely out of character, but you, Violet Clarke, seem to make me want to do things I normally never would. Say yes. Come to dinner with me."

Being around Asher felt a little like I was in a "Formula One" race car, with a driver that didn't know how to drive and was careening for a tight corner. He kept me off kilter and my head spinning as I held on for dear life.

"All right, yes. I'd like to go with you."

"Do you have an ugly Christmas sweater?"

"Umm."

"Don't worry. I'll make sure you have one before then. My mom loves us all wearing crazy sweaters." Asher walked away smiling like we hadn't just steered the conversation from his brother killing people to going to Christmas dinner. If that was not keeping me off-balance, then I don't know what was.

Not
even the
Devil could burn
the world like
I could

Chapter 25

I jerked awake and jumped up from the couch, ready for a fight. Light was pouring in the window, but that wasn't what woke me up. There was soft tapping coming from outside on the wooden deck. My eyes narrowed as a shadow moved underneath the front door. Whoever was out there was heading toward the window in the kitchen, and I quietly slipped my way into the front hallway. Peering into the kitchen, I fixed my eyes on the window as I waited.

The only person that ever visited me was Dora before she died. Other than that, I'd get feed delivered for the cows, but that was it, and that guy was not due for another week. The shadow of a reflection on the glass moved closer. Just before the person would come into view through the glass, they turned, and the tapping of feet began to head back the way they'd come.

Listening closer, I realized it was like they were tap dancing or something. The rhythm was all wrong for someone just walking. Who the fuck comes out into the middle of nowhere and begins dancing on a random property?

I pulled the hunting knife from the sheath that sat at my back and spun the blade in my hand. Well, whoever it was had better have a good fucking reason for being on my property, or they were going to meet my burn barrel in little pieces.

Marching for the front door, I whipped it open just as the person was about to pass in front of it again. I was ready to spring out the door like a wild animal but froze as my eyes landed on the petite blonde. I knew her, sort of. This girl was the one that was friends with Mathers's chick. The last time I saw her, she called me "The Dragon". It was kind catchy.

She didn't even pay attention to me as I glowered at her and leaned against the doorframe with a giant knife in my hand. Her feet made little tap, tap, tap sounds as she jumped from plank to plank on the wooden veranda while she softly sang a little tune that had no words I understood.

"Um...hello?"

Her big grey eyes rose to mine, and she smiled wide and then began to randomly giggle. She had one of those faces that, if you'd given her pigtails and a stuffed animal, she could've passed for a tall kid. The thing was, I'd seen her roasting marshmallows over a burning corpse. This girl had as many dark demons as I did and they'd manifested into...well whatever you called this state.

She pointed at me and squealed like she was seeing a rock star at a concert. My eyes went wide as she bounced on the balls of her feet, held her hands in front of her like she was a rabbit, and hopped toward me. All she needed was one of the Playboy Bunny outfits to complete the look.

"The Dragon, you're the Dragon," she said, like it was the most exciting thing to happen in her entire day. I inflicted many emotions on others, but excitement was not one of them.

"I am," I said, playing along to whatever little movie she had going on inside her mind. "How did you find me?"

Glancing around, I expected Mathers to pop out of the bushes or some shit. The fucked up game of dark tag I remembered us playing was going to haunt me forever. All I could say was that man needed to bear his ass to the sun more often.

She scoffed like what I'd said was the stupidest question she'd ever heard. "You're The Dragon," she said, with more emphasis, her eyebrows rising like that should explain all.

"Right...okay, how did you get here?" I looked around again, and there was no car or motorcycle, and it didn't look like anyone was on the road waiting for her.

"My vroom vroom," she said, rocking back and forth on her feet with her hands clasped together in front of her.

Yup, this conversation was as strange as the first time I'd spoken to her.

"Okay, let's try this. What's your name," I asked, just wanting to be done with whatever this was and then go shower.

I'd stayed in my car for two days waiting for Ms. Violet Clarke to come home, but her pretty roommate was the only person to come and go. Hungry and in need of good sleep, I'd come home to regroup and ended up passing out before I ever made it to the shower.

Now, I had to deal with this. Whatever this was.

She leaned forward and poked at the sharp point of my knife. "Ooh, pretty! I like shiny things. Can I have it?" Her eyes lit up as they focused on the sharp blade.

"What? No...look, what do you want? Did Mathers send you?"

I pulled the knife away from her finger before she could poke it again, then quickly tucked it into its sheath once more. It seemed like the safest place to have it right now was out of her line of sight.

The blonde's eyes went as wide as saucers, her mouth dropping open in a comical display. This girl could be a caricature, and right now, she was imitating the guy from that "Scream" movie. She spun around and proceeded to look around like monsters were hiding in my cow pasture. Sadly, I found myself looking, too. This girl needed to go. My crazy didn't need her crazy on top of it. That was way too much crazy, even for me.

"You know Mathers?" she said as she whipped around to face me again.

What the fuck kind of game was this? "Yes, I know Mathers, but who are you?"

She fluffed her hair and began to dance again. This time it looked like an Irish jig.

"I'm Ava," she said and then stopped and clapped her hands together, making me jerk. "Do you have cookies?"

"Yeah...but...." Ava didn't wait and marched under my arm, right past me, into my home.

This girl should be an assassin. She'd confuse the fuck out of everyone before she slit their throat and would probably do it with a smile. Mathers didn't need a whole biker club. Fuck, I didn't know why he even needed my help. All he had to do was unleash this ball of confusion and his problems would be solved. "Come on in, why don't you."

Slamming the door, I marched into the kitchen, where Ava was already rifling through all my cupboards.

"They're in this one," I said, opened a cupboard on the other side of the kitchen, and pulled down the four bags of cookies I had. They were nowhere near as good as what Dora would make me, but they filled the gap.

Ava smiled and grabbed all the bags before skipping away into my living room. Was this really happening, or was I having another night terror? It was hard to tell. I slowly wandered into the living room just as she flopped down on the couch and hit the remote.

"Oh no, no…" I marched across the small room to grab the remote control, but it was too late.

The television flicked on and there was one of my latest kills on the screen, their face frozen in a terror filled scream along with where I'd paused the video. I'd planned on enjoying this in private when I could jerk off, but apparently that was no longer happening. Ava hit the play button and the sounds of screaming filled the room along with the roaring crackle of my fire.

Like a moth to a flame, my eyes were drawn to the television, and I had to bite back the groan as the fire slowly closed in like a beast stalking its prey. My cock thickened instantly, and I really wanted to put Ava under my arm and kick her out, so I could enjoy this and then go shower.

"Wow, this is a great movie!"

Eyes snapping back to the little blonde, I looked her over as she stuffed two different flavored cookies into her mouth at once. Her eyes were transfixed on the screen, and as the flame began to lick its way along the man's jeans, she laughed and stood up, cheering.

"Whoop, whoop, whoop," she yelled with her fist in the air.

It was like she was watching an imaginary football game, not someone burning alive. Well, this was as entertaining as anything else, I guess. Consider me thoroughly interested to see what she would do next. Making my way over to the large recliner, I sat down, and my gaze flicked between the guy now swatting helplessly at his jeans as they melted to his body and the girl on my couch. I wonder what she'd think if I told her I masturbated on that couch.

"Ava?"

"Yes, Dragon," she answered but never looked away from the screen.

She pointed at the screen, and little crumbs fell from her mouth as she tried to talk again around the latest cookie victim. "This is a good part."

"Yes, it is." Leaning forward in the chair, I tried as best as I could to get her to focus on me. "Why are you here?" She blinked, and those grey eyes found mine. It was like staring into a bottomless pit of confusion. "Do you know why you're here?"

"Well, duh," she said, and then screamed and threw both hands in the air. "Gimmie a B, B. Gimmie a U, U. Gimmie an R, R. Gimmie an N, N. What does that spell? Burn him."

She waved her arms around and jumped, managing to do some sort of cheerleading splits thing, and sent cookies flying in every direction. She landed, looked around at the carnage of broken cookies, and her eyes filled with tears.

This was one of those very rare moments that I wished I'd paid more attention in therapy. I might have known what the fuck to say or do.

"It's okay," I said softly and took a step toward her.

"Don't move," she said and held up her hand.

My foot froze in the air, midstride, as she dove to the ground and grabbed the cookie piece I was about to step on. She dusted it off and shrugged before putting it into her mouth.

"I'll go get the broom. And clean up this mess," I offered and left to get the pan and broom.

I was bent over in the pantry when the light tapping noise closed in. She could play the part of Chucky or maybe that Annabelle doll because she was that fucking freaky as she tiptoed up behind me. I looked over my shoulder, and she was standing no further than a foot away. Habit had me watching her hands to make sure she didn't have a weapon. Maybe I'd worn out my usefulness, and Mathers intended to have this girl off me.

"I'm gonna make you new cookies," she exclaimed and then stepped over the top of me to get into the pantry.

"That's okay, Ava. How about you just tell me why you're here, and then you can get going. I'll even give you money so you can go and buy as many cookies as you want. How does that sound?"

"Nope. I'm going to make you cookies," she exclaimed.

Great, sounds wonderful. Shaking my head, I stood with the pan to go clean up the mess and returned to the living room.

"You don't have any chocolate chips, so I'm going to make peanut butter," she said from right behind me.

"Fucking christ all mighty. Could you stop doing that?" I said and turned, but she was already flitting off and not paying me any attention.

Sitting down, I turned off the video of my latest kill and turned on a real movie instead."I'm going to go shower," I called into the kitchen and made my way upstairs.

If this girl was sent to kill me...so be it. At least I would die clean.

Ava didn't answer but began to whistle. Walking into the bathroom, I locked the door and then checked it again before propping the laundry basket up against the door.

"What the fuck was I doing?" I mumbled and then stared at my reflection in the mirror.Quickly stripping, I jumped into the small shower and turned on the spray, not caring that the water was ice cold.

I hated the fact that it felt nice to have someone else living and breathing inside the house, even if it was a girl I barely knew. Of course, because I was a sucker for punishment, my mind drifted off into a little cloud and pictured a different set of grey eyes. What was it about Violet's roommate that intrigued me?

Was she beautiful? Yes, but I always passed beautiful women on the sidewalk, and they never caught my attention. At least not like this. I hated to even think of Adalyn and what she'd pulled on me, but my attraction to her was real, even if it hadn't been reciprocated. I felt that pain again now, and the anger burned in my gut. Reaching back, I hauled off and punched the hard tile of the shower wall until my knuckles split and started to bleed. Holding my shaking fist up, I stared at the blood dripping down my knuckles.

Who was I trying to fool? No one had ever wanted me or loved me, and that wasn't going to change. I was a hideous beast and no longer a man. I'd been reduced to a thing, and now I was The Dragon. Fire was the only companion that I needed. Thinking about a pretty brunette with grey eyes was only going to lead down one road, which was to more pain.

Pain was something I was used to and even accepted as part of life, but even I had my limits.

I finished rinsing off the soap, stepped out of the shower, wrapped a towel around my waist, and opened the door.

"Fuck!" I growled out as I almost ran into Ava. "Girl, seriously, you need to stop that," I said.

"The cookies are almost done," she said in a sing-song voice and smiled until her eyes found the scars on my chest and arms.

They were faded now, but the slight indents from where my father would burn me with cigarettes would always remain. Just another reminder of who I really was and what I'd become.

My body tensed, the muscles flexing as her hand reached for one of the scars on my pec. "Bad men hide in sheep's clothing, and not even the shepherds or wolves can keep them at bay. Only the ravens will stop them, but even they will be too late."

My brow rose at the saying that obviously held meaning for her. Her finger gently traced the outline of the scar and then did the same to the one on my arm. I wanted to smack her hand away, but I couldn't bring myself to do it. She wasn't horrified by what she was seeing, and the touch of another person was nice. Her finger was featherlight, but the warmth was searing in a pleasant way, and I had the urge to close my eyes and sigh.

"Thank you," I said, not sure what else to say as she removed her hand.

"He ruined me," she said, and laid her hand over her stomach.

I didn't have to be a rocket scientist to have a basic idea of what kind of fucked up shit had been done to her to make her mind break. As her head lifted and her eyes found mine, I saw the person she'd been hiding in the shadows. She was still in there but was tucked behind all the layers of fantasy that allowed her to live her life with no fucks given.

"You're not ruined," I said, cupping her cheek.

Leaning over, I kissed her softly. It was barely more than a pec, and I wasn't sure why I did it, but it felt like the right thing to do. "One day, you'll come out from hiding, and you'll see how strong you really are."

This was way too much emotion and feely shit for me, and before she could say anything else, I walked around her and headed to the spare room where I kept my clothes. When I emerged and went downstairs, I had to admit that the house smelled fantastic. Once more, I envisioned the feisty Dora in the kitchen baking up a storm.

The older woman had touched my heart in ways that I couldn't explain, but she managed to make me feel human, like a man worth having around, not simply the monster.

Rounding the corner to the kitchen, I saw two pans of cookies out cooling, and it looked like more were in the oven.

Ava was nowhere to be seen, but she had to be here some-where. My question was answered a moment later when I heard her coming up the stairs from the basement. She burst out the door with a wide smile on her face and carrying one of the bricks of C4.

"Look, I found Play-Doh, but you only had grey," she chimed cheerfully.

"Umm…how about I take that? You wouldn't want the cookies to burn," I said, and her face morphed into horror as she tossed the brick of explosive my way and dashed to the oven. Okay, I needed to invest in a lock for that door. I hid the brick behind some cookbooks on the shelf in the kitchen.

"Ava, did you remember why you're here?"

"I came to see you," she said.

Maybe she just wanted to see me. The thought of someone wanting to see me 'just because' once more pulled at me in ways I wasn't expecting. Was I lonely?

"Oh, here." Ava pulled a folded envelope from the back of her jeans and handed it over with a smile.

Or maybe she didn't just want to see me. I didn't bother to ask who it was from, there was only one asshole that would send me a letter. I tore it open and pulled out the handwritten note. Wow, Chase could write, and it looked like fucking calligraphy. That was impressive. I'd have to tease him about his pretty handwriting the next time I saw him.

Hey, D,

I have a job for you. I know you said no more jobs, but this one is up your alley.

Below is a list of three names. Each one comes with a very large sum of money.

I'll wire the money as soon as the job is completed. Do your homework, and you'll see these guys are fucksticks. Sorry for the letter, but I had some technical issues and didn't trust to call or text.

I never know when those fucking FBI assholes are listening. In case you're still tempted to say no, I've doubled the payout for each target.

You'll need to drop by and say 'Hi' at the clubhouse when I get back. We can have a shot or ten.

Your Cherry Popper

Fucking Mathers. I stared at the list of names committing them to memory before walking over to the sink and holding the paper over it as I set it on fire.

"Light show! Oh, we can do fireworks. I love fireworks."

I looked over my shoulder at Ava as she pulled the latest batch of cookies out of the oven. How many people she thought she was baking for was beyond me.

"Do you mean actual fireworks, or are you talking about a fire, like a building burning down?" The fact that I needed to clarify that statement said a lot about both of us.

She shrugged. "Either. Did you know my friend is pregnant? She's going to have a baby."

"That's usually what being pregnant means," I said, pulling a bottle of water from the fridge. "You want one?" I asked, holding out a bottle to Ava, but she shook her head no. "Is this Mathers's girl?"

"You know Mathers?"

The bottle paused on its way to my lips. Not this again. "Are you sticking around for a little while?" It was safer to simply change the subject.

"The Dragon wants me to stay." She smiled and then walked over and stuffed a hot cookie in my mouth. "Naughty Dragon," she murmured and gave me a wink.

As soon as she was out of the room, I spit the scalding cookie out into my hand and chugged the water. I quickly blew on the cookie and proceeded to stuff it back into my mouth before she returned. There was a good chance she'd start crying, and I didn't know what to do with her tears.

"Huh, this is really good Ava," I said, once the tastebuds returned to my mouth.

She'd made them with peanut butter, banana, and oatmeal. I turned at the sound of rain and stared out at the shower that was passing through, even though there didn't seem to be a cloud in the sky.

"Yay! Rain!"

The front door slammed open, and I stepped into the hallway just in time to get Ava's shirt in my face as she flung it off her body. Pulling the pink shirt off my face, my mouth dropped as she flicked her bra off and then wiggled out of her shorts. She was apparently going commando and sprinted out my door with nothing but her pink sneakers on.

Well, this was great, I'd managed to go this long without the cops coming up my driveway, and I was going to be taken down by a naked girl dancing in the rain in my front yard. There was something oddly magical about her freedom. For as free as I now was, parts of me remained locked up in a dark room with no one but myself.

She spun in a circle and headed back with her tongue out as she caught the raindrops. She looked at me and waved wildly.

"Bye, Dragon."

"What about your clothes?" I called after her.

"But it's raining," she said like I was being ridiculous and then waved. She pulled a small pink scooter out of the bushes where it had been hidden from sight.

Ava put on her helmet and got on the scooter in her birthday suit. She whipped out of my driveway and along the road.

There were some things in life I'd pay money to see, and the looks on all those that passed Ava as she whipped past as naked as the day she was born, was at the top of my list. I could picture her waving at all the open mouths and not even noticing the gasps, shocked looks, or turned-on expressions. She was truly unique.

Closing the door, I picked up her clothes and put them in a pile on one of the kitchen chairs. There was no way to tell if she would come back for them or not. Looking around the kitchen, I scratched my head.

"What the hell am I going to do with all these cookies?"

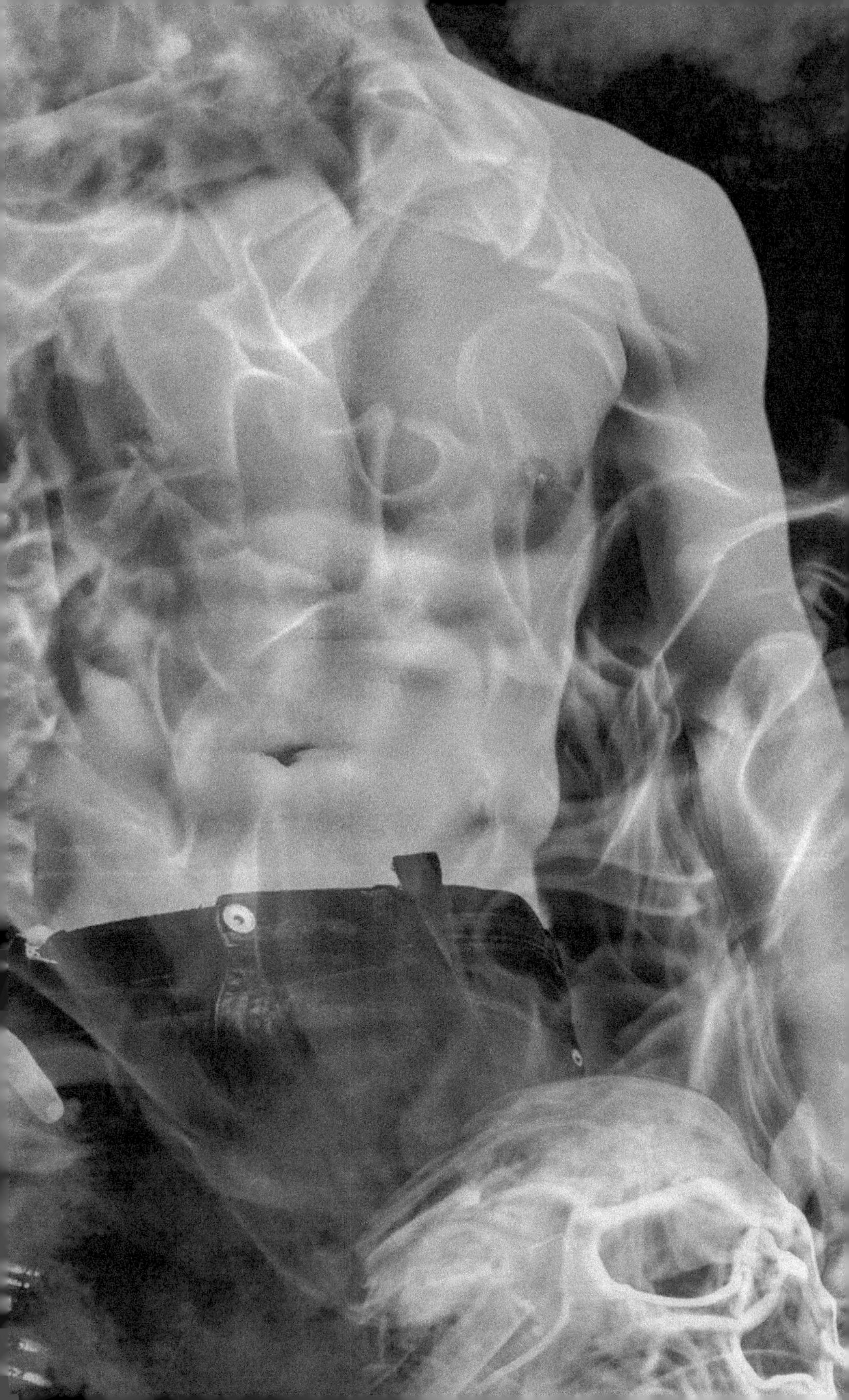

Chapter 26

Okay, I had to admit this was a lot harder than I thought it would be. I'd shopped thousands of times. Style was something that I took seriously, and I liked to look my best. Buying for someone else...this was new. I didn't even buy clothes for my mom. She loved cats, reading, and cooking. There were more than enough gifts to choose from in those three categories to allow me to stay very far away from clothing.

I hadn't bought a girl a gift since my senior year of high school, and that was only because my mom said it was the right thing to do. That wasn't entirely true. Gifts had stopped after I got serious about my new lifestyle a year after high school. Gifts meant I was serious about someone. At least, that was how I felt about it. It also became clear early on that you didn't buy gifts—other than sex toys—unless you wanted to move into a more committed relationship, which I'd never wanted. At least not until recently. It was still blowing my mind that I was even considering this.

Holding up the ugly knit sweater, I stared at the red nose of the cartoon reindeer image, and it took a second for the realization to sink in. The tradition of Christmas and the idea of gifts had never been a thing until Derek and me ended up at the Giltberts'. They didn't have much money, but they always had a great meal and we'd spend time together playing cards or some other board game. They would also find a way to get the two of us a little gift.

"All right, boys, I wanted to get you each something for Christmas," *Mr. Giltberts said, getting up from the dining room table as we helped* *Mrs. Giltberts clean up. Derek's body tensed, and I grabbed his fore-* *arm, the muscles tight under his skin. Gifts in our home had meant* *something entirely different, and it always ended badly.*

"It's okay. He's not dad," I mouthed and Derek nodded the muscles *slowly relaxing.*

I loved my brother with all my heart, but he'd changed since we *ran. We used to hangout all the time, but now it was like the sight of me* *annoyed him. Maybe it did. It was as if the scar on his face was eating* *away at the brother I knew.*

"Here we are," Mr. Giltberts came back into the room with a huge *smile on his face.*

His hands held two small boxes that obviously Mrs. Giltberts had wrapped because they looked perfect with little curly ribbon and neatly tucked edges of paper.

"It's not much," he said, rubbing the back of his neck as we took the offering.

Derek and I stared at one another for a moment unsure what to do. Derek had gotten me gifts over the years, but they were never wrapped. I was pretty sure he'd pocketed them to give to me, but I didn't call him out on it. He was nice enough to get me something. I usually ended up drawing him something. It was stupid, and I felt stupid handing my big brother a folded piece of paper with drawings on it as a gift.

If he hated it, he never showed it. Derek would always smile and rub my hair, telling me how much he loved it. He pinned them up on his side of the room, and my heart swelled.

"It's okay, boys, you can open them," Mrs. Giltberts said from behind us.

She was smiling wide and wiping her hands on a tea towel. Looking at Derek, I gave him a shrug, then pulled the end of the ribbon, and the pretty red color fell away from the package. Derek was not far behind me, and soon we were lifting off the tops of the small boxes in unison.

"Wow! This is for me?" I was unable to hold back the joy as I stared at the Swiss Army Knife.

It was one of those that had like twenty different things, and I lifted it out of the box like a trophy. Mine was black, but Derek got the same one in red, and even he couldn't keep the smile off his face.

"Yes, of course. You're young men, and you'll never know when you need a tool to get you out of a jam." He laughed at his own joke. It was a *weekly tradition that we all had to sit around and watch MacGyver. "Especially here on the farm. There is always somethin' that you're needing to have a knife or screwdriver for. I just wish we could give you more."*

Shocking me, Derek stepped forward and hugged Mr. Giltberts. The man stood there as wide-eyed as me, and it took a moment before he returned the gesture. Derek wouldn't let anyone other than me touch him since we ran. This was a miracle all on its own, and Mr. Giltberts' shocked expression melted away into a smile.

I hated having to leave their home after Derek was taken away. They didn't have any parental rights and were apparently considered too old to be fostering. It was ridiculous, but as it turned out, I ended up with a good family. I wondered all the time how they were doing or if they were even still alive. I'd driven past the old farm a number of times, and it never looked like anyone was ever home.

"Did you need any help," one of the salespeople asked, jerking me out of my thoughts. I turned to face the woman that had spoken, and as soon as I did, she glanced at the sweater in my hands. "I don't think that one will fit you," she said and gave me a teasing smirk.

Looking down at the sweater in my hands, I couldn't help but smile. "Is it that obvious that I'm a little lost? I didn't realize there would be so many to choose from," I said.

"I'm assuming this is supposed to be a fun gift?"

"Yes. Family tradition."

She smiled and stepped toward the large table with the wide assortment of sweaters. "What color is her hair?"

"Blonde."

"And eyes?"

"Sky blue."

"That is very specific of you," she said as she dug around through the piles.

"Is that a bad thing?"

"Nope. She is just very lucky. Most of us only ever get, umm…I think they're blue. No, maybe green. Oh shit, how am I supposed to remember?" She mocked in a guy's voice. "Does she have a good sense of humor?"

"Yeah, actually, she does." The corner of my mouth turned up at the thought of Vi. I loved her quick tongue and dry whit.

"Well, in that case, I think this one would look best on her." She held up a bright red sweater with an image of Santa's sleigh and reindeer flying across the sky. It even had little snowflakes on it. She flicked a switch, and all the little bulbs lining the sweater lit up and began to flash.

"Oh yeah, that's the one. Thanks."

I had no intention of stopping for anything else, but for whatever reason, I found myself walking into the jewelry store. Moving from one case to the next, I stared at all the glittering items. Rings of all sizes sparkled back at me, but that seemed like the wrong message. We weren't at ring status yet, but…my eyes caught sight of the case with pendants inside. Now, this was much more suitable.

"May I help you, Sir?" My eyes never left the pendant that seemed to be calling me.

"Yes, can I see that piece there?" I said, pointing to the flame that was created with rubies and diamonds.

"Gladly, Sir." He reached into the case and pulled out the

pendant that was not bigger than the tip of my baby finger. It was stunning with the way the light reflected off of it.

"I'll take this one, and I want it engraved."

By the time I left the jewelers, I couldn't be more excited about my gifts for Vi. Grabbing my phone from my pocket, I hit Vi's number and loved that she picked up right away.

"Please tell me you're not calling because you have another fire?"

I laughed. "What...the fire investigator is sick of fires?"

"No, but I could use a break, or a vacation, maybe both. My mind is still spinning. I found six more cases so far that fit the criteria you laid out. I think you're really on to something here, Asher. I do want to take a closer look at the sights that haven't been cleaned up yet."

I got in my truck and listened to her explain what she found out about the cases, and the entire time all I could think was that I loved her voice. She could be reciting the phonebook, and it would make me want to lay her out and fuck her.

"Sorry, I'm totally rambling on and on, and you haven't gotten a word in."

"I'm always willing to talk shop with you, but how about we do it over dinner? I can help you finish off those piles?"

"Actually, my brain needs a break, but I'd love it if you came here. There's someone I'd like you to meet." Her voice trailed off like she was nervous. My instant reaction was to say no, and that was not where our relationship was, but I'd invited her over for Christmas, hadn't I? "You don't have to," she said as the seconds ticked on.

"I'm just wondering what to bring for dinner," I said, pushing down all the nagging little thoughts that kept wanting to creep up.

At some point, I had to step away from my parent's issues and what that trauma did to me. I wasn't my father, and Vi was nothing like my mother, but that old fear wanted to claw its way up my throat as the sound of their voices, and furniture breaking tried to surface in my mind.

"Are you sure, Asher? You sound tense, like something is wrong," she said softly.

There was no anger or judgment in her voice, but I squeezed the steering wheel harder.

"I'm good. I promise."

"Okay," she said, but didn't sound convinced.

It was weird having someone see me. I never let people see me. In fact, it was always my job in the relationship to see everything about them and anticipate what they would feel or think."Well, there is no need to bring anything with you. My friend, who I want you to meet already made dinner. She's a damn good cook."

"Sounds good. I'll be there in ten," I said and pushed the button on the wheel to hang up the phone. Holding up my hand, I realized it was shaking. No, I wasn't letting this shit control me anymore.

Chapter 27

Violet

"Hmm," I said, hanging up the phone.

"Hmm? What's hmm?" Beck turned to face me, and I couldn't help but smile at the little splatters of sauce she had all over her face.

"I don't know. I can't put my finger on it. Asher just didn't seem himself."

"Vi, the guy, straight up told you he doesn't do relationships, and now you want him to meet your best friend after he invites you to go there for Christmas. I mean, those are big steps for anyone, let alone someone who doesn't do relationships."

"Yeah. Am I moving too fast? Should I not have invited him or said no to Christmas at his mom's?"

Beck was already back to making her creation which smelled divine. She could cook anything she set her mind to, but the Italian food she made was seriously worth killing for.

"Do you think you're moving too fast?"

"How am I supposed to know? I mean, my last real boyfriend was Jeff during senior year." I sat down at the island and couldn't help playing over the last few weeks.

"Jeff? You mean the guy that always wore the same rock T-shirt to school every day and brayed like a donkey when he laughed?" Beck turned her head and gave me her patented, 'have you lost your mind' look. "You went out on like three dates because he begged you and offered to do your math homework." She shook her head. "I'm not even sure how you managed to make it to number three. That guy was off. Plus, did you see the way he looked at cats? I'm telling you that one is a serial killer by now."

"Oh my god, stop." I couldn't help laughing. "He was a decent guy, just a little different."

"Different? Vi, the guy ate peanut butter and honey sandwiches with dill pickles. If that doesn't say it all, I don't know what would. Just disgusting."

"Okay, back to my question about taking things too fast."

Work was easy for me. I knew what to look for and how to analyze it. It was all very clinical. I also knew how to handle the guys that hit on me when I had zero interest, but this was different. I liked Asher a lot, so what he thought mattered. This was why I didn't date—too much emotional turmoil.

"I can't tell you if you're moving too fast, but if you're unsure, you should talk to him," Beck said.

"I hate logic."

"Ha! You love logic, just not with relationships."

"Okay, I hate that you know me so well," I said and smiled as I stood and gave her a hug from behind. "I don't know what I'd do without you."

"Girl, you're gonna make me cry."

I would've continued to pester her, but a knock sounded at the door. My body heated like I'd stepped into a five-hundred-degree oven, and the fluttering sensation in my belly staggered me. They had me grabbing for my stomach. Wow, this was crazy.

"Well, open the door, don't leave him out there," Beck whispered when I didn't move.

Taking a deep breath, I opened the door just as Asher was about to knock again.

"Hey," I said, my voice coming out breathlessly as I stared at him.

Asher didn't say anything. His eyes just roamed over my face before he took me by surprise and cupped my cheeks, dropping his lips to mine. In his standard Asher fashion, he managed to make the rest of the world evaporate. My soul felt lighter and calmer with him around. It was hard to explain and seemed insane to say out loud, but this man was quickly becoming the piece I'd been longing for and yet never knew I wanted.

Asher broke the kiss and pulled me close to his body as he whispered in my ear. "I'm going to give you one of my hoodies to wear, and then I'm going to fuck you in it."

If I hadn't already felt like melting, I sure as hell did now.

"Well, hello. I need a damn fan. That was hot as hell," Beck said.

I'd totally forgotten she was even here, and even though I knew my face would be red, I couldn't stop my stupid smile. Glancing at Beck, her hip was leaning against the counter while she fanned her face with the tea towel, and I suddenly wasn't sure this was a good idea. If anyone were going to embarrass the shit out of me, it would be Beck. I wasn't sure Asher was ready for that level of crazy just yet. I gave her a stern look that begged her to behave. Not that it helped.

"Well, come on in, Mr. Sexy. Vi, when you decide you're going to date, you definitely know how to pick 'em." Beck walked over and held out her hand as Asher stepped into the apartment. "I'm Becky, but honestly, you can call me whatever the fuck you want."

"Beck!" I scolded and covered my eyes like that would help the trainwreck that was coming.

If Asher was uncomfortable, he didn't show it. In fact, he laughed, his smile lighting up the entire kitchen as he held out his hand for Beck to shake.

"Nice to meet you, Becky. I'm Asher, and I brought this to have with dinner. Since I didn't know what we were eating, I grabbed red and white." He held out the bag of wine.

"Thank you," she said, shaking his hand. "You don't do threesomes, do you?"

"Beck! Oh my god." I grabbed my friend and pulled her away from Asher before she could traumatize me any further. "What? I had to ask."

"Just make yourself comfortable. I'll be right back once I kill my friend," I called out as I dragged Beck around the corner to my bedroom and closed the door. "You behave."

"I was behaving. You have no idea what I wanted to say."

I rolled my eyes at her. "Girl, I'm serious...I like him and...."

"Violet Clarke." Beck held up her finger, stopping me mid-sentence. "Let's get one thing straight. Good-looking or not, if that man out there can't take a joke or like your friends for who they are, then they are not worth keeping. You hear me?" she cocked her hip, daring me to disagree with her.

She had a point. I wasn't about to get rid of my friendship with Beck for him. If he was going to be in my life, he needed to be okay with my best friend because she was human and my only family.

"Fine, but can you tone down the flirting? I know you don't mean any harm, but...." I crossed my arms over my chest.

"You're jealous," she said, smiling wide. "Admit it. You don't like someone flirting with him?"

"That's ridiculous," I scoffed and looked away from her eyes.

"Okay, then it shouldn't be a problem. I wonder what he'd say if I offered to—"

I held up my hand and glared at my friend. "Okay, fine, you're right. I don't like it. You happy now?"

Beck grabbed me and hugged me like she was trying to give me the Heimlich. "I'm so happy for you," she whispered. "Now, come on, I'll be pissed if my sauce is burning."

We walked out into the kitchen, and it looked like Asher had lived here his whole life. The table was set. He had turned on the music and was sipping a beer as he stirred the sauce.

Beck looked over her shoulder at me and mouthed. "He's a keeper," which was code for 'don't fuck this up.'

"I hope you don't mind, but I thought I'd make myself useful," Asher said, backing away from the pot.

He sat on one of the tall stools, and as soon as I was close enough, he wrapped his arm around my waist and guided me to his knee. The moment I sat down, it was like we'd just met all over again. The adrenaline spike made my heart pound like a drum while his arm, which had snared my waist and held me close, made me want to melt into his body. God, he smelled good, and he was so incredibly warm. It felt strange in this oddly perfect way to sit with him like this.

"No, this is great. I was worried about it burning. Thank you. I hope you like Italian 'cause I've made potato focaccia rolls, grilled antipasto with a garlic bean dip, and a tasty arugula salad. Oh, and of course, a three-meat fettuccine." Beck smiled.

I'd never realized how much she loved cooking until this moment. How many other things had I missed while I was running on the same treadmill in my mind?

"Wow, that sounds incredible," Asher said and offered me his beer to sip. "So what do you do for a living, Becky?"

"Call me Beck, all my friends do, and I'm a nurse. I'd thought about being a social worker, but seeing all those sad kids all the time in horrible situations would break me."

"It was Beck's family that I went to live with when my family was killed," I said. "We were practically sisters before that, but she's been looking out for me since then."

"Oh please, girl, we look out for each other. Now Asher, do you have any single hot friends?"

I shook my head as Asher laughed.

"I have one, but honestly, if I had a dog, I wouldn't set it up with him," he said, making us all laugh.

Luckily, he didn't take offense to anything Beck said or did. By the time we finished dinner, I'd laid my hands on my stomach because it hurt from laughing so hard.

We'd ventured over to the couch and were currently in the middle of a movie. Beck was fast asleep at the other end of the couch, and I was nothing but a ball of nerves sitting in the dark, curled up beside Asher.

Even though Asher was sitting with his hand on my leg, I almost jumped out of my seat when he gave it a little pull. I glanced at him, and he gave my leg another small tug. Guessing what he wanted, I shifted it, so it was lying across his lap and, I turned to lean against the arm rest.

Asher grabbed the throw on the back of the couch and laid it out over my leg. Even though he kept his eyes on the television, I knew the slight lift of his lip told me he was up to something.

I sucked in a ragged breath as his fingers softly trailed along my leg and set my skin on fire. He stopped as his fingers brushed the bottom edge of my shorts and then traveled down my leg again. Biting my lip, I turned my head away from the television, and Asher's eyes flicked to mine.

I knew I was in trouble.

There was that commanding gleam in his eye that paralyzed me and made it hard to breathe. How could one man inflict such ragged emotion with nothing more than a glance? There was no doubt that the look was an order.

He didn't need to say it. He wanted me to remain quiet and hand myself over to whatever he chose to do. I may not have understood this side of him when we first met, but there was no denying that I liked it. The jitters that had never quite settled took over again. This time, they paused in my chest and made my heart race. Everything about him had a profound effect on me. Even the way he casually ran his hand through his hair had me wiggling in my seat.

The touch started out innocent as he massaged my ankle and then my calf, but the look he was giving was another story. That heated stare warned me of what was to come, and I didn't care. I wanted whatever he chose to do.

I was just starting to relax when his hand began to explore the length of my leg. Nervousness had me shuddering as his hand slid from my ankle to the button on my shorts, and with a quick twist, the button popped free. The zipper was next, and everything around me seemed to evaporate.

"Relax," Asher mouthed and shifted lower on the couch.

Of course, the movement slid my leg up higher on his body, and the hard lump under my leg made me want to straddle his lap. Although I was sure Beck would be the first person to cheer me on, I wasn't about to do that while she slept a few feet away. But, damn, it was tempting.

"Lift up," he said, his voice barely a whisper.

I did as he asked. My ass lifted up off the couch, and he gave my shorts a hard tug. I bit my lip to keep myself from yelping as the force had my arms giving out. I ended up in his lap and inches away from his face.

Asher didn't just kiss me. No. It felt like he was devouring my mouth as he kissed me hard. His hand gripped the back of my neck and deepened the kiss further until I was completely breathless.

"Slide back," he mumbled against my lips as he broke the kiss.

My head was spinning, and it had nothing to do with the two

glasses of wine I had with dinner and everything to do with the intoxicating man I was sprawled across, but I pushed myself back, and my shorts slid further down my legs.

"We can just go to my room," I whispered, and he smirked before shaking his head no.

I lifted my gaze to where Beck was still peacefully sleeping and then back to Asher. I opened my mouth to protest again, but he placed a single finger over my lips, and the words died in my throat. He shook his head and gave me a stern look.

Could I get up and walk away? Yes.

Could I insist that we go to my bedroom? Yes.

The question was, did I want to do those things? No.

The thrill of getting caught was an adrenaline shot to the arm, and my body agreed. This time, his warm hand traveled up my thigh to the narrow line of my thong. His hand moved slightly under the blanket, making me feel like I was a teen again as we tried to hide our make-out session from his parents.

I moaned as his thumb rubbed little addicting circles over my clit, but he took his thumb away and gave me a hard look. Nodding that I'd keep quiet, he started again, and I pressed my lips together hard to keep my mouth shut.

The tiny piece of useless material was moved out of the way, and my breathing was so fast that I thought I would pass out. This was not a normal reaction, or was it? I had no idea anymore. Asher stirred up an entire pile of 'I don't have a clue' in my head.

Pulling up the sweater, I stuffed it into my mouth to keep myself from making any noise as he slowly slipped a finger into me. The world could've blown up around us, and I wouldn't have noticed. All that existed was Asher and his demanding personality.

The actors on the television laughed loudly and then cheered about something. The sound blasted out a little louder than the rest of the movie, and Beck stirred slightly at the opposite end of the couch.

Asher froze until he was sure Beck wasn't awake, but he flexed his finger the entire time we waited. He loved to torture me.

It was frustrating and undeniably delicious. He was able to read me better than I could've ever read myself, and he proved it with each rotation and slide of his fingers. Swirling and pinching, he pushed deep into me, driving me higher, but never enough to let me fall off the other side of the peak I was chasing.

As I sunk deeper into the couch, my knees splayed out far as the constricting shorts would allow. I didn't want him to stop. Laying my head back on the arm of the couch, I enjoyed the sweet bliss of the moment rather than trying to rush for the finish line.

The rhythm Asher set got faster, and it didn't take long before I was panting. I tried to keep the mewling noises quiet, but it was so hard. As another little sound escaped, Asher placed his hand over my mouth and tapped a finger on my lower lip. My body responded to his command without having to ask. My mouth opened enough for his finger, and I sucked on it hard as the peak inched closer. When Asher added a second finger, I lost it. The sensations were too much, and the climax hit with force.

I had to bite down gently on his finger to keep quiet. I thought he would stop, but he kept up the same slow and teasing routine before ramping it up and pushing me over. Damn, he was good, and I didn't even want to know how he became an expert.

The movie finished, and as if she'd been connected to the movie Beck's eyes opened. Scrambling to look relaxed and tired, I leaned into Asher as my heart wildly pounded as he continued to wiggle his finger inside of me.

Such a jerk and yet I wanted to moan with the incredible pleasure. Asher laid his head back on the couch with his eyes closed and looked perfectly serene.

"You two look so cute," Beck whispered and smiled at me.

She stood and blew me a kiss before disappearing down the hall. I was not sure cute was the word I'd use at this moment. I slumped, taking a deep breath. I looked at Asher and immediately swallowed hard.

"Stand up and take your shorts off," he said. Asher whipped the blanket off, shedding it as easily as the sweet, sleepy persona he'd been sporting.

I stood and loved the flare of desire that was in his eyes. He stared at me like I was the sexiest woman in the world. I'd never been the type to need a man's affection, so it felt strange to crave that kind of attention. Yet, there was no denying that I wanted that look in his eyes as much as I wanted the rest of him. All of him.

Bending over, I grabbed the shorts to unhook my foot. Hands gripped my hips, and I yelped. I hadn't seen or heard Asher move, but he was standing behind me and pressed himself firmly against my ass.

Dropping the shorts to the floor, I stood and moaned as he

wrapped a hand around my throat while the other pulled me closer to his body.

"You're a naughty girl, Vi," he said.

His voice was so low that it rumbled along my skin. It didn't matter that he'd already made me come multiple times. I was ready to go again. "Do you know why you're naughty?"

"No," I managed to squeak out.

"Because you teased me. Because you make me want to throw you down on the couch and fuck you hard until you scream and wake up your friend. Because you're so fucking sexy that from the moment I arrived, I've been hard and want to be buried deep in your hot pussy."

Oh, dear lord. All I could focus on was the raw need raging through my body. Asher pulled back on my neck until my back was bowed, and I was looking up at the ceiling. I could feel his lips at my ear, and I shuddered.

"I want you to know that the old me would've done just that. I wouldn't care if your friend was in the next room. I wouldn't care if it was your parents or your local priest. I would've made you scream the walls down and then let you explain what you were doing."

I swallowed, not knowing if it was a threat, a promise, or just a warning, but at this moment, I realized my moral compass was completely broken.

If he wanted to fuck me until someone called the cops because they thought I was being murdered, then I'd do it. He said I was naughty for tempting him, but I could say the same thing. I felt wanton and needy for him in a way that words alone couldn't express.

"Would you let me if I told you that's what I wanted to do, Vi?"

"Yes," I breathed out through his tight grip.

"You're so sexy, my little Firebug. I am going to fuck you right here, but I'm not going to embarrass you." His hands dropped from my body, and I wanted to cry and tell him never to let go. "Turn around," he ordered, and I spun to face him. "Undo my jeans and remove them."

He didn't need to tell me twice. Gripping the front button on his jeans, I pulled hard, and both button and zipper opened in one go, drawing a smirk from Asher.

"Good girl."

He wiggled his hips. I bit my lip as they slipped down his legs. Damn, he had great quads. He wasn't the type to miss a leg workout, that was for sure. My eyes could roam over all that hard muscle and perfectly cut legs all day.

As my eyes traveled back up from his feet, I realized he was going commando. Everything in me wanted to reach out, wrap my hand around his cock and get down on my knees in front of him, but instead, I held perfectly still. The way he was staring at me, I knew it was a test. He wanted to see if I would jump the false start line before he'd given permission.

Asher smoothly stepped out of his jeans and leaned close to my ear, but he didn't touch me. I shuddered as an electrical charge traveled over my body. Even when he wasn't touching me, my body was anticipating when he would. Asher knew exactly what to do to keep me teetering between craving more without it being too overwhelming. I knew it was simply who he was, but it seemed completely unfair that he had this kind of superpower.

"What do you want, Firebug?" he asked and then proceeded to blow a tiny stream of air down the side of my neck.

"I want you to fuck me," I whispered, my eyes fluttering closed.

"How?" Bending just enough, he was able to blow a little stream of air over my nipple. Unable to stop myself, I moaned as my nipple hardened.

"I want to ride you," I said, impressed that my voice didn't shake.

"Very well." My eyes opened just in time to see Asher sit down on the couch, his hand wrapping around his cock as he stroked it for my viewing pleasure. "You like watching me stroke my cock, Firebug?" I nodded. "I want words. No more head nodding."

"Yes, I like it," I said, my eyes fixed on the hand, slowly moving up and down with as much control as he did everything else.

Asher smirked, and the flickering of the television light only added to the dark, intoxicating look. Men like him were the reason women wrote romance novels. Men like him made women swoon at their feet and pissed off all the men who tried to be the same way but instead ended up acting like assholes. They didn't understand the difference. Hell, neither had I until I met him. There was a cavernous gap between those that simply smacked their women's ass like they were scolding an animal and what Asher was. The two were light years apart, and I knew I was just scratching the surface of what he could do to me if I let him.

Asher held out his other hand, and I placed mine in his, but the simple act did nothing to settle my erratic breathing. "Then come and take what you want."

I quickly straddled his lap. Pushing up onto my knees, I stared down into his eyes. "Lagoons," I said, and one of his eyebrows rose.

"Your eyes remind me of a clear lagoon and how it can still grip you with its undeniable beauty, even on an overcast day."

I looked away, unable to hold his stare. My body flushed with heat at the silly comparison, but Asher cupped my face, and before I took my next breath, he crushed our lips together. The moan that ripped from my chest sounded like a wild animal, and maybe I was. Maybe that was what he'd reduced me to, but whatever it was, I knew that I wanted him right that second.

Our tongues battled as they explored one another's mouths. Taking a chance, I reached between our bodies to grip his hard cock. Asher didn't tell me I was naughty or pull away. Instead, he groaned into my mouth, and I couldn't resist any longer, sitting down on his hard shaft.

"Oh fuck," I whispered and dropped my forehead to his shoulder.

With each inch by delicious inch, my body lowered onto his.

"Now, now, Firebug, we don't want to wake your nice friend, do we?" Asher asked, his voice laced with humor. "We must be quiet," he teased, yet there was a hidden order in those four little words.

I finally bottomed out, shuddered, and gasped in a sharp breath as he filled me up. I wasn't sure how but he was pressing right on my G-spot and every little movement was making me want to scream as I came all over him.

Lifting my head, I was inches from his face and that intimidating stare. As our eyes locked, I truly understood. The desire to let go was strong. The image of simply handing myself over to Asher to do whatever he wanted with my body and mind was like a siren's call to my tired mind and overworked body. He wanted control, and in this intimate moment, I wanted none. The urge to toss away the reins of my life and let him have the wild horses as they ran was exactly what I wanted, even if I hadn't recognized it in the beginning.

"Ride me, Vi. Fuck me the way that you want, and use my cock for your own pleasure. Make yourself come. I want to feel you come all over me." Asher let me pick the pace, but once I settled into a rhythm, he helped my ass bounce up and down until the world around us melted away.

The stress of the job, the dark memories of my past, and even the fears of my future all dissolved into dust and drifted off along with my worries.

"Asher, oh fuck," I mumbled.

The words tumbled out of my mouth on repeat as the orgasm built. A hand clamped over my mouth a second before Asher sucked one of my sensitive nipples into his mouth. I screamed as I came hard, but thankfully the sound was muffled due to his quick thinking. The waves of pleasure didn't want to stop, and he wouldn't let me slow down.

Asher's hot mouth was firmly sucking on the sensitive bundle of nerves while his tongue flicked over the end, driving me crazy. As my movements labored, he gripped my ass firmly and effortlessly held me up just enough to thrust into me at his own pace. I buried my face into his neck, my mouth hanging open in a silent scream as my body soared toward another release.

"You feel so fucking good, my Firebug, so damn tight," Asher groaned out softly as he released my nipple only to move to the other one.

"Ahhh," a small yell left my throat, and he moaned around my nipple.

Even though I couldn't understand him, I still got the message to be quiet. Fuck, it was so hard as his cock drove up into me at a blinding pace. The world began to get fuzzy again, and I laid my head back to stare at the white ceiling, which could've just as easily been a blanket of stars, and let my mouth hang open in a silent scream.

"Come on, Firebug. One more time. Come for me, that's an order. I want you to come all over my cock like the good girl you are."

His words were magic because the release I'd been closing in on slammed into my body. As soon as Asher felt me starting to come, he let go, and I had to bite my own hand to muffle the screams as he hit every sensitive spot inside my body.

With a growl, Asher pulled me down hard into his lap and pushed up hard as he froze. His face was the picture-perfect image of desire as he came. I could feel each of his releases, and for whatever reason, I couldn't wrap my mind around it. I loved that he wanted to come inside me.

Slumping, I wrapped my arms around his neck and held on tight as my poor heart pounded out of control.

"Fuck, Vi, you're amazing," Asher said as he stroked my hair. If I'd been a cat, I would've purred for him.

I simply wrapped my legs around his waist when he stood and bent over. I figured he was grabbing our clothes, and honestly, I could've cared less one way or the other.

This was bliss, and I never wanted it to end.

Violet

The insistent chime was making me want to kill someone. Why, why, why did my phone have to be ringing before the sun was even up, yet again?

"You gonna get that?" Asher asked. "I don't care, but if not, can we at least turn off your ringer or kill it?"

"I don't want to move," I mumbled into his chest. The phone stopped ringing, and I sighed until it started again. "Son of a bitch."

Rolling away from the warmth of Asher, I grabbed the phone and stared at Mitch's name. It would've been an understatement to say I was tempted to do Asher's suggestion and heave it across the room.

"This had better be important," I grumbled into the phone.

"How about the police caught your arsonist."

That had me sitting up straight. "What?"

"The guy got sloppy at one of the scenes and left a print behind on a can of accelerant," Mitch said, his voice filled with excitement.

Asher sat up and stared at me, and instead of trying to explain the question in his eyes, I hit the speaker button.

"Hmm."

"Hmm," Mitch said. "That's all you have to say when I tell you that the police cracked the largest serial arsonist case in history? That there won't be any more crazy long shifts or being woken up in the night for a long time...hopefully."

"I'm sorry, Mitch, but I won't believe it until I see it. I want to see everything that the cops have," I said, my mind going through the evidence I had found or the lack of it. It seemed strange that this guy would get caught leaving behind a handprint.

"Vi, it's over. Trust me. I saw what they have. The cases are closed." Mitch tried for the 'I'm the boss' tone he would use when he really wanted me to drop something, but there was no way that was happening.

My hand balled the soft duvet up, and I met his tone with my authoritative voice.

"Mitch, I've done nothing but pour over these files again and again, and you know what they all have in common? Other than fire before you decide to be a smart ass."

A chuckle from the other end of the line told me he would've gone there. "What do they all have in common, Vi?"

"No evidence. The cameras I found watching the fires are a dead end. They lead nowhere other than to a million routers with no end in sight. The accelerant and C4 can't be traced. Fingerprints? Nope. Hair or anything at all? Nada. Cameras from around the area never picked up anything unusual. This arsonist always manages to get in and out of any building, home, or industrial area like a ghost. A ghost, Mitch. And you're telling me he suddenly left behind a hand-print? Sorry, I don't believe it."

Asher was nodding beside me, and it felt oddly comforting to know that he had my back.

"You're not going to take me at my word, are you?" Mitch said.

"Not a chance in hell. I want to see this supposed evidence," I said, and Mitch sighed loudly from the other end of the line.

I could almost see his furrowed brow as he pinched the bridge of his nose and shook his head. Sometimes, Mitch really reminded me of my father. They'd been best friends, but it was like Mitch had taken on the father figure role when I came to work for him. It was a bad habit that I'd been trying to break from the moment that I arrived.

"Fine, take a look, but Vi, let me be perfectly clear here. The mayor wants this case wrapped up. He is done with the fear spreading across the city and does not want to answer any more questions about why the police are so incompetent at finding this guy. So, unless you're a hundred percent positive this is not our guy, not ninety-nine percent, a whole hundred, this case remains closed. Do you understand me?"

I rolled my eyes and shook my head at the ridiculous statement. "So what you're saying is that the mayor would rather sweep the potentially real arsonist under the rug to save political face? What about catching the killer that is actually terrorizing his citizens?"

"Vi—"

I cut Mitch off. "Fine, I hear you—one hundred percent sure or nothing. Check. What precinct am I going to?"

Tossing the duvet off, I swung my legs over the side of the bed, but before I could stand up, Asher wrapped his arm around my waist and hauled me back into his body. His chest was pressing into my back. Right then, all I could picture was flopping over and going back to sleep, wrapped up in his arms.

"Whatever they have can wait a few more hours, you need to rest," he whispered into my ear.

We'd been up until like an hour ago, so I knew his concern was genuine. But it still seemed strange to have him telling me what I needed. Turning my head, I looked over my shoulder at Asher, and he lifted an eyebrow in challenge. He was daring me to say that he was wrong. Man, I hated that he wasn't.

"I'll bring everything to headquarters in a few hours for you to see. Meet me there at ten. Oh, and Vi? You only have the day to look it over. The mayor is planning on calling a press conference tomorrow about the arsonist's capture."

Man, this felt like the scene from *Jaws* where everyone in power at the town told all the citizens they could go back in the water because it was safe when they knew it wasn't. People ended up dying in the movie because of that decision, and this seemed just as dangerous.

"Alright, I'll see you then." Hitting end, I set the new time on my alarm and placed the phone back on the night table. I gave Asher a mocking glare. "What did I tell you about ordering me around outside of the bedroom?"

He kissed the side of my neck. "Technically, we're still in the bedroom. Besides, it's for your own good."

Asher kissed my neck once more, and I shivered, tilting my head to give him better access. He wasn't playing fair. I could feel myself weakening. Not that my resolve was all that strong to start with.

"You work too hard and push yourself to be the best all the time," he said and then nipped at my earlobe, making me moan. "You're running yourself ragged."

It was horrible that he already saw what Beck had been saying for months. "If you want to solve all those cases you're so passionate about, then you need to take care of yourself, too."

Asher pulled gently on me until I relented and laid down. He leaned casually on his elbow, looking down at me and even that casual pose oozed self assurance.

How did someone do that?

Staying so confident and assertive all the time must be exhausting, right? Lifting my hand, I brushed my fingertips over the rough, five o'clock shadow, and a devilish grin spread across his face.

"What do you think you're doing?" I asked as he lifted the covers and slipped underneath. "I thought I was supposed to be resting?"

Even as I said the words, I couldn't have stopped the smile that spread across my face.

"This is taking care of yourself." He shifted, so he was lying between my legs, and he kissed his way up my stomach until his head poked out from under the blankets. "It is a fact that this is as good as any spa treatment."

"Is that so?"

"It is. This therapy is known to relax the body, ease away all stress, and stop the running thoughts that have decided to take up residence in your mind." That impish grin was back, and his eyes were filled with the same mischief.

"Wow, that is some therapy. Since it is such a miracle, it must be doctor recommended."

"Oh, trust me, it is," he said and slipped back under the blankets.

How had I gone so long without feeling any real connection to someone? Beck and her parents were different, they were family, but Asher soothed a part of my soul that I didn't realize needed him. What scared me was that I'd opened myself up. I understood what I was missing, and with that understanding came fear. I didn't want to go back to who I'd been.

My heart swelled with Asher around, and it pounded harder, making me feel alive. It terrified me to my core that it could all be ripped away.

Burn

I didn't bother to get dressed up for this visit to the office. It happened to be my day off, so sneakers replaced heels, jeans instead of my dress skirt, and a comfortable hoodie instead of my blouse. The hoodie was Asher's and way too large. All I needed was a belt to make it look like a dress, but Asher said he loved it on me. I didn't know what it was about cuddling into a man's hoodie, but damn, was it super comfortable.

Looking down, I glanced at our hands and how Asher had taken my hand to walk into the building. Was it wrong that I loved the fact that he was showing off that he was with me? Plus, this felt like an intimate step for him. It wasn't that he was holding my hand. It was how he'd taken it and how even now, he was running his thumb over my skin like he was suffering from the same "disease" I was and I simply couldn't get enough of him.

The door to the boardroom was open, and we made our way inside. I would've paid a million dollars to have been able to take a photo of the look on Mitch's face when he saw me and then Asher. His eye followed our arms down to our linked fingers before his mouth fell open.

"Hey Mitch, this is Asher West he is one of our fire Captains. He came to the car fire that killed Sarah," I said and Mitch held out his hand for Asher to shake.

"Nice to see you again, Mitch."

"Nice to see you again as well, Asher. I've seen your reports, and you always do exemplary work."

"Thank you, I try to make sure that we don't leave a stone unturned," Asher said.

Stepping away from Asher, I wandered around the massive table that had pictures laid out. My eyes immediately found images of many of the fires, as well as newspaper clippings and digital printouts from other news sources. There were pictures of the guy's bedroom, and it looked like an homage to the fires. Pictures were covering the walls from the fires and those working them. There were images of different fire trucks and stations and the firefighters trying to put out the blazes. All of them laid out like this seemed like a window into what hell would be like—such fire and brimstone imagery.

The two men were busy talking, but I didn't hear a word if they were speaking to me. Now, shifting through evidence was when I felt the most focused and useful. My work gave me purpose. It made me feel like I was helping those left behind, helping someone else since no one had been able to help me. With slow steps, I made my way around the end of the table and froze as I spotted the apartment building fire. There was a photograph of me mid-flight, as I jumped from one fire escape to the other. It looked staged, like there should've been a huge air mattress or a net underneath. My stomach rolled as I stared at the image. What if I hadn't made it or the railing ripped away? I really could've died.

Picking the photo up, I looked at it and then up at Asher. I may never have met him if it hadn't been for this fire and what I did. However, the possibilities of what could've happened if I'd fallen had me swallowing a grapefruit-sized lump in my throat.

I had to put the image down before I thought about it too much and moved on to the mug shot and the copies of what the officers found for the handprint. The man in the image was slender with a narrow face and features that reminded me of a scarecrow. His eyes were overly large for his face, and his hair stood out in all directions like he'd gripped a powerline. He was missing a tooth but smiling in the mug shot.

This man was certainly unwell mentally, but I didn't think he was our man.

"So what do you think?" Mitch said, and I looked up at him and Asher as they both stared at me.

"This isn't our guy," I said flatly.

"Vi, look at all this evidence. He had images all over his room, including on the ceiling of the fires. He made collages out of the pictures and...." Mitched walked over to the table and held up a photo of what seemed to be a table full of voodoo dolls.

Each one of them was wearing a little miniature version of a fire-fighter's uniform. He also grabbed another image I hadn't yet gotten too that was a miniature version of Miami. The buildings, streets, trees and even little people looked eerily lifelike, but it was the homes and other buildings that had burned that were creepy. He'd obviously set fire to his miniature city to make sure that it matched.

"Okay, I can agree that this doesn't look good," I said.

"Doesn't look good? Vi, this is our guy. You couldn't ask for more compelling evidence. This is a gold mine."

"What do you see, Vi," Asher asked and crossed his arms over his chest as he gave Mitch a look. I didn't quite understand the male-speak, but it felt like Asher was telling Mitch to shut up and listen without saying the words.

"What I see is someone that loves fire. Do I think they may have tried to set a fire? Yes, but..." I grabbed some photos and held them up. "This is the work of a fan. He feels more like a groupie. You know, one of those people that follows the band around, praying for a chance to get backstage?" Mitch narrowed his eyes at me. "Look, I know what this all looks like. I mean, I have to agree with you that, at first glance, I'd say this is our guy. But I've been deep into the files, and what I see on this table is the opposite."

Mitch groaned and leaned on the boardroom table. "Why?"

"I can't put my finger on it exactly, but the arsonist that burnt down the apartment building and the subdivision on the golf course had one thing in common. They felt personal. They felt like an attack that specifically went after people or a person. This handprint was found on a can of accelerant and left at an old, abandoned house. Do those two things feel the same to you? I think this guy wants to be our arsonist. he may revere him, and even be gearing up to try his own, but the actual man setting fires and killing people all over the city? No."

"I can't go back to the mayor's office with, 'my fire investigator says it doesn't feel right.' I need evidence, Vi."

I held up my hands and looked around. "Mitch, I'm not a miracle worker, and I just got here. I don't even have the original items or the confession interview that says this man did it. How can I give you solid evidence?"

Mitch shook his head and even though he didn't touch me, Asher moved around the table and strategically stood by my side. I appreciated his support, but was happier that he wasn't interfering or jumping in to try and save me.

"Fine. You can stay here all night if you want to look this over, but at noon tomorrow, the mayor will announce the arrest if you haven't found anything new."

Mitch turned and marched out before I could even put my next sentence together. This was completely unreasonable.

"I'll go get us some lunch and extra-large coffees. It looks like we're going to need it," Asher said and gave the top of my head a kiss before he, too, walked out and left me alone with the piles of photos and reports.

Great, a little over twenty-four hours to prove my theory. Nothing like having this man's life in my hands. If I didn't find something else to prove his innocence, he was going to prison for the rest of his natural life. Nope, no pressure at all.

Not
even the
Devil could burn
the world like
I could

Chapter 29

Derek

I decided to take Mathers up on his offer. The list was way too enticing to pass up, but it meant that I couldn't watch Violet until I finished the job. Divided attention would cause errors, and I didn't make errors. Somewhere along the line, I'd decided that the only way they were locking me up again was in a coffin. Until that day, I was going to continue my work and do it to utter perfection.

Benny was first on my list. I didn't think that was his real name, but it was what he went by on the streets. This guy was a bad dude. Ironic that I was the one thinking that, but it was true. Everything from drug running to assault, rape, and murder was under his name.

So, my first question was, what was the reason Mathers had given him to me? It didn't take much digging to come up with the answer. It was because some of Benny's business dealings were encroaching on Lost Souls' territory. Chase had even lost a couple of guys over the last month to Benny's crew. If Chase Mathers, leader of the Lost Souls, killed Benny, it would start a whole damn war. But...if the crazy ass arsonist targeted Benny and his crew, well, that was another story.

There was a certain appeal to having the crime organizations around town know me as The Dragon. I liked that they were genuinely terrified I'd turn my attention to them. If I got off on that shit, I'd have a whole slew of reasons to stroke my cock, but unfortunately, power and popularity was not what I sought. At least not that kind of power.

I didn't give a single fuck about gang or motorcycle club turf wars. But, this Benny had a particular sexual appetite that Chase knew would piss me the fuck off. He was an asshole for exploiting it, and I'd pay him back at some point.

I didn't care, most of the time, what one piece of a shit human decided to do to another, but you add a kid in the mix, and my body burned with white-hot rage. I'd managed to do an initial survey of Benny's hideout with some strategic diversion at their stash house. It was amazing how quickly they fled like little insects when they thought their money and drugs were going to go up in smoke.

I'd utilized my time wisely and was currently staring at a live feed of some girl that couldn't be any older than twelve, giving my target a blowjob. My teeth ground together as he roughly manhandled the girl until she cried. Every instinct in my body cried out to storm the place and kill everyone other than the two girls he was keeping in the basement.

Taking a deep breath to calm my anger, I put the phone down. Watching this only made me want to lose control, and I needed them to sleep. Other than the two guards sitting in the kitchen with the television on, I would have no one to get in my way.

So cliché. Couldn't they sit in the living room or maybe the dining room to switch it up? Why was it that all the bad guys in movies would park themselves in the kitchen with a television, fast food containers, and a deck of cards? I'd been watching way too many old movies lately.

I flicked on the radio while waiting for the sun to get lower in the sky so I could make my move. I might as well have something to listen to in the meantime.

Breaking news.
The arsonist that has been plaguing our city has been caught.
The police found his residence and are now in the next stage of arresting the accused.

I sat up a little taller in the seat, my eyes flicking to the mirrors, but all remained quiet. Grabbing my phone, I turned on the feed to my home, and all was quiet there as well.

It has been months of fear.

We were all living with the knowledge that anyone could be the next target.
This serial arsonist was attacking all of us, and we will sleep easier now that this man is off our streets. This nightmare is finally over.
The mayor announced just a few short hours ago that the man hunt is over and that we will once more be able to breath a little easier.

I scoffed at that comment. If they had an arsonist in custody then great, but they were going to be sadly mistaken when they realized that they had the wrong one. A deep chuckle rippled from my mouth at the thought.

We are unable to release his name at this time, as the investigation is still ongoing, but he is the most prolific serial arsonist in history.

My chest puffed out at the compliment.

The case should be quick and just for all the victims since the man has already confessed to the fires and the murders.

My lip pulled up as I growled at the radio. It was one thing to arrest the wrong man. It was a completely different thing for him to take credit for my work. My hands tightened on the steering wheel. No, this would never do.

The rage continued to simmer throughout my body, creating an energy that refused to be contained. I was done waiting.

Pushing open the car door, I grabbed the small pack I needed and marched across the street and down a walkway that connected the streets. There was an overgrown bush poking through the fence, and I stuck my arm inside and grabbed the baseball bat and my second backpack. The hideout was essentially a shithole of a home that Benny didn't stay at all the time, but tonight was Wednesday, and the intel I'd gathered said he always came here to play with the girls midweek, without fail.

It was a rundown piece of shit of a neighbourhood. One of those spots that the cops knew had drugs, gangs and whatever else going on, but a lone officer patrolling this area would be like waving a red flag in front of a bull. The chances of the officer making it out alive were somewhere between slim and none. Even if the girls had happened to escape, they'd never actually be free. They'd be caught before they made it to the end of the street.

My hand slipped into my pocket, and I pulled out my phone to check the camera feed. Sure, enough, Benny was with each girl chained in the room and sleeping on the floor like large dogs with him. Meanwhile, he slept comfortably in a king-sized bed. This would be the last night that he slept so soundly.

Pulling the black mask down into place, I became one with the shadows. Through my freedom, I'd learned that I needed to be unseen. The ability to blend with the crowd when I didn't belong had become my art.

Stepping from one shadow to the next, it felt like I was playing a child's game. I dipped low under windows and made sure to avoid the range of the motion detectors that would flash on if I moved into their line of sight. There were multiple cameras set-up, but I'd brought my handy scrambler with me and currently had it in my backpack. It would seem like nothing more than a static glitch as I passed by the place.

Reaching the back door for my target, I pulled out the key I'd made earlier and slipped it into the lock. With a soft click and the whispered whoosh of the door opening, I was inside the house. What was it with bag guys that they felt like they had to live like pigs. The place was disgusting with dirt and grime so thick that you felt yourself getting a disease just staring at it. Bags of garbage that reeked lined the back hall. Were they planning on simply burying themselves in garbage or once the house got too full simply move to the next?

I shook my head as I closed the door behind me. The television was indeed on in the kitchen, the sound of laughter from some sort of sit-com drowning out any sound my boots may have made as I moved. The house was dark except for the light that was glowing softly from the kitchen area.

"I need ta take a piss. I'll be right back," one of the guards said.

"Again? Man you need to get that shit checked out. It's not normal to go that often."

"Whatever."

Stepping into the enclave that had a door leading to the basement, I became perfectly still as the man heading to the washroom walked right past my hiding place. I could make out his face clearly as he sucked in on the cigarette hanging from his mouth. The little tip glowed brightly in the darkness. He belched loudly, disappearing inside the small bathroom that stank of piss. It was rank as he opened and closed the door.

Moving quickly, I snuck from my little hiding spot and stepped into the kitchen behind the guy sitting at the table.

"Hey can you grab me a beer," the guy asked as the board under my foot squeaked.

"No more beer for you," I said my voice low and raspy.

The guy only got his head partially turned when my baseball bat connected with the side of his head. One blow and the guy was out cold or dead. I didn't really care which as long as he remained quiet. Falling forward, I saw his body hit the table and smash into the pizza boxes that were probably from their dinner tonight. A little bit of blood dripped from his nose and I swung the bat around in my hand tempted to take another strike, but I heard the bathroom door open and the fan turn off.

If this idiot had been paying attention, then maybe he would've stood a chance. I managed to get into position beside the door before the glowing cigarette made it around the corner.

"You want a beer man," the guy called out. Of course, there was no answer. "Yo, did ya fucking pass out again?" The glow came closer to the door. "Fuck man, you know that the last time you fell asleep the boss lost his shit when he found out."

Once more the oblivious man marched past me, and into the kitchen he came. The guy was a big man, not quite as tall as I was, but he obviously spent a great deal of time working on his arms and chest, because he looked like he could audition for a wrestling movie.

"Fuck, I told you…" The guy grabbed his friend's shoulder and then paused when he noticed the blank stare and the blood.

He spun around, but I was already prepared and jabbed the baseball bat hard into his windpipe. The cigarette went flying as he groped at his throat. His eyes were wide with panic as he stumbled back and dropped to his knees. He was already dead. That blow was hard enough to crush his windpipe, but the little demon that lived in my mind pushed for more violence. It had me swinging the bat for the side of his face.

The sound of bone crunching under the blow was delightful. It was like an appetizer to an expensive steak meal. I waited until he collapsed face-first on the floor, his fingers twitching before I made my way toward the electrical panel and the device that I'd already installed. Unzipping my backpack, I pulled out a brick of the C4 and finished setting up the timer.

Thirty minutes would be more than enough, and proceeded to close the panel door. Making my way to the stairs, I stared up at the wooden mountain and cracked my neck. I spotted the first tiny dot I placed on them that blended in with the rest of the scuffs and dirt. Placing my foot on the mark, I was glad the stair made no noise. With steady precision, I climbed the most treacherous part of the entire journey.

Benny liked to sleep with a gun under his pillow, which meant if he woke up before I had a chance to incapacitate him, then things were going to get a whole fuck load nosier and deadly. The adrenaline surge would be fun, but I didn't have that much time. Reaching the landing, I rounded the corner and did the exact same act with the marks I'd placed on this floor. Having a dirty home really could kill you.

The door was closed, but I'd already broken the lock with a quick jimmying inside the handle, and as I suspected the handle turned with a touch of resistance and then smoothly turned to open. There Benny was, sprawled out naked as a jaybird on the bed. Like anyone actually wanted to see that.

The one girl to the left of the bed sat up straight, the handcuff and chain jingling slightly as she moved. I put a finger to my lips and prayed that she could see the action with the only light coming from the small nightlight and remain quiet. The nightlight was of a naked girl bent over, showing off her ass, so it looked like her pussy was glowing. Class, this guy was nothing but class.

Stepping toward the bed, I stared down at Benny's body. I had no idea why people liked to sleep naked. If your house was ever on fire, then you were running out of there in your birthday suit. Definitely not what your neighbors wanted to see. The girl closest to me shifted away so her back was in the corner as she wrapped her arms around her knees. Raising the bat over my head, I took aim and froze as his eyes popped open, and he pulled the gun from under the pillow to point it at me.

"Whoever the fuck you are, you're gonna wish you never stepped..." I ducked as his arm jerked up and a bullet lodged itself into the ceiling.

The girl on the opposite side of the room, who I thought was asleep, was now screaming like a pint-sized banshee. She'd moved as quick as lightening and had wrapped the chain holding her around his neck.

Benny's arm swung around wildly, and the gun fired again. This time the bullet was too close for comfort as the lamp beside the bed exploded from the impact of the stray bullet. Jumping into action, I brought the bat down hard on his wrist, and he screamed and stopped fighting the girl long enough for her to take a tighter hold. I picked up the gun in my gloved hand and stepped away to set it out of reach before returning to the bed.

I was going to help. I'd planned on beating the living shit out of the man and then setting the house on fire. However, there was something so poetic about how his body was sprawled on the bed, thrashing as the girl pulled with all her strength, choking the life out of Benny.

His eyes found mine and silently pleaded for help. Instead, I placed the end of the bat on the floor and continued to watch the show until his body stopped twitching. Benny stared up at the ceiling. The girl was still yelling and pulling and making one hell of a racket, not that I blamed her. Making my way to the closet, I opened the door and grabbed two sweaters and socks from the drawer. There was another drawer with boxer shorts in it, and I tossed one set at the girl, quietly staring from her corner perch before moving around the bed.

The girl seemed more like a feral animal than a human. She snarled at me as I squatted down.

"If you want to live, then put this on and follow me out of the house. It's set to explode in..." I glanced at the timer on my wrist that was synced to the bomb. "Twelve minutes."

I held out the clothes to the girl, and she stared at them and then up into my eyes.

"Why should we trust you?"

It was the stupidest move I'd ever made, but I pulled the ski mask off my face and purposely turned my head to show off the ragged scar on the right side of my cheek.

"You have no other reason other than to know that I, too, was abused." I turned my eyes back to hers. "And now I kill those that hurt others. You've also seen my face, and I must trust that you keep my identity a secret." Dropping the clothes in front of her, I pulled the mask back into place and looked around. "Where does he keep the key for your cuffs?"

"Over there," the girl pointed to a box on the tall dresser in the corner. Dumping the contents, I found the keys and returned to the quiet girl. At first, she was shaking but held out her hands. The cuffs fell away, and I stood and made my way to the second girl. Her eyes were still wary as she finished pulling on the clothes I'd given her. She held out her hands, and I slipped the little key into the lock, freeing her.

Benny let out a dying wheeze, and although he was good and dead, the sound made the girl jump. But I smirked as she balled her hand into a fist and slammed it into the middle of Benny's face.

"Fucking asshole, I told you I'd make you pay," she growled and then flicked her gaze up to me. "My name is Raven, and that's Cindy." She pointed to the girl that was like a mouse in comparison to Raven.

"DW. Okay, let's go."

"What about all the other guys?"

That gave me pause. "How many are there?"

She shrugged. "Usually ten or more in the house."

Well, that didn't give me a good feeling. I never bothered to check the basement and there was no time now.

"Is the basement soundproof?"

Again, Raven shrugged. "I don't know, but that's usually where they take people to kill them, and we never hear anything up here."

Okay, that was a good sign, but I wasn't taking any chances. Making my way to the bathroom, I pulled it open and stared at the short roof that lead to the backyard.

"We better go this way." I pointed. "We really need to go. We don't have much time left. Whoever is left in here will die in less than five minutes."

That got the girls moving. Cindy was first. I helped her up and out of the window before doing the same for Raven. The window was a tight fit for someone my size, but with a hard push, I was able to squeeze through and then looked around before jumping down to the ground.

"One at a time, jump, and I'll catch you," I whispered. A light turned on inside one of the other rooms besides the kitchen. Shit. "Hurry up."

Cindy jumped, and she gave a little scream as I caught her, setting her down on her socked feet. Raven was next, and I caught her easily as she leaped off the roof.

I could hear yelling inside, and knew that the two guards in the kitchen had been found. It wouldn't be long before they headed upstairs— it would be their final minute. Not caring if they wanted me to or not, I grabbed the girls around the waist and lifted them off the ground as I ran for it. I counted down in my head and hated that I was setting off all the motion detectors as we went.

Ten

We reached the walkway.

Nine

I turned the corner and sprinted toward the next street over.

Six

I burst out onto the next street over.

Three

I ran along the sidewalk and across the street to my truck.

One.

I sat the girls down just as the house exploded with a rumble that would be heard for miles. Car alarms went crazy as the fire and smoke rose into the air, along with debris that landed as close as a few inches away from us.

"Wow, fuck. You weren't joking," Raven said, as she stared at the back of the house that was now fully engulfed in flames.

"I don't exactly have a great sense of humor." I looked down at the girl as she smiled back up at me. I put my hand in my pocket and pulled out what I had in cash. "Here, this is enough to get you to the police station and get something to eat."

Raven took the small wad and then linked her finger with Cindy's hand. They ran a couple steps before Cindy pulled Raven to a halt and looked back at me.

"Thank you," she said so softly that I barely heard it. It was the only two words she'd said since our encounter, but I nodded, and they took off again.

Making my way to the car, I slipped behind the wheel and waited until I was three roads over before taking the mask off.

"Send a text message to Cherry Popper," I said to my phone. "One chicken has been cooked. Two more to go."

"Message sent."

Now, on to the next target. I had a Ms. Violet Clarke to deal with, my brother to kill, and now a man claiming to be me. I would find a way to teach that liar a lesson.

Too many things to do in a day and simply not enough hours to do them all.

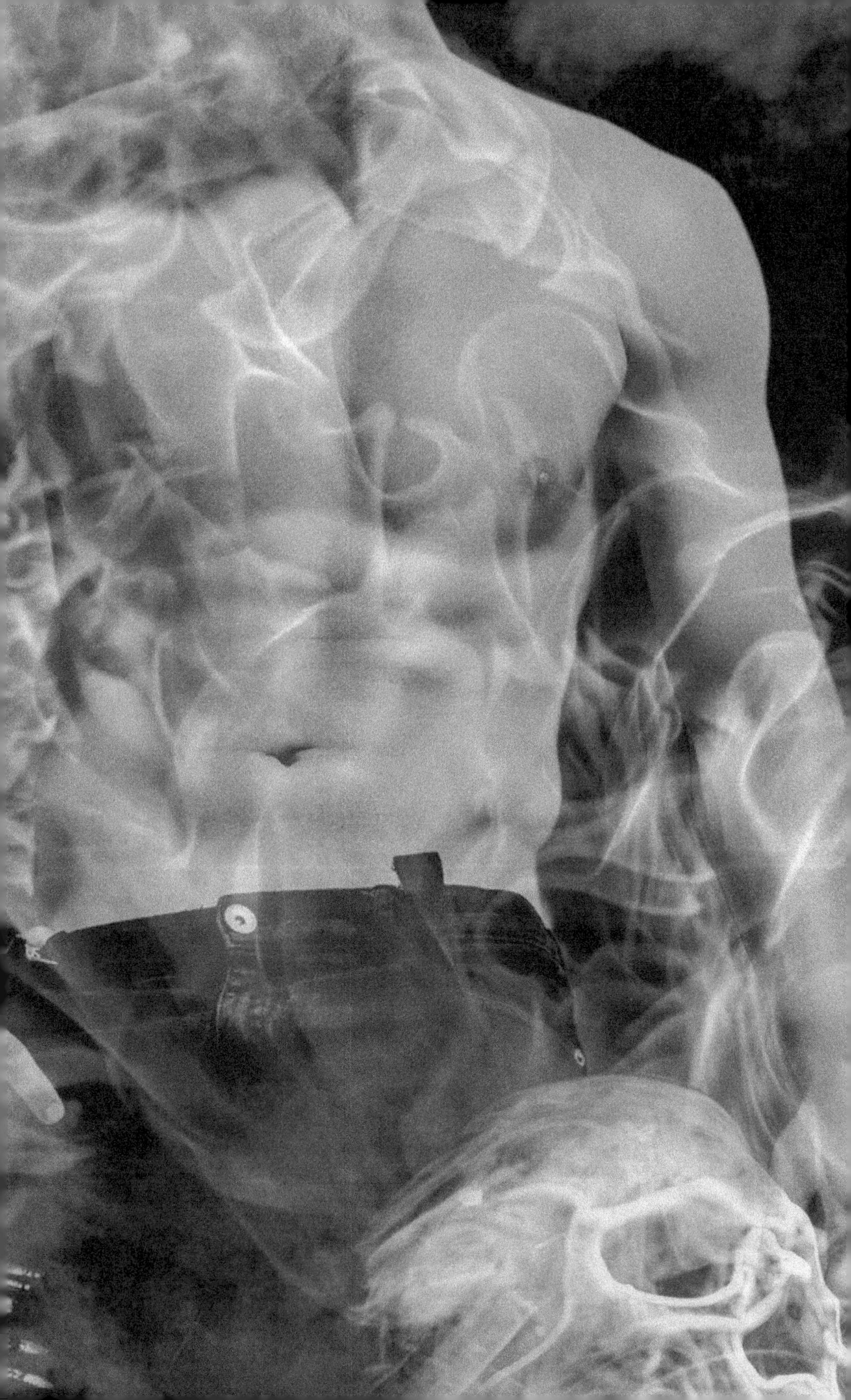

Chapter 30

Asher

I glanced over at Vi, sitting in the passenger seat of my truck. Even though she was sitting quietly with her hands in her lap, I could tell she was stressed. There was an energy that I was picking up on from her. It screamed that she was bottling up a pile of rage.

Reaching out my hand, I held it open for her to link fingers with me, and she sighed as soon as she touched me. I loved that. It was a shot to my system to know that I could affect her the way I wanted.

"You have to stop stressing about it, Vi. They had their minds made up no matter what you said. The only thing that would've stopped them was if you'd marched the real arsonist into the precinct and handed him over."

She mumbled, "idiots," under her breath, then turned to look at me. "All right, I will try to stop thinking about it and the big mistake they're making. Tell me about your family."

"The family gatherings when my mom was still living in Miami were huge, but now that she is in Jacksonville, they are much smaller. My cousin, who you met, Monique, and her partner Sylvie will be coming and doing the cooking. My foster-sister, Sabrina, and her husband, Andrew, will be there, but that's it. Ryan my foster-brother is in the military and at the moment he is overseas."

"Sounds perfect."

"I think you'll really love the spot. It's right on the water, and we will have our own room, and as you've seen, Monique can cook one heck of a feast. We're totally spoiled."

Vi smiled at me and my chest warmed with the look she was giving me. I'd stopped asking myself why she was so different from everyone else. There was no explaining feelings or attraction, but there was something about Vi that made me feel like I'd found what I'd been seeking. She was something that my heart needed, but I'd never realized that it did.

"Are you sure that everyone is going to be okay with me coming? I mean, we haven't been together very long," Vi said. Her cheeks pinkened, and I could see she was nervous, but she had no reason to worry.

"Honestly, they're going to be ecstatic that I brought someone home for them to meet. When I said I'd never done this, I meant it. When I told my mom that I was bringing you to meet them, I thought she fainted on the other end of the line, it was so quiet." I smirked as Vi laughed.

"I know it's not a holiday conversation, but can you tell me more about you and your brother and what happened?" Vi nibbled on her bottom lip as she stared at me.

Even though the story was painful, I wanted her to know. She was the first person I felt I could even confide in about what happened and how it made me feel without being judged.

"Well, it all came to a head three years after we ran. Derek had really tried to be okay. I want to stress that my father had done so much damage that even though we were with this really nice old couple that had shown us nothing but kindness, he never got over the pain and trauma. It ate at him like cancer. I could see it growing inside of him a little more each day."

Vi gave my hand a little reassuring squeeze.

"I'd wake up in the middle of the night, terrified that he'd slipped out of the house and what he might do. This one night, while we were sitting around the dinner table, I just knew. He'd been acting really out of sorts for a couple of weeks, but that night he was happy, lighthearted even. That wasn't my brother. If there were a picture in the dictionary for doom and gloom, it would've had my brother's picture."

Vi gave a little giggle that made me smile at her. She curled her legs up under her, looking so perfect and beautiful sitting beside me. At some point, I had to thank Wheels for pushing me to take the leap because she was worth every second.

"So then, what happened?"

"I just couldn't shake it and didn't sleep, so I knew when he got up from bed and got dressed. I asked him where he was going, and he glared at me and told me to go back to sleep. He said he'd planned to meet up with a friend at a party. Honestly, he couldn't have said anything that would've set off fireworks or alarms faster. My brother didn't have friends, and he hated parties. Most were terrified of him or were sadly grossed out about his scar and wouldn't even go near him. That pissed me off so fucking much. They had no idea what he'd endured to have that scar. How he'd saved me over-and-over again."

As if sensing I needed it, Vi let go of my hand and began rubbing the tight muscles in the back of my neck. I took a deep breath, the nervousness I always felt in the pit of my stomach thinking about that night churned now, and I had to work to push it down.

"I laid there for a little while longer, but it became too much. The panic was so intense that I leaped from the bed. I just knew I had to find him and took off on my bike to hunt him down. I checked all our usual spots, and nothing. But then I saw a glow in the distance, with smoke rising into the air like a signal and—"

I stopped and stared over at Vi, my lighthouse in a storm.

"Derek had gone too far—I peddled along the path through this small forest and dropped my bike just before running through the trees. This house was on fire that was not far from where we were staying. And I just knew it was him. My gut screamed that it was him." Vi's hand stopped massaging the back of my neck.

"Did you say you biked through a forest to a house fire?" Vi said, her eyes wide.

"Yeah, it was fully engulfed. A couple of girls about my age were screaming outside of the house, and my stomach dropped. There was nothing I could do but stare at the fire. I needed to find my brother and stop him before he did anything else and took off. There was no telling what he'd do next or where he would go, but I had to try."

I ran my hand through my hair as the memories flooded back, and the words continued to tumble from my mouth. "I biked to my parent's house like my instincts guided me and pushed me to go as fast as possible."

My eyes found Vi's, and they were a mix of shock and a dark pain that mirrored my own. "It was like he'd finally gotten brave enough to do what he really wanted."

I so badly wanted to pull the truck over to the side of the road and pull Vi into my lap so I could hold her.

"What...what happened next," she asked softly.

I shook my head as the image of my father's bloody body flooded my mind. I didn't love my father any more than Derek did, but the gore of his crushed skull had turned my stomach then just as the thought of it did now.

"The front door was open, and my father was sitting in his usual chair, but there was a crowbar at his feet. There was so much blood, and I couldn't recognize his face anymore. It...it was bad. I was too scared to look more than a glance at what Derek had done, and my fear wouldn't let me get any closer to the man who had been more monster than father to see if he had a pulse. I knew I had to try and stop Derek from doing anything else. I veered around my father's body and stared at the television screen that was smashed and covered in blood. If there was any more noise, I didn't hear it until the shrill scream of my mother ripped through the house. My mother had screamed many times at the hands of my father, but this was different."

I shivered and Vi grabbed my hand, giving it a kiss.

"The scent of burning flesh was instant, and I sprinted the final feet to the door. I was screaming for him to stop. Derek heard me coming, and as I ran into the room, he hauled me up over his shoulder like I was a sack of potatoes. My mother was tied to the bed, her arms above her head. She was screaming as she burned. I have no idea what he used on her, but it burned hot and fast. That was the last image of my mother I had before Derek ran from the house with me yelling and flopping around."

A tear trickled down my cheek.

"I couldn't let him kill people, Vi. I loved my brother with my whole heart. So burning random garbage was one thing, but burning people was another."

"So you turned him in?" she said, her voice sounding shocked.

I looked over at her. I couldn't tell if she liked that I turned my brother in or not. Her face was twisted up in an expression I didn't understand.

"Yeah, it was the hardest thing I'd ever had to do. He was my brother, my protector, and we were close, but...."

"Is that why you decided to become a firefighter?" She pulled our linked hands to her chest like she was needing something to hang on to.

"Yeah, I ended up in foster care. The Giltberts we'd been staying with, were considered to be too elderly to care for me, which was bullshit. They'd been taking care of Derek and me just fine, but that didn't stop the social worker from taking me away from them and putting me in a new home. There was another friend of theirs that had tried to take me in, but she was of the same age and her husband was already passed on, so that was how I ended up at Monique's house. As it turned out, that was how I met my mom, who wanted to take me in permanently. Luckily, I landed with an amazing family. They made sure I got an education, and I owe who I am today to them."

Vi suddenly burst out in tears. The sobs were so raw and painful that I could feel her pain from the other side of the truck.

"Vi, what is it? What's wrong?"

I looked over at her as she held my hand like she was terrified to let go. She was scaring me, I didn't know what I'd said to set her off like this, but I quickly flicked on the signal, pulled the truck into one of the many beach entrances, and parked. Undoing my seatbelt, I tossed the center console up and slid over to pull her shaking body into my own.

"Hey, what's going on, Vi?" I rubbed her back as she wrapped her arms around me and hung on as she cried like there was an endless supply of tears.

"Did...did the house sit on a golf course," she finally asked.

"Yes. Why?"

Vi pulled back, her eyes searching my face. She cupped my cheeks before leaning in and giving my lips a soft kiss.

"Vi, you need to talk to me," I said as she broke the kiss. "Please, you're worrying me."

"It was you," she said. "And you didn't do it. All this time, Beck was right. It wasn't the guy in the hoodie." She leaned back and covered her mouth as she smiled as more tears flowed from her eyes.

"What?"

"The fire..." She started and then stopped, collecting herself.

"The fire you found, the one with the two girls screaming?" She turned her head and looked at me, and the lightbulb hit.

"Oh god. That was you, wasn't it? That was your house?" My head began to spin, and I laid it back on the headrest. What were the chances that the one woman I'd have a connection with ended up being my brother's first victim? I covered my eyes with my hand, not even sure what to say. "I'm so sorry, Vi, I...."

"No, don't. You just gave me peace. I've searched for my parents' killer from the moment it happened. I always thought that it was the boy I saw standing by the forest before he ran off. I became obsessed with the search and wondered why the person just disappeared." She shook her head.

"Beck kept trying to tell me that maybe the person that started it was already caught, but I didn't believe her. I was convinced they were still out there setting fires all these years, and I was determined to find him and put him behind bars."

We stared at one another, and so many things clicked into place for me. We connected on so many levels, but she was the only person that truly understood the same pain, the same pain from the same night. We suffered it differently, but some of it was the same.

Reaching out, I cupped her cheek and ran my thumb over the soft skin. Vi leaned into me slightly, and my heart skipped a beat.

"I'm sorry I couldn't stop him. I wish I'd done more."

She shook her head, and unclipping her seatbelt, she got up on her knees and leaned in, giving me a kiss. I wrapped her up, pulled her into my lap exactly like I'd wanted to, and kissed her like she was going to disappear.

"I may wish that too, but the entire situation is complicated, and you did the right thing and called the police. I'm just shocked I never heard anything. Anytime I spoke to the police, they said they had no news."

I lifted my shoulder. "I don't know why they would say that to you. I gave my statement and watched Derek put into the back of the cruiser, but after they moved him to a hospital to treat him, I couldn't find him anymore."

"What do you mean?"

"Just that. It was like they'd wiped Derek away or lost their notes, and no one would talk to me. To this day, my brother and where he went are a complete mystery to me. I never saw a trial or anything. My mom called multiple times, and no one ever had any answers until one day, we stopped calling. Honestly, I wonder if he was killed and they swept it all under the rug. The killer kid had got what he deserved sort of thing."

"Still, that's weird for there to not be any trail of what happened to him," Vi said and leaned back slightly.

"It is." I shook my head at the painful thought. No matter what my brother had done, he was still my brother. "I have friends on the force and get this, they say they can see him being booked in and that's all there is. No other notes or evidence. He was simply wiped away."

"We'll figure it out. You have me now, and I don't give up. Besides, if we find him, I want to know why my parents. What did they do that would make him so angry that he would attack them?"

I shook my head. "I don't know. He never mentioned anything about anyone other than our parents. Could've been a random choice, but if we find him, I also want to know the answer to that question."

Leaning forward, I placed a soft kiss on her lips. "We better get going, or we're going to be late for dinner. You don't want to see Monique's anger over her food getting cold." I gave her another soft kiss. "Are you okay?"

"Yeah. For the first time in a very long time, I feel okay. Maybe we were always destined to meet Asher West. The universe is coming full circle."

My lip curled up in a sly smile. "Maybe you're right."

I couldn't express what was in my head or chest, but all of it said I wanted this woman forever. Violet Clarke was officially mine, and I was never letting go.

Chapter 31

Violet

For the rest of the drive to Asher's mom's house, I wavered back and forth between being happy and crying. It was this overwhelming sense of relief but also allowing myself to finally grieve and take a step to put that part of my past where it belonged. I had a feeling that what he told me was going to take a lot longer to process than the time we had left in this drive. My emotions had become like a leaf blowing in the wind, and I ended up going wherever mother nature decided to take me.

I couldn't stop staring at Asher. He was the boy I'd been looking for all this time. It just wasn't for the reason I thought. Sometimes when weird things like this happened, I just couldn't help thinking that the universe really did have a plan for our lives. It felt like there was this massive puppeteer sitting up in the clouds who loved screwing with us by pulling the strings.

Flipping down the visor in the truck, I gave myself a once over to make sure it didn't look like I'd been crying my eyes out. That didn't seem like a great way to meet Asher's mom for the first time.

"What do I call your mom?" I said, realizing that he'd only referred to her as 'mom.'

Asher smiled. "My mom's name is Elizabeth, but she likes to be called Lizzy. If you call her Elizabeth or Mrs. Pinchin, she will make you do the dishes."

He laughed as I stared at him, trying to gauge his seriousness. Asher jumped out of the truck and grabbed our bags. It seemed odd to me that the first time I met his family, I was going to stay with them for a few days. It was their tradition to come here for the entire holiday, and I didn't feel like bringing my own car to do the five-hour drive back alone like I was the single party pooper. So here I was.

As I hopped out of the truck, my feet barely touched the ground when the door to the pretty seaside home burst open with a loud shriek. Startled, I jumped as a woman came running out of the house with her hands in the air, but she had a big old smile on her face.

"Is that my baby?" she called out like she was trying out for cheer-leading practice.

I watched, shocked and fascinated, as Asher's mom gripped him in a massive hug, and then she physically rocked him from side to side. I was positive she would've picked him up off the ground to swing around if she'd been strong enough.

"Look at you, oh my god! Every time I see you, you get more handsome."

Before Asher could answer, his mom turned her eyes to me. I now understood what it was like to be an animal frozen by a set of headlights. Her eyes lit up as she saw me, and she pulled away from Asher to jog around the truck to where I was standing. I'd been completely wrong if I thought I was safe from the wild bear-like hug. "You must be Violet."

"Hi, Miss....I mean Lizzy. Nice to meet you," I said, on a wheeze as I tried to draw in a breath.

"Ah, I see my boy, here, explained the rules to you. That is a good thing. I'd hate to have you designated to clean up duty on your first visit." Lizzy laughed and gripped me by the arms. "Dang, you're pretty. Asher, you have good taste when you finally decide to settle down."

"I'm not sure I'd classify us as settled down," I said, but it was like I'd never said a word.

"Asher, Hunny, can you get all the luggage and bring it in? I'm going to give Violet here a tour," Lizzy said and guided me toward the front door.

She didn't wait to see if he had heard or if Asher was even going to do it. She just assumed what she said would happen, but she did it with such enthusiasm and a glowing smile that would make even the coldest person want to hop to the task.

"I hear you love it here," I said and her arm tightened around my shoulder as she gave me a squeeze.

"This place is a godsend. The gators I could do without them, but the rest of it is amazing. There's a beautiful big old deck out back, and it can hold twenty people easy. You'll see what I mean."

As soon as we stepped into the house, I was assaulted by the delicious aroma of pasta and garlic. My stomach rumbled at the thought of food. I'd been too nervous to eat lunch, and that poor decision was creeping up on me.

"Did Asher give you the itinerary?"

"Umm..." I started, but Lizzy was already on a roll.

"Well, it's going to start with dinner tonight and sitting around telling stories and singing carols. Then we'll play board games until we can't hold our eyes open while we stuff our faces with all the homemade baking. Then Christmas morning, we will have ourselves a large country styled breakfast and open gifts, and then we'll head out on the boat for the day and relax while Monique makes a gourmet version of a traditional Christmas meal. Don't worry. She hates to go out on the water, which is ironic since her restaurant is on a boat. Have you been to her restaurant?"

"Umm..."

"If you haven't been, then make sure Asher takes you. The food is outstanding." She smiled wide, and I took a deep breath like I'd just stepped off a fast-moving train.

"Mom, let Vi breathe," Asher said as he walked into the house behind us with all the bags under one arm.

"Oh, stop, Asher. It's not every day you bring someone home for me to meet." Lizzy lowered her voice so only I could hear. "He's never brought anyone home to meet the family. Whatever you're doing, keep doing it," she said and laughed as she tightened her grip on my arm as if she was hugging it.

Even though it felt like her enthusiasm had run over me, she seemed like a genuinely amazing person. Her blonde hair had white mixed in and laid in ringlets over her shoulder and was held together with a teddy bear scrunchy.

Her glasses were pushed up on her head, and they were lined with little rhinestones, making them glitter. She was wearing a simple linen jumper that reminded me of the style artists would use to paint. But, it was her smile that had me smiling back and her caring eyes that had me relaxing in her home.

"Oh wow," I said as we turned the corner to the open concept living room.

There was not a spot that hadn't been decorated. It was like the spirit of Christmas had decided to throw up in the spacious room and leave behind everything and anything. Not a single thing matched. Yet, just like Lizzy herself, you couldn't help but admire and like the confusion that assaulted your senses.

"Do you like it? I know I went a little overboard, but I just wanted everything to feel perfect and special," she said, the first hint of doubt slipping into her voice.

"It's beautiful. I feel like I just stepped into Santa's workshop," I said and smiled at Lizzy. She beamed back.

Something dinged and Lizzy practically jogged off. "My cookies, I'll be back."

I sighed as Asher's hands gripped my hips and then wrapped his arms around my body as he pulled me into his tall frame. He kissed the side of my neck and my stomach fluttered with a nervous energy that he always seemed to invoke in me.

"Thank you," he whispered into my ear.

"For?" I turned my head to look at him and his lips found mine.

By the time we came up for air, I couldn't remember the question I'd asked.

"For being kind to my mom, she can be a bit...much, but she means well."

I looked around the room, my eyes landing on the bushy tree that was as wide as it was tall and decorated with so many ornaments. I wasn't sure how it was still standing. My eyes moved onto the flashing lights strung from every available space to the television. The station was set to a crackling fire, and then I looked at the Santa that moved. His one arm was in a waving position, and the other held up a sign that said, 'Welcome to the North Pole.'

"It may be a lot, but it's perfect. It's like a Christmas paradise, and your mom...." I looked around his shoulder to make sure she hadn't snuck back into the room. "Is so sweet and...you're very lucky."

The corner of his mouth tugged up in a sad smile. "I really was, you know. My brother always protected me, and then I found the Giltberts and then Lizzy, who I truly do feel like she's my mom." He rubbed the back of his neck. "I just wish...I need to know what happened to my brother. I know he did horrible things and hurt you, but I need to know if he's still alive or...."

My emotions were conflicted. On the one hand, if I'd been him, then I'd want to know if my brother was okay no matter what, but on the other, I was elated that the person responsible for my parents' horrible deaths was put in jail to pay for what he'd done. It was hard to hold the opposing emotions in my chest, but I planned on helping find out the answers no matter what.

"So sorry about that, but I can't have the sugar cookies burning.

They're Asher's favorite," Lizzy said as she whirled back into the room. "Oh my gosh, don't you two make the cutest couple. Give me a sec now, don't move. I want a picture." She dug around in the large pockets of the jumper, and as I flicked my eyes up to Asher he once more mouthed, "I'm sorry."

Moniqua and her partner Sylvie were the next to arrive, and as soon as they stepped foot in the house, the bubbling excitement that Lizzy had managed to contain for half a glass of rum and eggnog evaporated. We just got her calmed down again when Sabrina and her husband, Andrew, arrived. She reminded me of Beck in some ways, but Lizzy even had Beck beat when it came to the high-level energy.

Asher and Andrew were sitting out on the deck while Lizzy went to bed early so she could get up early to enjoy the Christmas breakfast. That left me alone with the other three women. Now, most social individuals would find something in common and manage to make a semblance of a conversation. However, I stared at them as they reminisced and talked about Sabrina and Andrew's new house and how Sylvie's IVF was going well.

They hoped to be pregnant in a few months...I was way out of my element. Sure, they were talking about normal life things, but these were not the things lead fire investigators discussed or people who'd spent almost their entire life focused on burnt buildings and arsonists.

I felt like I had nothing to contribute, and I suddenly realized what Beck had been saying. I hadn't understood how consumed I'd become in my hunt for Asher's brother. It really had clouded everything I'd done from that one life-altering moment when he chose to kill my parents.

At this point, I didn't even know who I was without that investigation.

"What about you, Violet?" Sabrina asked, and I blinked and looked at her and the other two women.

"I'm so sorry. I didn't hear what you said. I zoned out." As soon as the words left my mouth, I realized how that sounded. "I have this work thing, and I was thinking...it doesn't matter what I was thinking about. What did you ask?" I felt terrible as Sabrina's face fell. Well, so much for making a good impression on all of Asher's family.

"We were talking about special Christmas moments. Did you have one you'd like to share?"

"Oh...um." I took a sip of my drink.

I was pretty sure Asher was trying to get me drunk because he kept making new concoctions. This one had a very distinct coconut flavor with chocolate and coffee.

"Well, I guess my favorite Christmas moment was when I was twelve. I turned into a brat of a teenager the following year, and my parents and I didn't see eye-to-eye on anything, but the year before was magical. At least it felt like that. It felt very much like being here with all of you."

The three women smiled, so I continued.

"My parents had decided to go away for Christmas that year, and it started out as a disaster. We were trying to make our way to Colorado and to the cabin they'd rented. It was going to be at the base of one of the mountains, and they had this large water park that I could use, but we never got there."

"Oh no, what happened?" Sylvie asked, her eyes tearing up. She waved a fan at her eyes. "Don't mind me. It's just all the hormones they're pumping into me. I cry at commercials about soup." We all laughed, and another little part of me relaxed. "Continue on, please."

"We were all packed and had the tow behind the trailer we'd rented all ready to go, but we never even made it out of Florida when we hit an alligator. The scaly gator had decided to lie on the road just over a hill. My dad couldn't see it, and as soon as he crested the hill, he slammed on the brakes, but the weight of the trailer pushed us, and bam! We went right over the gator."

"Oh my god, did you drive off the road?" Monique asked.

"No, but it was close. Luckily, my dad had put himself through school by driving trucks and kept us on the road, but it was terrifying. We got the rig pulled over, and my mom, who was an animal advocate, jumped out of the truck and ran for the gator to see if it was okay."

I shook my head at the memory of my father screaming for her to stop. I loved my mom, but she always tried to rescue the next person, animal, or plant. If there was a level higher than advocate, that was my mom.

"Of course, the gator was not dead and didn't take kindly to the woman yelling for someone to call a veterinarian or touching it. So the gator managed with its last dying breath to grab hold of her arm." The three women gasped, their hands going to their mouths. "I'm sure you can imagine how well this went. We ended up at emergency for hours, but luckily, she only needed like twenty-five stitches."

"She's so lucky," Sabrina said.

"Tell me about it, but that's not the end of it. We were almost through Texas when we were hit with a freak snowstorm, and the roads turned into skating rinks. People were in the ditches everywhere, and emergency vehicles passed us going both directions when suddenly, we were in the middle of a pile-up. No one was hurt, but the trailer with all our stuff flipped off the road, rolled down a steep ditch, and smashed. Other than our suitcases of clothes we lost almost everything that we brought with us."

I laughed as I thought about the look on my dad's face as we stood at the edge of the road.

"I'm not sure I want to see what number three is if this was number two," my dad said, making me smile.

"So what did you do?" Monique asked as she rubbed Sylvia's back, tears streaming from her eyes.

"We ended up in this tiny little motel in the middle of nowhere for the rest of our trip."

"I thought you said this was a wonderful memory," Sabrina asked, her face holding the same shocked expression as everyone else.

"That's the thing. The motel we ended up at was run by this elderly couple that also had an old family ranch. They invited us in to spend Christmas with them and their family. There had to be fifty people there. We ate like royalty. There was just so much food, and everyone was so warm and welcoming. They made us feel like we were always meant to be there."

I smiled as the memory filled my head. "A couple of them sang and played the guitar or piano. I didn't know you could make "Jingle Bells" a country song until that day. I learned how to play horseshoes and got to ride a horse for the first time. Would you believe that each of them gave up a gift to give to us so we had something to open on Christmas morning?"

I quickly wiped away the tear that was sliding down my cheek with the memory that was so potent that I could still taste the gingerbread cookies.

"It was the best Christmas ever. I didn't realize at the time that it would become such an important memory for me or how it helped shape who I became growing up. However, I'll always be thankful to that random family and their generosity to people they'd never met before and never saw again. For me it was the true meaning of Christmas."

"Wow, you need to turn that into a book. That was the best story ever," Sabrina said. "Definitely tops Andrew dressing up as a sexy Santa," she teased, making us laugh again.

"What's this about me in a sexy Santa outfit," Andrew said as both he and Asher walked in from outside.

"Just that I like the look of your ass in the assless chaps," Sabrina said.

I hadn't laughed this much or hard with anyone other than Beck in forever.

"Okay, that is enough of that. I'm off to bed before I flood the house with all these damn tears." Sylvia stood, and Monique followed.

"It was great meeting you, Violet. See you in the morning." The two women left, and with some sexy teasing, Sabrina and Andrew did as well.

Asher stepped up behind me, and his hands felt amazing as he massaged at the tight muscles in my neck.

"That feels incredible," I said, my head dipping forward.

"I have a few other ideas of how to relax your body tonight," he said, his voice taking on a suggestive tone.

Standing from the chair, I slid my hands up his chest until I was able to wrap them around his neck. "Is that so?"

Asher smiled the sexiest, wicked grin I'd ever seen as he dropped his lips to mine and kissed me, leaving me breathless. Pulling away, he got close to my ear, his five o'clock shadow deliciously rubbing against my cheek.

"I may have packed some kinky Christmas toys. I think you're going to make a very sexy Mrs. Claus," he said, making me want to melt. He held out his hand, and I quickly put mine in his, but I couldn't stop looking at his handsome face. I was beginning to feel more for Asher than was safe. I knew it, but I didn't want nor plan to stop the emotions storming through my heart.

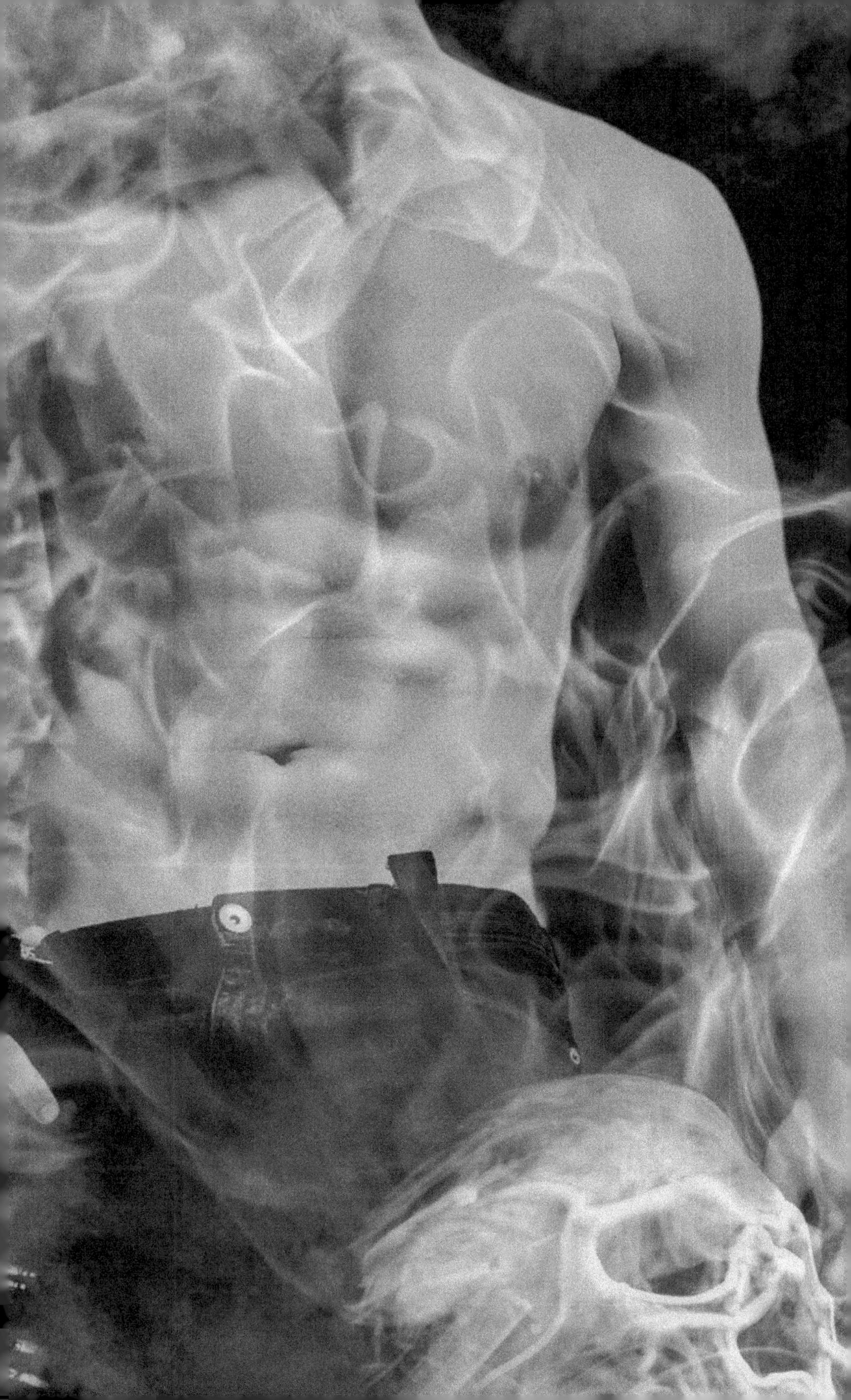

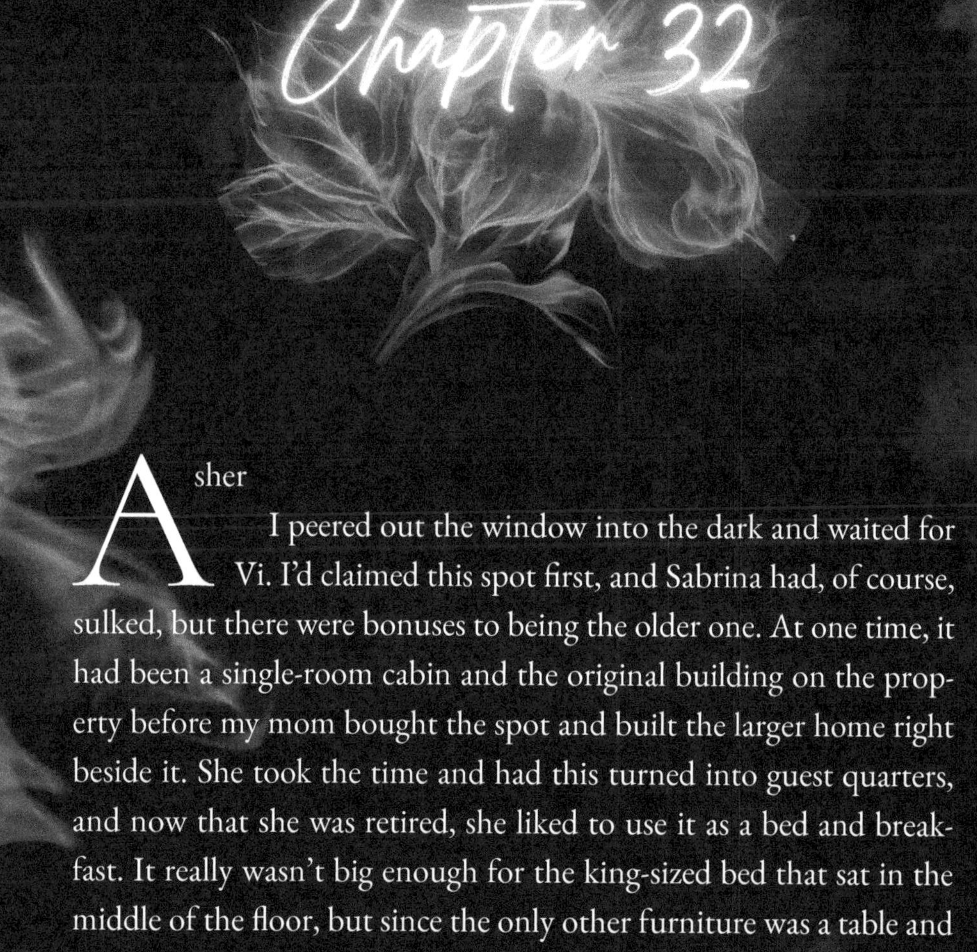

Chapter 32

Asher

I peered out the window into the dark and waited for Vi. I'd claimed this spot first, and Sabrina had, of course, sulked, but there were bonuses to being the older one. At one time, it had been a single-room cabin and the original building on the property before my mom bought the spot and built the larger home right beside it. She took the time and had this turned into guest quarters, and now that she was retired, she liked to use it as a bed and breakfast. It really wasn't big enough for the king-sized bed that sat in the middle of the floor, but since the only other furniture was a table and two chairs that sat looking out toward the water, it could handle the comfortable bed.

The moment that Vi stepped out of the small bathroom, I knew that deciding last minute to buy this outfit had been a smart idea. The bright green outfit could've passed for a seductive elf bikini with white fur trim, but it was the special additions to the outfit that made me want to break anyone's face if she ever stepped out in public wearing it.

She blushed a brilliant shade of red as I approached her and slowly looped around her as I admired just how perfect she was. Vi had an amazing ass that many women would pay for the cosmetic surgery to have, and the already scant material left most of her lush cheeks bare. It only accentuated their perkiness and made my hands itch to feel the soft, round flesh in my hands. I feasted on the look and immediately decided that, at some point, I was fucking her ass while she wore them.

Vi stood quietly and didn't move as I circled her a second time like I was a predator looking for the vulnerable spot to attack. Her eyes followed me, and it fucking made me rock hard to see the desire in those blue depths. If I had sprinkled her in sugar and cinnamon, she would've been my own personal cookie that I had no intention of sharing.

Stopping in front of her, I glanced down at the hard nipples poking through the holes cut in the material just large enough to show off her precious buds and the pink areolas that were begging to be sucked.

"You're never allowed to wear this anywhere anyone other than me can see you," I said.

A single eyebrow rose as her eyes flashed with the challenge, and I had a sudden urge to put her over my knee and tan that sexy ass for the defiant look. "Are you trying to tell me what to do outside of the bedroom again?"

"Maybe, but if you do, I'll end up in jail because I'll kill anyone who looks at you in this." I stepped in closer to her so she had to look up at me. "Is that what you want? For me to kill everyone that looks at what's mine?"

She licked her lips, and I could see the defiant part of her wanting to say something witty and sarcastic, but the part of her that she'd given over to me was keeping her mouth shut.

"Answer me, Vi," I said and softly traced a single fingertip down her arm and watched the goosebumps bloom in the wake of my touch.

"Would you really kill them?" she asked, her face showing the same skepticism her voice did.

"Do you really want to test it? I've never felt murderous before, but the thought of another man looking at you makes my blood boil." The truth of the words was shocking, but every single word of it was true.

I gripped the back of her neck, and she sucked in a sharp breath as I held her firm. "The thought of another man touching you brings out a monster in me that I didn't know existed," I said, my voice threatening as images of a man touching her flashed behind my eyes. I had no idea what the fuck had gotten into me, but Vi and everything about her was mine.

Vi's eyes flared with a dark passion as she licked her lips. "I will only ever wear this outfit for you," she said, and the corner of my mouth tugged up.

Even as she said the proper answer, she found a way to be sexily defiant, but it was partially what had me wanting her so badly. She didn't need me in her life. She'd already made that abundantly clear. She was more than willing to allow herself to explore this side of who she was and wanted me to be the one to bring her inner sex deviant to the surface, but she didn't want nor need me if she so chose. It was oddly refreshing.

Dropping my head, I ran my tongue over her left nipple and could feel the subtle tremor that she tried to hide. Swirling my tongue over the sensitive peak, I waited until she let out a tiny gasp before I moved on to the right one. Making sure not to touch any other part of her body that would be craving to be touched, I sucked on the nipple harder as Vi panted but didn't move from the position.

"Such a good girl, you are my little Firebug. Spread your legs wider." Vi did as I asked and stepped out a little more with each leg, making me smile.

I went back to enjoying her nipples like they were little gifts under the Christmas tree for my own pleasure as my fingers slipped between her parted legs. The second little feature this outfit had was the premade slit that stretched from the front of her pussy to her rosebud, which gave me free access to what lay under the soft green material.

If the small cottage we were in hadn't been so quiet, I would've missed the soft gasp as my finger slid along her wet slit. She was very ready for whatever I wanted to do to her, but what I wanted was for her to lose herself in the moment and be forced to hold off her climax until I slid my cock inside of her. I intended to test her resolve tonight and push her limits to see what she could take.

My finger continued to softly trace along her lips before dipping inside of her heat. The muscles quivered around my finger as I studied her face and watched her breathing. It had become an obsession to memorize. Everything about her body and what set her on fire was worth studying. Each time we were together, I learned a little more, and each time I found myself as entranced by her as the time prior.

Dropping my lips to hers, I swallowed down the moans she was trying so hard to hold back as my finger picked a steady pace. "You like that?"

"Yes," she said without hesitation.

"Do you want more?" I asked my lips brushing hers.

"Yes."

As soon as she said the word, I stepped back from her and loved the panicked look that flashed in her eyes as she sucked in her lower lip. It was easy to tell that she wanted to ask what was wrong, but she kept quiet.

"Get down on your knees," I ordered.

Vi didn't even give me a dirty look that I'd been half expecting as she lowered herself down.

"Well, I'm waiting," I said and glanced at the way too Christmasy flannel pants I'd put on after my shower. Vi reached for the pants, and I stepped back out of her reach. "Hands behind your back and use your teeth." A thrill raced through my body as she crawled closer and clasped her hands like she was told. Those amazing blue eyes found mine as she looked up at me a moment before moving in with her mouth to bite the end of the string holding the pants in place.

I ignored the pounding of my heart and the blood that was racing through my veins and how excited just a glance from her made me. Vi pushed all the buttons on my control, and I was quickly figuring out that I never wanted her to stop being exactly who she was.

Others I'd trained to become something else, but with Vi, it was more of molding her into the person she craved to be while giving me what I needed. It was a balance and one that I was enjoying immensely.

With a hard tug, the bow I'd tied came free, and the flannel pants pooled at my feet. Taking one more step back, I sat down on the edge of the bed and locked eyes with my beautiful temptress.

"You know what to do," I said, and I leaned back on my arms and loved that her eyes never left my cock. She went to touch my legs with her hands, and I shook my head at her in a warning. Vi wiggled her way between my legs, forcing me to spread them wider until she was pressed against the bed. She stared down at my cock, which had been hard most of the night thinking about this moment, and I groaned as she drew her tongue up my shaft.

She did the same thing a few more times and proceeded to swirl her tongue over the head of my cock, with a cheeky grin on her lips the entire time. Once more, I was tempted to tan her adorable ass, but the problem was she knew exactly how to toe the line now, and I didn't have quite enough to punish her over.

"You're a good little cock tease," I said as she sucked one of my balls into her mouth and treated it like it was her favorite treat. "Fuck, you're such a good girl," I growled as she switched and gave the other one the same treatment.

Her mouth was wonderfully hot, and she had skills with that tongue of hers. Reaching out as she went to switch again, I gripped her hair in my hand and pulled her face away from my cock.

"Enough of that." I pushed the cock out toward her. "Service it properly now, and you don't stop until I tell you to stop."

Vi nodded, and I released her hair, but I was nice enough to keep my cock out in a position that was easy for her to slip in her mouth. I didn't even mind that she took an extra second to lick the droplet of precome before she lowered her mouth down around my shaft. I held back the groan this time.

She needed to work for it. I couldn't stop staring at her lips as they moved along my shaft. They were the prettiest lips I'd ever seen and were starting to get puffy from the friction. I knew exactly how sexy they looked when they pinkened up from the extra abuse.

"Good girl, my Firebug, just like that," I praised. "Can you take it all?"

She looked up at me but wisely kept my cock in her mouth as she moaned and nodded slightly. She was going to have to get an extra special gift at some point for her obedience. I could feel her swallowing, and it took a few tries, but soon my cock disappeared, and her nose touched my abs. This time I did groan as her throat muscles worked at gripping me.

"I'm going to fuck your face, Firebug," I said and grabbed her hair again. I waited for a breath to see if she'd fight me or say it was too much, but when she stayed relaxed and compliant, I pulled up on her hair, and she sucked in a deep breath. I gave her a moment before I started, and once I did, I didn't hold back. I was rough on her mouth as I lifted my hips to meet her mouth. More than once, her nose slammed into my abs. Tears were running down her face as the sexy sound of her mouth sliding up and down my cock echoed loudly in the room.

It felt too fucking good, and I needed to stop her before I came too early. Pulling up again on her hair, this time, I made sure my cock fell from her mouth. Leaning forward, I kissed her hard, my tongue invading her mouth as my cock had. Those lips of hers were bright pink and puffy by the time I was done.

"Get on the bed and spread your legs," I said, my voice deeper with the strain of holding back.

This time, I did reach out and I smacked her on the ass as she crawled up the bed.

"Such a tease. Don't push too far, or I'm going to put you over my lap," I threatened, but she didn't look too concerned as she bit her lip and slowly rolled over onto her back. She spread her legs the way I asked, and as she bit the tip of her finger, all I could think was that image would make a hell of a December calendar page.

"You think you're pretty sassy, don't you?" I said, and she lifted a shoulder, the grin still pulling at the corner of her mouth.

I slid over to the bag I'd brought for the trip and pulled out a device I had to have as soon as I saw it. Turning around, I held up the contraption that looked like a large butterfly with a stubby three-inch cock in the middle. Picking up the small bottle of candy cane-flavored lube, I poured a healthy dose on the device. Vi didn't look so confident as I walked toward the bed holding out my prize for her to see.

Kneeling on the bed, I moved between her legs, but her eyes never left the new toy. "Do you know what this is?"

"No."

"This is a remote stimulator," I said, and took great pride in leaning forward to pull one side of the elf panties aside to fit the wing under the material that was going to hold it in place.Vi moaned softly as the miniature cock, which was easily the width of my wrist, was slipped into her pussy before I tucked the remaining wing under the other side of the underwear. It was a unique design that would add the maximum amount of pleasure while never being seen if worn out in public. I really wanted to take her out on a date wearing it as I controlled the remote. The visual was strong in my mind. I craved to see the look on her face as she tried to hold off an orgasm....so fucking good.

She lifted her head and looked a the simulator that was long enough in the front to sit against her clit with its little rubber ridges. I lifted a brow at her, and she swallowed audibly.

"You don't get to come until I say you can. You can't touch your-self, and you can't make a sound. If you do, then I will double the amount of time this stays on you." Standing from the bed, I turned the chair by the window to watch and sat down. "Fifteen minutes are on the clock. If you can last the fifteen, then I'll give you what you really want, but if you don't...."

I gave a nonchalant shrug and let her mind decide what would be an appropriate punishment. Whatever she came up with would prob-ably be far worse than what I would've done to her.

Smirking, I held up the little remote.

"Hmm, lets see what this does." I hit the rotate button and Vi's eyes went wide as the fake cock began to move around in a circle inside of her.

It didn't take long before her breathing changed, and I flicked the device off. Watching her body and knowing the precise moment to turn the simulator on again was a skill that I thrived at and I now knew all of my sweet little Firebug's cues.

"Or how about this one."

The front wing began to vibrate on her clit that I knew by now would be very swollen and sensitive. Vi gasped and gripped the sheets hard. I turned it off and then back on again and made sure to leave it off long enough that the climax she was searching for continued to be just out of reach. Flicking off the second button and hitting the third one without warning this time, Vi almost leapt off the bed as the back wing that was nestled against her rosebud began to vibrate and move in a circular motion.

I savored how her mouth dropped open as she continued obeying the rules. She was so close to screaming. I flicked it off again and glanced at the time. The moment her body relaxed and her breathing started to settle, I hit the alternate button, and all three stimulations started up and then stopped at different times.

"You're doing so good. I think we can turn this up, say...three... no five more notches. Let's see how well you do with that."

The flicker of fear crossed her face but was wiped away as the first stage of the device hit. Now, this was a show I could watch forever. Gripping my cock in my free hand, I began to stroke it for her viewing pleasure and to help ease some of the pain building in my balls. More precome dripped from the end, and I quickly spread it around to lubricate the entire length of my shaft.

"Mmm, this is so good, and what an amazing show," I said and spread my legs wider to give Vi a perfectly unobstructed view of what I was doing.

She bit her lip hard enough I could see the lower lip turning white as she continued to remain quiet. Holding up the remote, I smiled as I clicked the intensity up to six. Vi's back arched, but it was her hips that continuously pumped up like that would help get the device deeper. That had me transfixed. Once again, I made a flourish of pressing the intensity up, and for the first time, I could hear it hum as it vibrated fasted on either her clit or her rosebud and the only down-time was the few seconds that the cock would rotate inside of her.

Clicking it up to level eight, Vi snapped her mouth together and closed her eyes as she screamed, but it remained muffled. Technically, she made a noise, but she didn't openly scream or open her mouth. I hit the max. This time, the device began to jump around under her elf underwear, and I counted to ten in my head. Flicking it off, I counted to twenty and then started the process over.

I stared at my phone in disbelief as the timer went off to announce Vi lasted fifteen minutes. I turned off the device for the last time tonight and had to admire her sheer determination. On the one hand, I was proud and loved that she managed to do what I'd asked, but on the other, I was looking forward to teaching her a lesson. Apparently, that would not be tonight. It was easy to see how strung out she already was, and part of being great at what I could do was knowing exactly when enough was enough.

A soft sheen of sweat glistened on her skin. I stood and looked down at her and smirked at her clenched fists and closed eyes as her chest rose and fell at a rapid pace. Standing at the end of the bed, I continued to stroke my cock and waited for her to open her eyes. It took a couple of minutes, but when the device stayed dormant, and I didn't say anything, I could almost see her mind begin to race as she wondered what was coming next.

One at a time, she opened her eyes, and like a magnet, they were drawn to what I was doing. She wiggled slightly on the bed, her expression silently begging me to let her finally come.

"You were such a good girl, Firebug. I'm impressed," I said, and her eyes lit up with the compliment. Fuck she was sexy. "Take the bottoms off and remove the toy," I said and watched as her shaking hands reached for the waistband of her underwear. Vi rocked her hips up and slipped them off, and I grabbed them from where they dangled on her ankle. They were damp, and with a groan, I wrapped them around my cock and stroked it with the soft and now slick fabric.

Fuck. I was close and shuddered as my hand continued to work. I watched Vi slowly remove the toy from her pussy. She moaned as the last of the thick cock was pulled free, and Vi flopped back on the bed, panting hard.

Leaning forward, I took the toy from her hand and set it and the underwear aside to be dealt with later. Turning back to the bed, Vi hadn't moved. Her body was splayed open for me to stare at, but she looked completely spent.

"Is that enough for tonight?" I asked, something I rarely did. I knew she would say no, but I wanted to hear her say she wanted more. She shook her head no.

"You can speak."

"No, I'm not done, just catching my breath," she said, the smile returning to her lips.

"Then what do you want?" I forced myself to let go of my aching cock before I came all over her. The thought held a certain appeal.

Her next words were as if she'd read my thoughts. "I want you to fuck me here." She pointed to the valley between her tits. "And I want you to come all over me."

"Is that all you want?" Vi shook her head no. She looked away from my eyes to gaze out the window. "Whatever you want, it's yours. Just name it."

"I...." Vi cleared her throat. "I want you to make love to me." That I hadn't been expecting, she pulled her knees up and hugged her knees as she looked up at me.

It took a lot to shock me, and what she said had, but what shocked me more was that I wanted to give her what she wanted. There were very few things that I'd been certain about—being a firefighter was one of those things, and wanting to be a part of the kink lifestyle was the other. Deciding that I wanted to take six months and travel the world was another certainty that I wanted and was going to make happen, but falling in love and everything that went along with it was not one of them. The life I'd seen between my birth parents and, ultimately, what happened to my brother had set me on a course of being sure that was something I never wanted.

Yet, here I was, staring into Vi's blue eyes, and I couldn't picture being with anyone else. I couldn't imagine being comfortable enough with anyone else to bring them here to this little haven with my mom and meet those I now call family.

I took a step back from the bed as it became clear and the reality rocking my system to its core.

"I'm sorry, that...that was a terrible request." Violet jumped from the bed. "I don't even know where that came from." She grabbed for the hoodie that was lying on her travel bag. "Really, I'm sorry, I have a big mouth, and I was just caught up in the moment. It's way too soon for things like that," she said, her voice muffled as she pulled the hoodie over her head.

My brain finally decided to kick into gear, and I grabbed the top of the hood and pulled the sweater back off.

"What are you doing?" she asked, her eyes following where I tossed her hoodie.

Vi's brows knit together as she stared at me, her face flushed and her silky blonde hair wild like she'd already been fucked hard and fast. She was the most stunning sight I'd ever seen. From the moment we'd met she'd stolen the air from my lungs and now they didn't want to work at all without her.

I was unable to get the words free from where they were lodged in my throat, so instead, I cupped her face and kissed her softly. Trailing my fingers down her sides I wrapped my arms around her body, and held her tight against me. I sighed into her mouth as her soft skin rubbed against mine. Gripping her ass cheeks that I'd been dying to touch all night, I pulled her up my body until she wrapped her legs around my waist.

Vi chuckled as I crawled onto the bed with her hanging from me until I laid her down so her head was on a pillow. Settling my weight on her body felt right and exactly where I was supposed to be.

Lifting my head and breaking the kiss, I stared down into her eyes.

"It's not a stupid request," I said and smoothed back some of the wild strands of her hair. "I never dreamed of loving someone or making love to someone like most do."

I kissed the corner of her mouth as I moved my hips around until I could feel her pussy lips part for me. She moaned softly as I kissed the other side of her mouth.

"I didn't dream of having a family of my own." Dropping my head, I captured her lips as I pushed inside her, and we moaned together. "Until now."

Vi's walls were gripping and releasing me like they were massaging my cock, and the control I'd managed to gain was quickly slipping. The feel of her breasts rubbing against my chest as we kissed made me tremble with a desire to consume her entire body. I wanted to make every inch of her mine, and keep it that way.

Vi whimpered into my mouth as I kept my pace even. Her arms wrapped around my neck and held me tighter, and I could feel every part of her body tense right before she came. I swallowed down her moan that started with my name and ended the same way.

That was what I always wanted from now on. No matter what we did, I wanted her to say my name and say she only wanted me when we were done. Not because I told her to say it but because that was what she wanted.

"Come for me again. I want to feel you come all over me," I growled into her ear, and her body shivered against mine.

"Yes, I want to come all over you," she said, her voice breathy.

"Roll onto your side," I said, pulling out and laying down behind her as she moved. Grabbing her leg, I flung it over myself and couldn't get back inside her fast enough. Gripping Vi's chin, I kissed her hard as I continued to work her body over. My release was closing in, and I wanted to give her what she'd requested. Slipping my hand down her body, I tweaked her clit, which was quickly swelling, and softly rolled it between my fingers.

"Oh fuck," Vi said, breaking the kiss. "Yes, keep doing that, oh, fuck, Asher," she screamed and arched her back as she came again. Her nails dug into my hip, where she was grabbing. It was the most delicious bite of pain. The moment the waves of her climax subsided, I slipped from her body and loved that she rolled onto her back, and her eyes were glazed over with the intense pleasure. There was not a sweeter look.

Straddling her body, I got myself settled between her breasts, and she pressed them together, holding me snugly. There was no holding back now, my control was gone, and I thrust hard between the soft mounds and groaned as she opened her mouth so my cock could slip into her mouth with every forward thrust of my hips. I grabbed the old metal headboard that was beginning to bang loudly as the bed squeaked under the abuse. My muscles tensed, my jaw clenching as the orgasm hit.

The pleasure was so intense that it stole the yell from my throat. Dropping my head, I stared down at Vi, who leaned forward to suck my cock into her mouth, and shuddered at the sight of her cheeks hollowing as my come coated her neck and chin.

Slumping against the headboard, I caught my breath but refused to look away from the woman that I could say for certain I was falling in love with, or maybe I'd fallen already.

"Think you are up for round two on that shower?" I asked, already picturing having her again up against the wall.

"Only if you fuck me in there." She smiled.

Oh yeah, I'd definitely fallen.

Not
even the
Devil could burn
the world like
I could

Chapter 33

Derek

Why was I doing this to myself? Was it a sick fascination to continue to pour salt into the ever-growing wound that had become my life? Searching my image in the rearview mirror, I took in the stupid Santa hat I'd picked up on a whim and then wiped away the juice from the southern fried chicken I'd picked up at a local diner.

"Merry fucking Christmas to me." I mumbled as I polished off the last of the mashed potatoes and gravy that tasted exactly like they looked, which was like a pile of dog shit. Tossing the takeout container on the floor of the truck, I picked up the bag that held my dessert. I pulled out the lone piece of key lime pie and took out my lighter. My first birthday outside of the Asylum, and this was how I chose to spend it. Stalking my brother and eating food that I wouldn't feed to farm animals, but it was all that was open in the area.

Turning my head, I looked at the window of the small cabin that had finally gone dark and lit my lighter. I held it up in front of the pie since I didn't have a candle.

"Happy fucking birthday to me."

"Happy fucking birthday to me."

"Happy birthday, you fucking monster. Happy fucking birthday to me."

I blew out the lighter, and the truck was plunged into darkness. "Well, brother, this is the closest I've been to you for my birthday in nine years. Did you even think of me today? Bet you didn't. I bet you were too busy to be bothered to think about your brother."

Picking up the piece of pie, I bit into it and was shocked that it tasted half decent. I glanced at the bottle of whiskey I'd picked up.

"Do you know how much trouble you caused?" I asked the bottle as I polished off the pie. "Do you know how many nights it was because of you that I ended up sitting in the emergency room on my birthday?" I shook my head. "I bet you don't give a shit. I'm nothing but a memory you wish you never had. Probably you don't think of me at all anymore." I wasn't sure if I was still talking to the bottle or my brother. Didn't matter wasn't like either were listening.

An ache constricted my chest, and I hated that it hurt. Nothing my brother did, or does, should hurt me anymore. He lost that right when he left me for dead at the hands of that whack-job doctor and his sidekicks.

The minutes on the dash ticked on and my fingers drummed

along the top of the steering wheel as the anger sparked and began to burn brighter.

"Fuck this shit," I growled out and flicked the hood up on my jacket before hopping out of the truck. Once outside, I pulled on the black leather gloves. The grass was dried out and crunchy, and I could picture this entire area raging with fire as it spread from one lawn to the next.

I loved spots like this.

The areas where the people didn't like to see their neighbors any more than I did, and they had a wide girth of trees lining either side of the property. It was great cover, and I was able to slip easily from the road to the shadows of the tall trees. Then, I veered off and headed to the cabin.

There was still a light on in the main house, but I knew that Asher was in the small visitor's cabin. I'd seen him take a suitcase in when I did my earlier drive-by. Getting low, I stepped slowly toward the window and listened for any sound coming from inside. Peering in, I realized that the spot was much smaller than it even looked from the outside, and my brother was no more than six feet away from me.

"What the fuck?" I whispered as I stared at the blonde curled up next to my brother. Like a fucking magic trick, there was Ms. Fucking High and Mighty Violet Clarke. This was the best fucking birthday gift. I could remove both problems in one go.

My gaze shifted back to Asher, and he looked the exact same as he had when we were kids. How many times had I sat up at night and watched him sleep as I listened for sounds of our father moving around. I made sure he stayed safe, I made sure he could sleep just like this.

It was strange how people could age and yet look identical to their younger self. I felt like I looked like a monster while he still looked like the perfect golden boy, still sleeping peacefully. The stupid ache was back in my chest as I stared at his relaxed face, and my hand shook around the lighter in my pocket. I'd planned on setting the place on fire, wanting to see how good of a firefighter he really was, but I couldn't do it.

It didn't make sense.

He'd turned on me. He'd abandoned me, and here he was with a new family, a beautiful girlfriend, and a job like a normal person while I was lurking around in the shadows, unable to be a part of anything. I had no one.

Find your brother, reach out to him, and heal the wounds that lie between you. You are each other's only family now and all you have left. Don't make light of that.

Dora's dying words played on a loop in my head, and tears pricked at my eyes. Crouching down, I smacked at the side of my head and silently screamed as I tried to push the pain away. Seething, I got up and stomped back to my truck, not caring if the entire house saw me.

Slamming the door, I ripped off the balaclava mask and yelled as my fist found the dash over and over again. Starting the truck, I peeled away from the curb and raced for anywhere that was not here. A large sign came into view that announced it was a park with washrooms and a picnic area, and I drove into the lot, gravel flying. The tears were streaming down my face as I parked and grabbed the bottle I'd been traveling around with like it was my passenger. In a way, it was. It always had been just in different forms.

But tonight, it was going to be my companion.

Cracking the lid, I tossed it aside and chugged back the disgusting liquid that burned going down. I liked the burn. I like everything that burned, which made it feel like all the anger and sins were being seared away. I flopped down on one of the benches and watched the odd car pass. This was an out-of-the-way area, and if I wanted to, I could walk down to the water and let the alligators have me. That would end all of this. Maybe I'd finally find some peace in the nothingness that would follow.

Gripping my head between my hands, I put my elbows on the table and let the memories that wanted to bombard me come to the surface.

"Derek?" Asher whispered into the darkness of our room. I didn't sleep much, and when I did, it was only when I was sure father was passed out or not home. "You still awake?"

Rolling my eyes, I sat up to stare at my brother across the room. I could just make out his outline against the plain white wall of the room.

"Yeah, what's up?" I asked, keeping my voice low.

There was a rustling from the other side of the room. A moment later, Asher was hopping up onto my bed with me. I was about to tell him, no fucking way, I was sleeping with him again. He was getting too old for his big brother to be holding him at night so he could sleep, but instead he held out his hand.

It was too dark to tell what he was holding, and I leaned over to my night table and grabbed the miniature flashlight I'd stolen from the convenience store. Flicking it on, I stared at Asher's favorite football card. He'd spent months looking for this card and had to trade away almost all of his others to get this one rookie card of his favorite player. I looked at it and then up into Asher's eyes.

"Okay, what about it."

Asher looked down, his face falling. "I'm sorry, mom and dad forgot your birthday again. I want you to have my card as your birthday gift." He lifted his shoulder. "I don't have anything else to give you."

My chest warmed as I stared into my younger brother's face. "I don't need your card. I don't even like football. You keep it. It means a lot to you."

He grabbed my hand and placed the card on my palm. "No, I want you to have it. I love you, Derek, and I have nothing to give you to show you how much you mean to me. This is what I have. It's all I have. Take it. Please."

How the hell was I supposed to say no to that? Nodding, I closed my hand and wrapped it around the card. "I'll keep it with me always."

I gulped for air as more memories hit one after the other. Ones that I'd long forgotten and others I tried to forget. Suddenly, something cold pressed into the side of my head.

"Give me your fucking money, man, and that bottle," the unknown man said.

"Not a good time, friend. You may want to move along," I said, giving him a chance to walk away alive. People had really fucking bad timing. Then again, most humans were shitholes and deserved to burn.

"Are you fucking stupid, man? I have a gun to your head."

"Does it look like I care?" That should have been this idiot's cue to run along. Don't mess with people that don't care if they die. That should be the first thing you learn before you decide to be an asshole.

He pressed the gun harder into the side of my head. "Just give me your fucking money, man. I don't wanna have to kill you."

The turmoil that had already been brewing in my gut erupted. Jerking backward, I leaned back on the picnic table seat and grabbed the asshole's arm. Pushing it away from me, I hauled off and cracked him as hard as I could on his exposed ribs. He cried out in pain as my fist found the sensitive spot just under his chest cavity, and the gun went off with a loud bang. That shit had my ears ringing.

I stared in horror as the stray bullet took out one of the headlights on my truck

"Are you fucking kidding me?" I bellowed and stood gripping the guy's arm so hard he cried out, but I was beyond caring. He started this. He could've walked away, I gave him the opportunity twice to fuck the hell off, and he didn't. "Do you know how much one of those antique lights cost?"

With a hard jerk, the guy landed face-first on the table. "Do you know where I can get one? I don't!" I raged as I thought about Dora and the smile she had on her face when I restored the truck. "You piece of shit," I growled out and smashed his arm against the table hard enough that he let go of the gun.

I hated guns. They were a cheap and a chicken-shit way to kill someone. You want to fight, then fight but use your fists. You want to kill someone than have enough balls to do it right and slit their throat or burn them alive. Now, if you could stomach that, then you were worthy of the kill. If you have to shoot a gun and then run, you're nothing but a cheap imitation.

"I'm sorry, man," he whined, but it was too late for that.

I could tell the guy was a tweaker in the dim light of the lone lamp post. His eyes had dark circles and were sunken into his head, while his cheeks showed off every bone in his face. Terror stared up at me, but the hurt and the rage were too potent for me to see straight.

Grabbing the whiskey off the table with one hand and yanking the guy with my other arm, I dragged him toward the large garbage barrel. His struggles were pathetic at best. The girl from the warehouse had more fight than this guy.

"Please, man. I'm sorry. I'll leave you alone, man."

"You almost put a bullet in the side of my head so that you could get high. No, I don't think we're all right, man," I drawled, my tone sarcastic.

I kicked over the green barrel. The top flew off, and the garbage inside, spilled out onto the ground.

"You know what my father always told me?"

"I don't care, man, just let me go," he yelled and pulled hard on his arm.

I had my hand wrapped around his bicep like an iron shackle. My boot found the middle of his stomach with a hard kick that drove all the air from his lungs and stopped him from struggling. I released his arm, and he crumpled to the grass in a ball. Sitting the barrel upright, I tossed in whatever I knew would burn fast and hot.

Life choices. It all came down to our decisions, didn't it?

My father chose to beat the shit out of me and drink heavily, and he found himself an early grave at the hand of the son he chose to hurt. If you could call it that, those that treated me like shit at the hospital got what they had coming to them, too. Each one burned alive as they screamed for forgiveness. This man chose to do drugs, and this was where the road led him.

What would his life have looked like if he'd chosen a different path?

No one would ever know, but it probably would've been a fuck load better than being burned alive inside a barrel with garbage. Life choices were important. That really should be taught more to kids.

He hadn't tried to get away as he continued to wheeze on the ground, but I wasn't taking any chances and cracked him across the face with a hard right hook. His body went limp in his semi-conscious state. The man weighed nothing as I picked him up, and I stuffed him feet first into the barrel. He groaned and slumped down.

I could almost picture the guy's appearance before the addiction took control of his mind. Without asking, I'd assumed he was estranged from his family. Maybe he didn't have a real friend left because the only people that would hang around him were others with the same addiction. Could you trust and call someone a friend who would sell their soul for the next high?

Putting my hand in my sweater, I pulled out the small canister of accelerant I'd planned to use on the cottage and my brother, squirted it all onto the guy in the barrel, and then tossed it in with him. Grabbing the bottle of whiskey, I took a large swig before the rest was poured on the guy's head.

"Pleeease, man."

Another time and place, on any other night, I may have stopped myself from hitting the igniter on my lighter. Instead, I pulled it from my pocket and flipped open the lid to hit that little wheel. A soft whir and click would be the last thing this guy heard before he died. Well, that and his own screams as I tossed the lighter into the barrel.

The screaming was instant, and I stepped back as the heat flared and soared into the night sky as my creation came to life. He knocked the barrel over as he thrashed around inside, and I stared at his body as he rolled around on the ground. I waited until only the twitching of the smoking carcass remained before I walked away.

For whatever reason, I didn't get the same enjoyment out of this kill that I normally would. Pausing, I bent and picked up a small brown wallet that must have fallen out of the guy's pocket and flipped it open, but the sound of a siren in the distance had me closing it and putting it in my back pocket before marching for my truck. I'd forgotten about the gunfire, and you couldn't be too careful even though I hadn't touched it. Grabbing the gun off the picnic table, I flicked the safety on and ran to the truck.

I glanced at the broken glass from the headlight and swore again. Fucking kid, fucking choices.

Chapter 34

Violet

I'd never pictured wearing an ugly Christmas sweater and being happy, and I certainly had never dreamed about meeting someone like Asher or his family and wanting to be part of their lives. Yet, here I was, and I couldn't be happier.

Breakfast had been massive, and by the time we were done, I didn't think I could handle being out on the water and not be sick.

"You sure you don't want to come," Asher asked. I could tell he was disappointed, but the thought of being sick over the side of the boat and not enjoying Christmas dinner didn't sit right.

I picked up the charm on the necklace Asher gave me and played with it between my fingers. "I might be a daredevil, but my stomach knows its limits after two helpings of breakfast. I'm going to nap and keep Monique company." I stepped in close to his half-naked body and wondered if I was crazy for not going with them. Any excuse to see him shirtless in the sun was a good one. "Besides, this way, I'm well rested for after dinner," I whispered and wrapped my arms around his waist.

"Is that so? I'm looking forward to dessert as well." When he smiled, I followed suit before he kissed me, leaving me completely speechless.

"Come on, Asher, we got to go if we want to make it back in time for dinner," Sabrina called out.

"I guess that's my cue."

"I promise next time I won't eat so much so I can go," I offered.

"Next time, huh?"

Clearing my throat as the warmth spread across my cheeks with the blatant assumption.

"I like the sound of that." Asher said and smiled.

"Today, Asher, or we are shoving off without you," Sabrina said again. This was apparently her tradition, and she was very protective over it.

"You better go. I don't need to be the catalyst of a family feud," I teased.

Asher kissed my forehead, then turned and jogged off to the dock and the boat waiting for him. I waved as I watched it speed away and walked back to the main house. The smells in the kitchen were already making my mouth water despite having just eaten. Monique liked to do things a little differently and would prepare a traditional Christmas dinner but also smoked a pork-wrapped turducken. I had no idea what exactly that was, but my mouth began to water when she was describing it.

"Monique, you need any help?" I called out as I walked into the kitchen. A pot was boiling, and her knife was on the counter with the vegetables she was cutting, but I didn't hear her anywhere. "Monique?"

I walked out of the kitchen into the hallway and tried to decide which way she'd go.

She would've had to go toward the front of the house and the living room or down the hall to the bedrooms. Deciding on the living room first, I made my way to the room I'd deemed the 'Wrath of Christmas' in my head.

I wished I'd asked Asher how many people were going to be here. They'd all gotten me a gift while I'd only got a gift for Lizzy and Asher. Luckily, Asher had been thinking ahead and picked up gifts for me to give everyone.

He was used to taking care of everything, whereas I liked to do things for myself. Asher's need for control in all areas was going to be a challenge for me. I can see us locking horns over this at some point. Mind you, the smiles and excitement everyone had over 'my gifts' was as exciting as me seeing what I'd gotten them.

"Monique, you in here?"

I poked my head into the room that somehow looked even more like Christmas had exploded inside the walls, but I didn't see her anywhere. I couldn't picture her leaving a boiling pot on the stove, and an eerie feeling crept down my spine. I was being ridiculous. She probably just had to run to the bathroom or decided to get changed.

With each footfall toward the other end of the house, my nerves became more frayed. Why was I so nervous? Shaking it off, I poked my head in the first door where Sabrina and Andrew were staying.

"Monique?"

Moving on, I knocked on the closed washroom door.

"Monique, are you in there?"

There was no reply, and I turned the handle to find the door unlocked and the light off. I swatted the light switch and jumped back, but the room was empty. My heart was hammering inside my chest, and horror movies and serial killers kept playing through my mind regardless of the sun streaming through the window.

The next room was Lizzy's master bedroom, which now held a whole new meaning for me. I smirked at the thought of Asher making me call him Master. The room was as bright and colorful as the owner, but there was still no Monique.

Had she left and forgotten the pot was on?

"Monique?" I called out as I reached the room where she was staying with Sylvia. All was quiet, she wasn't lying down, and my concern spiked.

Marching back toward the front of the house, a door that I'd assumed was a closet opened just as I was passing by, and I screamed and jumped back, making Monica scream and grab for the railing.

"Oh shit, I'm so sorry," I said and grabbed for her arm, so she didn't tumble down the stairs.

"You just scared the shit out of me," she said, laying a hand over her heart.

"Same. I couldn't find you and had all sorts of crazy thoughts racing through my head," we both laughed.

"The cold cellar is downstairs. You can't hear anything down in that room." She held up a canvas bag. "I was missing some vegetables." My heart returned to normal as Monique flicked off the light and closed the door. "Were you needing me?"

"No, I was just wondering if you needed me. I feel terrible that you're cooking this massive meal on your own."

Monique laughed.

"Don't feel bad. First, I hate the boat. To be honest, I hate the water, too. I decided to do the restaurant on the yacht because it came at a great price and was already outfitted with an amazing kitchen. I know crazy, but I don't notice the water on the big boat. Not being able to see more than a couple of inches down into the water freaks me out, but Sabrina made everyone go after Lizzy moved here, and it has become a tradition."

Monique shrugged as she cut vegetables at a lightning-quick pace. I stared at her hand with my mouth hanging open. I'd have been here for days trying to get it all cut, but it seemed like seconds, and most of the vegetables lay in small pieces on the cutting board. She tossed a small piece of carrot into her mouth before turning to look at me with the massive knife in her hand. "Second, I love to cook. This is my passion and helps me escape from all the stress. With the business, IVF, and Sylvia struggling with the thought of it not working, this gives me time to collect myself."

"All right, I'll leave you to it then. If you need me, I will be taking a nap." I held open the door and then stopped and turned to look at the woman who was already focused on her task.

"For whatever it's worth, I hope that the IVF works. You two would make great parents."

Monique turned and looked like she might cry, so I slipped out the door before things became awkward, or we both ended up bawling our eyes out.

Kids. The thought of kids had always horrified me. I wasn't parenting material, or at least I thought. Now, I wasn't so sure. I could picture having kids with Asher. I could picture them having his amazing eyes and a wicked smile that would let them get away with murder. I could also picture a very protective Asher scaring off any boys that came sniffing around our daughter.

Smiling, I stepped into the cottage. The hair stood on the back of my neck a moment before a thick arm wrapped around my throat. I'd taken self-defense, and I'd spent time training with all men, but as my windpipe constricted, my mind was blank other than sheer panic.

Slamming my elbow back, I caught the person in the gut. Other than a slight groan, it did nothing to loosen the grip. My eyes focused on the window across the small space, and I could see a large bear-like man looming behind me. My adrenaline spiked, giving me an extra boost. Kicking back, I caught the guy in the knee.

The groan was enough to tell me I'd injured him, which only encouraged me to bring my heel down on the top of his boot, but that only seemed to hurt me as sharp pain radiated up my leg. Shifting from left to right, I caught him again with a pair of elbows, and the arm released me just enough that I could turn in his grasp and use his massive chest to push off and break the last of his hold.

Stumbling back, I dashed for the bathroom, the only other spot with a door since the exit was blocked and I fumbled for my phone. For his size, he was fast, and with a maneuver that would've impressed any professional wrestler, the man snatched me by the hoodie of Asher's I was wearing. He wrapped his other hand around my throat and slammed me to the floor.

I stared up into the dark hood as the leather glove tightened around my throat. Clawing at the arm didn't do anything. I tried to get a good kick in and almost succeeded until he put a knee on my chest. Pain exploded throughout my body with the weight that felt like a boulder, and the lack of air told me I was dying. This man was going to kill me.

Reaching up, I kept trying to find a way to push this monster off me and somehow got a hold of the hood covering his face. I yanked it off, and the shock froze me in place as I stared into eyes that looked identical to Asher's—taking in the dark hair and the scar on his cheek before finding his eyes again. This was the boy from Asher's family picture I'd seen.

"De...rek?" I whispered through the tight hold and his brow knitted together in what seemed like confusion before the darkness clouded my vision.

Burn

Asher

"Vi, you're going to be so happy you didn't come," I called out as I neared the cabin.

I couldn't stop laughing at Sabrina's face as she pulled in her line expecting a fish and had a massive snake on the end. Of all things that she could've caught it had to be a snake. She hated them with a passion. Her scream was so loud as it burst from the water as if it was pissed about being caught on a fishing hook. We all jumped as it landed on the back of the boat and thrashed around. It took a net and some very quick hands to get it cut loose and back into the water.

"You'll never guess what happened."

Pulling open the screen door to the cabin, I stopped and looked around at the empty space.

"Vi?" I'd already been to the main house, and she wasn't there.

The bathroom door was open, and I was worried that she'd slipped or something. I ran over, but it was empty. What the hell? My eyes scanned the room, her small luggage bag was still there, but something shiny caught my eye. I crouched to pick it up. My fingers gripped the pendant I'd given her for Christmas, and panic had me shooting to my feet and running out the door, looking for any sign to give me a clue.

"Vi?" I yelled like that would be helpful even though I knew it wouldn't. I just had this bad feeling.

"Asher, what's wrong?" My mom came running out of the main cabin, closely followed by everyone else.

"She's gone. Someone has taken her," I said, and everyone just stared at me like I wasn't speaking the same language. "Did you not hear me?"

I whipped out my phone and dialed 911. "I'm calling the police."

"Honey, don't you think you're overreacting? She could be out for a walk," my mom offered.

"Her necklace was on the floor."

"That doesn't mean that she was abducted."

I held up my finger to hold off whatever she was going to say next as the operator came on the line. I didn't mean to be rude or dismiss her logic, but I just knew it wasn't the case. I had no proof, but the churning my gut was telling me. It was the same feeling I got whenever the house would get quiet after dad had one of his rounds with mom. You'd think that all was safe, but it was only the calm before the storm. Then he'd burst into the room. I had that same sick feeling now and had to take a deep breath to calm the fear that was slowly bleeding into anger. If someone hurt her....

"Nine-one-one, what's your emergency?"

"Yes, I need to report an abduction. This is Captain West from the Miami fire station 126."

"Okay, Mr. West. Who is missing?"

"My girlfriend, Violet Clarke," I said. Why hadn't I told Vi that she was my girlfriend? She probably would've liked that.

"And when was the last time you saw Ms. Clarke?"

"About two hours ago, maybe two and a half," I said as I tried to do the math in my head.

"I'm sorry, Mr. West, but the individual has to be missing for twenty-four hours before they're considered missing."

My mouth fell open. "That's ridiculous. I'm telling you someone took her. I found her necklace on the ground in our cabin."

"Was there any other sign of a struggle or forced entry?"

"Well, no, but that doesn't mean anything. Her clothes are here, and she doesn't have a vehicle. I'm telling you that something is wrong. I'm a firefighter, for christ's sake. I know when someone is overreacting. I'm not overreacting," I yelled.

"Please calm down, Mr. West."

I bit my fist and walked away from the five pairs of eyes watching me.

"I'm sorry, but this is very distressing," I said, trying to stay calm.

"I will dispatch an officer to come to speak to you. They should arrive in approximately thirty minutes."

"Thirty minutes?" I pulled the phone away from my ear and stared at it in disbelief. "She could be anywhere by then. I need to speak to someone now."

"That is the closest officer, Mr. West," the operator said.

All I wanted was to lose my shit on them and swear every word I could think of, but I managed to pull myself together. The police thinking I was the one losing it was not a good start.

"Fine, I understand." I quickly relayed the location and hung up the phone only to begin pacing the backyard. My eyes found Monique.

"How did Violet seem to you?"

Monique shrugged. "She seemed fine. She offered to help me cook and then said she was going to take a nap. I haven't seen her since."

"And you didn't see anything or hear anything suspicious?" I asked, glaring at her.

"No, I had Christmas music on and was in the cooking zone. A bomb could've gone off, and I wouldn't have heard it."

"Shit."

My mom walked toward me and tentatively reached for my shoulder like I was some wild animal she was trying to console.

"Asher, sweetie, you need to take a breath. I know you're scared, but...."

"I'm not scared." I squeezed my phone tighter. "I'm angry. If someone has hurt her, I'm going to kill them."

I marched away from my mom and ran back into the cabin to look for any other clues. Realizing I was still in my boating clothes, I stripped out of my swim shorts and pulled on a pair of jeans and a T-shirt. I was just putting on my sneakers when my phone dinged.

Grabbing it, I saw a text from Vi and sighed. When I opened it, there was an image of her tied up and gagged on the floor of a vehicle. Her eyes weren't open, and she had a mark around her neck.

Thump, thump, thump.

My heart pounded hard as my blood pressure rose. I couldn't stop staring at the image that confirmed my fear to be true. There had been a small piece of me holding out hope that she would wander down the driveway after a nice walk and wonder what all the fuss was over.

My eyes drifted down to the message that accompanied the image. I read the message a half dozen times.

No police or I'll burn her alive and send you the video.
Meet me where the baby rabbits used to play.
We have unfinished business.

What the fuck? What kind of message was this? My mind raced as I tried to figure out what the person could mean by baby rabbits.

. . .

"*Derek, come quick. You have to see the baby bunnies,*" *I yelled out the barn door.*

"*It's just rabbits,*" *he called back, putting the wheelbarrow down and walking toward me.*

"*I know, but they are so tiny, just little balls of fur.*" *We'd never been allowed a pet, but here at the Giltberts, we had more animals than I could even keep up with. Dogs, cats, chickens, cows, rabbits, and goats always ran around and needed tending to.*

Derek walked over to where I was standing and stared at the pen of grey balls that could've passed for the furballs that popped off Gizmo when he got wet. Derek lifted a brow as he looked in the pen. If you didn't know him, you would've said he was unimpressed, but the little curl of his lip and the look in his eye told me he thought they were just as cute as I did.

"*Now we will have a bunch of baby rabbits to play with,*" *I said.*

"*Great, well, you better pick one out you want to keep and then hide it before Mr. Giltberts decides to eat them all for dinner.*"

"*Shut up, man,*" *I said as Derek laughed.*

"Holy shit, it can't be," I said, but even as my mind was telling me it was impossible, I grabbed the keys to my truck and ran for the door.

Chapter 35

Violet

The dream was always the same, but instead of running after a faceless boy, this time, I was chasing Asher through the woods. I yelled his name to stop, but he didn't seem to hear or see me. I ran faster, waving my arms, trying to get his attention when the forest burst into flames around me. I skidded to a halt and screamed for Asher to stop as he ran straight into the blaze.

I jerked awake and tried to gasp but found my mouth covered with tape. The images still danced like a vivid movie behind my eyes. The hair on the back of my neck stood as the dream gave way to reality. Someone attacked me. No, not someone, Derek. The man that took my parents from me and Asher's brother, the one we thought was locked up in some prison.

I blinked and stared at the roof of a vehicle as it bounced around. My head hit the floor, and I winced in pain. The sharp pain made it feel like I was being stabbed in the eye. How the hell had he found us? When did he get out? Why the hell was he taking me? I had too many questions. The sound of gravel pinged the underside of the... truck. It was too large to be anything else, and yet it wasn't a modern style. The area was too tight, and the seats had that old leather smell, not to mention the roof was just painted metal.

This was one of those moments that I'd randomly thought about after watching a true crime show or a horror flick. What do you do when a bad person has you? Do I kick the doors and try to make a lot of sounds, potentially piss Derek off more, but try to get someone's attention? Or do I play possum and maybe be able to rationalize with him from doing...I had no idea, but considering he needed to abduct me to make it happen said a lot about how this was going to go.

My decision was made for me when the truck slowed down a moment later. I could see trees lining either side, and my pulse went through the roof as the truck was pulled into some sort of garage or shed.

I pressed myself into the floor as hard as I could when Derek's large arm gripped the back of the seat I was lying behind. He peered at me, those eyes so intense that it felt like I would burst into flames from his stare alone.

"Good, you're awake. I'm surprised you didn't scream or kick the shit out of my truck. You seem like the type," he said and opened his door.

Good was not the word I would've used to describe this situation. The slam of his door shook the vehicle, and I tried to swallow down the terror that was clawing at my throat. I had decided I was never going to date, and then when I did, I met the two people who had haunted my dreams for years in different ways. What kind of luck do you call that?

The back door opened, and he looked larger now than he did in the cabin. I tried to ball myself up like that would somehow help. Derek grabbed the ties he had wrapped around my ankles and, with a single jerk, had me out the door and over his shoulder like I weighed nothing.

He carried me out of a large shed, and a couple of things struck me right away, despite the fading daylight. The first was that we were on a farm, and the second was that we were in the middle of nowhere. Even if I could break free, how far would I have to run to find another person before he caught me again?

I closed my eyes as vomit tried to rise. Maybe I'd been the target all along. Maybe my parents died because of me, and like some reaper, he was back to finish the job. Derek dropped me as unceremoniously as he'd picked me up, and I groaned as my tailbone came into contact with the hard dirt floor. My back and head slammed into the hard wooden beam behind me, and once more, my head screamed from the abuse. Derek knelt, and I realized he was somehow tying my already secure hands to the beam.

The smell of animals and mold bombarded my senses as a lone pigeon took flight telling us off for disturbing it as it went. I held still as he gripped the tape covering my mouth between his fingers and gave it a hard pull.

"Ahh," I yelled with the sting.

We stared at one another, neither of us saying anything for what seemed like forever.

"I see you've been looking for me. Did you like my work?" he asked like we were two old friends talking about the weather. I'd been in many different situations over the years with friends, but somehow they had never tied me up in a barn before.

"I know your brother," I blurted out instead of answering the question I didn't have an answer to that wouldn't unravel the situation further.

"Oh, I know. I know everything, and I couldn't have planned the two of you finding one another any better if I tried," the way he said that didn't give me any comfort.

I licked my lips. "Your father did that to you, didn't he?" I asked, nodding toward the side of his face. "Asher told me all about the abuse. I'm sorry for that, I am, but what happened to you didn't have anything to do with me. If anything, you hurt me," I said, the first real threads of anger seeping into my tone.

Derek smiled and traced a finger down the side of his face to follow the line of scared tissue. "I bet he told you his version, the one where he was the hero," Derek snarled.

"No, he told me he'd be dead if it hadn't been for you."

Derek stayed quiet and stared at me. "My father made me, you know. I go by Dragon now, and fire will never hurt me again. It's my pet. I would thank the man if he weren't already dead." He turned his head and showed off the second line stretched toward his ear. They stood out on his handsome face, yet somehow, they suited him and made him look rugged. "He made me strong."

"He made you into a fucking killer," I said and then swallowed hard, wishing I'd learned to think before I said shit.

"Depends on how you look at it. I see it as cleansing the world of the shit that is running rampant. You didn't say, did you like my work? I mean, I've kept you busy enough. Watching all of you run all over town as you chased your pathetic tails was amusing," Derek said, and it hit me.

He wasn't talking about my parents and what happened years ago. He was the serial arsonist that we'd been hunting all this time.

"The police say they caught the right guy," Derek scoffed and rolled his eyes at me.

"You didn't believe for a single second that they had the right guy. The weasel they have in custody is a wannabe copycat, and not a very good one at that. Fucker is trying to claim my actions for his own glory, but that's fine. He can have it for now." He shrugged. "It will be more entertaining this way when they realize they have the wrong guy and have to start all over again."

I didn't like how he was talking. The way he spoke made it seem like I wasn't a threat, and if I wasn't a threat, it meant I was dead. That was the only way I wasn't going to go straight to the police.

"Meh, your work is good, but I've seen better," I lied, not sure why I was pushing this guy's buttons. Then again, I had nothing to lose at this point.

Derek smirked, and at another time and place, I would've said it was sexy.

"You know, Violet Clarke, it's a shame I have to kill you. I like your sass. I can see why Asher likes you. Just so you know my brother can be a real ass. Loyalty is not his strongest trait so you better watch out," I couldn't tell if he was trying to joke with me or not.

"It seems to run in the family," I said and once more kicked myself in the ass, but Derek laughed the sound jovial as he smiled and rubbed the back of his neck. This was too weird, even for me. It wasn't every day that you met the person that killed your family, but this situation was one of those that I could never have planned for.

"I don't know why you have to kill me. It's not like I've ever done anything to you. You killed my parents. I lost everything, and yet here you are, tying me up like I wronged you. You can go fuck yourself."

Derek rocked back on his heels as I glared at him and pictured all sorts of fun and new ways to kill him.

"I need to kill you because it will hurt my brother. This is his payback. I was just going to kill him, and you would be collateral damage, but then I thought this was kind of poetic. A full circle kind of thing." My blood was boiling as he continued to talk. "You know, I watched you for weeks," he said. "Back then, I mean. I watched you sneak out of your window and run off into the woods almost every night. I could almost time my watch by when you'd make your great escape." He moved his fingers like they were a person running and smiled at me.

I wanted nothing more than to be able to wipe that smug look off his face.

"Why did you do it? Why did you kill my parents? They didn't even know you!"

"Ha!" Derek yelled and stood. "Did you really think I just came across your house and decided, yup, that's the family I want to kill?"

"I didn't know what to think. I was fourteen, and I've spent my entire life looking for you," I yelled. "I wanted you to pay for what you did."

The laugh that tumbled from his mouth wasn't a happy one. "Oh, I paid. I paid more than you could ever even imagine."

I sucked in a deep breath as I stared at his face. Ghosts were haunting those bright blue eyes that were clinging to the fabric of who he was. Pulling back on my pain, which was the hardest thing I'd had to do, I thought about all the files that Asher and I had poured over and the one thing they all had in common. People that abused others, people that had wronged another in a way that most would find unredeemable, but the fires that were tied to cases involving children were the most horrific. There were a few exceptions, but they were not the norm.

"Please. I've spent the last ten years wondering why. Why them? Why my family?"

Derek stopped pacing and stared down at me, his eyes were angry, but there was hurt that lay beneath the anger.

"Because your parents knew. They knew that Asher and I were being abused and didn't do anything about it, even when they had the chance."

My mouth fell to the floor, and anger had me lashing back. "Take that back. It's not true."

"Oh, it is true. It's very fucking true."

"I don't believe it. My parents had their flaws, but they would never condone child abuse."

Derek stomped toward me, and I couldn't stop from leaning back as he squatted and grabbed my face. I cringed as he squeezed my jaw hard. I didn't remember being hit, but my face felt all bruised.

"You have no idea," he snarled, and my anger wavered slightly. "Your mother came to my house all the time, made friends with my mother, and never helped take us away from the abuse. You want to know what would happen every time she showed up and stayed long enough that my father got home?"

Derek released my jaw, and I could feel the rage building inside of him.

"He'd hurt you and Asher," I said.

"No, he'd hurt me. Asher only got touched once. I wouldn't let him hurt my brother. That bitch you called mother knew what my father was like. I'd told her, Asher had told her and even my mother had opened up about the beatings we endured and yet...what did she do? Nothing!" He stomped away and then wheeled around, his large body shaking. "She knew he'd hurt us, and she'd stay until my father got home. That's a sadistic bitch, that's not a good person."

He looked away from my eyes, but I could see the pain he was hanging onto. He felt betrayed. As his eyes swung back to mine, it was as if he'd sucked the air out of the room. Like a flick of a switch on and off he swung between eerily calm and enraged, and each time it came back, it burned brighter inside of him.

"I saw your mom one day driving home. She was singing away to a song in the car without a care in the world. It wasn't right that my father got to do what he did, and your mother, who was supposed to help, did nothing and then got to head on home to her perfect life, forgetting about us. She got what she deserved."

I narrowed my eyes at Derek, I had no idea about what my mom did or didn't do at work, but she didn't deserve to burn alive for it.

"I see your anger, Violet. I see the hurt in your eyes at losing your parents. A part of me is sorry for your pain. I had nothing against you, but whether you want to believe it or not, your parents were evil. They hid behind masks of smiles and popularity. You want to know what your father did? It wasn't just your mom, you know. I was after both of them."

I looked away from his eyes, my heart beating hard with anger and confusion. How could even a tiny part of me feel bad for this man? He'd taken everything I loved and shaped me into this person, this...obsessed shell.

Derek wandered back over and squatted down once more.

"What did he do?" I asked, my voice soft. A part of me didn't want to know. Was he going to tarnish my parents' memory further?

"He was a family court judge."

"I know that," I said and wished I could move my arms. They were starting to go numb.

"I wasn't finished. He was a judge that liked to give children back to their abusive homes."

I opened my mouth to argue, but Derek held up his finger and growled like a dog, freezing the words in my throat.

"Don't say it's not true. You don't have a fucking clue. Did you go sit in court and watch your precious daddy work? Did you ever ask him about his job? Did you even once consider that every decision he made affected another's life?"

I closed my mouth. I didn't know. I'd never been to his courtroom. The thought of sitting there all day and listening to legal stuff had seemed boring.

"I did," Derek said. "I sat in the back of his court for days and watched families plead to have someone arrested or restraining orders put into place. I watched children cry on the stand, and your father had the nerve to say that parents deserved the right to be with their kids."

Derek burst to his feet, and I flinched as his massive fist hit the pole I was tied to. The whole building sounded like it groaned with the abuse. Dust and dirt fell onto my head, and I coughed and choked on the particles.

"The parents' rights!" He bellowed so loud that it echoed in the large open space. "What about the children's rights?"

He marched away, and when he turned back to stare at me, I saw the face that all those that died at his hands saw. There was a fissure in his mind that had broken. When, I didn't know, but I could see it in his eyes as he tried to rein it back in like he was arguing with someone else.

"Didn't I have rights? Didn't my brother?"

Even though I didn't want to, all I could picture was a young Asher terrified and hiding from his father, and I hated how that sat like a rock in my stomach. I hated that Derek was making me feel bad for him and what he'd done.

"So now you're planning on killing me to get back at your brother. Do you even know that he talks about you all the time?"

"Bullshit."

"It's the truth. He loves you, Derek."

"Shut up!"

Derek picked up a canister, and I shivered as I stared at the red metal can. He walked to a far wall and a large pile of loose hay before setting it down as if he was preparing his stage. All the other kills had been the same. The perfect angles, wind, or accelerants were used to make the fire travel at his will.

"I chose you before I knew you were with my brother. That's just a bonus."

"Why? What the hell did I do other than my job? You pissed off that I was hunting you and getting close?"

Derek laughed as he lit the first old-style lantern. I quickly realized he had them placed all around the barn and the thought of burning alive became a lot more real in my mind.

"You weren't close to catching me. I thumbed through all your notes and theories, and I mean, you were on point with some of them, but who I was...." Derek looked over at me as he replaced the glass topper of the next lantern. "You had no clue. I would've gone months or years without you coming close."

"Gloating now? You didn't seem like the type," his glare had me reconsidering my life choices. You'd think I'd learned by now not to poke at the bear.

"You're right about that. I'm not the type to gloat, which is why I know you weren't close. I don't leave behind calling cards, and I certainly don't stick to patterns."

I shook my head. "Fine then, why me," I asked, exasperated as my head pounded harder with the start of a migraine.

"Because you tried to save Sarah. I mean, she died in the end, but you did ruin my first attempt," he said casually, as if we weren't discussing a person's life.

"The apartment across from me? That's what this is about?"

"Yes. You don't know how many times I watched you jump from your balcony to Sarah's like you were trying out for a staring role in an action movie. Over and over again, I watched as you rescued my prey. My pet didn't get to eat, so you needed to be punished."

"Okay, can we be real here for a moment? What did you think someone would do if they saw that and thought they could help?"

"Why didn't you just stay out of it? She deserved to die for what she was doing. Why would you want to help her? You're just like your parents."

I'd never wanted to yell 'yes' and 'no' at the same time before.

"If what you say my parents did is true, then no, I'm nothing like them." I snarled and tried to shift around the beam enough to keep my eyes on him.

With the setting sun, the barn was beginning to glow softly. On any other occasion, I would've said it was romantic, but there was nothing romantic about this.

"Then tell me why you'd want to save a child abuser?"

I opened my mouth and closed it again. It felt like no matter what I said. This was a lose-lose situation.

"I didn't know she was hurting her daughter until after. I interviewed Kim with Asher, and he was the one that saw it in her. I didn't."

"You should have!"

"Maybe, but I'd only met them a handful of times."

"I'd never met her, and I knew."

"Only because you suffered like her!" I yelled back, my chest heaving as we stared at one another. "For as terrible as you say my parents were, I was never abused. How was I supposed to know? I feel terrible that I didn't, but I never saw anything or heard anything...Derek, I would have called the cops if I'd thought Kim was being hurt for even a second." I took a deep breath as I tried to collect myself from the well of emotion. "Do I really seem like the type that would be okay with that? Did you find anything on me that would suggest I like abusive assholes?"

He didn't say anything as he finished lighting the final lantern. Derek picked it up and walked toward me with the metal handle swinging from his hand. No horror movie could properly portray the fear that was coursing through my body.

"So is this it? You're going to kill me now?"

"No." A flush of relief washed through me as I thought that I'd gotten through to him. "I'm waiting on our audience to arrive. Asher needs to see you burn."

If I'd had any hope of making it out of this alive, it died with those words. He was far more delusional than I'd originally thought.

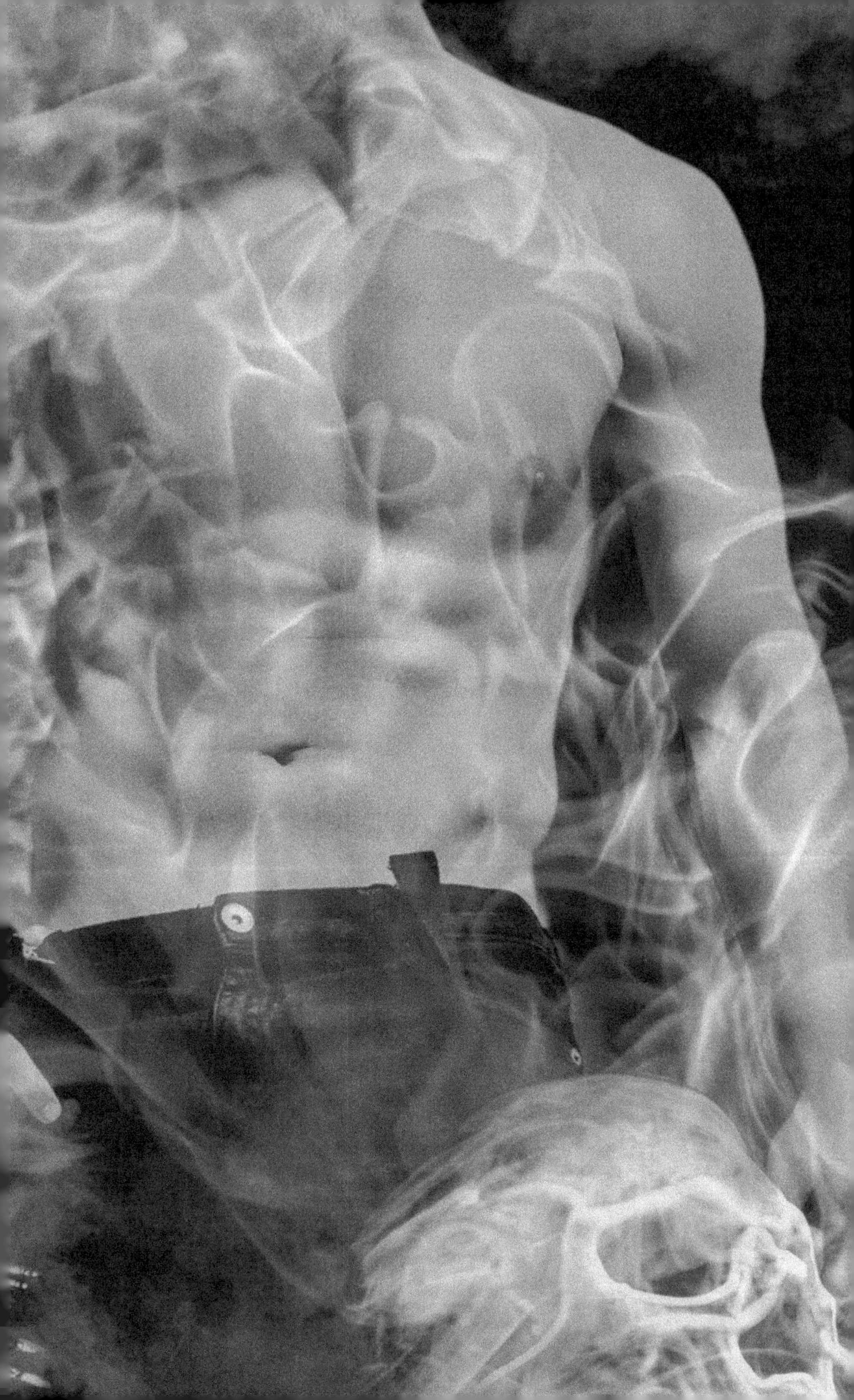

Chapter 36

Asher

The drive back to Miami had never felt so long. The adrenaline and dread coursing through my body kept my foot pressed to the floor and praying that I didn't get stopped. I didn't know if I'd even pull over.

So many things were falling into place and making sense. I felt stupid for not seeing the signs of who this was. It was like, from the very first fire he set, I knew my brother had been taunting me. Telling me he was back and just waiting to see how long it took for me to figure the puzzle out.

He always did like puzzles. It was the one thing he would sit and work at every night. Once he completed one, he'd pull it apart, put it in the box to shake up, and start all over again.

I turned onto the gravel road that led to the Giltberts and I didn't think it could get any worse, but as soon as the big old barn on the hill came into view with the soft glow coming from inside, my stomach rolled. What did he have planned?

I'd been tempted to sneak my way up the driveway, but I could see the motion sensors lining the driveway, and the only other way in was too dangerous in the dark. I'd had more than one scare with an alligator on this property.

Parking the truck, I grabbed the tire iron off the floor in the back and jogged for the large open door. I could hear talking inside, so I slowed down and tried to listen to what was being said.

"No point in slinking around in the dark, Brother. I know you're out there," Derek called out, and a wave of fresh emotion lanced my heart.

It was really him, he was here, and he was alive. I wanted to hug him and tell him everything I had been longing to say for years. Instead, I walked through the large doors and saw Vi tied up, her face covered in dirt, and all I could think about was how much I hated him for putting me back in this position all over again.

My eyes locked with Vi's before they swung back to Derek, who was casually leaning against a support beam. He looked so different and yet exactly the same. Gone was the scrawny teenage boy, replaced with a man that filled the room with his presence.

"I should've known it was you," I said. "You left me so many clues, but I just didn't think that my brother would be capable of killing that many people so callously."

His nostrils flared. "So what, no warm welcome? You're not

coming across the barn and hugging me like old times and telling me you still love me and have missed me?"

"Honestly, I would've if you hadn't been terrorizing all of Miami and then taking Vi." I held the hand with the tire iron toward where she was sitting. "Did you really think I would be happy about any of this?"

"The complete opposite, actually. I wanted you to suffer," Derek said.

My mind raced. "Derek, you killed two innocent people and then our mother. I mean, dad, I could see after what he did to you, but mom? She didn't deserve that. She was just as much of a victim as we were."

"She was no mother to me. Don't use that word for her. She was nothing more than the devil's whore. She could've run, or she could've tried to stop him when he did this." Derek pointed to the side of his face.

"No, she left the room and let him do whatever he wanted," He took a deep breath.

" If you hadn't stopped him...it doesn't matter now. They got what they deserved," he said with a smile.

"And, just so you're caught up, I already explained to Violet here why her parents had to die." I glanced at Vi before turning back to my brother.

"Funny enough, that wasn't a question you thought to ask before you turned me in to the cops. Then again, I shouldn't be surprised coming from the brother that didn't bother to visit me. You certainly showed your true nature." Derek pushed away from the beam.

"Not such a perfect pretty boy after all. You have a dark streak in you too."

I shook my head. "I tried D, but I was fourteen. They took me away from the Giltberts, and when I ended up with Lizzy we tried to find you, but by then, no one could find you. It was like you'd disappeared." I stepped further into the barn and took in the lanterns and gasoline container.

"You are my brother. You were supposed to protect me like I protected you," Derek screamed, his hand shaking as he pulled a lighter out of his pocket.

"Instead, you turned your back on me. You left me for dead in that place."

"What place, D? I didn't know where you were. The police reports were gone. No one would give us any answers." I held up my hands, realizing I was still hanging on to the tire iron, and I dropped it on the ground with a thud.

"Do you remember the asylum fire months ago? Wasn't in your district, but I'm sure you heard about it." Derek flicked open the lighter and closed it again, the clicking sound loud in the quiet barn.

I glanced at Vi, who was sitting like a statue, except for her eyes that were bouncing between us.

"Yes, I remember. That was you?" I asked.

Hundreds had died in that fire. It had burned so hot and damaged so much that it was days before anyone could get inside to inspect it.

"You asked where I'd been, well now you know. They locked me up and proceeded to torture me like I was a fucking lab rat." His hand was shaking now. "They tortured me over and over again. I'd scream your name, and begged that you'd come for me."

He shook his head and it felt like a weight sitting on my chest. I'd feared what had happened to him, but to know that all this time my worst fears were true, hurt like a stab to the heart.

I stepped closer to Vi as Derek's eyes drifted off to a corner of the barn like he was remembering or maybe seeing things I couldn't.

"You okay," I whispered, and she nodded.

"What are you doing?" Derek asked and stepped sideways, putting himself between Vi and me.

"Cut her loose, D. She didn't have anything to do with what happened between you and me, and she doesn't deserve to die. It's me you wanted, so let Vi go." Derek's eyes went to my old knife as I pulled it from my pocket.

He flicked the ignition, and the little flame came to life in his hand. He held it over Vi's head, her eyes wide and terrified. It was then that I noticed her clothes were damp.

Shit. Gasoline.

"D, stop this! If you want me, here I am. Kill me and end this once and for all," I said, my hands going to my chest. Fear filled me as I stared into his eyes and silently begged him not to do this. "I hurt you. I thought I was helping, but you're right it's all my fault that you ended up in that fucking place." My eyes begged for his mercy. "Please don't hurt her."

"I couldn't do it. I couldn't kill you. I walked around your house, touched your things, and sat in your chair." My face must have shown my skepticism.

"It's true. I watched you sleep just like I did when we were kids.

Then again, at your new family's place, the family you traded me in for." The anger was still there, but his voice wavered.

"I watched you through the window, and I still couldn't do it, but it was a stroke of luck that you'd decided to fuck my other target. Now, I get to hurt you without killing you...just her."

Derek looked down at Vi, and I thought about what I'd learned in all my research about the fires.

"D, you're no longer that scared, hurt kid. You can be better. You have been better. You've been going after those that hurt others. Vi is not one of those people, and if you let yourself believe me for just one second, you'd see that neither am I. I've never stopped loving you, D, and I've carried around the pain of my decision all these years."

"She needs to die," he said, but his voice was softer as his hand shook violently.

"No, she doesn't. Vi never hurt you. She's never hurt anyone, please D," I begged. "Don't do this. If you still feel anything for me as a brother, then please don't do this."

Derek lifted his eyes to mine, and I took a deep breath as the lighter closed. Vi slumped against the beam, a terrified whimper coming from her mouth. His eyes suddenly turned dark, and he ran at me, colliding like a football player taking down his opponent.

"Fuck," I swore as my back slammed off the wooden boards, and his fist connected with my jaw. My teeth rattled with the hard impact.

"You should have let him kill me," Derek roared as he landed a second solid blow to my jaw.

"I couldn't. I love you. I couldn't let him take my brother," I yelled back as I blocked the next hit.

"Love? You call this love?" Derek pointed to his face. "I'm a monster! I was made into a thing to be stared at and feared." He gripped the front of my T-shirt and shook me hard.

"No one can love this. No one could ever love me, not even you. Even you were scared of what I'd become!"

Thrusting my hips up, I managed to move him enough to roll us over, but before I could say anything, I was knocked to the side and off his body. I shook my head as Derek stood, and I expected to get a boot in the ribs. I dabbed at my face and blinked as I stared at the red blood.

Derek's sudden scream had my head jerking up. He was wielding the tire iron that I'd brought in, and with each swing, one of the lanterns he had set up went sailing through the air and crashed against the wood.

"Derek, stop!" I yelled as one after the other fires began to ignite all over the barn.

He was beyond hearing as he screamed and yelled out profanities about someone dying. I didn't know what he was talking about, but I had to get Vi out of here. I ran to Vi and grabbed my discarded knife.

"My hands are tied to the post," she said as I dropped down behind the post and proceeded to saw at the rope.

"Fuck, he had to use the thick shit," I swore as a lantern sailed passed my head and smashed into the old pile of hay. The glass shattered on impact and as if setting what was housed inside free, the little flame began to devour the hay and sending flames shooting into the air.

The smoke was thickening, and we were both coughing as the rope finally broke free. My eyes burned as I picked Vi up in my arms and ran for the door coated in bright orange flames like a decorative arch.

I stopped just before we were outside and looked over my shoulder at Derek, who was still raging and smashing the tire iron off everything he could.

"Derek! We have to go," I yelled, but he didn't hear me.

The high beams began to groan as embers fell from above like rain. I bolted out the large barn doorway, knowing I'd go back in for him.

"I'm so sorry. I'll be right back," I said, setting Vi down. I couldn't take the time to cut her free.

"Go. You have to stop him from killing himself," Vi said.

"Asher, don't leave me again," Derek yelled for me.

I ran full speed for the barn that was now almost fully engulfed in flames. I skidded to a stop and had to dive away from the door as the main beam crashed to the ground.

"Ash, help me. I love you, Brother. I'm sorry," Derek screamed. "Don't leave me like this."

"Derek, I can't get in." I ran around the side of the barn as more groaning and crashing came from inside. "Derek!" I lapped the building looking for another way in, and my chest constricted. I couldn't breathe. No, this wasn't happening. My brother couldn't die like this. "Derek, answer me!"

I was a firefighter. I knew that no one could survive the smoke, let alone the heat, without protection, and yet I still tried to peer through the raging flames to find my brother.

"No!" I screamed and went to my knees as the walls caved in and, one by one, folded in on themselves.

"Derek," I whispered, rocking forward and grabbing the dirt as the pain gripped me. Nothing had felt real, seeing his face, knowing he was alive. It all became real as the fire roared, sending flames and smoke into the air. I could hear the distant call of a fire engine and knew someone had called for help, but it was too late. Getting up, I walked toward Vi, she had tears streaming down her face, and once more, I collapsed to my knees.

"Asher, I'm so sorry," she said, and I felt like I was on autopilot as I cut the bindings on her hands and feet. As soon as she was free, she hugged me tight, and I buried my head into the side of her neck and let it all out. The tears wracked my body as I physically experienced the loss of my brother for the second time.

She gripped me hard as I rocked against her like it was the only thing keeping me from drowning in the sorrow that wanted to swallow me whole.

"Is going to be okay," Vi said. "I've got you."

Epilogue

Violet

"Are you sure you're okay?" I jerked out of the memory of the barn burning to stare at Beck. Her eyes were shrouded with worry. They had been since Asher and I made it back from the farm, and I called her on the way.

"Yeah, I will be. It still seems like a dream that turned into a nightmare. I mean, Asher and I went from strangers to lovers, to wonderful Christmas holiday, and then having to save one another. I mean...I don't even know what to call that." I turned my head to look at Asher, sitting by the water with his mom.

It had been a week, and he'd barely spoken. I'd catch him crying when he thought I wasn't looking. I knew his pain. I understood that loss, yet I felt lost as to how to help him.

"Yeah, when I said you needed to add more excitement to your life, this was not what I had in mind," Beck teased but reached out and gripped my arm as she smiled at me.

"I'm worried about him," I said, nodding toward Asher. "He's trying hard to pretend he's okay, but I know he's not. He feels responsible for all of it, and it's eating at him."

Beck's fruity drink rattled as she swirled it around. "You love him, don't you?"

I glanced over at Beck and then back to Asher. I didn't know why I was watching him. Maybe I was waiting for him to break or show that he was doing better. Whatever it was I couldn't say, and I knew I was hovering, but the panic I felt when I couldn't see him was real.

"Yeah, I love him, Beck. I know it hasn't been that long, but...the emotions are so strong, and this situation with my parents and his brother, which in reality should've driven us further apart, has only brought us closer together." I rubbed my eyes.

"Then just keep being here for him. It's all you can do right now," she said. "He will find the other side of the sadness and will figure out a way to cope. You did, and it didn't happen overnight."

Nodding, I decided to change the topic. "How are things going with...um...I'm sorry, what's his name?" I shook my head. "I'm sorry, I'm a terrible friend right now."

Beck snorted. "Actually, calling him 'what's his name' is perfect. Let's not talk about him." She crossed her arms over her chest.

"Oh, that bad, huh?"

"I won't bore you with the details right now, but I dodged a bullet, and I'm happy you haven't found a new apartment yet. I was going to ask if I could have my old room back?"

I laughed. "Girl, you can always have a room, anywhere, anytime with me. Besides, I spend all my time here with Asher anyway. I'm not sure if he wanted me to move in, but he gave me drawers to put clothes in and cleaned out half his closet, so I'm taking that as his way of offering even though he hasn't said the words."

"Girl!" Beck squealed, and Asher and Lizzy turned around to look at the commotion. "Sorry, I'm just a loud, obnoxious friend," Beck called out to them, and I laughed.

Asher smiled, and it was good to see. He was so sexy, but it was like Derek dying had rubbed a bit of shine off of him. Like part of him died along with his brother, and it broke my heart.

"That is very good indeed. Means he's serious about you," Beck said, and we sat back in the comfortable chairs and let the silence fill the space.

I had so many mixed feelings when it came to Derek that it was probably going to take ten therapists and the next twenty years of my life to unpack it all, but at the end of the day, I could see the pain in him. Whatever had happened had damaged him beyond anything I could've imagined.

I'd always thought that whoever had killed my parents had done it because they were simply evil, but now that line in the sand had been shaken up, and I didn't know which side I stood on. Was he right about my parents? Could they have done more and didn't, or were they trying but in all of his hurt and pain, he wasn't able to see the good they were doing?

I guess that was a question that was never going to get answered.

Asher stood and stretched, and I couldn't help but smile as Lizzy chatted away excitedly as Asher offered her his elbow.

"Damn! He is hot girl. Is it just me, or does the sun make him sexier?" She leaned closer in her chair. "If you ever want to share, let me know. I'd fuck you to have a taste of that," Beck said, and I rolled my eyes at my friend.

"We're thinking of grabbing some dinner at the new Caribbean place you mentioned," Asher said when they were close enough.

"Yeah, that sounds good," I said as his phone beeped.

He took the phone out to read the text, and I jumped up and went to him as the color drained from his face.

"What? What is it?" He handed me the phone.

Unknown: *We have unfinished business.*

Thank you for reading Burn With Me. Book Three in the Trilogy Burn Me Down will release in 2023. Be sure to follow me on BookBub or Goodreads for more details as they come available.

THANK YOU

Thank you to all those that decided to pick up this book and read it. It is only with readers continued support that Indie Authors, such as myself, are able to keep writing which is why your reviews mean so much to us. If you enjoyed this book, please consider leaving me a review.

BROOKLYN

If you like it dark and edgy then look no further. Brooklyn Cross has always had a deep passion for writing that stemmed from a wild imagination. When she is not busy typing away about the next character you will fall in love with, you can find her walking with her dogs on the farm and sipping a hot cup of coffee.

In addition to getting her degree in business she was highly competitive in the equestrian sport of dressage, with aspirations of an Olympic dream. She is an entrepreneur at heart and has coached and trained many of a riding enthusiast or their wonderful mounts, but always found herself drawn to writing full-time.

"Writing is what I love. I just want to be authentic with my characters. To tell a story that others can immerse themselves in and enjoy, but also relate too. If I can make you smile, laugh, cry, or your heart pound then I have done my job. To drop people into my worlds and for a short time have you live alongside my characters, is what I have always wanted."

CROSS

Below are the links that you can use to find me if you'd like to follow me on my social media platforms.

Book Bub: Brooklyn Cross Books - BookBub

Goodreads: Brooklyn Cross (Author of Dark Side of the Cloth) | Goodreads

TikTok: Author Brooklyn Cross (@authorbrooklyncross) TikTok | Watch Author Brooklyn Cross's Newest TikTok Videos

IG: Brooklyn Cross (@author_brooklyncross) • Instagram photos and videos

FB Group: Crossfire - A Brooklyn Cross Reader Group | Facebook